To: Darrin Witocki

Darrin — sorry we didn't meet at
Jill's party.
I know she thinks you're a
great boss and she's learned
a lot from you.
Hope you enjoy the book.
Robert McDowell
5-25-05

LOOSE CANNONS

LOOSE CANNONS

Robert Mc Dowell

Writer's Showcase presented by *Writer's Digest*
San Jose New York Lincoln Shanghai

Loose Cannons

Published by Writer's Showcase presented by *Writer's Digest*
an imprint of iUniverse.com, Inc.

For information address:
iUniverse.com, Inc.
620 North 48th Street
Suite 201
Lincoln, NE 68504-3467
www.iuniverse.com

This work is a novel.
Any similarity to actual persons or events is purely coincidental.

ISBN:0-595-09312-4

Printed in the United States of America

To my wife, Mary, for tolerating me all these years.

1

When the tiny white blip first appeared in the soft green glow of the small, round radar screen, the captain of the Connead Braith was not unduly alarmed. The equipment was old and more than once had malfunctioned, showing blips briefly and intermittently at a range where he knew there was nothing to cause the display. Usually these ghost blips went away after ten or fifteen minutes. Even though this blip was different, in that it was showing at the outer range of the scope, the captain expected it would soon vanish from the screen.

After thirty minutes passed, with the blip still showing, and moving closer to the Connead Braith, the captain became concerned. He doubted there was another vessel afloat with radar worse than his own. They should have picked up the Connead Braith by now and altered course. But they hadn't, and although the other ship was still miles away, the captain knew it couldn't be chance that put it directly behind them and closing fast. They were well away from commercial shipping lanes and too far from the coast for the vessel to be a fishing boat.

Hoping for an answer that might calm his mounting unease, the captain turned to his engineer. "What d'ye make of it, Bernie ?"

The engineer shook his head. "I don't like it. What are they doin' out here?"

The captain nodded his head slowly. "Aye. That's what I was wonderin'. Looks like they want t' make contact. Keep an eye on things while I go an' tell our, ah, passengers."

Leaving his bridge, the captain climbed down to deck level and walked toward the stern of the boat. Years of experience kept his stride perfectly balanced as the ship rolled in the heavy ocean swell. Even in the weak light of the few naked light bulbs sprinkled around the deck, he had no trouble negotiating the ropes, capstans and hatches which a landlubber might have thought were randomly scattered about. Reaching the last hatch, he climbed down and made his way between wooden crates to the back of the hold. This part of the boat was clear of cargo and served as the crew's quarters. There were half a dozen hammocks strung between the beams of the hold, a table and some chairs, with a small galley and toilet off to the right.

Four men were in the hold, playing cards at a small, square table, which folded down from one wall. Each had a bottle of Guinness in front of him. The captain knew this was how he would find them and resented it, even though he was being well paid to carry these people and their cargo. The men all looked up when the captain entered the area.

"Captain," said one of them. "Pour yerself a bottle an' get in for a couple o' hands."

The captain shook his head. "Yer stakes are too high for me."

"Ach, c'mon, captain," said one of the other men. "Ye're goin' t' be rich when we get t' Cork."

"There's a ship behind us, closin' fast," stated the captain.

"It's yer bet," said one of the men to the companion on his right. Then to the captain, "What's so unusual about there bein' a ship behind us? This is the Atlantic Ocean after all."

A couple of the card players snickered.

"They'll probably turn away from us, won't they?" the man continued.

"We aren't anywhere near a shippin' lane or fishin' ground," answered the captain. "An' it's continuin' t' close in on us, even though they must know we're here by now."

The man laid his cards face down on the table and leaned back in his chair. "What are ye sayin'?"

"Just what I said," replied the captain. "I thought ye'd want t' know."

The other card players now gave their full attention to the captain. "How far away is it?" asked one.

The captain shrugged. "Maybe five miles."

"And how long before it catches up to us?"

"That depends," answered the captain. " We're runnin' three quarter speed, and if we hold steady they'll catch up to us in about an hour. Even if we go to full speed, it'll be an hour and a half at most. Of course, that assumes they don't speed up."

"So, if it isn't a fishing boat or an ocean liner, what is it?" asked the first man.

"My guess'd be it's the American Coast Guard," said the captain slowly.

There was a stirring among the card players and they turned to face the first man, who was obviously their leader. His face took on a solemn look. "What could they want?" he said, as much to himself as to anyone.

"I don't know," the captain responded. "But a couple o' things might happen."

The card players looked at him expectantly.

The captain continued. "Maybe you're right, an' they'll veer off. Or, maybe they're wonderin' why we're so far from the shippin' lanes and they'll pull up alongside just t' make sure we're not havin' any trouble." He paused. "Or maybe they'll want to come aboard. Check us out for drugs, or…" He left the sentence unfinished.

There was a tense silence.

"What are we goin' t' do, Andy?" one of the card players finally asked the first man.

"What do ye suggest, Colin?"

"Make a run for it?" Colin responded weakly.

"Ye heard the captain say we can't outrun them," Andy answered.

"What about fightin', maybe lobbing a couple o' mortars?" suggested another of the card players.

"Don't be crazy!" sputtered the captain. "We try anythin' like that an' we'll bring the whole U.S. navy down on us."

The leader turned to the card player on his left. "Ye're the only one that hasn't said anythin', Kevin."

Kevin sucked in a breath. "If we can't outrun them or outgun them we don't have much of a choice. We'll have t' bluff it out. Maybe the captain's right an' they just want t' see if we're OK. Or maybe they're lookin' for a specific boat an' when they're sure we aren't it they'll go away. There's a better chance o' that than them comin' aboard lookin' for drugs. I mean, we are headed away from the American coast."

Andy nodded. "Captain?"

"Kevin's right. We've no choice," the captain stated.

"Anybody else?" asked Andy, looking to each card player in turn. None of them responded.

"All right," Andy continued. "That's it then. Let's cover the stuff up as best we can, in case they do take a look down here."

The men threw their cards on the table and drained their drinks. They then set to work retrieving tarpaulins and covering the Connead Braith's cargo at the other end of the hold.

———

It was a little more than an hour before the Coast Guard cutter pulled up alongside the Connead Braith and drenched the boat in blinding spotlights. A bullhorn warned that the boat would be fired on if anyone moved. The hearts of every man on the smaller vessel sank.

The next bullhorn announcement ordered that the speed of the Connead Braith be cut and that everyone on board move to the stern of the vessel. The captain, on the bridge with his engineer, nodded at the latter to comply. They then joined the four card players on deck. There were several whooshing sounds followed by the clank of metal on the deck in front of the group.

"What are they doin'?" Andy asked the captain.

"That'll be grapplin' irons, which means they're comin' aboard," the captain answered glumly.

The men on the Connead Braith were unable to see what was happening because of the dazzling spotlights trained on them. They could hear noises from the deck in front of them, but had to shade their eyes and refocus before they could make out that six U.S. marines had boarded the Connead Braith, with automatic weapons drawn.

The marines approached the crew of the Connead Braith. "Hit the deck!" one of marines yelled, waving his weapon back and forth. "Lie on your stomach and put your hands behind your head! Now!"

The crew of the Connead Braith looked at each other. The captain cleared his throat. "What…

"Shut the fuck up, Mister! Hit the deck! Now!"

The captain quickly lay on the deck as instructed, with his companions immediately following suit.

The marine walked along the deck and pointed his weapon at the captain's head. "Anybody below deck?"

"No," the captain answered.

The marine nodded. "Yoblanski, keep these guys covered. Stevens and Scarella, check out the hold. Compton and Lansford, hook up the winches. One of you come to the bridge and let me know when everything's ready."

The marines went about their assigned tasks while their commander walked toward the front of the boat. Climbing into the bridge, he picked up the radio headset. Tuning the dial he began reciting, "Cuckoo to Mantis. Come in Mantis. Over"

He flipped a small switch on the headset and heard some static. It cleared and he heard a voice. "Cuckoo, this is Mantis. Report your situation. Over."

"Securing target. Winches in place. Awaiting further instructions. Over."

"Bring one prisoner. Kevin Boyce. Confirm instructions understood. Over."

Scarella appeared on the bridge and formed an 'O' with the thumb and forefinger of his right hand. The marine leader nodded to show that he understood. "One prisoner. Kevin Boyce. Also can confirm target now secure and winches in place. Are you ready to receive cargo? Over."

"Yes. Begin transferring cargo. Over."

"Understood. Stand by to receive. Over and out."

"Standing by. Over and out."

Laying the headset on the bridge console, the marine leader said to Scarella. "Let's get this over with," They both climbed down to the deck level and went back to where the men of the Connead Braith lay, under the threatening guns of the other four marines.

"You two," barked the marine commander, touching the captain and Kevin in turn with his boot, "Stand up, and keep your hands behind your head."

The two men did as they were told.

"Search them," the marine commander said to Yoblanski.

Yoblanski laid his gun on the deck behind him and searched the men. He found a gun stuffed into the waistband of Kevin's trousers, in the small of his back.

"Take them below and have them start passing up cargo," the marine commander said to Scarella.

Scarella motioned with his gun for Kevin and the captain to head for the nearest hatch.

The marine commander prodded the engineer and Andy with his boot. "Stand up and keep your hands behind your head."

The men did as instructed and Yoblanski performed his search. He found nothing on the engineer but Andy had a concealed gun like Kevin had.

"Stevens, send one of them below to help with passing the cargo up. The other one can hook the cargo onto one of the winches."

Approaching the last two men lying on the deck, the marine commander issued the same instructions, and watched as Yoblanski searched them. Each man had a gun this time. "Have these two hooking cargo onto the other winches. That'll take care of all the work. We can sit back and wait till they're finished."

The transfer of the cargo went quickly, and the marine commander went to verify that there was nothing of interest left in the hold of the boat. While below decks, he went to the Connead Braith's fuel tanks. From his breast pocket he removed a round, black object, no bigger than a hockey puck. The front of the object had a timer dial, and the commander turned a small knob on the side of the object. He set the bomb to explode in one hour. That would be enough so that no one on the Coast Guard cutter would see the explosion, but the radar operator would still be able to confirm that the Connead Braith had indeed vanished from his screen. He jammed the bomb into the narrow gap between the fuel tanks, pushing it back out of sight. Satisfied, he returned to the deck.

The commander had the men of the Connead Braith line up on deck. "Which of you is Kevin Boyce?" he asked.

"I am," Kevin replied.

The marine commander studied Kevin for a moment before saying to Yablonski, "Winch him up."

Before Yablonski could take a step, Colin, on Kevin's left, spun around and punched Kevin in the face, at the same time screaming "Ye traitorous bastard! I'll fuckin' kill ye..."

Swinging the butt of his weapon up, Yablonski smashed it into Colin's mouth. There was a crunching of teeth and bones, and an immediate spurting of blood. Colin sank to the deck on all fours, clutching his mouth and choking.

Kevin ran the back of his hand along his lower lip where Colin's punch had landed. A thin line of blood smeared his hand. Grabbing him by the arm, Yablonski led Kevin over to one of the winches. Kevin looked terrified.

"Hang on to the hook for dear life. Lock your finger together through it. It'll only take a minute," said Yablonski. "Ready?"

Putting his hands through the large hook, Kevin locked his fingers together as tightly as he could. "Ready."

Yablonski hit the button on the winch control and Kevin was pulled up into the binding lights of the Coast Guard cutter.

One by one the marines were winched up to the cutter in the same manner. The commander was the last to leave. There was a bullhorn warning to the men of the Connead Braith not to move or they would be fired on. The marine commander had an awkward moment when he had to cling to the hook with one hand and hit the winch control button with his other hand, but he managed the maneuver and also disappeared into the cutter's spotlights.

"What now?" said the engineer to no-one in particular.

"They'll disconnect the winch cables and hopefully we'll go our separate ways," said the captain in response. "Are you all right?" he added to Colin, who was still on his knees clutching his bloodied face.

Only a grunting sound came in reply.

"We'll take care o' ye, Colin. But we daren't risk movin' yet," said Andy grimly.

The spotlights from the cutter snapped off and it was a few minutes before the eyes of the men on the Connead Braith adjusted enough to make out the dark shape of the cutter pulling away from them. They stayed where they were, watching the lights of the cutter recede into the Atlantic darkness. Five minutes passed Before the captain said, "I think we're OK now."

———

For an hour the men on the Connead Braith tended to Colin and cursed Kevin Boyce. Finally, their leader, Andy, had brought them back to reality. "Talk's cheap, but chances are we'll never see that bastard again."

It was then that the bomb exploded, igniting the fuel tanks. The burning stern of the Connead Braith sucked in water, forcing the bow to rise on end. Under the tremendous pressure, the boat snapped in half, forming a large upside down V. The boat spat huge clouds of smoke and steam before, hissing in futile protest, she slid under the waves.

2

The man wore the uniform of a Metropolitan Police constable, but he wasn't a Bobby. The costume would allow him to get away quickly, without drawing attention. He had chosen this disguise himself, and found a gratifying irony in masquerading as a protector of the people he was going to kill.

Sitting by an open window on the seventh floor of the Empire Insurance building, he looked down into Bryson Square. His chances of getting away increased with the number of people on the streets, and the crowd gathered below was smaller than he had hoped. Still, he wasn't worried. He had supreme confidence in his plan, and was certain he'd be safe long before panic and confusion subsided enough to allow the authorities to react in a way that might threaten him.

The banners on display in the square represented the usual groups of agitators and malcontents; the Young Socialists League, the Committee for a Nuclear Free Britain, Greenpeace, the Trades Unions Congress, Liberals for Democracy, and lesser known but more extremist bands of disaffected, mostly young people. The man sneered inwardly at them all.

He would gladly have fired indiscriminately into their midst, eradicating as many as he could, but unfortunately that couldn't be part of the plan. He had to concentrate on one specific target.

The man had a clear view of the raised platform where two of the chairs were still empty, awaiting the arrival of the main speakers who would address the rally. A young woman, dressed in denim shirt and jeans was at the microphone, gesticulating wildly. Although he couldn't make out her words, the man could tell from her tone and from the crowd's reaction that she was stirring them up, priming them for the main event.

Raising his rifle, the man leaned forward and rested his right elbow on the pigeon-stained window sill. Squinting into the rifle's telescopic sight, he fixed its crosshairs on the young woman on the stage. He had a perfect sight line. Turning a fraction of an inch to his left, he aimed at the first empty chair, and then at the second one. Again, nothing impeded his aim. Relaxing back into his chair, he returned the rifle to its resting place on his lap.

Believing that a critical part of planning an operation like this was to envision success, the man once again ran through what was about to happen.

The police had already erected a roadblock on Musgrave Road, which entered Bryson Square from the west. The limousine carrying his targets would come that way, escorted by police motorcycles front and rear. The convoy would be waved through to the square and the limousine would pull up behind the platform. Its passengers would be led to the rear of the stage where they would wait a moment while the crowd, buzzing with rumor of their arrival, was whipped into one final frenzy. The two men would finally stride to center stage amid tumultuous cheers.

The Prime Minister would receive a thundering ovation. After ending twelve years of Tory rule, he was the undisputed darling of the Left and would bask in glory. His companion, the Northern Ireland Minister, would ride the swell of emotion to cement his place as the designated deputy who would one day assume the mantle he so desperately coveted. Of course, he'd have to deliver on his promise to extricate Britain from the mess in Northern Ireland, and thus end the IRA bombing campaign in England.

The man with the rifle didn't know who was paying for this job, although he suspected one of the extremist Protestant paramilitary groups might be behind it. They were not as efficient or daring as the IRA and it made sense that they would put out a contract for the job. But the man didn't care who was behind it. Money was what mattered to him and he would be well paid for this job.

He guessed the Northern Ireland Minister would speak first. The Prime Minister would sit in one of the empty chairs. When the crowd was fully concentrated on the speaker, the man would raise his rifle and squeeze off one shot which would shatter the speaker's forehead and send him flying backwards. The Prime Minister would reflexively turn to look toward his colleague. A second bullet would smash into its target before anyone could react.

The bloody scene his actions would soon create did not disturb the man. He had served in Vietnam and had seen what Americans did to the Vietnamese. Worse, he had seen what the Vietnamese did to each other.

He had no doubt that from this distance and trajectory, two shots were all that would be required. He had been trained as a sharpshooter by the FBI and had proved his skill with unerring accuracy in many hostage situations during the past ten years. He would not fail because if he did, he would not be paid, and that was unthinkable.

Satisfied that the shooting would pose no problem, the man continued to imagine what would happen next. Before the crowd realized what had occurred, he would have thrown the rifle from the window, peeled the gloves from his hands, stuffed them into a tunic pocket, and be across the room and out into the corridor. That would be the time of greatest danger. He would follow the corridor to the elevator, ride down to the ground floor and walk to the back door of the building where a car would be waiting.

If he did encounter someone between leaving the seventh floor window and getting to the car, he was sure they wouldn't interfere with a policeman. Nor would they later be able to give a description. They would remember only a Bobby.

The same driver who brought him to the building, would take him away. The man knew nothing about the driver, but more important, the driver knew nothing about him, except that he was on a big job. Once in the car he'd have three blocks to strip off the police uniform and change into the business suit which held his passport, airline tickets, money and the key to a locker at Heathrow Airport. He'd be dropped at Haymarket tube station and would take a train to the airport.

At Heathrow he'd go to the locker, retrieve his luggage and check in for his flight to New York. He should arrive at Heathrow about two hours before departure. By then the police might be watching for known terrorists, but he was neither known nor a terrorist. Even if something should go wrong, he could always produce his diplomatic papers, although he wanted to avoid that.

He'd be home in time to catch the evening news broadcasts on television and expected to be the lead story.

The man assured himself that, compared to some other jobs he'd undertaken, this one would be a stroll in an English country garden. Most of the police didn't even carry guns. He turned his attention back to the square below and cradled his rifle. It wouldn't be long now.

The man did not imagine that he himself would be dead within twelve hours.

———

The man's escape had gone as planned and he now relaxed aboard the Boeing 747 which would whisk him back to New York. The seats on either side of him were empty, and he figured that by raising the seat arms, he might be able to lie down and sleep away the time between London and New York. His luck didn't hold, though. The last passenger to board took the seat on the man's left, toward the aisle. Worse, he proved to be the talkative type.

"Hi! You from New York?" the new arrival began.

The man nodded affirmatively, but reluctantly.

"Jesus! What a country, huh? Can you believe that weather? How do people put up with that all year? And the food! How can they eat that stuff?"

The man offered no encouragement.

"And talk about a hard sell! I'm in computers, I.C.O. We're trying to get a toehold in the market here, but Christ, I couldn't sell at cost! They want it for nothing! What line of business are you in?"

The man studied his fellow passenger for a moment. He imagined replying that he was in the business of assassinating people, and was there some way a computer could help with that line of work? Instead, he said, "I'm really bushed and I'd like to get some sleep."

He slid over into the seat beside the window, leaving an empty seat between himself and the computer salesman. Snuggling against the corner of his headrest and the window, he closed his eyes.

Surprisingly, he slept through the whole flight, being awakened finally by a stewardess as they began their descent into Kennedy. The computer salesman had moved a couple of rows back and was now assailing some other poor guy about what a relief it was to be back in the good old USA and how he didn't care if he never heard of Europe again.

When the plane finally jerked to a halt and the 'Fasten Seat Belt' sign was extinguished, the man stood and retrieved his briefcase from the overhead compartment, then headed up the aisle to exit the plane. He had no other luggage and would be able to get through customs long before his fellow passengers had retrieved their checked luggage from the bowels of the terminal. He knew that a lack of luggage might make him more suspicious to customs, but the explanation he always used hadn't failed him yet.

First off the plane, he hurried along the tunnels and corridors which led to the customs area. Slowing his pace, he looked at each customs desk in turn, finally heading for the one where he noticed the agent check his watch. A small chance, but the agent just might be about to finish a shift and would want no delays to keep him late.

"Good morning, sir," said the agent. "Passport, please."

The man handed it over.

""How long were you in London?"

"Just a couple of days. Business trip." They always asked if the trip was business or pleasure.

"I see." The agent tapped the keyboard of a computer on the desk. "No other luggage?" he asked, keeping his eyes on the computer screen.

"No. I go to London quite a bit and keep an apartment there." They always expected an explanation.

"I see." The agent looked up from the computer screen. "Would you open the briefcase please?"

The man complied and the agent poked around inside, then closed the briefcase and handed the passport back. "Thank you, and welcome home, Mr. Traynor." He smiled and glanced at his watch again. The man picked up his briefcase and headed to the main terminal.

———

Eddie "Butt Burner" Ralton got his nickname from something he had done to a girlfriend with a cigarette lighter. A drug addict from the age of fourteen, Eddie had graduated from robbery to murder to support his habit. The police knew he had committed the murder but had no evidence that would stand up in court, and since the victim had been a drug dealer, they weren't too concerned about it anyway. Instead, they bluffed Eddie into believing they had him cold for the murder and offered him a deal. If he would snitch for them, they'd deep six the murder rap. Eddie thought he was in heaven.

Over the years he proved effective in setting up drug busts, and all he asked in return was a steady supply of drugs, which the police were happy to provide.

This current gig though, wasn't a drug bust and it hadn't come from Eddie's usual police contact. The man who approached Eddie about it yesterday was a stranger who knew about the murder rap. He wanted someone killed, which didn't faze Eddie, especially since the stranger promised $5,000 for the job. Eddie had no choice anyway, since the stranger made it clear that if he didn't perform, Eddie would go down for life, with no possibility of parole. Eddie pegged the stranger as a Fed, maybe FBI or CIA, but he didn't really care.

So Eddie came to be at Kennedy airport, with a snub-nosed .45 caliber pistol stuffed in the pocket of his grimy overcoat. He had a photo of his target and as he lounged against the wall of the international flights terminal, he studied the picture. He didn't care who the man was or what he had done, only that the guy looked old, maybe fifty, and should present no problem. Eddie had already decided he'd make the hit on the sidewalk, outside the terminal and escape by going back into the terminal and losing himself among the crowds inside.

Glancing at the flight arrivals screen he saw that finally flight NW108 from London had landed at Gate 18, just as he'd been told it would. He walked to the gate, and found a spot toward the back of the crowd waiting for the flight, but from where he could see everyone who came off the plane.

Recognizing his man immediately, Eddie trailed him across the main terminal, his heartbeat quickening as he drew closer. Keeping one hand in his pocket, Eddie caressed the smooth, cold metal of the gun. When they reached the main exit Eddie closed the distance between them to a couple of feet. Glancing around, he noted there were no police or airport security nearby. They'd be more concerned with the entry and exit gates to the customs area and the aircraft.

Walking through the sliding door onto the pavement outside the terminal, the man stopped for a moment, looking around for the taxi line. Passing him, Eddie used the man's hesitation to survey the sidewalk. Still no cops.

Making up his mind, the man started to his left. Stepping in front of him, Eddie drew the gun from his pocket and fired repeatedly. The first two bullets hit the man in the face and the next four found his chest. By the time the man's body hit the ground and the first screams were coming from passers-by, Eddie had stepped back into the terminal and cut to the right. He didn't run, but moved quickly through the crowds, at the same time peeling off his trenchcoat.

Heading to the nearest restroom, Eddie went into an empty stall. He removed a baseball cap from a pocket of the trenchcoat. Pulling on the cap, he forced his shoulder-length hair through the hole in the back, so it formed a pony tail. Next, he removed a pair of plain glass spectacles from the trenchcoat and put them on. The stranger had thought of everything and Eddie was sure no-one would recognize him. Pulling the gun from the trenchcoat he stuffed it into a pocket of the leather jacket he wore. Finally, he threw the trenchcoat across the toilet bowl and left the restroom.

Heading away from the main terminal exit where he knew there must by now be pandemonium, he went to a side exit. On the sidewalk, he found himself at the head of the taxi line, a hundred yards from the airport shuttle bus. He walked to the bus and climbed aboard. The bus pulled away from the international terminal and Eddie got off at the domestic terminal where he took a taxi back to Queens. He was home in time for lunch.

On the sidewalk outside the main terminal, the dying man knew he'd committed a cardinal error. He hadn't covered his back, and the people who had hired him didn't want any witnesses. He remembered that as a kid in school, he'd learned that the people who built the tombs of the Pharaohs were killed and buried inside so that the secrets of the tombs would never be known. Then he died.

3

Belfast is a hard city, an exaggeration of its rugged environment. Tall office buildings ape the towering granite peaks that ring the town on three sides. Back alleys cutting between ghetto row houses echo the ravines that gash the nearby mountains. The perpetual smog which hangs over the city parodies the mist that usually shrouds the surrounding hills and valleys. Gray asphalt streets reflect the cold, threatening Irish Sea which constantly pummels the city's eastern edges.

On such a street a black car, deliberately chosen to be inconspicuous, coasted up to an intersection and parked. From above, the car looked like a squat cat, crouched between the smoky rowhouses, waiting for unsuspecting prey.

Switching off the car's engine, the driver looked at his watch. "Right on time," he murmured to his passenger.

Although only in his late twenties, the driver had a prematurely receding hairline which he tried to disguise by brushing his jet black hair toward the front. Brown marble eyes and a sharp nose gave him a bird-like look, and thin lips suggested that he lacked humor. His body appeared

19

gaunt, almost skinny, but implied a wiry toughness. The unmistakable throatiness of a scouse accent could be heard in his voice.

The two men sat for a moment, listening to the cracking and hissing of the cooling engine block.

"They built the Titanic here," the driver stated, keeping his eyes on the street to his right, which rose in a hill above them. The driver knew the street ended at a pair of huge wrought iron gates, although from where he sat he could see only the top spikes of the gates.

"Yes," responded the passenger without interest. He too had his eyes fixed on the hill.

The passenger was about twice the age of the driver. His hair was steely gray, like a scouring pad. The small veins which scored his cheeks heightened his ruddy complexion. He had soft blue eyes and a slightly bulbous nose, beneath which was a well-groomed mustache. He was handsome for his age, with a body that was also in good shape. He spoke with a public school accent, which is to say that his voice couldn't be tied to a particular region of the country, but would be recognized as upper class. He might have been viewed as the stereotype of a typical British army officer, although it had been years since he'd been involved with the army in a way that most people would consider typical.

"Funny thing is," continued the driver, "They're proud of it."

The passenger pondered this anomaly. "Well, they don't have much to be…" he began, before the sharp, shrill shriek of a siren shut off his sentence. He straightened in his seat. "Here they come. Keep your eyes open," he said to the driver while keeping his own eyes fixed on the hill to his right.

They both watched the spikes at the top of the hill slowly recede from their view. The massive gates were swinging open, and from the crest of the hill a flood of workers began to flow down the street toward the car. The torrent of men spilled off the pavements, overflowing into the street and spreading down the hill like a dark stain.

The bicyclists passed them first, deftly weaving their way through the crowd then freewheeling down the hill. The driver and his passenger concentrated on the sea of faces now streaming around the car.

"Here he comes," said the passenger, touching the driver lightly on the arm. "He's just about to pass the lamppost."

Glancing to the other side of the street, it took the driver only a moment to identify their quarry, who was walking quickly down the hill, hands dug into the pockets of his pea jacket. A steel thermos was tucked under his left arm. Although his head was lowered against the wind, there was no doubt he was their man.

"Let's go," the passenger ordered.

They got out of the car and the driver took a step directly toward their target. The passenger put his arm out, restraining his partner. "Take it easy, he'll come to us."

Leaning against the hood of the car, they kept their eyes fixed on the man.

The subject of their attention was about forty feet away when he saw them. Recognition made him stop abruptly, causing a man hurrying behind to bump into him, knocking the thermos into the gutter. He picked it up, keeping his eyes on the men by the car, then started toward the other side of the street, cutting across the current of the crowd. The passenger jerked his head at the driver, who responded by walking quickly at an angle, to cut the man off.

Wading through the crowd, the passenger headed directly for his target, whom he confronted as they both reached the pavement.

"Hello, Billy," grinned the passenger.

Billy looked for an escape route. There was a tall wall to his right and the driver was rapidly approaching from his left. Realizing he had nowhere to go, he stopped again. The driver came up and the three of them stood for a moment, the crowd streaming resentfully around them. Billy looked uneasy. "What d'ye want?" he spat.

"We thought you'd be happy to see us again, Billy," answered the passenger, feigning disappointment.

The driver snickered at his partner's tone.

Billy noticed the looks the three of them were getting from the passers-by. "Do we have t' stand in the middle o' the street like this?" he muttered.

The passenger nodded, conceding Billy's point. "Come on, we'll give you a lift home." He motioned in the direction of the car.

Looking over that way, Billy saw a group of four men watching them across the street from where the car was parked. "All right," he said, "But can we act like mates? We're bein' watched."

"Of course," said the passenger, wrapping his arm around Billy's shoulders and leading him toward the car. "After all, we are mates, aren't we?"

The driver, on the other side of Billy, snickered again.

Billy tried to appear relaxed as they approached the car. Forcing a smile, he was relieved to see the group of four lose interest and continue on their way.

"Suspicious people in Belfast," remarked the driver. "But I suppose they've a right to be."

The passenger and Billy got into the back seat of the car. Starting the engine, the driver began to slowly navigate his way through the crowded streets. Billy was careful to keep his face turned away from the window and cradled his thermos nervously. "Take the next right," he instructed the driver.

"I know the way to Dundonald street," came the curt reply.

"How d'ye know where I live?" Billy raised his voice, trying to sound indignant.

"We can usually find people when we want to," answered the passenger. "You're looking good, Billy. Better than the last time we saw you."

Billy winced. "Am I under arrest?" He tried to sound defiant, but his voice betrayed fear.

The passenger raised his eyebrows. "Why? Have you done something we don't know about?" He grinned, then shook his head. "No, Billy, you're not under arrest."

"What then?" asked Billy, defensively.

The passenger patted Billy on the shoulder. "Relax. We need your help. That's all."

Billy's eyes narrowed suspiciously. "How could I help ye?"

The passenger studied Billy for a minute. "We want you to visit an old friend of yours," he said finally.

"I have no friends," snapped Billy. "Ye know that."

The passenger looked hurt. "How can you say that, Billy? You have us." He smiled humorlessly. "And, apparently, Joe Mallory."

Billy hesitated for an instant, wondering how much they knew about himself and Mallory. Could they know he and Mallory wrote to each other once in a while? Slowly, he said, "Joe Mallory? From Mountjoy? Sure I haven't seen him since I got out." Strictly speaking, that was true.

"Yes," stated the passenger. "But we also know he took a liking to you in prison, went out of his way to help you. Some might say he treated you like a son." He leaned closer to Billy, peering into his eyes. "Why was that, Billy? Why would Joe Mallory be interested in you?"

Looking away, to avert the passenger's eyes, Billy made no response to the question. The passenger relaxed back into his seat. "Never mind. What matters is that Mallory must consider you a friend."

Billy sighed, but still avoided looking at the passenger. "Why d' ye want me t' go an' see him?"

The passenger looked out his window. "Do you read the papers, or watch the news, Billy?"

Billy sagged into his seat. "Who doesn't in this city? Everybody wants t' know whose body was found last night, or which o' yer neighbors had a bomb factory in his house. Aye, I stay home an' watch the news like most people that don't want t' be on the streets after dark."

"Then you'll know somebody tried to assassinate the Prime Minister in London a couple of weeks ago, and killed the Northern Ireland Minister in the process."

"Aye," retorted Billy, "What of it?"

"Her Majesty's government doesn't like its Ministers being killed," answered the passenger.

"What's it got t' do wi' Joe Mallory? D'ye think he did it?"

"Maybe it has nothing to do with him," responded the passenger. "Or maybe everything." He turned to face Billy again. "We think the IRA did it, but they deny it, which is strange. Usually they're happy to claim credit, especially when this operation, as they'd call it, went so smoothly. So we're beginning to wonder if some of their boys are freelancing."

"An' ye think it's Joe Mallory?" There was disbelief in Billy's voice.

"I didn't say that. We just need you to pick up something from Mallory that might help us with our, ah, inquiries."

Billy's voice became deeply suspicious. "What d' ye want me t' pick up?"

"We don't know what it is," the passenger answered. He grinned at Billy's obvious exasperation.

"Then what makes ye think he's got somethin' t' be picked up? An' why would he give it t' me?" Billy sneered, "I'd think the IRA would be cheerin' whoever killed yer Minister."

The passenger pondered that for a moment. "Maybe not. Things are pretty much going their way at the peace talks, and they don't like the heat they're feeling from the assassination. We've hit them and their sympathizers pretty hard. They can't move around easily and their sources of money have dried up. They're also afraid we might bring back internment. Maybe Mallory wants to give us something that will lead us to look elsewhere and lay off the IRA."

"Joe Mallory wouldn't grass on anybody," Billy snapped.

"I suppose you'd know about that," said the passenger quietly.

Billy's face flushed. Embarrassment and anger welled up within him, but he bit it back. "What makes ye think Mallory will give me anythin'?"

"He told us he would. In fact, you're the only person he'll give it to."

Billy looked stunned. "Me? Why? Ye must have people who could go an' get it?"

The passenger sighed. "I suppose he doesn't trust our people like he trusts you. We do have people infiltrated into the IRA just like I'm sure they have people working among us. I don't know why he chose you." He turned to face Billy again. "Look, this isn't difficult. You go to Cork, meet him, get what he's got and bring it back here. Then you go back to your anonymous little life and live happily ever after."

"Easy for ye t' say! Ye know as well as I do Mallory's in charge of an IRA cell. Ye think his friends aren't goin' t' wonder what I'm doin' there? Or am I just suppose t' walk in an' say 'Hello. I'm here t' pick up somethin' for British Intelligence.'? Them bastards wanted t' kill me in Mountjoy!"

The passenger sat impassively. "Are you done? Because you're beginning to piss me off." His tone sounded ominous. "Wasn't it Mallory who stopped them from killing you? He wouldn't do that in the hope that he could lure you down there years later so you could be killed, would he? He'll take care of you again. He already took a risk contacting us, so he must be anxious for us to have whatever it is he's got. As for any nosy people you run into, you'll both have to deal with that. Tell them you're on the run from the law up north and have nowhere else to go. That'll impress them."

Billy shook his head. "Why should I go t' Cork just because Joe Mallory wants me to? I don't remember anybody askin' me about it!"

The passenger continued to look straight ahead. "You'll do it," he said quietly. "Because if you don't, word might get out about Dundalk, and what you did to your buddies. I don't think the IRA or UVF would be very happy with you. One side or the other would get you, and from what I know of them, you'd be glad when they finally snuffed you out." He turned to face Billy and glared at him through narrow eyes. "And I would tell them, Billy, you know that."

Sagging back, Billy closed his eyes. "Ye bastard, why can't ye leave me alone?"

Turning toward Billy, the passenger grabbed him by the lapels. "It's not our choice! You think we'd choose a piece of shit like you?" he snarled.

Seeing the fear and surrender in Billy's eyes, he relaxed his grip and brushed at Billy's collar, smiling coldly. "Mallory expects you on Wednesday. We'll pick you up at nine o'clock at the corner of Newcastle and Island streets."

"Why Wednesday?" Billy asked.

"Because that's what the man said. We'd like it to be today, but he's calling the shots. At least you'll be able to go to work tomorrow and ask for the rest of the week off. One last thing, Billy. Don't do anything stupid, like a midnight flit. Something like that might reflect badly on Linda and the girl. What's her name, Susan?"

Billy became rigid and the color drained from his face. "What d' ye mean?" he said quietly, already fearing the answer.

The passenger shrugged his shoulders. "I understand your ex-wife and daughter have a nice life in London. Linda's got a good job and Susan's doing well in school." He narrowed his eyes again. "Be a pity if things started to go bad for them. Like maybe there'd be a report of child neglect or abuse and Social Services would have to be called in. They might have to protect the kid by taking her away from her mum."

Hatred showed in Billy's eyes. "Ye bastard," he whispered.

The passenger shrugged again. "Let him out here," he said to the driver. "He can walk the rest of the way." Then he turned to Billy again. "Remember, Billy, nine o'clock Wednesday morning, corner of Newcastle and Island streets."

"Why can't ye pick me up at me house?"

"You've a new neighbor in your street, Billy. John Piggell. Do you know who he is?"

"No. Am I supposed to?"

The passenger shook his head slowly. "You should pay more attention to your neighbors, Billy. Piggell's a commander in the UVF. His people are watching who comes and goes in your street. That's why we didn't wait for you there today." He paused. "If I were you, Billy, I'd think about moving before they find out what you did. Maybe we can help you with that when you get back from Cork. No need to worry about it until then, eh?" He smirked.

Billy slid out of the car, slamming the door behind him. He stood on the sidewalk, breathing heavily and watched as the car pulled away from the curb. In a sudden fit of anger and frustration he hurled his thermos after it. It didn't come close to hitting the car. For the second time that day, Billy reached into the gutter and retrieved his thermos.

There were two taps on the door before it swung open and Larry poked his head through. He was in his mid-twenties, tall and gangly, with a mop of golden blond curls. His blue eyes, Roman nose and pasty complexion marked him as a Swede, and his persistently serious expression added to the stereotype. Bernadette had trouble recalling seeing him smile and was sure she'd never heard him laugh. He'd been with her for about two years, which was longer than any of her previous aides. Today's college graduates seemed to tire of public service quickly unless it offered a chance for power in the very near future. Working for Bernadette, who was neither a Republican nor a Democrat, held no such promise. She was surprised Larry had lasted this long, but grateful. He was thoroughly efficient and usually non-demanding.

"I have the Speaker's secretary on line one," Larry announced.

"Put it through," Bernadette answered.

Larry withdrew and swung the door closed.

Inching her chair up to the desk, Bernadette waited for the red button on her phone to flash. She deliberately did not pick it up until the third blink. "Hello, this is Bernadette Mallory," she said, more loudly than she meant.

"One moment, please, Representative Mallory, I have Speaker Sullivan for you." The secretary sounded effortlessly professional and efficient. To her, this was routine.

Bernadette waited, aware of the greasy feel of the receiver in her palm, which betrayed that this was not a routine call in her mind.

"Hello. Bernie?" came a voice she recognized as the Speaker of the U.S. House of Representatives.

Bernadette had talked to him in person a few times before, at congressional and charity events. They made polite small talk then, saying nothing of consequence, but she knew his gravely voice well, having sat through many of his speeches in the House. Although he was a powerful man, or perhaps because of it, she resented his use of a nickname for her. It was condescending, assuming a friendliness which did not exist.

"Yes, this is Bernadette." She stressed her name. "How are you, sir?"

"Well, I tell you, Bernie…You don't mind if I call you Bernie?"

He was determined then. "No, not at all," she conceded.

"Good. I'm as well as can be expected." He coughed and wheezed. "Mind you, I'll feel a damned sight better when this election is over. I'm too old for this flitting from city to city, day after day, shaking hands, giving the same speeches over and over again. And smiling, always smiling. It's depressing. I'm afraid one day someone will tell me some terrible news, and I'll still be smiling, it's become such a fixture on my face. Time some of you young'uns took over this campaigning crap." There was a pause while he wheezed some more, catching his breath.

He had obviously forgotten that she was not a member of his party, or maybe he deliberately wanted to make her feel that she might as well be. She felt obliged to fill in the pause. "Come now, Mr. Speaker, no-one could do it as well as you. I heard the speech you gave to the Bar Association yesterday. That story about the president and the judge was marvelous. You haven't lost your knack for delivering the punch line."

"Ah, you're good at the flattery, Bernie. Must be full of the blarney like myself. It's impossible to lose once you've kissed the stone, but you'd know all about that, being from county Cork, eh?"

Bernadette forced a laugh. "Yes, I know what you mean." She wished he'd get to the point.

"Well Bernie, I'll get right to the point. Gary asked me to call and let you know how much he appreciates what you're doing with the committee."

She wondered why Gary couldn't call himself. It would have been a nice touch.

"He would have called himself, but you can imagine how hard it is to find a spare minute, with the election just a month away and the polls neck and neck," the Speaker continued, then paused, expecting an acknowledgment.

"Of course," Bernadette said. "I understand."

"Anyway, he wants you to know, and so do I, that we're one hundred percent behind you on this. We'll go to the wall on it if we have to." He hesitated again.

Bernadette decided that his talking like this was not only meant to convince her that 'they' were on her side, it was more insidiously designed to make her commit to being on 'their' side. "Thank you, sir. That's very encouraging." She hoped there was no betrayal of sarcasm in her voice.

"Have you learned anything more about the money?" he asked.

"No, nothing, just what you've read in the press." Even if she had, she would not have told him, but as long as they were pumping her for information, she realized that two could play that game and boldly continued, "Do you know anything that might be of help, sir?"

There was an odd silence at the other end of the line, as if he had put his hand over the receiver. She waited.

The Speaker's voice dropped to a conspiratorial whisper. "Our best guess is the money will be laundered through the CIA to a Cuban exile group in Florida. The theory is they will provoke something with Castro that would allow us to send in the marines. Seems like a small amount to finance an operation like that, and it would be a gamble for Ganera, but with the race so close, you never know. No incumbent has ever lost the presidency during any kind of war situation. It's an old trick.

The point is, that appropriation means an awful lot to them and we need time to find out what it's for and kill it without damaging ourselves in the process." Another wheezy pause before he continued, "I don't want to put you under any more pressure Bernie, but the whole election could turn on this."

'Thanks!' Bernadette thought, 'No pressure there.'

"I intend to hold out for a full disclosure about the money," she said.

"That's great, Bernie. Exactly what we need. One final thing, this hasn't been discussed openly, you understand, but if things work out, Gary might consider you for a post in his administration. Of course, I don't know how you'd feel about that.

Mind you, that stuff in the paper this morning was news to me. I mean about you wanting the Irish ambassador job. Anything to it?"

Bernadette sighed. "No, sir. It was news to me too. I've never considered such a possibility."

"Well, just thought I'd ask. You're meeting with Ganera this evening aren't you?"

"Yes, at seven o'clock." She would spare him the trouble of asking, and wanted this conversation to end. She was shocked that they seriously considered she might hold out for some personal reward. They were so caught up in their power games that they couldn't comprehend someone simply doing their job. The idea was alien to them. The Democrats wanted to prevent it only because it would dilute their own power. They would do the same thing given the chance. Probably had already.

"Well Bernie, I have to be going," the Speaker said. "If I don't get a nap I'll never make it through this evening. Remember now, we're with you all the way, and let me know how things go tonight, OK?"

Bernadette deliberately did not answer the question. "Good luck with the campaign," was all she said, before a click at the other end told her he'd already hung up. She had no doubt he'd contact her to find out what happened at her upcoming meeting with the president. "And thanks for calling. I appreciate it," she said into the dead receiver before setting the phone down.

The Speaker of the House needing a nap struck her as ridiculous. It belied the image of bustling energy that he worked so hard to project. She thought it pathetic, this worn old man, bone tired from traveling, arm muscles sore from grasping hands, throat raw from talking, maybe even lips hurting from kissing babies, resenting the whole business, needing naps to maintain his facade of vigor. She despised the lack of dignity it showed.

Still, she couldn't deny being excited by his hint at a post in the administration if things went the way the Democrats wanted. Such an offer would not influence her vote on the appropriation, her conscience would dictate that, but if she was rewarded for it, so much the better. And if the president dropped a similar hint tonight, she'd be in a 'can't lose' situation and that thought pleased her. She was tired of seeing younger, less qualified people being put in charge of the reins of government just because they voted the party line. She had accepted that she would not be given a more powerful post while she remained outside the party structure, but now it seemed she might finally have a chance, and without joining either side.

She pressed the gray button on the side of her phone to summon Larry. Seconds later, he leaned into her office again.

"Hold my calls, Larry. I need an hour to think about some things."

"Sure," he said, "How'd it go?"

"Until I can sort things out, all I can say is that it went."

Seeing his disappointment at her unwillingness to confide in him, Bernadette smiled. "Don't worry. I just want to have everything straight in my mind before we discuss options."

"Yes, of course," he replied, looking confused. "Can I ask you something about the bank account?"

"Can it wait? I have a lot to think about right now."

Larry hesitated, then turned and closed the door behind him.

Bernadette sat with her chin cupped in her left palm. Her right hand picked up a pencil and wrote the roman numeral 'I' on a yellow legal pad. She imprisoned the number inside a tight circle. After doing it, she remembered one of her old schoolteachers telling her that people who numbered things that way betrayed an inner frustration, that they felt trapped. She drew a second circle around the first one.

She knew she should make notes for her meeting with the president, anticipate questions, draft answers, but she couldn't concentrate. Her mind roamed back over the events that had put her in this situation. All the way back to college, and to Mike.

She had first laid eyes on him at Boston College, in 'Econ 101'. He came bursting into the room five minutes after the class had started, clutching books and papers under one arm and swinging a battered brown leather briefcase from his other hand.

His hair was a perfect ginger, uncombed and in need of a trim. Thick, black-rimmed glasses dominated his face, magnifying his eyes and making him appear to be permanently gawking. the bridge of the glasses was wrapped with white tape. His slight build was accentuated by the loose-fitting sports jacket and baggy pants he wore. His shoes were badly scuffed.

He appeared breathless as he squeezed through the door, and bumped against several students as he tried to close it behind him, causing quite a commotion. The professor, who had just begun to offer a textbook definition of economics groaned at the disturbance.

"Mr. Cabell," the professor said wearily. "So, we are to have the pleasure of your company again?"

The newcomer spun around to look at the professor. In the process he dropped the book and papers he had been clutching. He ignored them. "Yes. Sorry I'm late," he muttered.

The professor addressed the class. "For those of you who don't know, this is Mister…no, sorry…Comrade Mike Cabell, avowed communist, or as he prefers, avowed socialist and disrupter of classes. Did I get that right, comrade Cabell? You are a socialist and not a communist?"

Cabell glared at the professor. "Yes. There are no communists in the world. Yet." He positively spat the last word.

"Yes, yes. I know." The professor waved a hand at Cabell and turned his attention back to the class. "You see, fellow comrades, comrade Cabell has been known to interrupt classes at every opportunity so that he can wax poetic on the theories of comrade Karl Marx. I am going to deny comrade Cabell that opportunity by summarizing those theories for him. With that out of the way, maybe this class can proceed as it was designed. Any objections, comrade Cabell?"

"I..."

The professor did not wait to hear what Cabell had to say. "No? Good." Again the dismissive wave.

Bernadette felt sorry for Cabell, who was flushed with embarrassment, giving his face a deeper color than his hair. He looked pathetic, standing with his book and papers scattered around his feet.

The professor faced the class again. "Comrade Marx proposed and comrade Cabell believes, that the economic development of society is not only predictable, but inevitable. I believe the progression is...correct me if I'm wrong, comrade...the progression is from caveman hunter, to feudalism, to capitalism, then socialism, then communism, and finally some kind of perfect anarchy.

Now, remember that this development is inevitable, and there is no shortcut. Society must, pass through each stage. Bear in mind also that even the good comrade will admit that each stage is better than the previous stage. Correct?" He turned to Cabell, who squirmed without moving, and made no reply.

"Good. So, our society, as you are all aware, is presently in the capitalist stage and must inevitably, according to the comrade, evolve into the socialist stage. Now, assuming this is true, which I don't, you might wonder why communists, er, socialists, would bother fighting it. They concede that it's a necessary stage and they believe it will inevitably be replaced by socialism. So, tell us, comrade Cabell, what are you hoping to accomplish if we're all doomed to socialism anyway?"

Cabell narrowed his eyes noticeably. "Because we want to get to socialism quickly. There's no reason to wait. Capitalism has served its purpose and people are being hurt by it." Each word dripped with venom.

"I see. Well, would you agree that a good plan for hastening the downfall of capitalism would be to learn as much about it as possible? Identify its weaknesses?"

Cabell saw the trap clearly, but couldn't avoid it. "Yes," he said reluctantly. "But…"

"Good. Then I trust that is where you will focus your efforts." There was a veiled threat in the words. "Because, comrade, if you don't, you will have a very big problem." The professor fixed Cabell with an icy look. "That ends all discussion of Marxism, socialism, communism, etcetera in this class. I don't want to hear the words 'bourgeois', 'revolution' or 'establishment', and I will not tolerate disruptions. You will allow your fellow students the opportunity to get what they paid for, a chance to learn something about the economic system of this country. There will be no protracted arguments and no politicking. If there is, you will be removed from the class with a failing grade. Is that understood, comrade?"

Flushing redder than ever, Cabell narrowed his eyes again and looked around the room as if to say 'You see? This is what we're up against.' The only response he got was some titters from his fellow students. "I understand all right," he responded between clenched teeth.

"Good. Now find a seat. We've wasted enough time. I don't want socialism to take over the world while we're waiting for you." The professor smiled at this final dig and more giggles sounded from the students.

Dropping to his haunches, Cabell gathered up his papers and book. Rising, he looked around the room. The nearest empty seat was beside Bernadette, on her left. Cabell zigzagged toward it, stumbling over feet and swatting people with his briefcase as he negotiated the narrow spaces between the rows of chairs. Finally flopping into the empty seat, he placed the briefcase between his legs and began sorting his papers on his lap.

The professor shook his head. "Are we quite ready, comrade?"

Cabell didn't look up. "Yes," he said between thin lips. Under his breath he muttered "Bourgeois bastard!"

Bernadette avoided looking at him but she almost burst out laughing. The guy had convictions, or something.

Cabell laid his papers on the writing board attached to the chair arm. Sliding the book he had been clutching into his briefcase, he pulled out the course textbook. "What page are we on?" he whispered to Bernadette.

She hesitated to be identified as even talking to him, but did feel some sympathy for him and after all, couldn't ignore the simple question. "No page," she whispered, keeping her eyes on the professor, "He's just starting."

Cabell glanced at his watch, then held it to his ear. "Must have stopped. I thought I was a half hour late," he muttered. Then, more loudly, but still a whisper to her, "Means I'll have to listen to more of this capitalist bullshit than I thought." He gave her a slight nudge.

She couldn't tell if it was intentional, and glanced at him instinctively. He was looking right at her, with a conspiratorial twinkle in his eyes. She didn't know how to react, so did what she thought was the safest thing and smiled, then turned her attention back to the professor. She didn't realize that to Mike Cabell, political pariah, a smile was like a roar of encouragement, and he wasn't used to encouragement.

From time to time Bernadette glanced furtively at him. Throughout the class he muttered to himself and wrote furious notes, often thickly underlining words and making large exclamation points. Once in a while he caught her eye and nodded at her knowingly, as if they shared some secret. She found it unnerving, but also slightly exciting. He wasn't bad looking and had an air of impishness that she found attractive. She was also drawn to him because he was an outcast, much as she felt herself to be, although for different reasons. She was simply shy, so much so that she hadn't struck up an acquaintance, much less become friends with anyone on campus. She was in fact lonely, although she would have denied it.

When the class ended, he stood and began trying to stuff his loose papers into his briefcase. Instead he dropped them into her lap. Blushing, he mumbled apologies and delicately tried to retrieve the papers.

"Let me help you," Bernadette said. "Hold the briefcase open."

He did so and she managed to stuff the papers in.

"Thanks," he mumbled. Then, looking her straight in the eye, he said, "Could I buy you a Coke or something?"

It was so unexpected that Bernadette didn't know what to say and just stared at him. His face reddened again and he looked away, then turned to leave.

"All right," she said quickly. "A Coke sounds good."

Cabell turned and looked at her in surprise, then his face lit up. "Great! Here, let me carry your bag." He reached for Bernadette's bag.

She smiled. "I thought communists believed in women's liberation?"

Cabell's look told her he didn't understand the remark. "I think you already have enough to carry. I'm OK," she explained.

"Oh, right," he agreed, nodding slightly.

They found a table at the back of the cafeteria and Cabell fetched their Cokes.

"Do you smoke?" he asked, pulling a strange looking pack of cigarettes from his jacket pocket.

"No," Bernadette answered.

"Mind if I do?"

"Depends what you smoke. Those look like weird cigarettes."

Cabell held the packet toward her. "They're little cigars, from Cuba."

Bernadette took the pack from him and examined it. There was a picture of a girl on the front. In one hand she carried a scythe. Slung over her other shoulder was a rifle. "They don't look like normal cigars" Bernadette said, simply.

Cabell pulled a cigar from the pack. It was short and thick, with black tobacco. He tapped the end of the cigar against the table top. When he lit it, the smell reminded Bernadette of burning rope. Blowing out the match, he dropped it in the ashtray, then leaned back and inhaled deeply. "I don't care how thy look, or taste, come to that. I'd just rather give my money to Fidel Castro than to R.J. Reynolds."

He was careful to exhale the smoke away from her and Bernadette was grateful for that consideration. "How do you get them? You got a friend over there, or something?" She sounded disbelieving.

He leaned across the table. "You're not in the CIA, are you?" he grinned.

Although his smile indicated it was a joke, his penetrating gaze made Bernadette feel uncomfortable. Maybe he was paranoid enough to be serious. She looked away. "I thought smoking was a bourgeois habit," she stated. When she looked at him again he appeared insulted.

"I'm joking," Bernadette said quickly. "I don't mind if you smoke."

"Just because a doctor smokes doesn't mean he can't treat cancer," Cabell said seriously.

"You take things too seriously," she said. Then, to try and get the conversation going again, she added, "How do you get cigars from Cuba? I thought we banned imports from there?" She was relieved to see him smile naturally again.

"I order them through a Canadian catalog company and have them sent to a friend in Winnipeg. He sends them to me. I also get other stuff. Flags, posters, books. In fact, I've one here you should read." He bent over to rummage in his briefcase.

"I don't read Spanish," Bernadette said, jokingly.

"It's in English," Cabell answered solemnly. He produced a thin, white volume and held it out to her. "You should read it if you really want to understand economics, instead of the bourgeois crap they feed us here."

Bernadette took the book from him. It was the Communist Manifesto by V.I. Lenin. "I don't know," she said slowly, "I don't have a lot of time..."

"Take as much time as you need," Cabell interrupted. "You can return it whenever you want. Maybe you'll learn something from it, and isn't that what we're here for?"

Bernadette nodded in resignation. "OK. It can't hurt I suppose." She slid the book into her bag. "You really are a communist then? I've never met one before." She felt stupid when she said it.

Cabell smiled at her evident naiveté. For the first time Bernadette noticed that he had a cute dimples. "I'm a socialist, remember? There are a few of us around and we don't have horns, despite what professor Jorgas would have you believe."

"Do they all treat you like that? The professors, I mean."

"Pretty much. They try ridicule because they can't deny the truth." Suddenly he sat bolt upright. "What time is it?"

Bernadette looked at her watch. "Five after twelve."

"Christ! I'm supposed to be in Lincoln Hall at twelve!" He ground his cigar into the ashtray, picked up his briefcase and stood to leave. "How about another Coke tomorrow?"

He had that same pleading look. She hesitated, unsure that he was someone she wanted to become involved with, but he did interest her. "Sure," she answered finally, "Same time, same place?"

"Great." He turned to leave then spun back to her. "I don't even know your name."

She smiled. "Bernadette. Bernadette Mallory."

"Irish, eh?"

Bernadette nodded.

"Michael Collins was a socialist. I'm…"

"Mike Cabell," she interrupted, "I know. Professor Jorgas introduced you to the class. Remember?"

"Yeah, bourgeois bastard. I've gotta run. Tomorrow, then?'

She nodded. Cabell turned and sped off through the lunchtime crowd, bumping and jostling people, making his exit in the same manner he'd made his entrance into her life. Bernadette smiled to herself. There was something she liked about comrade Mike Cabell.

They met every day that week. Bernadette began to read the book he had given her and they talked about it. She understood it to be a brilliant theory, but he believed it to be an inevitable blueprint for humanity.

At the end of the week he invited her to a meeting of the Socialist Youth League. She was reluctant at first, but he pointed out that it was a chance to make new friends, so she finally agreed to go.

There were about a dozen of them, although now, only four remained in Bernadette's memory:

Merwyn, a black guy, also a student. Street-wise and as passionate as Mike but not as eloquent. He and Mike were best friends. Bernadette's impression of Merwyn was that he might be a homosexual, which caused her to wonder about Mike, who so far, had not made any kind of romantic overture to her.

Dan, an older white guy who ran the group's printing press. He was unemployed, chain-smoked, and only spoke when someone spoke to him.

Barry, another white guy in his late twenties. He volunteered that his parents were wealthy and he was a 'perpetual student' to avoid having to work in his father's business. It was plain that Mike didn't like him and Bernadette's initial impression was that Barry was insincere.

Carol, a white girl a little older than Bernadette, was another student. Very attractive and a militant feminist. She seemed friendly enough, but Bernadette sensed an embarrassment, maybe a shared secret between Mike and Carol.

The meeting did not go well. The group argued over most things, including who was in charge, even though everyone agreed that Carol was chairperson. There were two factions, with Mike and Merwyn on one side, and Barry, Dan and Carol on the other. The first group called the other Stalinists and were in turn branded as Maoists. Bernadette could have laughed when they stopped arguing long enough to talk about the one thing they agreed on; they were the vanguard of the socialist movement in America and were leading a revolution.

After the meeting Mike talked to Bernadette about the people she had just met. Merwyn was OK. Dependable, but extreme. Liable to get the group into trouble with the law. Dan was a fraud, only involved because he received a free annual trip to Moscow, compliments of the Soviet Union. The group tolerated him because he was the only one who knew how to operate the complex printing press and wouldn't let anyone else near it. Barry was the worst and would betray his mother to save his own skin. He was definitely not to be trusted. Carol was an opportunist who played the different personalities in the group against each other. Mike claimed that was how she came to be elected chairperson. He was convinced she would be gone as soon as she found someone rich to marry.

Bernadette couldn't imagine the group organizing a frat party, never mind a revolution, but said nothing to Mike. Unbeknownst to her though, they did have one thing going for them. They were in the right place at the right time.

It was 1982. President Reagan had smashed PATCO, the air traffic controllers' union, thereby dealing a crippling setback to the labor movement. He was proposing to pay for a huge increase in defense spending by equally large cuts in welfare programs. Although college students in those days were not the radical activists their parents had been in the sixties, the Socialist Youth League, despite its schisms, was able to stir up opposition to Reagan's policies. They organized marches, sit-ins and protests. Bernadette remembered the exhilaration of posting flyers around campus in the middle of the night, and fleeing when campus security showed up.

She felt the same excitement at student rallies and demonstrations, becoming confident enough to take the podium on occasion. Becoming more comfortable in front of the microphone, she discovered she had a rare talent for public speaking and was able to fire up a crowd, and get them to donate money or volunteer time to help with "the struggle".

She remembered when the president came to town. Mike, Barry and herself made a huge sign reading "Ray Gun aims to hurt women and children". Despite the heavy security and the efforts of the police to keep the president's route into the city clear of protests, they managed to climb a huge freeway billboard and wait until the presidential motorcade appeared before unfurling their banner. They got away too. The incident received national media coverage, mostly because of the alarming breakdown in security. 'What if they'd been trying to assassinate the president?' the press wondered.

It was widely known among the student body that they were the ones involved in the incident and they became campus heroes. Because of her way with words, she was the one the local media sought out when they wanted a controversial opinion on any issue. She became a local media star. Mike encouraged her, content to stay in the background, planning strategies and events to further their cause. Her crowning achievement came when she led a sit-in in the chancellor's office. The national guard was called in and there was a standoff for a week. Her political status was established, and now came her real opportunity.

The area around the university was a ghetto and there was an election for a vacant city council seat. Although Mike had always mocked the electoral system, he realized that with all the attention Bernadette had garnered from the media, the time was ripe to move to the next level of involvement. He encouraged Bernadette to run for the seat and organized a voter registration campaign. Bernadette won the election easily, appointing Mike as her aide. During all this time he showed no romantic interest in her and she had resigned herself to the fact that his passion was reserved for politics.

Two years on the city council gave Bernadette a small sip of power which she found addictive. She learned the art of politics well and was able to influence Mike toward moderation which would ensure her re-election. She guided him away from the Socialist Youth League and toward a more community-based philosophy. Mike went along because, Bernadette realized, he too was smitten with the trappings of power. She assured him, and herself, that they weren't selling out, they were maturing.

Bernadette did such a good job of handling constituent concerns and building coalitions that by the time her term was up she was in a position to eschew the chance for re-election to the city council and run instead for the higher position of county commissioner. Her fund raising skills proved decisive and she won the election narrowly. With the increase in power came a craving for still more.

Four more years passed before that fateful day, the memory of which still made Bernadette wince.

She had gone to the office one evening to pick up some papers she wanted to review before the next day's board meeting. She remembered being surprised that the office light was still on. When she entered the room she found Mike and Carol, whom she hadn't seen for a couple of years. Mike was sitting on his desk, leaning back on his elbows. His pants were down around his ankles and Carol's head was between his legs, her long hair bobbing jerkily. Recalling the scene still cut Bernadette like a razor.

Bernadette did not create a scene, but she would have vengeance. She had simply turned and left, ignoring Mike's pleas to let him explain.

She immediately fired Mike and began planning her campaign for the following year's election. It became an obsession when Mike announced he would run against her.

She understood that minority and women's issues were becoming the focus for change. Running as an independent, she gathered support from the groups she'd worked with. Most importantly, she understood the need to raise money and was good at it. She beat Mike handily, and savored his concession speech, especially the fact that Carol was absent from his side when he delivered it. So it was that politics, which had brought Bernadette and Mike together, became the battleground where they were torn apart.

In his bitterness Mike turned to drink and slid into alcoholism. He staggered in and out of treatment centers where he would scream that if they knew who he was, they wouldn't do this to him. In rare, sober moments, he would sob uncontrollably, like a child exhausted from fright. Carol simply disappeared.

Bernadette immersed herself in the power which was now hers alone. When her term on the county board was nearly up, a women's group suggested that she run for a seat in the U.S. House of Representatives. They needed a feminist candidate and there weren't any around with her experience. Most importantly, they would finance her campaign. Bernadette accepted their offer and was elected.

She had held the seat for nine years now and her seniority had gained her a position on the special appropriations committee. Luck had placed her in an even better situation. There was a Republican/Democrat deadlock over who should chair the committee. As an independent, and as the only woman on the committee, Bernadette was the logical compromise choice, much as both parties hated to give up the power that went with the position.

That was how she came to be in this present situation, where a paltry appropriation of one hundred million dollars, stalled in the committee she chaired, meant an awful lot to both parties in this election year. Bernadette could break the deadlock, which was why both the Speaker and the president wanted her ear.

Being in such demand caused her an inward smile. It was quite an accomplishment for a girl raised in poverty, half a world away.

The rising wail of a siren from the street below interrupted her reverie. Stepping to the window, Bernadette pulled aside the thin, white curtain. Large snowflakes were falling. A police car, red light flashing, skidded through the intersection and swerved wildly on its way down 'M' street. She watched it disappear around the corner, the siren echoing more and more faintly. Traffic, which had pulled over to avoid the crazy squad car, began to move again, creeping along the iced streets.

On the opposite sidewalk Bernadette noticed a mother bending over, knotting a scarf around the chin of her uncooperative toddler. Bernadette thought of her own mother. How would she have reacted to all this? To the president's attacks in the press, painting Bernadette as selfish, conniving, unpatriotic?

Ever since that night, years ago, when she told her mother she was embarking on a career in politics, the old woman had made her disappointment clear.

"Politics! Have ye learned nothin' from all that education? I thought what happened t' yer father would be lesson enough about politics!" She wrung her hands. "I should've known his bad seed was in ye an' would sprout one day, whether I moved ye t' new soil or not."

"Oh, mother!" Bernadette had replied condescendingly, "That was Ireland. This is America. Things are different here. Father was caught up in centuries-old feuds, forced to take sides. This country's young. People are open to fresh ideas and new approaches. And didn't you always say America was a land of opportunities, especially for women?"

She could still see her mother's smarting look. "Politics allows only two opportunities. The first one is t' become a crook like the rest o' them, obsessed wi' money an' power an' corrupted by their addiction. Oh, ye think it won't happen t' ye. That ye can remain pure an' help people. It won't work, Bernadette. The system won't allow it.

Or there's the other opportunity as ye call it. Ye might be successful at first. It might even continue for a while, but the day will come when yer of no use t' them, when yer in the way, or they need a scapegoat. Ye'll find out then that talk's cheap, just like yer father did. An' like him, ye'll find out too late."

She grasped Bernadette by the arms. "I know what I'm talkin' about, Bernadette. I was young once too an' as full o' idealism as ye are. Yer father an' me met at a meetin' for 'The Cause'. Finally, I understood what was goin' on, but he never could. Who d'ye think keeps all that fightin' an' killin' goin'? Not terrorists. Not the IRA. Not men like yer father. It's politicians! They need it that way t' keep their power, an' every generation they use misguided people, then they cast them aside. Ye may not end up exactly like yer father, Bernadette, but ye'll end up hurt. Yer not their kind an' they'll use ye like they used him, believe me."

Bernadette hadn't believed. Had tried to convince her mother that she knew what she was doing, that it was what she wanted. But the old woman was not to be convinced. Her girl, the focus of her life, for whom she had worked and saved to create a new life, had betrayed her. Spitefully, she declared politics to be a taboo subject between them, thereby effectively insulating herself from most of her daughter's life.

Now, in the comfortable quiet of her office, Bernadette wondered if her mother's bitterness was because she wanted her own dreams and ambitions realized through her daughter. Or if it was because she, Bernadette, had sided with her father in some unknown spiritual battle against her mother. She did not want to think about these things because she could never know the answers, so she tried to think of something else.

Her breath steamed the office window and she watched the circle of condensation shrink rapidly on itself until it disappeared. She imagined her father's sad face behind the glass, the way she had last seen him. In prison. The glass there had been bulletproof. How old had he been then? She was twelve at the time, so he would have been about forty. He had looked twice that, with slumped shoulders, bowed head, and thinning hair. The aging effect was heightened by the gray, wrinkled prison uniform that was several sizes too big. Her child's mind had wanted to know why he had to wear such clothes. She understood now that it was a deliberate indignity. It must have been a special pain to him, who had regularly asserted that no matter how low a man felt, he could always retain some pride by at least dressing well.

That was what made him so furious when his only suit wasn't redeemed from the pawnbroker's in time for him to wear on weekends. Or was it that he felt inadequate because his pay wasn't enough to support them from one week to the next? In either case, Bernadette now knew, it was his dignity that was pawned for a few shillings.

She cringed at the memory of the pawnshop. The furtive glances to make sure no neighbors saw her enter, and the place itself, with dark, musty little booths which were supposed to ensure privacy, but which instead gave a feeling of entrapment. And the fly-paper. It was everywhere and Bernadette still remembered the dried out shells of flies and wasps stuck to the yellow strips.

It was bad enough on Thursday evenings, when she was sent to redeem the suit, but it was worse on Monday mornings when she had to accompany her mother to pawn it again. Then, neighbors couldn't be avoided. Most of them were there too, pawning clothes, clocks, rings, the prized accumulations of their poor lives. Although everyone knew that everyone else was there, friends and neighbors did not acknowledge each other in the pawn shop. That would be embarrassing.

Bernadette found it even more humiliating to observe the bartering between her mother and the pawnbroker, who, although he had arrived from England over twenty years ago, still spoke with an accent. The ritual was always the same. Her mother would ask five pounds for the suit. The old pawnbroker, magnifying glass in one eye, would cluck his tongue, shake his head and shrug his shoulders. He would pick up the suit, drop it on the counter and push it back towards her mother.

"Clothes," he would mutter, gesturing around the shop with his arms. "What can I do with so many clothes?"

Her mother had told her that when he spoke loudly he was in no mood to negotiate. When he was willing to raise his offer he talked softly, so that his other customers wouldn't know he could be bargained up.

"What if you don't come back for these clothes?" the pawnbroker would continue, "How am I expected to sell them? Am I to hope that someone who happens to fit these clothes and who happens to like the pattern of this suit will come into my shop?"

"Sure ye know I'll be back in for it on Thursday. I always am. It's not like ye'd have t' sell it, an' ye know it's worth more than the five pounds," her mother would answer.

"To you, maybe. Not to me." He would pick up the suit again. "Tell you what, it's not good business but I'll do you a favor this time. I'll give you two pounds."

Her mother would protest and the pawnbroker would state that was his final offer, take it or leave it, he had other customers to attend to. Always her mother would become afraid, and plead for three pounds at least. Enough to buy dinner. The old man would finally agree, muttering about charging another ten pence interest.

Her mother knew he wouldn't, and always left the shop feeling she had provided a fine example for her daughter to follow when dealing with pawnbrokers. They were, after all an integral part of life.

Bernadette never had gotten to ask her father about the prison clothes. Never even got to say goodbye to him properly. Her mother had grabbed her hand and led her from the large, cold room where other families were touching palms to the thick glass partition and blowing kisses through it.

Years later, her mother told her that her father had wanted it that way. Already facing twenty years in jail, the visit from his wife to say that she was giving up on him and taking the girl to a new life in America had finally broken him. His pride though, would never allow him to admit it.

Bernadette understood now what it must have been like for them. And how it must have felt for her mother when her final written attempt at reconciliation was killed by the terse letter they received in response. It said, "You were right to take the child. She should have no part of this life and should not even know of it. Do not bring her here, even for a visit. We have separate lives now."

Bernadette could still picture the crumpled, lined page, looking like it had been torn from a school notebook. The words were in black pencil, formed with large, childlike letters. Her mother had never spoken of him again, and Bernadette was left to wonder what had become of the thin man who used to balance her on his knee, asking the same riddles over and over again in a whisky-slurred voice, and beaming and rewarding her with pennies when she got the answer right.

A lump came to her throat and her mind surrendered to the falling snow which seemed like a comforting, thick blanket, smothering her memories. After a moment, she walked back to her desk and picked up the legal pad and pencil. Almost immediately she laid them down again. Her memories had depressed her and she couldn't make notes now. She felt drained.

Taking her purse from the bottom desk drawer, she opened the door to the outer office. Larry wasn't there. Crossing to his desk, she began to write a note, but before she could finish, the door opened and he came in. Bernadette crumpled the unfinished note into a ball and dropped it into the wastebasket by his desk. "Ah, there you are," she said.

"I just went down the hall to get some pop." He held up the can as proof. "Was there something you wanted?"

"I'm taking the rest of the afternoon off, to get ready for the president this evening. Anything we need to go over before I leave?"

"Well, Boyce from the Globe wants your reaction to the president's tirade this morning. I told him we had no comment." Larry waited for her approval.

"Good. Anything else?"

"The DC Teachers' Association called again, about the speaking invitation. I said I'd get back to them." He waited again.

Bernadette studied him for a few seconds. "I'll sleep on it," she said finally.

"They wanted me to call back today," Larry badgered.

"I'll sleep on it, and you will be able to give them an answer today." Bernadette smiled.

"I...I don't understand," Larry faltered.

"I'm going home to have a nap. I'll let you know about their invitation later."

Larry looked as if she were speaking a foreign language. "Don't you feel well?" he asked eventually.

"I feel fine. Don't worry, it's a trick I learned from an old dog." She smiled again. "You can hold the fort?"

"Yes, of course," he answered. "About the bank account…"

"There's money in the account isn't there?" Bernadette interrupted.

"Well yes, that's…"

"Well then, that's all that matters. I can't think about it right now," she interrupted again. "Anything else?"

"No," Larry sighed, "What about your meeting with the president? Will you be all right for that?"

Bernadette knew he wanted desperately to accompany her. It was a matter of status with the other congressional office aides, but she saw no point in his being there. Besides, he'd want to rehash and analyze everything immediately after the meeting, and she didn't want to be committed to his company for that long. "Don't worry. I'll be fine," she stated.

Larry shrugged his shoulders as if shaking off responsibility.

"Call me at five about the teachers' conference," Bernadette continued. It was a concession to his wounded look. She touched him on the elbow. "Why don't you take the afternoon off too? You've been under a lot of pressure lately. I can ask Bob to have Laurie cover the office."

"It's OK," he answered. "I've got a mountain of mail to get through. Besides, I have nothing better to do."

Smiling at his unwitting deprecation of their work, she finished buttoning her coat, picked up her purse and turned to face him. "I appreciate all the work you've done lately, Larry. I'm sure things will improve after my meeting tonight. See you tomorrow."

"Good luck!" Larry said after her as she stepped into the corridor.

The elevator door slid shut and Bernadette felt relief in her anonymity among the clerks, house pages, and assorted minions of the Washington bureaucracy.

5

Billy stopped in at Mc Kenna's Fish n' Chip Emporium on the corner of Dee street. Being Monday there was no line. Most people could only afford carryouts on weekends while they were still flush with Friday night's paypacket. He ordered a fish supper and watched as the battered cod and thick fries were dumped onto a sheet of newspaper, saturated in vinegar and heavily salted. Billy paid and picked up the hot, greasy package.

As he walked home, he noticed that the red, white and blue curbstones along the edge of the sidewalk were badly faded. Next July they would be painted again by the neighborhood kids who, he knew from experience, had quite a scam going by collecting money from each house on the street, to pay for the paint. Any money left over went for cigarettes and beer. No-one dared refuse to contribute, since they didn't want their patriotism called into question.

He also noticed the murals painted on the gables of those houses unfortunate enough to be at the end of a block. The murals were done with paint left over from painting the curbstones and usually depicted either King William of Orange crossing the river Boyne in 1690, or modern masked men with guns, representing paramilitary groups like the UVF. In Catholic areas of the city the murals would be of the pope, or masked men with guns, representing the IRA.

The houses which bore the murals suffered doubly by also having to endure the intense heat of huge bonfires which were ignited every July 11th at most of the intersections in Protestant areas. The owners of these houses often suffered broken windows, blistered paint and smoke damage as a result of the infernos, not to mention the risk of the roof catching fire from flying embers.

What Billy did not notice was that every house he passed, indeed thousands of houses for miles around, even in the Catholic areas, were exactly like his own, down to the red painted bricks of the front and the white painted bricks surrounding the door. The only difference was in the color people chose to paint the wooden window frames and doors. The houses had all been built by the Harland and Wolff shipyard around the turn of the century to accommodate the vast number of workers they needed.

Finally arriving home, he dug into his pocket, and extracted the front door key. Opening the door, he stepped into a small hallway. He was relieved to be home again, even if he was returning to an empty house. Throwing his jacket over the stair banister, he went into the scullery. His first order of business was to make some tea to go with his fish and chips. He filled a kettle with enough water to make two cups and placed it on the largest ring of the gas stove. He lit the gas, careful not to turn it to full power and have the hairs on the back of his hand singed as sometimes happened. Taking the tea canister from a shelf above the stove, he tossed two spoonsful of tea into the teapot. Next he buttered two slices of bread and threw them on a plate along with the fish and chips. While he waited for the kettle to boil he ate a few of the fries and was reminded why Mc Kenna's had such a poor reputation. The chips were undercooked, with a starchy aftertaste. He knew the fish would be overcooked, as if in a futile attempt to compensate for the chips.

'Not what is meant by a balanced meal,' he thought. 'I'll go the extra couple o' blocks to Gillespies in future.' He had told himself this many times before.

The kettle finally boiled and he made his tea. Pouring a large cup, he switched on the television and settled down to his dinner, placing a cushion on his lap on which to balance the plate, and setting his tea on one wide, flat arm of his chair. He ate with his hands, carefully selecting chips of just the right size to lay in a row on one of the slices of bread, which he then folded over to make a chip butty. He would make a fish butty with the remaining slice of bread. As he ate he tried to concentrate on the six o'clock news broadcast but his mind kept wandering to Joe Mallory and what he would tell his foreman tomorrow to excuse his absence from work for a few days.

Suddenly there was a loud knock at the front door, which startled him. He never had visitors and the week's coal delivery wasn't due until tomorrow. The knock came again, louder this time. Picking up his dinner, Billy stood, and placed the cushion and plate on the seat of the chair. Going to the window, he looked out, but could see no-one from that angle. Warily, he opened the door.

Two men stood on the doorstep. One of them nodded at Billy. "Evenin'. Are ye Billy Kingston?"

Billy's wariness turned to uneasiness. "Aye," he answered slowly. "D' I know ye?"

"I'm Harry Johnstone an' this is Roy Pearson." The other man nodded, while the first one continued, "We know a fella ye work wi' in the 'Yard, Jimmy Kincaid."

Billy signaled acknowledgment of the name and waited. In Belfast you didn't invite strangers into your house.

"We just moved int' the street. Ye've probably seen us comin' an' goin' the past couple o' days?"

"I don't mind other people's business," Billy replied. He thought they would be pleased with that answer.

"Aye, right," Johnstone continued. "We're here t' talk t' ye about somethin' that's all our business. Ye know there's been some IRA drive-by shootin's lately?"

"Thank Christ there haven't been any on this side o' the city," Billy said.

"So far there haven't," Johnstone agreed. "An' that's how we'd like t' keep it. We're settin' up checkpoints at each end o' the street so the bastards can't be shootin' our women an' children."

"Ye mean the army an' police're settin' them up?"

"No, they can't be everywhere at once, can they? We're doin' it ourselves. The men in the street, I mean. We already checked wi' the peelers an' soldiers, an' they won't interfere. Sure it's be less for them t' worry about."

"I suppose so," Billy said, not grasping the import of what was being said. "Are ye gonna be stoppin' people from comin' int' the street, then?"

"Only cars. We don't need t' worry about people walkin'."

"Well, I don't own a car so I don't need t' worry about it," Billy said, relieved.

Johnstone looked at his companion who smiled slightly. "The thing is," Johnstone went on, "Since we're doin' this for the benefit o' everybody in the street we figure ye won't mind helpin' out. We're askin' all the men t' take turns mannin' the checkpoints. Now I know ye've a job an' we don't want t' be interferin' wi' that. We thought ye could take the eight till midnight shift. There'd be four o' us on duty then."

Now that Billy understood, he cursed inwardly. This wasn't something he was being asked. He was being told to be there. He swallowed. "Would this be every night?"

"The IRA doesn't take time off," Johnstone replied caustically.

Billy saw no alternative. "Which end o' the street d' ye want me at?"

"Newtownards Road. They're settin' things up now. Like I said, if ye'd come at eight o'clock?"

Billy nodded. "Aye, all right. I'll be there."

"Good enough. We won't disturb ye anymore. We've a few other calls t' make. See ye at eight, then."

The men turned and walked down the street. Billy heard their knock at a house a few doors down. He closed and locked the door and went back to his dinner.

His immediate concern was not that he might be in any physical danger. All the shootings so far had been in west Belfast. There were few Catholics to fight with here on the east side of the city. Billy felt the UVF was using this as a way to make themselves look like protectors of ordinary Protestants. It also occurred to him that they were protecting their own commander's house, which might well become an IRA target.

He was concerned that he'd have to explain why, beginning Wednesday night, he wouldn't be around to man the checkpoint for a while. Whatever reason he gave as his absence from work would have to be good enough to be acceptable to the UVF without further explanation. He certainly didn't want to draw their attention to him. Luckily, he had a day to come up with something.

At eight o'clock he put on his jacket and walked to the corner of Dundonald street and the Newtownards Road, one of the city's major thoroughfares. Against one wall of the Red Hand pub a small hut had been built from wood and sheets of corrugated metal. Across the street stretched a thick plank with three rows of six inch nails driven through it, pointing upwards. It was a crude but effective deterrent. Any car driving over it would have its tires shredded. In front of the tire slasher was a Belfast corporation road work barrier, resting on two triangular sawhorses.

It was already dark, and it wasn't until he was within a few yards of the checkpoint that Billy recognized one of the two men standing at the barrier as Harry. It wasn't until he was within a few feet that he made out the rifle slung over Harry's shoulder.

"Billy," Harry greeted him, "D'ye know Ken?"

Billy didn't. He nodded at the other man, who returned the acknowledgment.

"There's one more fella supposed t' be here. I'd better go an' get 'im." Harry said.

He walked back down the street. Billy and Ken watched as he knocked on the door of a house which had a street lamp in front of it. They heard an agitated voice, but couldn't make out what was being said. After a few moments a small Pakistani man came out of the house. Billy knew the Pakistani drove an ice cream truck. He was the only Pakistani Billy had ever seen in person.

Harry turned and began walking back to the checkpoint. The Pakistani, shorter-legged, hurried at his side, all the while keeping up a stream of protests which Harry was ignoring.

"You are not understanding," gabbled the Pakistani, "I am not being part of these troubles as you are calling them. I am Muslim, not Protestant or Catholic. I sell ice cream and I don't care who is buying. I want only to work and bother no-one."

Harry stopped and looked at the Pakistani. "Listen, darkie. Ye live on this street, don't ye?"

The Pakistani looked perplexed. "Yes, of course I do. You are just bringing me from my house. And my name is being Ranjsee, not Darkie."

"Ye want yer wife an' kids t' be safe?"

"Yes, most definitely," said the Pakistani stoutly.

"Then quit whinin'. Every man in the street is doin' this. No exceptions. I don't care what religion ye are. Ye're in Belfast now an' ye do what we do."

The Pakistani muttered to himself. Harry rolled his eyes at Billy and Ken. He walked over to the hut and disappeared inside. In a moment he emerged. "All right, now, here's a torch for each o' yous, an' a whistle."

They each took the offered items and immediately all three turned on their flashlights.

"Don't be wastin' the batteries," admonished Harry.

Obediently they all turned off the flashlights.

"An' yous needn't be testin' the whistles either, they work too."

"Pardon me." It was the Pakistani again. "But I am not understanding. For what are we needing these things?"

"I'm gettin' t' that." Harry glared at him. "Here's how it works. Any car will have t' slow down t' turn the corner int' the street. They'll see the barrier an' stop. One of yous, step in front o' the car an' keep yer torch shinin' on the driver. Another one o' yous approach the car from the passenger side an' shine yer torch int' the back seats. Remember these IRA bastards might be lyin' in the back, holdin' a gun on the driver. An' check the boot too, them bastards've been known t' hold a hostage an' force the driver t' deliver a car bomb for them. The last one o' yous find out the driver's business. If he says he's pickin' up or visitin' somebody, one o' yous go down t' the house an' check it out. Don't let any strangers through just because they know the name o' somebody who lives in the street. Any questions?"

Ken spoke. "Aye, I've two questions. First, what if the car's just cuttin' through t' another street?"

"They'll have t' find another way through."

Ken nodded. "An', what'll ye be doin' all this time?"

"I'll be in that hallway," Harry answered, jerking his head in the direction of the pub. "An' I'll have this aimed at the driver's head." He tapped his rifle.

Ken was visibly shaken and took an involuntary step back from Harry. Not knowing how good of a shot Harry might be, Billy decided he'd be the one to check the passenger side and trunk of any cars. At least then the car would be between him and Harry.

"Any more questions?" Harry asked.

"Yes, please be excusing my ignorance. I am understanding the flashlight, torch as you are calling it, but I am not comprehending the use of this fine whistle." The Pakistani turned the whistle over in his hand, examining it as if he'd never seen such a thing before.

Billy was glad the Pakistani had asked the question. It had been on his mind too but he hadn't wanted to risk an obvious answer which would make him appear stupid.

"I'm glad ye asked that, darkie. The whistles are in case somethin' goes wrong."

The Pakistani waited, then realized that no further explanation was forthcoming. "I regret I am still not understanding, and please to remember my name is being Ranjsee and not Darkie."

Harry sighed. "Suppose a car's about t' turn int' the street, sees the checkpoint an' decides t' hightail it out o' here? Very suspicious, right?"

The Pakistani nodded in agreement.

"So, ye blow the whistle as loud as ye can."

Again the Pakistani waited and again there was no further explanation. "I regret to be so foolish, but still I am lacking something. What will this do, me blowing this whistle at a car which is speeding away?"

"When ye blow the whistle, the people at the checkpoints in the neighborin' streets'll know t' swing their tire shredders around ont' the main road so the car won't get very far."

Billy was surprised to hear there were checkpoints on other streets, although it made sense when he thought about it.

"Ye'd better hope the car's speedin' away from ye, darkie, because if it's speedin' toward ye, ye'll have t' jump faster and higher than a monkey." Harry laughed at what he considered an appropriate simile. "Any more questions?"

The Pakistani sputtered. "You are telling me that when these lunatics are driving a car at me or maybe shooting or bombing me, I am to be blowing a whistle?" He was becoming visibly angry. "Then I am telling you this is madness and I am not being a part of it. I am thinking I will be returning to you this bloody torch and this bloody whistle and I will be going home to my bed. Yes, that is what I am thinking I will do!"

Harry walked up to the Pakistani until he was within an inch of the shorter man's face. His voice had an unmistakable tone. "Do that if ye want, darkie, but let me tell ye something'. Ye know yer ice cream van?"

The Pakistani nodded. He had a look of fear in his eyes.

"Ye go home now an' that van'll never leave the street."

The Pakistani's expression turned to complete horror. After a minute he threw his hands up in the air and began walking in small circles. He kept up an incessant muttering to himself. Billy could make out an occasional "lunatics!" and "Muslim" from the chatter.

"I think that's taken care o' him," said Harry. "Anythin' else?"

Billy spoke. "Ye said there were checkpoints on other corners. Does the whole road have checkpoints at every street?"

"Not yet," Harry answered. "So far they're only set up at Dundonald, Chadolly an' St.Leonards streets, but the other streets'll start doin' it soon enough." He nodded toward the ramshackle hut. "There's a paraffin stove in the hut. It'll be bitter cold later. Some o' the women'll be bringing tea an' sandwiches about ten o'clock." Just as he finished saying this a car turned off the main road into the street. "Let's go," Harry said, then slid along the pub wall and into the hallway he had pointed out earlier.

Turning the corner slowly, the car stopped at the barricade. Switching on his flashlight, Ken approached the driver who rolled down his window. Walking to the passenger side, Billy shone his flashlight into the back of the car. The Pakistani, shaking noticeably, stood in front of the car, the beam from his flashlight shining jerkily through the windshield and showing the frightened faces of the old man driving the car and the even older woman who was his passenger.

"It's all right," said Ken loudly and with relief. "It's Mr. an' Mrs. Moore from number thirtyseven." Leaning into the driver's window he added, "It's all right now, Mr. Moore, there's nothin' t' worry about."

Mr. Moore was in his sixties. His wife, ten years his senior, looked cowed beside him and clutched her husband's arm.

"We're just keepin' the street safe for ye so them IRA men can't be comin' down here," continued Ken.

Mr. Moore nodded in comprehension and patted his wife's arm. "It's all right, Martha. These men are protectin' the street from the IRA."

His wife sagged visibly with relief. "Bless yous all," she muttered hoarsely, "Sure it's time somebody did somethin'. Ye can't depend on them peelers an' soldiers at all, can ye?"

"No, Mrs. Moore, that's a fact all right. We'll let ye on through now." He turned to the Pakistani. "Swing the nails back out o' the way." At the same time he hauled the roadworks barrier away from the front of the car.

The Pakistani muttered loudly but did as he was told, although he staggered under the heavy weight of the plank.

"Away ye go now, Mr. Moore. Sorry for the trouble."

"It's no trouble at all," answered the driver, easing the car forward.

"Bless yous all," repeated his wife, smiling and waving at each of them in turn. The car moved slowly down the street.

Harry emerged from his hallway. "Don't just stand there lookin' after them, darkie. Get the plank back in the street. Ken, put that barrier back." He watched while his commands were carried out. "Bloody lucky that was only an old couple who happen t' live in the street," he continued. "Billy, didn't I say ye were t' inspect the boot?"

Billy blushed. "Ach, sure there'd a' been nothin' there. That old woman woulda been a sobbin' wreck if..."

"An' what if she knew the IRA was holdin' a gun t' her daughter's head an' would kill her if they didn't hear the bomb go off in the next five minutes?"

"Sure Ken knew them," answered Billy. "They're just an old couple." Billy looked imploringly at Ken for support, but none was forthcoming.

"Ye've got t' be serious about this!" shouted Harry.

Billy didn't like the idea of an upset man holding a rifle. "Yer right, I'm sorry. It won't happen again," he said quickly.

Harry nodded. "All right, then. That was a first try, but let's get serious from now on, eh?"

The three conscripts nodded their heads in unison.

"I'm goin' t' sit in the hut for a while," continued Harry.

They watched him go inside and the Pakistani said, "Bloody lunatic!" but not loudly enough for Harry to hear.

Billy agreed with the Pakistani's diagnosis, but said nothing.

The rest of the evening was uneventful. Only a few cars pulled into the street and Ken knew all of the occupants except for one car which contained three young men. The checkpoint trio were nervous until the driver told Ken to call Harry over. Harry came and told them to let the car through. They were friends of his.

'UVF men,' Billy thought. This was confirmed when the car pulled up at the house Harry himself occupied.

At ten o'clock two women approached the hut. They carried trays with steaming cups of tea, cheese sandwiches and biscuits. They clucked over the men, blessing them and assuring them that they were greatly appreciated.

Over tea, Billy had his most uncomfortable moment of the evening. Harry asked where he was from. Billy had anticipated this might come up and had decided that if the UVF checked up on him, it didn't matter much whether he told the truth or lied. Either way they'd find out something wasn't right, so he told the truth. "I'm from Lisaleene, outside Newry."

"I know it. D'ye know a fella by the name o' Adam Bickerstaff?"

Billy cursed his luck. He hadn't imagined that any of them would have even heard of Lisaleene. "I don't recall anybody o' that name. Mind, it's been years since I was there."

"Bickerstaff's about your age an' he's lived on a farm near there all his life. Funny ye not knowin' him, Lisaleene being such a small place."

"I left when I was a wee lad," Billy said, hoping that would end the conversation. He was relieved when Harry nodded and let the subject drop.

At eleven thirty the pub closed and a small crowd of drinkers was turned out into the street. Included in the group were two men who were due to take the midnight to four checkpoint shift. They'd had just enough to drink that they were feeling charitable and offered to take their shift early. Harry told the Pakistani he could go. Billy surmised correctly that this was so Harry could be rid of him. The Pakistani scurried off without saying goodnight. Since Billy had a job to go to in the morning, Harry told him he could leave too.

On the walk back to his house it dawned on Billy why only three streets had checkpoints. That was all the UVF needed. They were guarding against the possibility that the IRA might enter one of those streets. From St.Leonard's street to the west, they could enter one of the houses, go through the back door and launch an attack across the alley. From Chadolly street to the east, they could attack the rear of the UVF house. From either street they'd have a clear escape route if there were no barriers.

Billy revised his opinion of the UVF. Perhaps they weren't so stupid. Given his situation, and what would happen if they found out who he was, this realization did not comfort him. He lay awake for a long time worrying about it, and about what lay ahead of him.

6

Bernadette dreamed of towering black rocks and white, crashing surf. A gang of seagulls squawked and fought over a dead fish, which had her face. She could make out a faint two-toned tweet among their coarse screeches and she strained to isolate its source. The sound grew louder. She woke up. The tweeting was urgent now. Rolling over, she picked up the phone. "Hello?"

"Sorry if I woke you, but it's five o'clock and you said I should call…" Larry waited for acknowledgment of his justification.

"Yes. Anything new?"

"Just the usual. Press calls mostly. Wanting to fan the flames…"

"Anything else?"

"You said you'd decide about the Teachers' Association."

"Damn! I completely forgot. I'm being picked up at six-thirty. Call me at six-fifteen. I promise I'll have an answer then, OK? I have to get a move on now."

"About the bank account…"

"Not that again, Larry! I just haven't time right now. I have to get ready. Call me back at six-fifteen." She hung up the phone to avoid a response.

She had already decided not to address the teachers' convention. She couldn't face one more group wanting her current notoriety to provide them with news coverage for their own narrow viewpoint. Why she didn't just tell Larry that, she couldn't imagine.

Stripping, she inspected her body in the full length mirror which hung on the back of her bedroom door. The wrinkles around her eyes bothered her. They seemed to have deepened over the past few weeks, but she told herself they only looked worse because she had just woken up. She cupped her breasts in her palms. They were still firm, but her belly was more pneumatic than she wanted. She liked the look of her legs, though. They were straight, long and still young looking. "Middle age," she thought. "You really should exercise, trim that midriff."

After showering, she sat naked before her dresser and began applying makeup, laying it on thickly between the wrinkles about her eyes. As she painted, she thought about what to wear, her mind skipping along the rows of dresses in her wardrobe. Too tight, too informal, no shoes to match. It would have to be the navy blue pleated skirt and pearl necklace again.

That decision made, she felt better, which in turn restored her appetite, reminding her that she was hungry. She wondered if they would feed her. Probably not, and there wasn't time to eat before going. She'd have to wait until later, maybe go to the bistro on the corner and spend some time alone. She fixed her hair and dressed. While she was searching for the only shoes which matched her outfit, the phone rang again. She looked at her watch, which showed six-fifteen. Sometimes she hated Larry's efficiency.

"Hello Larry," she sighed into the receiver.

"Hi," he answered hesitantly, "Did you decide about the teachers?"

"Yes. Tell them I appreciate their invitation, but regret I am unable to accept at this time."

"Bern...!"

"Please, Larry, that's my decision." She tried to sound like a boss.

He persisted. "I just think you should accept some of these invitations. They provide a forum to answer back and win some people to your side."

"I've made my decision, and haven't time to discuss it now. The car will be here in a few minutes and I'm still not ready. Goodbye, Larry, I'll see you tomorrow."

"Wait! The bank account…"

Bernadette sighed. "OK. What about the bank account?"

"There's more money in it than I can account for."

"That's a problem?"

"It's ten thousand dollars."

Bernadette gasped. "That's a lot to be off. Have you checked with the bank?"

"Of course." He sounded peeved that she imagined he had not taken that elementary step before raising it with her. "They're looking into it but it might take a few days."

"OK. so what's the big problem?" Bernadette asked. "They probably screwed up and they'll take the money out of the account before we can think about spending it. Or, we can hope it's not a mistake and some aunt I didn't know died and left me the money. It'll get sorted out."

Larry sighed. "Yes, I suppose so. I just wondered if you knew anything about it."

Now Bernadette felt peeved. "If I'd known about a ten thousand dollar boost to the bank account I'd have mentioned it."

"Yes," Larry said in a chastened tone. "Well, goodbye then." He sighed again. "And good luck."

"Thanks. I'll see you tomorrow." She hung up.

Poor Larry. She should get him a small gift to show her appreciation. A tie, maybe. She immediately dismissed the idea as too personal and went back to finding shoes to wear. Maybe she should wear boots for the snow? But if she did, she'd have to carry her shoes somehow. And where would she put the boots when she got to the White House? She couldn't just leave them sitting outside the door. She decided that since she would walk only a few steps to and from the car, she would forego the boots. She found the shoes she wanted and wiggled her feet into them.

She had her head tilted sideways, piercing an earring through her left lobe when the phone rang again.

"Good evening, Ms. Mallory." It was Horace, the doorman. "A limousine has arrived for you ma'am."

"Thank you, Horace. I'll be right down."

She finished putting on her earrings and slid her arms into her coat. She shook her head slightly, so that her hair looked a little more natural, not quite so made up. After a glance in the mirror, and another around the room, she left the apartment.

Horace saw her get out of the elevator and motioned to a gray-uniformed chauffeur who stood near the front entrance. The man took a final, long drag on his cigarette, opened the door and flicked the glowing butt into the half inch of snow which had accumulated on the sidewalk. Bernadette pretended not to notice.

"Good evening ma'am," said Horace, tipping his hat at her. "Anything I should say if someone calls on you?"

"Say I have a date," Bernadette responded, smiling and raising her eyebrows to indicate a joke.

"Very well, ma'am, have a good time," the doorman said.

He was a professional and would have said the same thing, in the same tone, if Bernadette had announced she was going to the moon. Bernadette smiled back at him. "Thank you, Horace." She went through the lobby door, to where the chauffeur held the car door open. She acknowledged him with a slight nod of the head and a murmured "Thank you."

Her nap had left her no time to think about the coming confrontation. Now, the realization of where she was headed hit her, and along with the smell and feel of the limousine's plush leather, made her feel out of her depth. She distracted herself by concentrating on the car.

There was a button on the arm of her seat. She hesitated, then pressed it, imagining it might reveal a well stocked bar. Although she couldn't risk the smell of alcohol on her breath, she wanted to see what the bar might contain. Instead, the darkened glass between her and the driver slid quietly down.

"Yes, ma'am?"

Bernadette caught the chauffeur's eyes studying her in the rearview mirror. "Sorry. I hit the button by accident. How can I make it close again?" She felt foolish.

"Just press the button again, ma'am. If you're sure there's noth…"

"No. Thank you." Bernadette quickly pressed the button, relieved to be isolated again. Settling back into the soft leather, her mind returned to the coming meeting and her stomach rumbled. "Damn! Why didn't I eat something?" she thought.

As the limo cruised along the darkening streets she wondered who else would be at the meeting. She knew she would be outnumbered but the Irish in her didn't mind that. Yet, she did not want this meeting. It reminded her of a trip to the headmaster's office during her first week in school. She had received six strokes across the hand with a thin bamboo cane. Her crime had been running in the corridor. The Jesuit Father wanted to make a point. Rules were to be obeyed and if they were broken, terrible and swift punishment awaited the culprit. It was the Christian promise.

Arriving at the main gate of the White House, the car halted at a red and white striped barrier which blocked the driveway. A marine guard approached. The chauffeur lowered his window and exchanged quiet words with the marine. The guard stepped back toward the back of the car and pressed his face against the rear window, peering at Bernadette, who looked straight back at him. Finally, the guard stood back and waved to an unseen ally. The red and white barrier rose smoothly and the car started forward. Bernadette's stomach growled again.

The limousine pulled up against the side of the building, opposite a side entrance. A figure stepped from the side door toward the car, opening an umbrella on the way. With light reflecting off the melted snow running down her window, Bernadette could not make out the figure distinctly, even as the person reached to open her door. It wasn't until she got out of the car that Bernadette saw that the umbrella was held by Bob Butz, White House Chief of Staff. She was momentarily shocked. Butz had made his hatred of her clear ever since she humiliated him at a committee hearing on the appropriation.

The scene flashed through her mind. Butz had stated that the appropriation was for supplies to government forces in Angola who were fighting a communist insurgency. That wasn't so bad, but among the items listed were heaters. For Angola? Bernadette had asked for an explanation and the Chief of Staff had tried to belittle her.

"Madam chair may not know that it can get very cold at night in the desert," he had said, beaming around the room.

Bernadette's reply was caustic. "Perhaps, but is the administration proposing shipping a desert to Angola?"

A ripple of laughter spread around the room, while a red-faced aide hurriedly whispered to the Chief of Staff. "I meant jungle, madam chair," the Chief said quickly. "It can get cold in the jungle at night." He toyed with his microphone and glared at Bernadette.

She met his look. "How cold?"

There was more giggling around the room. After consultations with several of his retinue the chief responded, "My apologies, madam chair. Due to a clerical error, that item is incorrectly classified as heaters." He offered nothing further.

"Just how should it be classified?" Bernadette asked, too sweetly.

The Chief's face flushed red and his eyes flashed hatred. "That particular materiel should be classified as flame-throwers," he said unwillingly, lowering his eyes.

She kept her eyes fixed on him. "I had trouble renaming the MX missile the Peacekeeper, but to call flame-throwers heaters is going a bit too far, don't you think?"

The Chief said nothing.

Bernadette's next comments made headlines the following morning. "You had better return to the White House, Mr. Chief, and get your story straight. Until you do, this appropriation stays frozen, heaters and flame-throwers notwithstanding!"

There was another outbreak of laughter and a rush of reporters to telephones.

The Chief snatched his briefcase and stomped from the room.

The Post, next morning, ran the headline "Administration burned by flame-throwers." She heard the Chief had a tantrum when he saw that, and swore to have her hide nailed to his wall.

This entire flashback took only an second, but it was enough to qualify as hesitation on Bernadette's part.

"The president is waiting," the Chief said tersely, holding the umbrella out to cover Bernadette's head.

She nodded and smoothed her jacket. "Take me to your leader. I'd just as soon be where there's some heat."

The Chief's eyes narrowed at the unintended barb, but he made no reply and they walked in tandem to the side door. Once inside, the Chief closed the umbrella and handed it to a young man who closed the door behind them. Bernadette's stomach rumbled again as she followed the Chief down a corridor. As she passed the rows of pictures of past presidents and patriots Bernadette glanced at each one, not seeing it, but using the framed glass as a mirror to check her appearance. Finally they reached the Oval Office and the Chief held the door open. Bernadette straightened up and walked in, trying to appear at ease.

The Secretary of State was seated opposite the door. He stood and walked towards Bernadette with his hand outstretched. "Representative Mallory, nice to see you."

Bernadette shook his hand, surprised by the tiny beads of sweat already on her palm. "Mr. Secretary, good evening," she responded.

The president was seated behind a huge desk to her left, phone in hand and feet on desktop. He motioned her over with his free hand, took his feet off the desk and said into the phone "Call me later with it." He replaced the receiver and stood up. He did not walk towards her. Bernadette realized she was expected to approach him, and did.

"Representative Mallory," the president said, clasping her one hand in both his. "Thank you for coming. How was the drive over?"

He was much older in person, with dark rings around his eyes and folds of skin under his chin. Bernadette thought it remarkable what TV could do with makeup. "Fine, thank you. It's still cold, but the snow is tapering off." She almost added that it was an honor to be here, but decided that would smack of fawning.

"How about some coffee? Something to eat? Cookies, maybe?" the president asked.

She desperately wanted something to eat, if only to stop her stomach from rumbling, but worried about sugar and crumbs sticking to her lips and falling on her clothes, so she replied "Thank you, just coffee would be good."

"OK," said the president. "I'll take a couple of ginger snaps, if you can find some, Bob."

The Chief of Staff nodded stiffly and slipped from the room. Bernadette sensed his resentment at being appointed waiter and wondered if it was a deliberate slap at him for her benefit.

"Please sit down," the president went on, sitting again himself. It provided him a position of authority to be seated behind his desk. "You know George?"

"Yes," she answered, glancing at the Secretary of State.

"Great. Well, I'm sure you know why we invited you here. I would like us to begin by forgetting everything that's been done and said so far. We made some mistakes in dealing with your committee, and I'm sorry about that. Some of my people are so loyal to me, they forget not everyone agrees with me. They don't understand people, like yourself, who question things." He paused.

Bernadette resented the last remark, but let it pass.

"As for all that stuff in the press, well, you know that most of what they print is a mixture of misquotes and speculation. Hell, I'm surprised they haven't put Peggy's illness down to pregnancy!" He laughed and the secretary followed suit.

Bernadette felt obliged to inquire "How is Mrs Ganera?"

"Oh, she's fine. Just a cold. Nothing serious."

The door opened and the Chief walked in, balancing a silver tray with a silver coffee pot, dainty white cups and saucers, and a plate piled high with cookies. He placed the tray on a dark, mahogany coffee table in the center of the room and began to pour. "Cream or sugar?" he asked, in Bernadette's direction.

"No thanks," she replied, taking the offered saucer and steaming cup.

"You like your poison strong," remarked the president.

No-one spoke as the Chief poured for the other two. He handed a cup and saucer to the Secretary of State and delivered the same to the president.

"I'll take a couple of ginger snaps," said the president.

Butz walked back across the room to get the cookies.

Bernadette used the lull in conversation to examine her surroundings. She had expected to feel overwhelmed by history in this room where so many fateful decisions had been made. She wondered how many unknown, furtive persons had been here to make secret deals affecting world events. However, she was not overwhelmed. The room seemed like a thousand other executive offices. Luxurious yet functional. Not awe-inspiring.

She noticed the scuff marks on the president's desktop. From the heels of how many former presidents? She wondered if the cleaning staff was instructed to leave the scratches and scrapes intact for history. Her stomach growled again, and she rattled the cup slightly, to hide the sound.

Coffee and cookies now distributed, the president stood and walked to the bay window behind him, nibbling at a cookie as he went. His back was to them. He cleared his throat and Bernadette sensed that the serious talk was about to begin. She blew gently on her steaming coffee.

"This whole matter has gotten out of hand," the president said to the window. "I don't blame the other side for wanting to make political capital out of it. I might do the same myself, except that in this case, it's too serious to become a political football." He paused.

Bernadette wondered why politicians always used sports terms. She glanced at the others and found they were watching her closely.

"I know that's not your attitude," the president added, pausing to get her confirmation.

Sipping her coffee, Bernadette said nothing, refusing to be patronized.

The president continued. "I read in the papers that you might be interested in the Irish ambassador post. Anything to that?" He turned to face her, to force an answer this time.

Bernadette looked down at her coffee cup, aware of the others still studying her, waiting for a response. She took a sip of coffee. Were they testing to see if she could be bought? "Dare I say, Mr. President, that I have never considered the job, have never actively sought it, and am not sure I would accept it even if it were offered?"

She looked up and smiled at the president. They were his own words, his verbatim response when asked four years ago if he would break the deadlock at the Republican convention by accepting the presidential nomination as his party's compromise candidate. There was displeasure in his penetrating gaze. Bernadette blinked and took another sip of coffee.

The president looked at the other men in turn, then pivoted back to face the window again. "This job carries tremendous pressures. Decisions sometimes need to be made based on information that cannot be made public, which makes it easy for others to second-guess. When I accepted the job of president, I agreed to assume the responsibility for such decisions. I don't shirk that duty, or delegate it, or share it. No-one else should be made to feel the pressure I agreed to take. However, you leave me no choice. No-one outside this room knows what you are about to hear." He stopped, to let the drama of his words sink in.

Not knowing whether to feel afraid or to laugh, Bernadette took a gulp of coffee to stifle either impulse.

"Why don't you tell Representative Mallory, George?" the president continued, without turning away from the window.

Bernadette looked toward the Secretary who slowly set his cup and saucer on the table in front of him, and gave a throaty cough. "Within the past two months, the Chinese have been moving a lot of military hardware into Fujain province, which is directly across the East China Sea from Taiwan."

Bernadette stiffened.

"Naturally, we are tracking this activity from our satellites."

"Doesn't this happen every few years? I've read about it in the past," Bernadette interrupted.

"It has happened before," the Secretary answered. "However, we have reason to believe something special is brewing this time. Have you heard the name Cheng Shaing?"

"The North Korean defector?" Bernadette responded.

"Yes, he was the number three man in the military and has proved reliable in everything he has told us so far.

Shaing claims the military activities in Fujain are related to a surprise move the Chinese are planning in an effort to influence our election..."

"Why? What would they gain from that?" Bernadette looked at each man in turn.

The Secretary looked back at her with pity. "When you deal with the Chinese," he answered, "You can never assume they are rational." He paused, looking towards the president, then went on, "There are three possibilities."

Remembering her earlier conversation with the Speaker of the House, Bernadette wondered if all bureaucrats and politicians were trained to look for exactly three possibilities.

"One, we know there is a power struggle going on inside the Central Politburo," said the Secretary. "It is possible that the army is being used to further the ends of a general Chou Li. He may be trying to embarrass the

present leadership to strengthen his own position within the politburo."
He took a sip of coffee.

"Possibility number two is that the Chinese believe they can influence our election. Whether to hurt the president, or to help him, we can't be sure."

"If you'll pardon my saying so, the president has annoyed China lately by calling for greater human rights. Why would they want to help him?" Bernadette looked from the Secretary to the president.

"Despite their public utterances, the Chinese might actually want this president to remain in office," responded the Secretary. "They might prefer that because of this administration's attitude toward Russia. Paranoid as the Chinese are, they might rather deal with a devil they know, instead of a new president who might be more receptive to overtures from Moscow. The Chinese have a continuing nightmare in which America and Russia form a military alliance against them." He paused again.

"And the final possibility?" Bernadette asked.

"The Chinese may feel they can emerge with something tangible from whatever it is they're planning. Perhaps even taking over Taiwan." The Secretary looked straight at Bernadette, waiting for a reaction.

She returned his gaze, betraying nothing.

"From their point of view," the secretary continued, "The worst that could happen from a limited military stand-off is that their action would be welcomed by some of their third world clients as relieving the pressure on them. North Korea and Vietnam, in particular. The Chinese may also feel that our allies around the world would not want us to risk a nuclear confrontation over an island, which everybody knows is really a part of China. Of course, we'd never acknowledge that, but it might strain relations with some of our allies who have large investments in China. Japan, for instance, has invested heavily in light industry. France has contracted to build nuclear power plants and other countries in western Europe are negotiating billion dollar deals for infrastructure. The Taiwanese also already owe billions of dollars in loans from the International Monetary

Fund. No-one would want to see all that put at risk because of a super-power confrontation."

"If Shaing knows what's really behind the maneuvers, why doesn't he tell us? Also, the Chinese must know that he knows and might tell us, so what are they likely to do in that case?"

The Secretary looked to the president, then to the Chief of Staff. "Why don't you carry on, Bob?" he said to the latter.

"Shaing is willing to tell us," the Chief stated. After a few seconds he added "But he says he needs one hundred million dollars."

Finally, the connection to the appropriation. Bernadette had expected better. "Talk about inflation," she said, "I can remember when one million dollars was the ultimate demand of spies, terrorists and kidnappers." She smiled and looked at each man in turn. None of them seemed amused.

"He claims he needs the money to bribe politicians and military officers so that there will be no confrontation and hence, no threat to the billions already invested or loaned," Butz continued.

"And let me guess," Bernadette said, "You don't want this to get out because, one, you aren't sure of the effect it would have on the election. Two, you need time to analyze the situation, and three, you are afraid of an outbreak of mass hysteria among our allies and bankers." She deliberately stopped at three points.

"The election is not a concern in dealing with this situation!" snapped the Chief. The president shot him a glance, which seemed to warn the Chief about his tone, and he softened it accordingly. "Look, if the president were concerned about the effect this would have on the election, he could probably guarantee winning by allowing the situation to develop so he could confront the Chinese. Yes, the public might be frightened, but that fear would make them likely to re-elect the president. They wouldn't switch to an untested president in the middle of a major crisis."

Bernadette recalled Speaker Sullivan's remark that no incumbent had ever lost the presidency during a war situation.

"But the president does not want confrontation," Butz continued.

"He believes we should use all means at our disposal to deal with this matter in a way that will not cause public alarm or trouble for our allies. It may cost us a hundred million to control, but if Shaing comes through, that would be a small price to pay."

"Then why not let the allies pay it? They're the ones who stand to lose," said Bernadette, evenly.

"Many of this country's largest multinational companies are involved in those investments, and the IMF loans were mostly made by American banks. One hundred million dollars is not much in the scheme of things."

"Then why not take it from somewhere else? I'm sure the CIA or the Pentagon has some money set aside for emergencies," Bernadette countered.

Butz sighed. "Those agencies have oversight committees made up of members of both parties. The Democrats would try to use it to their advantage. You, on the other hand, are an independent, with no party interests. We hope you can see the greater public interest."

Bernadette knew they were lying. If the president thought he had a sure way to win re-election, he would take it, public interest be damned.

"But I've already questioned the appropriation and drawn the attention of the press to it."

Butz narrowed his eyes but before he could say anything, the Secretary of State spoke up. "That may work to our advantage. Knowing how you've grilled us over the money, if you now pass the appropriation, they'll probably feel it must be OK and they have no reason to dig deeper into it."

Without looking up from her coffee cup, Bernadette asked, "What if Shaing is lying?"

"We will not release the money until he provides us with names and information so that we can verify that the situation can be controlled." answered Butz.

Bernadette looked at each man in turn. They all seemed uncomfortable. She thought about asking how they would verify the information, or why they trusted her not to share the information with the Democrats, but having decided it was all lies, she didn't want to waste any more time on this meeting. "I need to think about it," she stated.

The president sat down again and studied her. "Of course. We didn't expect an answer tonight, but time is short. Would you be able to give us an answer by Thursday? That would allow us a few days to implement another option if you should, ah, decide not to go along with us."

"Yes. I can let you know by Thursday," Bernadette replied.

"Fine," said the president. "That's all we ask." He looked at his watch. "I'm glad we had this chance to meet but I have another engagement. Perhaps you could come to Camp David some weekend so we could get to know each other better? Peggy would enjoy having another woman around."

Something about his last sentence sounded sexist, but Bernadette ignored it. His offer was not serious anyway. "Yes. I'd like that," she answered. Turning to the Secretary of State, she said, "Good night, Mr. Secretary."

Schultz nodded in return.

Placing her coffee cup on the table, Bernadette walked toward the door. Butz opened the door for her and accompanied her back down the corridor to the waiting limousine. Again they did not speak.

The president fidgeted with a long, thin pencil. Then, reaching under his desk, he pushed a button to shut off the tape that had silently recorded the meeting. "The bitch isn't buying it, is she?" he said matter-of-factly.

"No," replied the Secretary of State.

After twirling the pencil through his fingers a few times, the president snapped it in two. "Then we have no choice. Take her out of the picture. I don't want any more screw-ups on this, George. Make sure it's clean, and get rid of Butz."

"We'll have to keep him until after the election. We can't afford any controversy before then."

"That's true," agreed the president reluctantly.

"As for Mallory," the Secretary went on, "I anticipated her response and the first step has already been taken. Everything else is in place. I'll give the word to proceed immediately." He strode quickly from the room.

———

Although still hungry, Bernadette did not stop at the bistro. Instead, she soaked in a hot, foamy bath. Perhaps not eating, she thought, would help get rid of her midriff bulge. A headache was forming in her brow. She tried to ignore it and concentrated on the soothing water, but the dull throb in her forehead grew stronger. Stepping out of the bath, she wrapped a large towel around her shoulders and a smaller one around her hair. From her medicine cabinet she took a bottle of aspirin and downed three of the pills with a glass of tepid water. Then she walked barefoot to the kitchen, her wet feet sucking at the linoleum and leaving wet, skeletal prints behind her. Opening the fridge, she took out a package of Swiss cheese, cut a large slice and poured a glass of milk.

Her mother had always said that eating cheese last thing at night caused nightmares. On the other hand, just a few days ago she had read a magazine article claiming that dairy products encouraged sleep. Perhaps they were both right.

She dried off her body and hair, then slid into bed. It felt good to be naked under the covers. She drew the blankets up to her chin, curling into a fetal position. Her fists gripped the blankets until finally she fell asleep.

7

Billy decided to tell his foreman that his ex-wife and child had been in an accident in London. Not serious enough so that he had to leave immediately, but something that would be accepted as necessitating a trip over there for a few days.

He approached his boss as soon as he got to work. The foreman was deeply religious and visibly distressed at Billy's story. Billy was one of his best and most dependable workers and hadn't taken a sick day that the foreman could remember, so there was no problem getting the time off. Indeed, the foreman urged Billy to leave right away, but Billy said the earliest flight he could get was tomorrow morning and that would be as quick as taking a boat to Liverpool tonight and then a train into London.

Throughout the day Billy's co-workers expressed their sympathy as word of his situation spread. He felt guilty repeating the lie, and it made him nervous to invent details in response to different questions. What happened? His ex-wife and daughter were struck by a taxi while crossing a street in London. Were they seriously injured? His ex-wife had a broken leg and a fractured wrist. His daughter had a broken arm. How had he found out? His ex-wife's sister in Kent had sent him a telegram and he phoned her last night to get the details. One man wanted to know where exactly the accident had taken place because he used to live in London. Somewhere in Camden, Billy answered. That was all he knew. Another man asked if they would be suing the taxi company. No, the bastard didn't stop. It was a hit and run. This last lie elicited even more sympathy from those who heard it, whether because it made his family the victims of a crime, or because they'd lost the chance of getting big money from a settlement, Billy wasn't sure.

He knew that the broader he spread the tissue of details, the thinner it became and the more susceptible the whole story was to having a hole poked in it, so he was relieved when the siren sounded for the end of the workday. One good thing about his co-workers' questions was that he was better prepared to answer anything Harry might ask at the barricade tonight.

His worries in that regard evaporated when he told Harry why he wouldn't be available the next few nights. Harry was politely sympathetic but not really interested. "Don't worry about it," he said. "We've other men in the street can fill in for ye. In fact, we've enough that we might only need ye every other night. Ye just take care o' yer family."

Billy was relieved that things went so easily, but remembered to appear preoccupied and worried.

These feelings became real about halfway through his shift when Harry said, "Remember thon fella I was askin' ye about, Adam Bickerstaff?"

Billy tensed slightly. "Aye?"

"I saw him this mornin' at the dole. He lives up on the Knocknagoney Estate now. He doesn't know ye either, not personally."

Billy felt relief.

"But he thought he'd heard about ye," continued Harry. "That ye'd been involved in robbin' some bank down south an' were sentenced t' twenty years in Mountjoy prison in Dublin."

Harry appeared nonchalant but Billy was keenly aware of his fixed gaze studying Billy's face and waiting for a response. Billy forced himself to go one better than nonchalance. He laughed. "What? Well, he's mistaken. I couldn't have served twenty years in Mountjoy prison an' be here now, could I? Unless I robbed this bank when I was eight years old."

Harry continued to study him then finally said, "Aye, I suppose so. He's always gettin' things screwed up. Ye might as well go on home now. We can manage without ye an' ye've enough on yer mind already. Hope yer family recovers soon."

Billy thanked him and went quickly back to his house. He was afraid that Harry might dig some more into Lisaleene and who from there might have been involved in a bank robbery. You never knew what the UVF could find out. He'd be as well out of Belfast for a while and was now anxious to make this trip to Cork. Coming back might be a problem, though, if Harry did find out something while Billy was gone. He'd have to talk to British Intelligence about that in the morning.

8

The telegram arrived at nine a.m. and Larry signed for it. When the delivery boy stood waiting, Larry realized a tip was expected. Pulling out his wallet, he was annoyed to find the smallest bill he had was a ten. He shrugged his shoulders. "Sorry kid, you'll have to catch me next time."

Giving him a disgusted look, the delivery boy turned on his heel, slamming the door behind him.

Larry considered the telegram, turning it over in his hands and holding it to the light. He couldn't make out anything through the brown envelope. The only telegrams he'd known Bernadette to receive before were of the mass protest variety. This one was clearly different. Constituents who wanted urgent action usually phoned, so Larry deduced the telegram was likely of a personal nature. He debated what to do.

He deluded himself that he alone took care of all of Bernadette's business, public certainly, and sometimes personal. It irritated him that he had no idea what this telegram could be about, or who it might be from and he desperately wanted to know, but he hesitated. He sensed that the telegram was not good news and wasn't sure he should be the one to open it. On the other hand, it was after all, merely a piece of mail, and as Bernadette's aide, part of his job was to deal with mail. He'd opened her mail a thousand times before. What was so different about this? Yet, he couldn't shake his sense of foreboding.

Deciding the safest course would be to call Bernadette and ask if he should open the telegram, he glanced at his watch. He might just catch her. Dialing the number, he allowed it to ring six times before he hung up. She must have left already. That made him feel a sense of urgency. With Bernadette acting like she had been lately, if he didn't open the telegram he might never find out what it contained, and knowledge, whether business or personal, was a useful commodity in this town.

Tearing open the envelope, he removed the half sheet of paper and unfolded it. His eyes scanned the page, and he slumped into his chair. "Shit!" he said aloud. He read the telegram again.

"Main Post Office, Cork, Ireland.

To : Bernadette Mallory, U.S. House of Representatives, Washington DC, USA.

Father seriously ill. STOP. Asking for you. STOP. Dan Fogarty, priest.STOP. END."

"Shit!" Larry said again under his breath. He laid the telegram on his desk.

Bernadette had mentioned her father to him only once, about a year ago, when Larry had made a contribution to Noraid in her name. He thought Noraid was a charity for poor kids in Ireland but Bernadette threw a tantrum when she found out. She lectured him that the real purpose of Noraid was to buy guns for the IRA. He'd been in her shithouse for a week and it had scared him. When she cooled down she explained that her father had been involved with the IRA and was in prison because of it. She said nothing beyond that, but he knew enough not to inquire further.

Picking up the Yellow Pages he began thumbing through the Airlines section. Half an hour later he had made all arrangements. He hoped Bernadette would appreciate that at least.

————

Bernadette arrived at the office at ten minutes to ten. Larry knew the time precisely, because he had impatiently checked his watch every five minutes while waiting for her.

"Good morning, Larry," she said breezily, setting her purse on the chair by the office door and beginning to remove her coat and scarf.

Larry stood, not responding to her greeting. "Bernadette," he half-whispered.

She turned to look at him, the seriousness of his tone striking her immediately and causing her to freeze with one arm out of her coat. "What is it?" she asked.

"I'm sorry," he said, avoiding her eyes. "It's bad news."

Bernadette said nothing, but kept her eyes on him, not knowing what to expect . She slid her other arm slowly out of her coat sleeve and without looking, tried to hang the coat on its assigned hook. It fell to the floor. Letting it lie, she kept her eyes fixed on him as she stepped over to his desk. "What? Has the president declared me public enemy number one?" she said nervously, forcing a half smile.

Larry held out the telegram to her. "This just arrived."

She didn't take it right away. Her mind was racing to anticipate what the bad news might be. After a few long seconds, she reached for the piece of paper. Her eyes scanned it. Panic welled up in her chest and her facial muscles tightened. Reading the brief message again, she swayed backwards slightly, lower lip twitching and eyes blinking rapidly.

Larry felt awkward. "I've made a reservation for you on the Concorde, and booked a connecting flight from London to Dublin. You can be in Cork by nine am tomorrow, their time." His voice trailed off and he lowered his head. He didn't know what more to say.

Spinning away from him, Bernadette crossed quickly to the window. Afraid she was going to throw up, she cupped her hand over her mouth. In the glass she saw her father's sad face as she had last seen it, except that now he was calling to her. She turned away from the window, tears smarting her eyes. "I need to be alone," she whispered, her eyes closing tightly in a useless attempt to hold back the tears.

"If there's anything..." Larry began mumbling.

Bernadette interrupted him by rapidly shaking her head and at the same time waving him away with one hand. He walked to the door then turned. "I'll send a telegram back, saying you'll be there. Maybe it'll find the priest at that address..." His voice trailed off and he walked through the door, closing it behind him. He was relieved to be out of her presence. Standing in the corridor, he inwardly cursed his inadequacy, then turned and walked quickly away from the office.

Bernadette wept, and in her weeping found some relief, but it was not the release of grief that relieved her. It was that she was able to cry at all. She had always been afraid that when this moment finally came, she would feel no emotion. Her guilt about that made her sob more.

9

The tinny ring of his cheap alarm clock woke Billy at eight a.m. Dressing quickly, he made tea and toast. Now that morning had arrived, he wanted to get on with this. He threw a shirt, trousers, some underwear and a pair of socks into a small canvas grip. Looking around the bedroom, he wondered what else he might need. His eyes fell on the bible on his dresser. He picked it up and slid it into the bag. From the bathroom he took his razor, shaving soap, toothpaste and toothbrush. He had always been fastidious about his teeth.

Stepping into the street, grip in hand, his immediate, irrational fear was that he'd run into Harry, but the street was empty except for a neighbor who had chosen that early hour to scrub the sidewalk in front of her house, a task which Billy considered as productive as washing the sole of a shoe. He hurried quickly to his rendezvous.

The car was waiting and Billy climbed in quickly, anxious to be out of view. The same driver and passenger were in the car but today the passenger sat in front. Traffic was light and they were able to speed through the side streets, to the main road.

The passenger turned to face Billy. "Good morning, Billy. Did you have a good night's sleep?"

"As a matter o' fact, no," Billy replied testily.

The passenger's raised his eyebrows. "Why not? You're not worried about anything are you?"

Billy told him about the UVF checkpoint and his fears that Harry might dig into the Dundalk bank robbery.

The passenger stroked his chin. "That could be a bit of a problem. Still, we must have somebody who's letting them to set up these checkpoints. Somebody who can talk to them. We may be able to take care of it so they don't find out about you, or at least we should be able to warn you if they do."

"I won't be comin' back if they find out!" Billy snapped.

The passenger smiled. "Relax, Billy. We've always taken care of you haven't we?"

Billy scowled out his window in response.

Not encountering any security checkpoints, they quickly reached the outskirts of the city and joined the motorway, speeding up considerably. "We'll take you over the border to be sure you don't get hung up there," said the passenger. "After that, you're on your own."

"Why not just take me t' the station an' put me on a train?"

"You don't know much about the city you live in, do you? The army searches every passenger and their luggage on every train, plane, boat and bus heading into and out of Belfast. The Irish check it all again at the border. We'll drop you in the town of Dunfrior. You can get a train to Dublin from there."

"What if somethin' happens t' me after ye drop me off?"

"Don't let anything happen," answered the passenger. He reached into his jacket pocket and produced a small brown envelope which he offered to Billy. "Here's two hundred pounds in Irish bills. Don't spend it all in one place."

Billy was sure that if they were giving him two hundred pounds, they'd probably been allocated five hundred for costs, and pocketed the difference, but he said nothing, and stuffed the envelope into the inside pocket of his jacket.

"Remember this phone number," continued the passenger. "25582. Your name is Mr. Pigeon. When you call, ask for Mr. Baxter."

Billy frowned. "Who's he?"

"Me," replied the passenger.

"I thought yer name was Wilkinson?"

"It was, and now it's Baxter. Next month it'll be something else. Makes it harder for certain people to track me down. This is Mr. Richards, by the way." He nodded at the driver. "If I'm not available, ask for him. Got it?"

Billy nodded and the passenger continued. "Phone me tomorrow morning. If you don't, I'll assume you've skipped, and you know what that means." He watched Billy to make sure he understood.

"Yeah." said Billy sullenly.

"What's the phone number?"

"25582," sighed Billy.

"And your name?"

"I'm not a kid!" Billy snapped.

The passenger ignored the outburst. "Your name?"

"Pigeon! Walter bloody Pigeon!"

"Very funny," the passenger said, turning away. "Any questions?"

"What if I'm recognized by one o' them fellas that wanted t' kill me in Mountjoy?"

The passenger shrugged. "That would be bad luck. You'll have to depend on Mallory to protect you again."

"An' if Mallory's not around at the time?"

The passenger turned to look at him again. "What are you getting at?"

Billy looked out of the window, away from the passenger. "I want a gun," he said quietly.

There was silence for a minute, then the passenger laughed. The driver followed suit. "No gun, Billy," said the passenger. "We wouldn't want you hurting yourself."

"If I don't get a gun, I'm not goin'." Billy stated. He turned to look at the passenger. "It isn't going t' help either o' us if somethin' happens t' me. I need t' be able t' protect meself."

"Even if we wanted to give you one, Billy, where would we get a gun? It isn't something they sell at a petrol station."

"I can take his." Billy nodded at the driver, who shot him a glance in the mirror.

The passenger glared at Billy. "Give me your gun and clip," he finally said to the driver.

"But, chief…" whined the driver, glancing at his boss.

"Give it to me! The little shit hasn't the nerve to use it on us if that's what you're thinking."

Reaching inside his jacket, the driver produced a small, snub-nosed gun The passenger took it. The driver then reached into a side pocket and pulled out a small metal clip of bullets. He handed those over as well. The passenger examined the gun and bullets for a moment then handed them to Billy. "You be bloody careful with that," he said between his teeth. "I want it back unused."

Taking the items, Billy examined the gun. "What's this wee lever?"

"Christ! It's the bloody safety catch! When the lever is down the safety catch is off and you can fire the gun. You do know how to shoot?"

"Aim an' pull the trigger, I suppose," said Billy.

The passenger sighed deeply. "Hold it in both hands and keep your arms straight out in front of you. Your aim won't be steady if you try to shoot it with one hand like a cowboy, Jesus, I don't know…!"

Billy stuffed the gun in one jacket pocket and the bullets in another. "I don't want t' use it but I need it just in case." He decided to change the subject before the passenger had second thoughts about the gun. "How are we goin' t' get through customs?"

"We won't be going through customs. We're taking an unapproved road. The army patrols it but we know their schedule. Any more questions?"

Billy shook his head.

"Good. What's the number, who are you and when do you call?"

Billy sighed and recited the information.

"You know how we came up with Pigeon?" the passenger asked, smirking.

"I suppose it's t' do wi' carrier pigeons. Me bringing a message back t' ye," said Billy.

The passenger looked disappointed.

"Brilliant," snorted Billy.

They continued the journey in silence.

————

Dunfrior was a typical one-street town which, if the railway didn't happen to run through it, might have been abandoned long ago. It endured by serving as a stop for people in the surrounding countryside who wanted to take a day trip to Dublin. Belfast was closer, but nobody was interested in a day trip to that city.

Pulling up at the station's main entrance, the driver put the car in neutral, leaving the engine running.

"Here we are," announced the passenger. "You're on your own now. Take the train to Dublin and change there for Cork. You'll be able to manage that, won't you?"

Billy didn't deign to answer. "When's the next train?" he asked.

"How would I know? You'll find out when you buy the ticket."

"What if it isn't for hours?"

"Then you'll have to wait."

"Why can't ye take me int' Dublin? It's only another fifty miles."

"Afraid not. We've other things to do and I don't much care for being in the Republic. Makes me nervous. Phone when you've got the stuff from Mallory, then phone again when you know what time your train gets back to Dunfrior and we'll meet you here. We don't want you crossing the border with whatever Mallory gives you. They do a thorough search of people heading for Belfast."

Billy got out of the car. As soon as he slammed the door, the car backed up, turned around and headed back in the direction they had come from. Billy watched it disappear around a corner. Part of him wanted to stay with them and another part felt relief to be out of their company and on his own.

Walking into the station, he approached the ticket counter. After waiting a minute, he rapped loudly on the glass partition. A uniformed old man appeared from behind a row of file cabinets at the back of the office. He did not seem happy to have been disturbed and took his time walking over to face Billy through the partition. "Aye?"

"Can I buy a ticket t' Cork from here?"

"Single or return?"

"Return."

"Eighteen pounds." The old man began inserted a blank ticket into what looked like an old hand-crank calculator and began punching buttons.

Pulling the packet from his pocket, Billy held it below the level of the counter so the old man could not see the banknotes. Extracting a twenty from the bundle, he laid it on the counter. "D' I have t' change trains in Dublin?"

The old man yanked on a large handle at the side of the machine and pulled out the ticket. He inspected it before pushing it under the glass to Billy, while taking the twenty pound note at the same time. "Aye," he said in answer to Billy's question. At the same time he pulled open a drawer under the counter, placed the twenty inside and pulled out two one pound coins, which he pushed toward Billy.

"When's the next train?" Billy asked.

Closing the drawer, the old man leaned on the counter. He fixed Billy with a look that said "Are you going to keep me here all day answering questions?"

"Twelve fifteen," he announced finally, then waited, expecting another question.

"What time is it now?"

The old man pointed behind Billy, who turned. A huge clock glared down at him. As he looked, the large hand jerked and advanced to mark passage of another minute. Nine-thirty. Groaning inwardly at the thought of the long wait, Billy turned back to the counter. The old man still stood, glowering. Billy was going to ask if there was a pub in town, but was intimidated by the old man. Besides, he had more than enough time to find a pub himself, so he turned and walked out of the station.

Looking up and down the street, he decided to go to the right, where he could see shops. He found a pub on the next block, but it was closed. A sign on the door announced that it would open at ten, so Billy continued down the street and came to a small cafe. He entered and ordered a cup of tea. There were only five tables in the cafe and all were empty. One table had a newspaper lying on it so Billy sat there and began scanning the paper.

The tea was delivered by a plump, ruddy-faced woman who seemed to be the only person working in the cafe. "Ye'll be waitin' for the train, I daresay?"

"Aye," Billy answered without looking up from the newspaper.

"Aye, I could tell that. Dublin or Belfast?" the woman continued.

Billy decided she was asking where he was headed and not where he was from. "Dublin," he answered, and peered more intently at the paper to signal that he didn't want to converse. It had the desired effect. The woman shrugged and left him alone.

After a few minutes a plump, pasty-faced man in a business suit entered the cafe and sat at another table. The newcomer and the woman struck up a conversation to which Billy paid no attention. It did strike him though that they looked like a perfect match. Billy read the paper thoroughly, even the ads. Finally, he asked the woman what time it was.

She must have been used to the reason for the question. "Five past ten. The pub's been open five minutes."

Billy paid his bill and walked back to the pub where there were already three men crowding the bartender. Billy waited his turn and ordered a pint of Guinness. As he filled the glass the bartender said, "Waitin' for the train are ye?"

Billy nodded, paid for the drink and walked over to an empty booth. He slid into the corner. Despite telling himself that there was nothing to worry about, that this errand would be a piece of cake, he couldn't still the nagging questions and worries in his mind. Why had Mallory picked him? Would he be in danger? Would he ever be free of Wilkinson or Baxter or whatever his name was? Like a cat tormenting a mouse he'd try to put the questions out of his mind, then drag them up again and paw at them some more.

By the time he finished his second pint of Guinness the pub had filled up with a lunchtime crowd of mostly farmers who all seemed to know each other. After his third pint Billy was feeling good, and had enough false courage to be anxious for the train. He was relieved when the pub clock finally showed noon, and returned to the station, following the signs to the platform for trains to Dublin. There were about twenty people waiting, ranging from young couples with polished kids, to a couple of nuns, a few businessmen, and farmers with their wives.

The train was on time and half empty. Taking a seat in the last carriage, Billy placed his grip on the luggage rack above his head. The nuns entered his compartment. After watching them struggle for a minute to load their suitcases onto the luggage rack, Billy responded to their silent pleas for help by hoisting their suitcases onto the luggage rack. Although they thanked him, he detected a disapproving look on their faces and realized it would be due to the smell of alcohol on his breath. "Up yours," he thought. "If this was Belfast, they'd throw you and your luggage out the window."

The Guinness made him tired and he snuggled into a corner of his seat. The train gave a lurch and pulled out of the station. For a few minutes Billy watched the houses pass slowly by. As the train picked up speed, the houses were replaced by hedges and fields which zipped past the window. He struggled to keep his eyes open but the rhythmic swaying of the train and the clickity clack of wheels on the tracks proved overpowering and he dozed off.

He was awakened by one of the nuns shaking his shoulder. "Young man. We're here."

Billy looked at her blankly, totally disoriented for a moment.

"Dublin. Time t' get off." The nun smiled at him. "An' could we impose on ye again?" She nodded in the direction of the luggage rack.

Opening his eyes wide, Billy blinked two or three times. "Aye, sure. Thanks for wakin' me." Standing up, he hauled the nuns' suitcases down. "D'ye know what time it is?"

One of the sisters shook her head. "There'll be a clock in the station."

Each nun began to drag a suitcase down the aisle. A porter boarded the train and immediately came to help them, crossing himself as he did so. Retrieving his grip, Billy followed them down the aisle and off the train. He wondered why no-one had come to check his ticket while he slept. The answer became clear when he reached the end of the platform. A crowd of passengers stood at a gate where two uniformed railroad employees were checking tickets. Billy was annoyed. It would have been more efficient to have a conductor check tickets on the train, like they did in the north. He hoped this delay wouldn't cause him to miss his connection to Cork.

Finally reaching the gate, he handed his ticket over for inspection and asked what platform the Cork train left from.

"Cork, platform seven," the ticket inspector stated, as if programmed. Punching the ticket, he handed it back to Billy.

"D'ye know when the next train is?" Billy asked.

"There'll be a sign at platform seven. Now, move along please, ye're delayin' other passengers."

Billy considered responding that it was this stupid system of checking tickets that delayed passengers, but decided there was no point.

Dublin was the big, bustling station he'd expected. The main concourse was a melee of passengers and porters, rushing to end their journey or anxious to begin one. All kinds of people struggled with luggage and kids. It was pandemonium. Yet, despite it all, the trains ran on time, constantly shuttling people in and out of the city.

He threaded his way to platform seven, ticket clutched in hand. As he feared, the platform was deserted. A large sign stated "Cork" and listed the smaller stations the train would stop at. Beneath that the next departure time was shown as four-thirty. Billy looked around the station. A huge clock to his left showed that it was two-forty. "Well," he thought. "I'll have time to get something to eat." First though, he headed to the information counter and learned that the train would arrive in Cork at seven-twenty. He then walked over to the Railway Cafe on the main concourse and enjoyed a dinner of Vienna steak and mashed potatoes, washed down with scalding tea.

The journey to Cork was uneventful. Billy admired the lilting countryside, but with every mile his apprehension increased.

Cork station was not busy when the train finally pulled in. First, Billy needed a toilet, then he'd find a hotel room for the night. He'd take a taxi in the morning and the first half of his journey would be over. With any luck he could be back on a train to Dublin by midday.

Entering the men's room, he found only one other person there, washing his hands. Billy headed to the urinal. The man dried his hands and walked to the exit. Billy watched him leave, then went over to the row of wash basins, setting the grip on the floor between his legs.

The door opened and three youths entered, jostling and laughing. Seeing Billy, they became quiet. One stayed by the door while another walked down the row of stalls, checking each one. A small note of caution sounded in Billy's head. The third youth walked up to the sink beside Billy, pulled a comb from his hip pocket and began to comb his hair, humming loudly. Billy continued washing his hands. The youth who had been checking stalls came and stood behind Billy. The note of caution was now an alarm in Billy's head, but he had no choice but to brazen it out. He turned to the towels. Suddenly the youth behind him reached forward and grabbed Billy's arms, pinning them behind his back.

"Hey! What the hell!" Billy struggled but to no avail. The youth was strong.

His partner stepped in front of Billy and snarled, "Shut up or we'll kill ye!" He thrust both hands into the inside pocket of Billy's jacket.

The youth by the door opened it a crack and looked out into the station. "The porter's comin'!" he called to his partners.

Pulling the packet of bills from Billy's pocket, the youth held them in front of his face for a second, amazed that they had hit such paydirt. "C'mon!" he shouted to his partner.

The juvenile pinning Billy's arms spun him around and aimed a punch at his face. Billy instinctively turned his head and ducked. The blow landed on his neck. Off balance, he staggered back against the sink. He reached out to keep his footing, but the youth stepped forward and delivered a powerful kick to his crotch. Billy doubled over in agony and slumped to the floor, groaning. The youths fled from the room.

Billy lay stunned, nausea sweeping over him. The door opened and a porter entered, looking over his shoulder in the direction of the fleeing youths. When he saw Billy lying on the floor, the porter hurried over to him. "What did they do t' ye? It was them young lads wasn't it? I knew they were up t' somethin'. Are ye badly hurt?"

Billy felt shook his head. "No. I'm all right, I just need a minute." Grasping the edge of the sink, he pulled himself up. His left ankle caved in under him and he groaned at the sudden, sharp pain.

"I'll away an' call an ambulance an' the police," said the porter excitedly. "Stay where ye are."

Billy didn't want the police involved, especially not with a gun in his grip. "There's no need for that. I just slipped on some water an' winded meself. I've just twisted me ankle. If ye could help me up, I'll be fine."

The porter looked at him disbelievingly. "But them boys…"

"They were just horsin' around. One o' them bumped int' me an' I fell. They got scared an' ran off. There's no need for the police. Can ye help me up?"

The porter looked unconvinced but came over and helped Billy to his feet. Keeping the weight off his ankle by leaning on the sink, Billy said. "Thanks. I'm fine now. Could ye hand me me grip?" He nodded toward the bag under the sink.

The porter reached down and handed the bag to Billy. "Are ye sure? I better call an ambulance anyway."

Billy waved away the idea. "I'm fine. I just need t' sit down for a minute." He shuffled along the row of sinks toward the door, keeping his ankle elevated.

"Let me help ye," offered the porter, reaching for Billy's arm.

Billy waved him away again. "I can manage."

Reaching the end of the sinks, Billy gingerly applied some weight to his ankle. It hurt, but he managed to limp on tiptoe to the door. The porter hurried to open it for him. Billy nodded his thanks and limped across the concourse to an empty bench. Slumping into the seat, he placed the grip beside him. Pulling up his trouser leg and rolling down his sock, he examined his ankle. The porter peered at it too. It showed some redness. Billy touched it carefully, then pressed harder, which hurt and made him wince.

"Is it broke?" The porter sounded hopeful. "Can ye wiggle yer toes?"

Billy did, and flexed the ankle as well. "It's fine. Just a knock."

"Ye should have it x-rayed. It might be cracked."

Billy wanted to be rid of the porter. "Aye, true enough. I'll do that."

The porter seemed satisfied. "Yer sure ye'll be all right then?"

Billy nodded. "Aye. Thanks. I don't want t' keep ye from yer work."

It was the porter's turn to nod. "Aye, all right then." He turned and walked down the concourse, turning once to look at Billy and shake his head disapprovingly.

Billy was already concerned with other things besides the porter and the pain in his ankle. He'd been mugged, and now had no money. Instinctively he felt in his side pocket. The return ticket was still there at least, and he still had the grip and the gun. He considered his situation, checking the amount of change in his pocket which yielded three pounds and thirty pence. A hotel was out of the question then, but he might still be able to afford a taxi to Mallory's, and maybe even back to the station. If he picked up the package, he could maybe catch a train back to Dublin tonight, but then what? There might not be any trains to Belfast in the wee hours and he could end up spending the night on a bench in Dublin station. Apart from the discomfort involved, this did not appeal to him since he knew the police in any city hassled people hanging around railway stations all night. No, he'd tell Mallory what had happened and hope he could stay the night with him.

He examined his ankle again. The red was already darkening and the joint was beginning to puff up. Still, he saw no other choice, he'd have to go to Mallory's sooner or later. Heaving himself up from the bench, he picked up the grip and hobbled toward the information window to confirm his options. "When's the next train t' Dublin?"

"Twenty minutes, sir."

"An' the one after that?"

"There wouldn't be another one till five a.m."

Billy nodded. "Could ye tell me what time I could get a train from Dublin t' Belfast tomorrow?"

The clerk flipped through the pages of a large book of timetables, finally drawing his finger down and over. "The first train leaves Dublin at five thirty a.m. Then it's about every four an' a half hours. The last one's at nine p.m."

"Thanks. Where can I get a taxi?"

The clerk pointed to Billy's right. "There's a taxi stand right outside the main gate."

Billy limped off. When he reached the street, the air was noticeably colder. There were two taxis at the stand and Billy approached the first one. The driver rolled down his window and Billy handed the piece of paper with Mallory's address on it to the cabby. "How much t' go there?" he asked.

The driver turned on his interior light to read the address then handed the paper back to Billy. "Five pounds," he answered. Switching off the interior light, he reached back to unlock the rear door, then started the car's engine.

Billy hesitated. "I've only three pounds..."

"It's five pounds," said the driver firmly.

Billy sighed. "Could ye take me as far as three pounds will go?"

The driver looked at him with some disgust. "All right then, get in."

Billy climbed into the back of the cab. The driver removed a microphone from a clip on the dash. "Car six reportin'. Elsie, I'm on me way t' Limerick Road. No exact destination. Fare wants t' go as far as three pounds'll take him."

He pressed a button on the microphone. Billy heard a burst of static and a female voice. He couldn't make out what she said. The driver clicked the button again. "Aye, true enough. I'll be back at the station in about a half hour. Over." He returned the microphone to its clip, then pulled out onto the road.

They drove in silence. After a few minutes the driver turned on his wipers. "Startin' t' rain again," he noted over his shoulder.

Billy dejectedly watched the small drops of mist on his window become larger as the taxi drove through the deserted streets.

The rain was coming down heavy and steady when the driver pulled over. "That's three pounds worth," he announced, watching Billy in the rearview mirror.

Billy hesitated, unwilling to leave the warm cab and face the cold rain.

"Sorry, but everything's on the meter. I'd take ye the rest o' the way, but I'd have t' pay for it meself," the driver said.

Reluctantly, Billy opened the rear door and pulled himself out of the cab. He leaned against the driver's door while he counted out the money. "I'd give ye a tip if I'd any more money."

The driver said resignedly. "I guessed that. Ye've about another three miles t' go. I noticed yer limp, but if ye could manage it, it'd save ye about a mile t' go through the estate an' cut across the fields behind it." He nodded in the direction of a housing estate which began a few hundred yards ahead on the left. "The main road curves around the estate. If ye head straight across the fields ye'll come out at the road again."

Wiping the rain from his face, Billy looked toward the estate.

"Have ye no cap in your grip?" the driver asked.

Billy shook his head.

"Here." Reaching down to his front passenger seat, the driver handed Billy a peaked cap. "It'll keep yer head warm an' dry anyway."

"Thanks." Billy pulled the cap onto his already soaked head.

"Aye. Well, good luck t' ye." The taxi started forward slowly then did a U-turn and headed back to town. Billy watched it recede into the rain and darkness.

He began limping along the road toward the lights of the estate, hoping that maybe a car would come and he could hitch a ride the rest of the way. None did, and when he reached the main road into the estate Billy faced a choice. Wait there in hopes of hitching a ride, or take the cabby's advice. He reluctantly decided on the latter. Even if a car came, there was no guarantee it would stop for him, and even with his limp, the walk should take only about an hour. There wasn't a soul about on the streets of the estate, which wasn't very big. Billy was through it in about twenty minutes and began to limp across the fields.

He soon realized two things. The grass was long and soaking, and in no time his shoes and trouser bottoms were sopping. Also, without the lights of the estate, the fields were pitch black and he could barely see a few yards ahead. He hoped he wouldn't have any hedges or rivers to cross.

Limping along, he settled into a rhythm. Even the throbbing in his ankle became part of it, and his determination drove him on. He was almost at journey's end, he kept telling himself.

As time passed though, cold seeped into his bones and the throbbing in his ankle became an acute, worsening pain. He began to regret taking the shortcut and was feeling that he would have to succumb to his body's demands for relief when he heard the faint swish and hum of a car ahead of him. He saw a flash of lights in the distance. The road! He was almost there. His spirits picked up and his limping steps quickened. He didn't hear the sounds of any more traffic, but after about ten minutes reached the road. On the other side of it, across the fields, he could make out faint, stationary lights. The road curved to the left. The lights must be a cottage, Mallory's cottage maybe! He guessed it was about nine-thirty, and hoped the lights meant someone was still up in the cottage. Heading along the road with newfound strength, he reached the cottage after about fifteen minutes. A small, faded, handpainted sign announced 'Honeysuckle Cottage'. He'd made it! Approaching the cottage door, he raised his hand to knock.

10

When the priest touched her arm, Bernadette spun around, thinking it would be one of the beggars she had seen when the train pulled into Cork station. Then she saw the dog collar and at the same time the priest said, "Bernadette Mallory? Dan Fogarty. We went t' school together."

Studying him for a long moment, Bernadette tried to place the name. Then she remembered. The boy who brushed crudely against girls in the public swimming pool, and who had once been caught masturbating at his school desk. Now a priest.

From his face, she knew that she was too late. "Is he..." she choked.

"Aye, I'm sorry. In the wee hours o' Sunday morning, just after I sent the telegram..."

Biting her lower lip, Bernadette shivered.

Stepping forward, the priest embraced her. "I told him ye were comin' an' he understood. He passed on peacefully."

She clung to him, her eyes stinging and body shaking. They stood there for a few moments, the steady rain dripping off his hat and onto her shoulder. Finally, stepping back, she scraped at her red eyes and sniffled. "I'd like to see his...I'd like to see him."

"The priest answered soothingly, "They took him t' Brown's Funeral Parlor t' get him ready for the laying-out. They'll be bringin' him home this afternoon."

"I need to see him now," Bernadette stated with finality.

The priest saw her lower lip quiver and could hear the lump in her throat. He understood her need to see her father as close as possible to when he was alive. Nodding sympathetically, he cupped her hands in his, giving them a gentle squeeze. "Of course," he reassured her, "It's just up the street. I'll put yer cases in the motor an'. we can walk up there. The rain's easin' off now."

Picking up her two suitcases, he carried them to a battered, green Volkswagen bug. Setting the suitcases down, he raised the trunk lid and slid the suitcases in. They filled the small trunk. Slamming the trunk shut, he dusted off his hands and walked back to Bernadette. Sliding his arm through hers, he led her along the street.

As a child from the countryside, the city had seemed overwhelming, but now Bernadette was struck by the smallness of it, the narrow streets with no buildings more than two stories high, and the miniature store-fronts. The cars, designed for efficiency, not comfort or status, were tiny. Most noticeable was the lack of billboards and neon advertising, reflecting a discrete distaste for vulgar business.

"How was yer trip?" The priest sounded formal, as if required to make conversation but uncomfortable doing so.

"All right. I came on the Concorde." She didn't know why she added that except to reciprocate and keep up her end of the conversation.

"The Concorde, eh? Sure that's a beautiful plane."

"Yes." Bernadette could tell this conversation had nowhere to go, so she opened another avenue. "Will you be conducting the funeral service, Father?" It felt strange to call him that.

"Aye. Joe, er, yer father was a longstandin' member o' our flock at St. Patrick's. He'll be sore missed. This is Brown's now."

The long, brick building with its towering chimney stack in the back yard, away from the street, was more like a factory than a mortuary. Her childhood friends had said bodies were burned in the chimney stack, and that's what caused the strange smell in the neighborhood. She had believed it, and although she wondered what, then, was in the coffins people carried at funerals, she hadn't wanted to seem stupid by asking anyone.

Passing the gate which led to the area where hearses were parked, she suddenly recalled that her father had been a nightwatchman briefly at Brown's, before he worked on the docks. She remembered going with her mother to see him. Outside the watchman's hut stood a large oildrum with legs attached and holes punched in the side. In the drum a coke fire burned hotly. Bernadette remembered seeing the searing redness of it through the holes. Every few minutes her father would hold his hands out to the fire then rub them together, washing them with heat. Bernadette had imagined it would be nice to stand by a warm fire and be paid for it. She thought of her father in the building now, in eternal night, hands forever cold. Did anyone keep watch over him, she wondered?

On either side of the office entrance were two large windows, painted with a silver reflecting material which prevented bypassers from seeing into the offices, preserving the privacy of grief. The priest held the door open for her and they stepped into a dimly-lit corridor. The priest walked up to a door on the left. The door had a pane of stained glass with the word "OFFICE" painted in flowing script. Trying to open the door, the priest found it locked. He knocked, softly at first, then more assertively. There was no response. "Must be at lunch," the priest said apologetically. "Maybe Tom's in."

He crossed the corridor to another door. This one was plain wood and was marked "PRIVATE" in stern business lettering. The priest ignored the admonition and opened the door, beckoning Bernadette inside.

It was a sparse little office containing a desk, a file cabinet, and four straight-back chairs along one wall. On the desk was a collection of small model hearses and figures arranged in a funeral procession, complete down to a miniature coffin, borne by four of the tiny figures, one at each corner. Behind the desk sat a fat, bald man who looked up in consternation at their entrance. The man clumsily stubbed out a cigarette in the ashtray on his desk and stood up, waving to disperse the smoke around him. He was not used to clients entering his office. They usually had appointments, and were seen in his brother's impressively ornate office across the hall, but this was Father Fogarty…

"Father!" the fat man beamed, coming from behind the desk, hand outstretched. "Good t' see ye again." He kept one eye fixed on Bernadette.

"Tom," said the priest solemnly, "This is Bernadette Mallory. Joe's daughter."

The fat man's demeanor changed. He nodded slowly and looked sympathetic. He was thinking Brown's might be paid sooner than he'd expected. "Ms. Mallory." He held out a hand to her. "On behalf o' Brown's Funeral Parlor I'd like t' offer our sincere condolences."

Touching his hand limply, Bernadette nodded an acknowledgment.

Placing his thumbs under his waistcoat, the fat man puffed out his chest. "I think ye'll find that Brown's will do a…"

"Tom," interrupted the priest. "Can I have a word? Ye'll excuse us for a minute, Bernadette?"

Bernadette nodded and smiled weakly.

The priest led the fat man through the door of the office into the corridor. The fat man looked perplexed and blinked rapidly. "She wants t' see the body, Tom," whispered the priest. "I tried Dick's office but it's locked."

"Lunch," the fat man explained. "He'll be back in an hour."

"She wants t' see the body now, Tom."

The fat man's eyes widened. "I don't know, Father. I'm only the accountant. Dick makes all the arrangements an' deals wi' the families, an' anyway, I'm sure the, ah, departed's not ready." Then adopting the priest's conspiratorial tone he added, "If ye could just wait, we'll have him lookin' real nice in a couple o' hours." He looked hopefully at the priest.

"Tom, she's just arrived from America an' in her emotional state I think she should see him now. I'd appreciate yer help."

The fat man hated being put under this pressure by the priest and his face assumed a frown. "I see, but it's highly irregular, Father. We're not ready..."

The priest gripped him by the arm. "She needs t' see him, Tom. I can give ye a few minutes t' get him ready. Just the face is enough. Ye can cover the rest o' him. She doesn't want t' conduct an examination. Just a look is all."

The fat man sighed. "I see," he repeated, knitting his brows. "It's not normal practice, ye understand,..." He hesitated, but the priest offered no way out, so the fat man conceded. "I'll see what I can do. Mind, we'll need at least fifteen minutes."

The priest nodded reluctantly. "All right, but take care of it, Tom. I'd appreciate it."

The fat man nodded and hurried off down the corridor.

The priest returned to the office. "It'll be a few minutes," he said to Bernadette, who stood by the desk, gently brushing the top of the miniature model coffin with one finger. "Might as well have a seat," the priest continued.

Walking slowly over to the row of chairs, Bernadette sat down. The priest eased himself into a chair beside her. They waited in silence.

The fat man entered a large, brightly lit room at the end of the corridor. In the center of the room stood a large, stainless steel table with the naked body of Joe Mallory stretched out on it. A white label was tied to the big toe of his right foot.

In a corner at the far end of the room, two men sat smoking and drinking tea. They looked up when the fat man entered. He waved at them with a chubby hand. "C'mon boys, put them fags out. There's work t' do. The daughter's here an' she wants t' see the body."

"What!" exclaimed one of the men. "We just started our tea break!"

"Never mind that," snapped the fat man. "Yous can have yer tea later. Yous've fifteen minutes t' get him ready, so get a move on."

"Fifteen minutes?" complained the second man. "Sure he won't be ready in fifteen minutes!"

The statement made the fat man panic. "Yous're wastin' time!" he shouted. "Just clean up the face an' neck an' do somethin' wi' his hair. Yous can cover the rest o' him. She'll hardly want t' do an examination. Now, get busy!" He turned to leave the room then spun to face them again. "An' get rid o' that ashtray!" he commanded. He tugged on the lapels of his jacket, pulled his trousers up around his waist and hurried back into the corridor, slamming the door after him.

Behind him the first man said to the other "I don't know who's more trouble, the livin' or the dead."

Back in his office, the fat man explained that it would be a few minutes before they could enter the "Preparation Room", and began to hurriedly explain that what they'd see wasn't the normal way the departed would be displayed and he hoped they'd understand.

The priest held up a hand. "We understand, Tom," he said dismissively.

Trying to buy time, the fat man offered them tea but they declined. He attempted small talk about America, the weather. Neither of them responded enough to carry on a conversation and the he resented the priest for not helping him out. He considered raising the subject of payment but decided it was not the best time, with the priest there. As the long minutes passed, Bernadette grew agitated, getting up from her chair and pacing around the room.

The priest finally said "D'ye think we could go now, Tom? It's been fifteen minutes."

The fat man hated the priest for pointing this out. He glanced at his watch, hoping it would contradict the priest but it didn't. "So it has right enough. Aye, they should be ready now." Sounding unconvinced, he sighed and added, "This way, please."

He held the door open for them, then deftly, for someone his size, stepped around and led them down the corridor. He stopped at a door marked STAFF ONLY! POSITIVELY NO ADMITTANCE! in big, red letters.

"Let me just make sure..." the fat man muttered nervously. Opening the door, he looked into the room then turned to face them again. "Ye understand now..."

"Aye, Tom," interrupted the priest. "We understand. Can we go in?"

The fat man made a mental note that the priest owed him a lot for this. "Aye, of course," he answered, swinging the door open and stepping aside to let them through.

Bernadette entered slowly, her eyes wide and heart pumping. She did not feel the priest's guiding touch at her elbow, indeed was oblivious to everything except the sheet-draped figure on the steel table in the middle of the room. Approaching it, she made out the shapes that were feet, knees, stomach, shoulders. Then she saw the head. Her blood felt hot and pulsing and she shook nervously as she stepped to the table to see the face clearly. The priest stood close behind her, thinking he might need to catch her if she fainted.

Bernadette was shocked. The face was drained of all color and had a white, eggshell sheen to it. Gone were the mustache and beard she expected, although there was a pale outline where they had been. The hair was greasy and slicked back from the forehead, not like her father had ever worn it. The eyes were closed, but the mouth was open as if in a last, futile attempt to suck life-giving air. Wrinkles covered the whole face, accentuated by the thin paste that had been applied like a death mask.

She reeled slightly at the sight and the priest stepped forward to steady her. His hip brushed against the body, causing the corpse's arm to swing down from under the sheet. Recoiling in horror, Bernadette was transfixed by the swinging arm. The priest held her tightly, at the same time glaring at the fat man to do something.

Red with embarrassment, the fat man fumbled to stuff the protruding arm back under the sheet, but it kept sliding down again. Panicked, the fat man finally pulled the sheet away from the shoulders and folded the arm across the corpse's chest. Bernadette saw the stark contrast between the chest and the face. The former tanned and dull, the latter pale and waxen. The head seemed to have been grafted to the wrong body, but it was the shoulder which shocked her most. At the top of the arm was a hideous, black bruise as large as a fist. Imagining it was the rot of death, she turned away, feeling herself gag. The priest held her tightly to his chest and patted her back soothingly. "I'd like to go now," she muttered finally.

The priest led her from the room.

The fat man was unable to move for a minute. He was aghast at this bad luck and blamed the priest for it. He was the one who insisted they come in here and wasn't he the one who dislodged the arm in the first place? The fat man would have to answer to his brother when he heard about it.

"That's the first time I've seen one o' them wavin' goodbye," said one of the preparation staff. They had both stood back in the corner the whole time and now laughed heartily at this joke.

They were instantly silenced by the look the fat man shot them. "Get back t' work!" he snarled. "If yous want t' keep yer jobs!" He turned and hurried after the priest and the woman but they were already into the street and he decided not to pursue them. What could he say anyway? It was their own fault for not waiting. He regretted not having broached the subject of payment after all.

The priest led Bernadette gently by the arm. "Why don't we go to my house? Ye can rest up there. It's been a gruelin' day for ye."

Bernadette acquiesced with a slight nod, and they walked back to the priest's car, Bernadette seeing nothing but her father's corpse stamped in her mind. The priest held the passenger door open and helped her into the car. They drove out of the downtown area and into a neighborhood of terrace houses. Deciding she needed distraction from what she had just seen, the priest kept up a monologue about what a good man her father had been and how the all-forgiving Lord would set aside the sins of youth. Bernadette's ears heard but she didn't listen. Nor did she see the streets, houses and people they drove past. Her mind was numb, frozen by the picture of her dead father's face. "I don't even know how he died," she said to herself, but aloud.

The priest looked at her, and blushed. "Forgive me, Bernadette. Sure that's terrible o' me." He coughed slightly. "When they let...I mean when yer father was..."

"When he got out of prison," she helped.

"Aye, that. Well, he was a sick man. They added forty years t' him, squeezed it int' the space o' twenty. Squashed the spirit out o' him, like juice from an orange." He shook his head slowly. "The IRA treated him like a hero. They needed one because people were beginnin' t' see them for what they are. They used him t' make people feel guilty about all he'd done for them an' how they owed him somethin' in return. I tried t' keep him away from them, bring him back to the church, but he felt some kind o' loyalty t' them. Anyway, a couple o' them were with him when he...when it happened.

He had t' take all sorts of medicines, includin' morphine injections. The dosage had t' be just right, so one o' the sisters from St. Mary's would stop by t' give him that. The two men with him that night said that just after midnight they heard yer father coughin' an' chokin'. They found him givin' himself an injection o' morphine. They tried t' wrest the needle away from him an' it broke off in his arm." He glanced at her. "That's what caused the bruise ye saw."

Closing her eyes, Bernadette tried to shut out the image of her dead father's dangling arm.

The priest continued, "Me an' the doctor were sent for. Yer father regained consciousness briefly while I was wi' him an' was able t' make his confession." He glanced at Bernadette again. "The doctor says it would have been painless..." The priest's voice trailed off at the lie and he kept his eyes fixed on the road, not wanting to look at her again.

Imagining her father choking and clutching his throat, struggling for life, Bernadette wondered if he thought of her in those final moments.

"We're here," the priest announced, relieved. He swung the steering wheel around and the car made a sharp turn into a gravel driveway and stopped in front of a gray, slate house. The shock had worn off Bernadette but she was overcome by sudden fatigue and paid no attention to their surroundings, allowing herself to be led inside to a small living room. The priest guided her to a couch. "Sit there now an' rest. I'll make us a nice cup o' tea."

Bernadette nodded mechanically. The priest hesitated, then left her staring into space. When he returned with the tea she was slumped on the couch, asleep. He put a cushion under her head and lifted her feet onto the couch. She didn't stir, so the priest left her, creeping upstairs to his study to work on his sermon for the coming Sunday.

———

Waking suddenly, Bernadette was totally bewildered by her surroundings. A small cry escaped her lips, bringing the priest hurrying down the stairs at the sound. "It's all right," he soothed.

Beginning to remember where she was, Bernadette struggled to sit up, looking dazed.

"Take it easy now," said the priest, crossing to her side. "Are ye all right? That's not a very comfortable couch, I'm afraid, but I didn't want t' wake ye."

"How long have I been asleep?" Bernadette asked groggily.

"About five hours. Would ye like some tea now?"

She blinked her eyes widely. "No, but I would like to freshen up if I could."

"Of course. The bathroom's upstairs, first right."

Bernadette stood. "I'm sorry. I'm a lot of trouble to you. First the mortuary, then falling asleep on your couch..."

The priest waved a hand at her. "Ye've nothing t' apologize for. There should be clean towels in the bathroom."

"I'm afraid I'll need one of my suitcases…"

"They're still in the car. I'll get it. Which one?"

"The small one."

"Won't be a jiffy."

He left and she heard the crunch of gravel as he passed the window.

She stretched and yawned, then strolled idly around the room. On the wall opposite the window was a Sacred Heart painting. The young, bearded Jesus in the picture seemed to scowl at her. She turned to a small music cabinet on which was a photograph of a smiling woman holding a baby. Picking up the photograph she examined it more closely. The door opened behind her and the priest set her suitcase on the floor and crossed quickly to where she stood. Taking the photograph from her, he replaced it on the cabinet, then turned so that his body was between her and the photograph. Bernadette realized she had trespassed on something.

"I've brought yer case," the priest stated.

Looking into his eyes, Bernadette saw that he resented her having touched the photograph. "Thank you," she said quietly, then added, "I'm sorry, I didn't mean to pry."

The priest said nothing.

Bernadette turned and walked to her suitcase. Snapping it open she took out a small overnight bag. Closing the suitcase again, she turned and walked slowly up the stairs.

When she came back down about a half hour later, the priest had softened. "Feelin' better?" he asked.

"Much better."

"Would ye be wantin' somethin' t' eat?"

Bernadette shook her head. "I've no appetite."

The priest nodded understandingly. "Should we go on out t' the house then?" he asked tentatively.

"Yes. I don't want to impose on you any further," Bernadette answered as she replaced the overnight bag into her suitcase.

"Impose? Sure it's no trouble at all."

Picking up her suitcase, the priest held the door open for her with his other hand. Outside, Bernadette noted that the priest must have brought the car around to the door while she slept. She realized how tired she must have been, not to have been awakened by that. She got into the car while the priest put her case in the trunk, then climbed in beside her. It had stopped raining but the slate-gray sky held the threat of more to come. The priest started the car and turned onto the main street.

They drove in silence for a while before the priest said "D' ye see anythin' different about the ould town, Bernadette?"

"Well, there were no video stores when I lived here, and there seem to be more European cars," she answered.

The priest nodded. "Aye, that's because o' the Common Market. Of course, livin' here I don't notice the changes."

"You've changed too of course," Bernadette continued. "I would never have guessed you'd become a priest. Did you always want to be one?"

His body tensed and she sensed that she was intruding again, but he relaxed quickly. "No. I never imagined I'd be a priest, but the Lord works in mysterious ways as they say."

She waited, expecting more.

He glanced at her. "That photograph," he continued, "Was me wife an' child."

It was Bernadette's turn to tense involuntarily.

"The good Lord tested me," the priest went on. "He gave them t' me briefly. Then he took them forever."

Bernadette felt the uncomfortable feeling that comes when you know the answer to a question is bad, but you ask anyway. "What happened?"

The priest took a deep breath. "Car crash. I taught her t' drive meself an' she'd just passed her test the week before. She was proud o' that." His voice betrayed that he was reliving the time. He jerked back to the present. "She went through a red light an' a lorry hit them."

"I'm sorry," Bernadette stammered.

He nodded imperceptibly. "I blamed meself because I'd taught her an' she caused the accident. Tried t' kill meself but the old priest, Father Flannery, found me in time. I spent a while in hospital an' durin' that time the Lord showed me that he had a task for me, that I still had somethin' t' live for. I began hangin' around Father Flannery, drivin' him around, doin' odd jobs. He helped me get int' the seminary an' when I got out we both asked that I be assigned t' him. He taught me about ministerin' an' I took over the parish when he died about ten years ago. People probably call me the old priest now." He smiled. "An' what about yourself? Ye're a politician I understand. Senator, is it?"

"Representative. A bit less than a senator. I didn't plan it either. Just happened to be in the right place at the right time. Turned out I wasn't too bad at it."

The priest looked at her and Bernadette realized she hadn't exactly described a vocation. "I wanted to help people," she added belatedly. This time Bernadette gave the impression that the priest was intruding and she didn't want to pursue the conversation, so they drove in silence again.

When they reached the outskirts of town and landmarks became familiar, Bernadette's pulse quickened. Finally they turned into a greasy, rutted lane that she remembered well.

"Here we are," announced the priest.

Looking up, Bernadette saw the dirty, white cottage, still glossy from the recent rain. A thin wisp of smoke snaked from the chimney. The car jerked to a halt and the priest turned off the ignition. As soon as she opened the car door Bernadette's nostrils twitched at the dimly remembered sweet smell of burning peat. She noted the old milk urn which still stood by the door. It leaned to one side, where the bottom had rusted away. A spider's web, spangled with raindrops, stretched across the top of the urn. The large white and yellow flowers she had painted on the side as a child, were still discernible, though greatly faded. The tilted urn seemed like a small, squat sentry, dozing on the job.

Stepping in front of the cracked, wooden door, Bernadette pushed her thumb down on the rusted latch. The door creaked open. Before her eyes had adjusted to the dim interior, an old woman's voice cackled "C'mon in. Sure never mind yer feet."

The priest followed Bernadette inside, closing the door behind them. "D'ye remember Mrs. Slaugherty, Bernadette? She's been a real angel, helping out around here." Then he raised his voice in the direction of the old woman. "It's young Bernadette, Mrs Slaugherty."

"I mind her right enough. I haven't seen ye since ye were a wee girl, skippin' off t' school, mind." She got up from the three-legged stool she had occupied by the fire, chewing on her gums and nodding her head up and down. "I'm awful sorry about yer father. Sure it's a terrible thing, an' him so young."

Bernadette looked at the toothless old woman who was now wiping her hands on her grimy apron. "Thank you," she murmured.

The old woman cocked her head to one side. She obviously had not heard, but continued to nod and chew as if she understood.

"Ye'll have t' speak up, Bernadette. Mrs. Slaugherty's a bit hard o' hearin'."

The old woman nodded at the priest's words. "Aye, a wee bit hard o' hearin'," she confirmed.

Bernadette's eyes adjusted to the gloom and were drawn to some candles which flickered toward the back of the room. Brown's had finished their work and delivered the body home. There was a candle at each corner of the coffin.

Bernadette had forgotten it would be like this, with the body on display, amidst the chairs, ornaments and bric brac that represented the meager accumulations of a poor life. She soaked in the atmosphere, oblivious to the priest and the old woman. The silence was broken only by the steady ticking of an old Victorian clock on the mantelpiece, the same clock her father would wind ritually, each and every night. The ceremony was a statement to everyone that another day had officially ended and it was time for bed.

Behind the coffin, faded green curtains were drawn across the window which she knew looked onto a tiny back yard and to the fields and hills beyond. She had trudged those fields and hills on many long summer days, collecting wild flowers for her mother, sipping sweet, wild honey-suckles, and chasing butterflies without really wanting to catch one, just exercising a child's delight at the variety and beauty of nature.

The coffin was the only thing of beauty where she stood now. Its soft, polished mahogany glowed in the candlelight, and its large, brass handles and hinges reflected the candles' flames.

The priest coughed lightly and Bernadette was reminded of his and the old woman's presence, but stepped toward the coffin anyway.

The corpse's face shocked her anew. It was no longer white, but now appeared waxy yellow in the soft candlelight. She noticed a trace of caked, white cream on his sideburns. The slightly open mouth showed a glimpse of stained teeth. She was surprised to notice that the teeth were not glossed with saliva. The indifferent but final look of death sent another tremor of shock through her. She had seen the look once before, on her mother. Stepping backwards, she stumbled on the torn linoleum. The priest reached out and steadied her.

"There now, take it easy. Sit yerself down here." He eased her into a straight-backed, wooden chair by the fire. Speaking loudly again, he said "Maybe, Mrs. Slaugherty, ye'd be good enough t' make some tea for us?" He beamed at the old woman, who slapped her hands over her mouth.

"Sure I don't know what I'm thinkin' at all," she exclaimed. "I'll away an' put the kettle on this minute." She stepped towards the scullery.

"No!" Bernadette was immediately aware of how harsh the word sounded. The old woman clearly heard it too. Dropping her voice, Bernadette continued "I'm sorry, but I'm sure you've done more than enough already." She hesitated. "I'd like to be alone if I could." It sounded apologetic.

"Of course," said the priest, mildly. "Sure I should have known that. I'll bring in yer suitcases from the motor. Mrs Slaugherty has already made the bed for ye."

Bernadette looked from the old woman to the priest. She had not thought of staying in the house and now knew she could never do it with the body there. "I thought I would stay at the Starry Plough," she said quietly.

For a moment, the only sound was of the clock marking time. She knew they were surprised, maybe even shocked but she offered no explanation, only turning and staring into the fire.

"Well then, why don't I go on down there wi' yer suitcases an' make sure they've a room ready for ye? That'll be no problem, mind ye, there'll be nobody stayin' there this time o' year. Sure it's a better idea anyway. Ye won't be alone in the middle o' nowhere all night." It was an attempt to reassure her that the idea was acceptable. He raised his voice again. "C'mon, Mrs Slaugherty. I'll give ye a lift home."

The old woman hurriedly pulled on her coat and wrapped a scarf over her head. "I'm ready, Father," she said.

"About what time should I come back for ye, Bernadette?" The priest asked.

Bernadette continued to stare into the red, bottomless peat fire. "I thought I'd walk."

There was another moment's silence before the priest said, "Aye, fine. As ye wish. I've an umbrella under the seat in the motor. I'll bring it in. Ye'll likely be needin' it. Three miles is a fair walk an' it looks like it might rain again."

"I won't mind the rain," Bernadette answered softly.

The priest shrugged his shoulders. "Let's be off then, Mrs Slaugherty."

"Right y'are, Father," said the old woman. She pointed to the few peat briquettes lying on the hearth. "That's the last o' the peat. I'll send me man over wi' some more."

"Thank you," said Bernadette. She looked at the priest, then to the old woman. "I'd like to pay you for your trouble."

"Ach, away wi' ye," said the old woman, waving an arm at her and chewing her gums nervously.

Bernadette looked back to the priest. "Father, can you find out how much is due and to whom? For the coffin, preparations and whatever else…" Her voice trailed off as the priest held up the palm of his hand to her.

"Don't ye be thinkin' about that, now. Ye'll be embarrassin' people. There'll be time enough for that later. We'll be away now. Ye know where t' find me if ye need anythin'."

"Yes. Thank you both again." Bernadette returned her attention to the fire.

The priest led the old woman to the door and closed it quietly behind them. Bernadette heard the car doors slam, the engine cough into life, and the car drive off. Peace settled over her. Only the ticking clock remained for company. She sat, hunched before the fire for a moment, then picked up one of the peat briquettes. It felt dry and warm on the side that had faced the fire, but the bottom was cool and damp, the way she remembered peat. Tossing it onto the glowing red fire, she sent a stream of sparks shooting up the chimney, like pinpoint souls, freed from a searing pit. The peat hissed slowly, as if warning the gray smoke that began to rise from beneath it. Thin tongues of flame began to lick at the edges of the peat, carefully tasting this offering, before consuming it.

The clock struck four and Bernadette strained to hear the last chime echo away, to be overtaken by the steady ticking again. Imagining the lifeless clock to have a steady heartbeat, she resented that her father had none. She thought of "My Grandfather's Clock", a song she learned as a child, and how that clock had "…stopped short, never to go again, when the old man died." Reality seemed more challenging, in that life had to go on.

Getting up, she walked slowly over to the coffin. Pulling a chair up, she sagged into it. "Father," she whispered, but still causing the closest candle flame to buckle and weave in the disturbed air. "I tried to be here to say goodbye. I'm sorry I was too late." Tears came to her eyes and dripped onto his cheek. Breaking into large sobs, she fell forward, hugging the cold body, and burying her face in his chest.

Minutes passed and her sobs subsided. Straightening up, she wiped at her eyes, then bent over to wipe away the tears that had fallen on her father's face. "This is the closest I've been to seeing you cry." Forcing a smile, she stroked his hair. "But I remember putting tears on your face once before, when I couldn't learn my times eight multiplication tables and there was a test at school the next day. I cried and cried and you sat me on your lap and spent hours teaching me. I thought you were the cleverest person in the world. Far cleverer than any of the nuns at school.

I still remember that riddle in the newspaper. where it asked for the next number in the sequence twenty, one, eighteen and twelve. None of the teachers knew, not even old Bootsy the Mother Superior, but you looked and right away said "Five, 'tis the numbers on a dartboard, goin' clockwise." Of course the nuns wouldn't know that, but I was proud of you anyway."

She stroked his brow. "I could always get my way with you. Remember the Christmas I wanted a golliwog? I knew we were too poor for me to have it, but I yapped and whined and you finally got it somehow. I still have that golly." She stopped. "How could you not want to know me? Not want to share our lives? That was so stupid." She began to sob again but there was no response from the corpse. She studied his face, wondering what might have been with this stranger.

A soft knock sounded at the door. Looking up, Bernadette didn't register the source immediately. The knocking came again, slightly louder. Stepping to the door, she opened it a crack, then wider. It was an old, heavyset man. His weather-beaten face testified to the rows of potatoes he had planted, nursed and harvested over many years.

"Me woman said ye needed peat," he said flatly. " I'll drop it by the fire."

Nodding, Bernadette stood aside, holding the door ajar. Grabbing a swollen sack by the neck, the old man hoisted it in front of him, legs spread wide as he staggered toward the fire. He lugged the sack onto the hearth. "Got here just in time, looks like." He nodded towards the few remaining peat briquettes. Then, like a scolded schoolboy, he grabbed at his cap, and folded it into his fists, glancing towards the coffin, as if apologizing for the disrespect.

"Thank you," said Bernadette. "How much do I owe you?"

"Ach, away wi' ye woman! Sure it's little enough, an' someday soon it'll maybe need be done for me own woman." He looked towards the coffin again. "He was one o' us, an' we look after our own."

Bernadette could think of nothing to say.

"I'll be on me way then, unless there's somethin' else ye'll be needin'?" the man stated, squinting at her.

"No, nothing. Thank you again."

She had known this old man as an ogre. As kids they called him 'Old Slaughter', and his cottage was the 'Slaughter House'. The names were earned by his once chasing boys from his apple tree, ax in hand. She had always run past his house on her way to and from school after that. Sometimes, she would glimpse him at the window and her heart would pound in terror that he might chase her. She didn't know what to say to him now.

He stepped to the door, then turned. "I don't recall ye as a child, they all look the same t' me, but I'm sorry about yer father. They just wouldn't leave him alone." He stepped outside, pulled on his cap and tugged his coat collar up around his neck. Turning, he closed the door behind him.

Bernadette wanted to ask who wouldn't leave her father alone, but she was still intimidated by the man, still felt like a child in his presence. Pulling back the front window curtain, she watched him disappear behind the hedge, hands pushed deep into jacket pockets and body bent into the wind. It was getting dark already. She turned back to face the coffin. The candles flickered and she felt a cold draught.

Sitting on the three-legged stool in front of the now-blazing fire, Bernadette remembered how she used to lie on the cold linoleum, school-books spread around her, doing homework. Watching the peat burn, she recalled that sometimes, when fresh briquettes were added to the fire, slugs would appear and move around the top of the peat in frantic circles, before they shriveled up and melted. She would stare at the white stain that had been their life, for a long time. Now she thought about her father. Like the slugs, he too had been reduced to a mix of chemicals and like them, he also would finally sink into the peat. She hoped he would not be consumed by eternal flames.

Getting up, she walked to the scullery, as much to take the image from her mind as anything. Nothing had changed. There were the old sink and stove, and under the countertop was a garbage pail. Looking into it, she saw dried-out potato skins and tea leaves. The staples of his life. It was so depressing that she no longer wanted to be in the house, alone with the corpse. The scullery felt cold as a tomb, but she before she left she had to go upstairs and see her old bedroom.

Grasping the wooden banister she began the climb. The stair creaked beneath her feet. As a child, the staircase had seemed wide and high, but now it seemed designed for a midget. She reached the top and ducked to miss the low beam that ran across the ceiling. To the right was her parents' bedroom. Standing in the doorway, she peered into the semi-darkness. There had never been electricity. "Why d'ye want light in a bedroom? Sure ye just lie down an' close yer eyes t' block out the light anyway!" she remembered her father saying when his wife nagged about putting an electric light in the room.

Against the back wall was the same old bed, dented in the middle. Ahead was a small dresser, its mirror cracked and yellowed at the edges. To the right a tall chest of drawers stood. The room whispered to her of intimate couplings. She understood now those nights when she would lie awake and hear the muffled voices, the "Don't now, ye're hurtin' me!", and the resigned "All right then, but hurry up.", followed by the rhythmic creaking of the bed, gradually becoming faster and louder, peaking in short moans and labored breathing. She had been frightened that her father was hurting her mother.

She had been born in this room. Long ago it must have seemed romantic to her parents, especially to her mother's honeymooned eyes. A coat of paint, lace curtains on the window, a matching bedspread, some cheery pictures on the walls and it would make a cozy lovers' nest.

The years of wear and neglect made it squalid now. The stale air, she was sure, held her father's dying breaths and this thought produced a swell of nausea within her. Turning away, she walked quickly down the landing to her own bedroom.

That room was bare but for two sleeping bags spread on the floor and some beer bottles lying around. An ashtray lay, upside down, the trail of spilt butts and ashes like a comet's tail. She deduced her father's friends must have slept here. Looking to the top of the walls she saw that the thin border of brightly colored wallpaper was still there. It had been her rainbow when she lay in bed and imagined herself to be Dorothy, and her pillow Toto, about to depart Kansas for the land of Oz. Glancing around the room now, she felt a wave of disgust pass through her.

The whole house seemed suddenly hostile. On the landing, the long shadows of dusk looked like obstacles, creating holes in the floors and bars across the walls. She was afraid that she would be prevented from leaving.

From outside came the squawking of crows. She strained to look through the window in the hallway outside her room. They were gathering in the naked ash tree, fighting for their night's roost. She watched them, large and black, shoulders hunched like vultures. Turning to go downstairs, she smacked her forehead on the low beam at the top of the staircase, which knocked her back a step. Rubbing at the spot and sucking breath between her teeth, she went quickly downstairs.

The coffin now dominated the room, its sheen heightened by the blazing peat. The flames of the candles danced, as if mocking the stillness of death.

A scratching sound caught her ear. She listened intently. It came again, faint but certain. A chill ran across the back of her neck. She knew it was either mice or bats. They'd always had both. The sound seemed to come from behind the coffin. She remembered her crazy old aunt Lottie telling stories of wakes and funerals where the corpse sat bolt upright in the coffin. Whether the old woman had been trying to frighten her, or had actually imagined such events to be real in her gin-soaked mind, Bernadette didn't know, but she would rather have seen what her aunt had described than face bats whirling about her head. She hadn't seen one since she had left here and in her horror-haunted mind they were the size of eagles, intent on entangling themselves in human hair. The corner of her eye caught a dancing shadow and the nape of her neck bristled again. She relaxed when she saw it was only a large moth come to worship a candle flame, before being singed for its devotion.

Casting one last look around the room, she pulled open the door. A dark figure loomed before her, fist raised to strike.

11

Instinctively throwing her hands over her face, Bernadette stumbled back, uttering a cry of shock.

"I'm sorry," the figure blurted, "I was about t' knock. I don't mean ye any harm."

Slowly lowering her hands, Bernadette saw a man of about her own age, wearing an ill-fitting, peaked cap and a mid-length pea jacket. In one hand he carried a small grip. His face had a look of embarrassed concern. "Are ye all right?" he asked anxiously.

Putting one hand on her chest, Bernadette took a deep breath.

"I'm sorry," the man repeated, "Maybe I've the wrong house." He looked over his shoulder as if expecting to see another cottage.

Bernadette recovered enough to respond. "You gave me a start. Took my breath away."

Rain dripped from the peak of his cap onto his nose, which he self-consciously wiped with the back of his sleeve, then glanced over his shoulder again. Turning back to her he said, "I'm looking for Joe Mallory." His

voice had a touch of hope tinged with desperation. Shifting from one foot
to the other, he wiped at his nose again.

"This is his house," Bernadette said softly. "But I'm afraid my father
die...passed away..." Her voice trailed off.

The sudden jerk of the man's body registered shock and his face showed
disbelief. "I'm sorry," he finally murmured. He looked as if he were lost.

"Were you a friend of his, Mr...?" she asked.

The man's eyes blinked and he snapped out of his reverie. "Me name's
Billy. Billy Kingston. Aye, I'm a...was a friend o' Joe, er, Mr. Mallory."

"Well," Bernadette said. "Why don't you come in out of the rain?" She
stepped aside, holding the door open.

He hesitated. "I don't want t' intrude."

"You're soaking," she answered. "And it's cold standing here."

Billy glanced inside, eyes squinting dubiously. Then he blew into his
right fist and nodded. "Ye're sure?"

"You can dry off by the fire." Bernadette encouraged.

Stepping inside, he scraped his shoes on the tattered mat. Bernadette
noticed his limp. She closed the door behind them.

Suddenly seeing the coffin, Billy froze for a second, then turned to her.
"I am intruding. I'd best go," he said quickly.

"You're not intruding. Any friend of my father is welcome. Here, let me
take your jacket," Bernadette responded. She held out her hand.

He set his grip on the floor and unbuttoned his coat, allowing her to
slide it off his shoulders. Carrying the jacket over to the fire, she draped it
across the back of a chair. "We can dry your cap too," she offered. Billy
handed the dripping cap to her and she placed it on a corner of the hearth.

"Why don't you sit by the fire?" Bernadette said, pulling up a chair
for him.

Picking up his grip he walked across the room, glancing at the coffin,
then lowered himself slowly into the chair.

Bernadette could see now how shabbily dressed he was. He wore a drab,
olive sweater with gray patches on the elbows. The right patch was

unraveling. His baggy brown pants were worn shiny on the front thighs and wet around the cuffs. His boots were black, where they weren't scuffed or spattered with mud. She noted the white rims around his toecaps, where the polish had been worn away by his walk through the wet grass.

In contrast, his face was ruggedly handsome, square and clear-complexioned, with a masculine toughness.

Their eyes met for the briefest of instants, but in that time each felt a pulse of excitement and detected in the other that look which is both shy and inviting. Although both recognized it, neither acknowledged it. Bernadette broke the moment. "I'll make us some tea," she stated, flustered.

Turning his eyes to the coffin Billy asked softly, "When did it happen?"

"Early Sunday morning," Bernadette answered, then turned and walked to the kitchen, wanting to avoid the subject.

As she busied herself making the tea she wondered about the stranger. He was young to be a friend of her father, and why had he come at this time of night? And his accent, from the north?

"Milk?" she called over her shoulder. There was no reply, so she looked into the living room. He was kneeling by the coffin. Bernadette stepped over to the sink so as not to be seen looking at him. After a decent interval she began to deliberately make noise, setting the kettle down harder than she had to, closing cupboard doors, clinking cups, so that he'd know she was coming back. He was in the chair by the fire again when she walked back into the living room carrying the two steaming cups. "Milk?" she asked, as if for the first time.

"This is fine," Billy answered, accepting the cup she offered.

Pulling up a chair for herself, Bernadette sat beside him.

"How did it...I mean, what did he ..." Billy faltered.

Bernadette was embarrassed that she didn't have a short answer, like an illness she could name that would require no further explanation. "He'd been sick for a while and gave himself an injection by mistake." Instinctively reaching across her chest, she touched her left shoulder to indicate the injection point. "I suppose he didn't remember he'd already

had his morphine, or he meant to take a different medicine," she said, half
to herself.

A vague thought tried to surface from deep in Billy's mind, but he
couldn't focus on it and it disappeared like a ripple on water. "Was he
alone?" he asked quietly.

The question clearly surprised her. "Why do you ask that?"

Billy lowered his eyes to his cup. "He was always afeard o' bein' alone."

His answer hurt her. She was ashamed that this stranger had a more
private knowledge of her father than she did. "No," she finally answered,
her voice quivering. She took a deep breath. "Some of his friends were
here and tried to stop him. The needle broke off in his arm." She turned
away as the sight of the swinging arm in the mortuary replayed again in
her mind.

"I'm sorry, I didn't mean t' pry," Billy said sincerely.

Bernadette recovered. "It's all right."

Sipping his tea, Billy continued staring into the fire. After a moment of
silence Bernadette decided to take the initiative. "How did you know
him?" She turned to face him and their eyes met again. This time they
were both willing to hold the look longer.

"I met him in prison." As if this made him remember something, Billy
reached down and unzipped his grip. Pulling out the bible he had packed,
he held it out to her. "I was goin' t' return this t' him."

Bernadette recognized the bible immediately. Placing her teacup on the
floor between her feet she took it with a trembling hand. Clasping both
hands around it she pressed it to her cheek. Recognizing the intensely personal moment, Billy looked away.

Bernadette let the pages of the bible fall open and sniffed gently. The
perfumed smell of crushed flowers she remembered was gone. In its place
was a damp mustiness. She opened the front cover and tilted it towards
the firelight. A faint trace of handwriting remained but was illegible. She
tried to recall what it had said. Something about being a prize for her
father's perfect attendance at Sunday school. It was the only prize he'd ever

won and he was proud of it, even though he always said he'd rather have had the second prize candy bar.

Her father had enjoyed reading to her from this bible, especially the Song of Solomon. He liked the poetry, although his wife would cluck that those particular passages were hardly suitable reading for a child. Bernadette hadn't understood all the words but remembered that she liked the sound of them. Her eyes began to mist. "How did you get it?" she sniffled.

Billy shifted uneasily in his seat. "Yer father taught me t' read from that bible," he answered, flushing slightly.

Bernadette couldn't hide her surprise. "You couldn't read? Didn't you go to school?"

A bitter laugh escaped his lips. "School? I remember the day I was t' start school…Ach, but I shouldn't bore ye…"

"I'd like to hear about it," Bernadette said earnestly.

He hesitated but only for an instant. "Me mother got me all spruced up. Scrubbed me face till it glowed an' brushed me hair till it shone. Even cleaned an' ironed me clothes. She kept saying how handsome I looked. I was proud, but nervous about going t' this strange place she'd told me about where I'd learn new things an' make new friends."

Then me father came in from the barn an' asked her what was goin' on. I could tell somethin' was wrong by her nervousness. "It's Billy's first day at school. Remember, I told ye?" He snorted an' told her not t' be stupid. If I was old enough for school, I was old enough t' be helpin' out more around the farm. My mother argued wi' him, but he would have none of it. So I stayed home that day, an' the next, an' the next.

One day, a man showed up. Said he was from the School Board an' wondered why young Billy hadn't been t' school yet. Me father grabbed the man by the throat an' said young Billy wouldn't be goin' t' school an' if anybody showed up again, askin' about it, me father'd kill them. The man was terrified. Nobody ever came back askin' about young Billy an' school."

"That's terrible," whispered Bernadette.

Billy shrugged. "Me father couldn't read or write himself, ye see. So he didn't see the need for me t' learn. Or maybe he couldn't stand the idea that his kid would be able t' do somethin' he couldn't," he added bitterly.

Looking at him, Bernadette could se he did not want to pursue the subject. "Tell me about my father. Teaching you to read, I mean," she said softly. Her father had helped her with reading and she felt close to the stranger.

Billy cleared his throat. "I was in solitary, for me own protection. One day I found a small foil wrapper in me soup. Inside the wrapper was a note. I couldn't ask the screws, I mean the guards, t' read it for me an' the only other person I ever saw was yer father. He brought me food, so the next day I pushed the note into his hand an' whispered that I couldn't read. A screw was near, so yer father only nodded to show me he understood. A few days later he told me he'd received permission from the warden t' teach me t' read an' write. I thought he was crazy an' I'd never be able t' learn, but it was a chance t' break solitary for a couple o' hours a day so I played along.

He could tell I wasn't taking it seriously so he made me a deal. If he could teach me t' read a complete verse from the bible in half an hour, would I make the effort t' learn? I agreed, figuring I had nothing t' lose. Well, he did it. Mind, it was only a two word verse. 'Jesus wept'. Shortest verse in the bible, but he won his point.

The other thing he did was t' refuse t' tell me what the note in the soup said. Told me I could read it for meself an' the more serious I was about learning, the sooner that'd be." Billy stopped and his eyes narrowed.

Bernadette couldn't wait. "What did the note say?"

Billy smiled bitterly. "That I was a marked man an' I'd never leave there alive." He stared resentfully into the fire.

Bernadette studied him for a moment while screwing up the nerve to ask her next question. "Why were you in prison?"

Continuing to gaze into the fire, Billy gave no indication he had heard the question. Afraid she had offended him, Bernadette was on the verge of apologizing, when he closed his eyes tightly. Opening them again, he turned his head to look at her. His face was expressionless. "I robbed a bank."

Bernadette didn't know what to say. "You don't look like a bank robber," she finally managed.

He gave a hollow laugh. "I'm not. That's why I got caught."

"Why did you do it then?" Bernadette said, at the same time realizing how stupid the question sounded. People robbed banks to get money. "I mean, were you that desperate for money?"

"No," Billy responded. "In fact the money wasn't for me. Ach, but it's a long story. Ye don't…"

"Yes, I do," she interrupted. "I'm interested."

Billy hesitated, then shrugged. "All right then, but it's nothin' I'm proud of.

I'm from Lisaleene, just over the border near Newry. It's hardly big enough t' be on a map, about twenty houses, a petrol station, general store an' o' course, a pub. One thing it doesn't have is any kind o' religious building. No church, parochial school or gospel hall. There aren't many villages like that in Ireland.

It was a quiet place as ye might expect. Some smugglin' back an' forth across the border, but nobody thought anything o' that. There were five o' us teenagers in the village. Boys I mean. For excitement we'd hang out at the general store on weekends an' watch the day trippers from the big city on their way t' the beach. Well, Newry was a big city t' us. Anyway, they'd stop t' buy cigarettes an' petrol before they crossed the border. We wanted t' see the girls wi' their mini skirts an' hot pants. We couldn't believe city boys got to see that every day.

Even when the troubles began in Belfast an' Derry it didn't affect us. The nearest Catholics were in Newry, twenty miles away, which might as well have been five hundred. Oh, people talked about the things going on but they never imagined it would affect them." He paused to take a breath. "But it did. The soldiers rolled into the village one Saturday afternoon. They set up a checkpoint on the road t' the border. It was scary. The jeep an' the troop carrier had wire mesh over the windshields. Then the soldiers jumped out. They had blackened faces an' real guns. They knelt wi' their guns pointin' in every direction, protectin' their mates while they built a small sandbagged barracks that would be their post. The troubles had come t' Lisaleene.

After a while we got used t' the soldiers. Most of them were young fellas, eighteen or twenty years old. At first they were as nervous as we were. Their faces were tense an' they made no attempt t' communicate with the people o' the village. As time went by though, an' nothin' happened, they began t' relax an' became friendlier. Me an' me mates started playin' football with them. They were far better than us, but kind enough t' let us think we were almost as good. They always kept the score close enough t' make us believe we could beat them next time, but we never did." He stopped again, a faint smile playing in his eyes. Then his look turned somber.

"It happened on a Saturday morning. The week before Easter. Yellow gorse was bursting from the hedges an' newborn lambs skittered in the fields. It was sunny an' warm, one o' them days that convince ye the long winter is finally over an' summer isn't far away. I was headed t' the checkpoint for our usual game an' could see two o' me mates already there. One o' them waved t' me an' I broke into an eager trot. As I passed the general store I took a kick at a tin can in the gutter."

Bernadette noticed his heavier breathing and how his whole body tensed slightly.

"That's when the bomb exploded. Me ears popped an' the ground shook. For an instant I thought I'd caused it by kickin' the can. Then I fell an' smacked me head. When I gathered me senses there was total silence. I thought I'd gone deaf an' panic began to rise in me. I sat up an' looked around. Not only was there deathly quiet but nothin' was movin'. It was like I was the only livin' thin' in the world. I was terrified. I remember feelin' relieved when I saw that the cloud o' dust hangin' over the checkpoint was in fact movin', although very slowly. I watched it expandin' slowly like an angel o' death reachin' out t' embrace the town. It seemed t' hypnotize me for ages.

In reality it was only a few seconds before pandemonium broke out. People ran out o' the buildings. Women covered their mouths an' screamed while men ran past them, shoutin' an' swearin'. One o' them cradled me in his arms, yelling at me, askin' if I was all right. His eyes were wide wi' terror an' that made me feel scared but I finally managed t' nod. A woman came an' kneeled beside us. The man told her t' take care o' me an' ran t' the checkpoint. I looked after him.

There was no checkpoint anymore. It was just a gaping hole in the ground. Off t' the side the troop carrier lay upside down with its wheels spinnin' slowly, like an overturned bug weakly kickin' its legs. Large pieces o' jagged metal were scattered about an' juttin' from the hedges on either side. Above it all the dust cloud loomed like an obscene genie cranin' for a better look."

His voice dropped an octave. "Me two mates an' three o' the soldiers were blown to bits. The IRA claimed responsibility. As usual, they regretted the civilian casualties, but were pleased they were able t' plant five-hundred pounds o' gelignite behind a hedge an' detonate it from a safe distance. Hell, the soldiers had become so comfortable in the town, an' trusted the people so much, that the IRA could've planted it inside the checkpoint an' it wouldn't have been suspected."

Stopping again, he lowered his eyes to the floor. "At the wake for me two mates, two men I'd never seen before whispered about revenge. Whisky gave me the courage t' join them. They said we'd need some money t' pay for the retaliation an' the plan was to rob a bank in Dundalk. Banks in the north were too well protected an' anyway, it was fittin' that we steal Catholic money.

It was planned for a Monday afternoon. Saturday was market day an' the farmers an' shopkeepers would deposit their money on Monday morning. One o' the men would drive the getaway car an' the other would cover me while I scooped up the money. It sounded simple enough.

It was drizzlin' when we got t' Dundalk, but the main street was still busy. We had t' drive around the block a couple o' times before we found a parking spot close t' the bank. The two of us went in an' walked over t' the counter. We pretended t' fill out forms while we looked the place over. Nobody paid us any attention. There wasn't even a guard. I remember bein' surprised at how calm I felt, not scared at all.

Me partner gave me a nod an' stepped toward the door. He pulled a gun from his coat an' yelled for everybody t' stand still. Mostly they turned an' looked at him in disbelief. They didn't understand what was happenin'. I jumped over the counter an' began riflin' the cashier drawers, stuffin' the wads o' bills into a carrier bag. I moved fast, ignoring loose bills an' coins. I couldn't believe how easy it was. I had one drawer t' go when a door at the end o' the counter opened. I looked up an' saw an old bald guy pointin' a gun at me. Before I could react he fired, hittin' me in the shoulder an' knockin' me off me feet. I didn't feel anythin' until I was on the floor, then the burning pain sent a wave o' nausea through me an' I passed out."

He looked into Bernadette's eyes and smiled sheepishly. "I woke up in hospital wi' two Irish policemen in me room. Me partner had shot an' killed the old guy, then bolted, leavin' me lyin' there.

They made a big show out o' the trial. I mean, it was a big deal, a man being killed an' all, but they wanted t' show how tough they were wi' terrorists. That's what they called me, not just a bank robber, but a terrorist. The British always complained that the south tolerated IRA men robbin' banks in the north an' crossing the border t' safety. Well, now the south had a chance t' show that they wouldn't stand for terrorism either."

His voice took on a bitter tone. "At least, not when it was Protestants involved. They didn't have t' worry about anybody bein' sympathetic t' me like they might've been t' an IRA man, so they made an example o' me."

"By putting you in solitary?" Bernadette queried.

He gave another hollow laugh. "No. They did that because I was the only Protestant in the place. The other prisoners would have torn me apart.

Yer father was the only man I got to know. We became good friends an' he asked me to keep in touch wi' him after I got out, joked that it would help me keep up wi' me readin' an' writin'. We wrote t' each other every couple o' months."

"Do you still have his letters?" Bernadette asked, hopefully.

"I'm sorry, I didn't keep them."

"How long were you in for?"

"Long enough."

This last answer indicated to her that he felt he'd said enough, and in confirmation he stood up. "I should go. I've imposed on ye too much already."

She stood also. "Where will you go?" she asked. "I mean, you look like maybe you were expecting to stay here, it being so late ..." His embarrassed look confirmed her suspicion, and she quickly added "You can stay. There's a bed upstairs and you'll be alone. I'm staying at the hotel in town."

After the briefest hesitation, he said, "No. Thanks all the same, but I'd best be goin'." He reached for his cap and coat.

"Why be stubborn? You've nowhere to go and it's too cold and wet to be tramping around." Their eyes met again. "And I'd like to talk to you some more about my father,"

He made no reply for a moment, thinking, then finally admitted, "You're right. I've nowhere t' go, but still..."

"Then it's settled," she interrupted with finality. "Look, you were a friend of my father and he'd want you to stay. Right?"

Nodding reluctantly, he let the cap and coat fall back on to the chair. He was suddenly exhausted.

"Come on," Bernadette said, taking his arm. "I'll show you to the bedroom. You look like you're ready to drop, and I should be getting to my hotel."

He let her lead him up the stairs to the bedroom where she sat him on the bed. He tugged his right shoe off. She saw that he treated his left foot more gingerly and noticed the grimace of pain as he finally worked that shoe free. She remembered his limp. "You're injured," she said with concern.

"It's nothin', just twisted me ankle."

"Let me see," said Bernadette and before he could object, she sat on the edge of the bed and gently pulled his sock down. "It's swollen and badly bruised. There'll be no ice in the house, but I'll soak a towel in cold water and use that as a compress. It'll help keep the swelling down." She stood to leave.

"No, it's not too bad. Really. Anyway, I did it hours ago. It'll be swollen as much as it's goin' t' swell. It'll be fine if I can just rest it for a while."

Looking dubious at first, Bernadette finally accepted that what he said was probably true. "Still, you'd better have it seen to."

"It looks worse than it is. I had t' walk a few miles on it. It'll be better tomorrow." He lay down. "I am tired, though," he murmured.

"Of course you are," she coaxed. "Why don't you get under the covers?"

"I'll be all right like this," he said sleepily.

"There's a sleeping bag in the other room. I'll get it to cover you."

He muttered something but she ignored it and went to the other bedroom. Picking up one of the sleeping bags she shook it off then crossed to the window and peered out at the night. In the faint light of the window below she could see that it was raining steadily and the bare branches of the trees were straining against a strong wind. She regretted her bravado in refusing the priest's ride, but there was no helping it now.

She returned to where the stranger lay. His eyes were already closed. She draped the sleeping bag over him. He muttered something.

"What?" Bernadette whispered.

He muttered again. She couldn't make out any words, but his voice had a plaintive quality to it. Unsure if he was awake or not Bernadette whispered "It's all right. Go to sleep now."

He turned on his side, his muttering increasing in volume. Bernadette shushed him like she would a child. "It's all right. Go to sleep now."

Tiptoeing over to a chair in a corner by the foot of the bed, she whisperingly shushed him some more. His muttering died down and she relaxed. She'd leave in a few minutes after he settled down. She could use some rest herself anyway. Her eyes closed.

12

Waking suddenly, Billy was surprised to realize that he knew exactly where he was. Raising his head, he saw Bernadette slumped in the chair across the room, asleep. He felt embarrassed. How could he have imposed on her at a time like this? Yet he was glad he had stayed. He was attracted to her, but cringed at the thought of how he'd talked about himself. True, she had asked, but only out of politeness. It didn't mean she was genuinely interested. Her father had just died and she'd have more on her mind than Billy Kingston's life story. But he had found it so easy to talk to her, and had sensed an attraction to him on her part. In the cold light of day though, a feeling of caution stirred in him. He wasn't sure he could hope for or even wanted anything to develop between them. He'd had one ruinous experience with a woman already.

Besides, there was nothing he could do here now. He'd get to a phone, call Baxter, tell him what had happened, have him wire some money and be back home in Belfast that night. He would likely never see Bernadette again after today.

Realizing he didn't know where the nearest phone was, he considered waking Bernadette to ask. She looked especially pretty when she was asleep. Nice breasts, good looking legs. No, he wouldn't wake her. She'd have little enough time to be free of sorrow for a while. Let her enjoy it now. He'd scout up and down the road and if nothing looked promising, he'd come back and see if she could help him.

Quietly easing himself off the bed, and grimacing when he put weight on his injured ankle, he picked up his shoes, socks and grip and tiptoed from the room. The staircase creaked loudly and he stopped on every step to see if the sound awakened Bernadette, but he heard nothing from her. The clock on the mantelpiece showed seven fortyfive.

Sitting on the chair by the now dead fire he pulled on his socks and shoes. His ankle was bruised black and still swollen. It was tender to his tentative touch. He carried the grip into the scullery. Looking around, he found a towel hanging on the back of the scullery door. There was a thin cake of soap on the corner rim of the sink. He turned on the faucet and washed his face in the cold water, drying it on the towel. Opening the grip he found his toothbrush and toothpaste. Realizing he hadn't cleaned his teeth the night before, he cleaned them especially vigorously now. Satisfied, he rinsed off the toothbrush and returned it and the toothpaste to the grip, which he zipped closed. He considered for a moment. He didn't want to carry the grip when he went looking for a telephone, but the gun was in the bag, and he didn't want to leave it unattended. Nor did he want to take the gun with him. He finally set the grip, with the gun in it, under the sink, behind an empty bucket. It should be all right there, he wouldn't be gone long.

He thought about leaving a note for Bernadette, but decided he didn't want to search for a pen and paper and he'd be back soon, probably before she woke.

Slipping out of the cottage quietly he surveyed the main road. He had come from the right last night and hadn't seen any lights in that direction, so he followed the curve around to the left. His ankle still throbbed dully, but he gritted his teeth and ignored it.

He hadn't gone far when he saw a village up ahead. He tried to quicken his pace, but his ankle hurt too much. As he drew closer, he made out a cluster of houses, with a grocery shop and a post office. Outside the latter was a green public telephone kiosk. That's when he remembered he didn't have money to make a long distance call. He'd have to reverse the charges.

He looked around furtively before picking up the telephone and dialing the operator. Long minutes passed before the operator made the connection and he could hear her asking if Mr. Baxter would accept a reverse charge call from Mr. Pigeon. He heard Baxter's voice angrily agree. "Ye're through, now," confirmed the operator.

Billy heard a click and assumed she'd hung up. "Hello?" he said, tentatively.

"What the hell are you doing, reversing the charges?" Baxter exploded.

"I got mugged last night. I haven't any money."

"Christ! You are a real piss-up."

"I didn't know the cost o' a reverse charge phone call meant that much t' ye." Billy felt himself getting angry.

"It isn't the cost, you moron. How do we know the operator isn't still on the line?"

"I'm sure she's got nothin' else t' do but listen t' us! If you're that paranoid, call me back."

"That wouldn't help. If she's listening now, she's gonna listen when I call you back," Baxter answered gruffly. "Did you get the package?"

"He's dead," stated Billy.

There was silence from the other end of the line and Billy relished the impact his news must have had. "Dead? When? How?" Baxter finally said.

"Sunday. Drug overdose."

"Suicide?" Baxter sounded dubious.

"No, it was an accident."

"What do you mean?"

"He took injections for pain. Gave himself one too many."

"How do you know?"

"His daughter told me."

"His daughter? From America?"

"Aye."

"Damn big coincidence that he'd die right now," Baxter mused.

"What?"

"Come on, Billy. Somebody might have found out what he was going to give us. Maybe they took care of him and made it look like an accident."

Billy was silent for a moment. "I thought about that meself," he lied, but a small alarm related to Bernadette's description of her father's death went off in his head.

"What made you think about it?" Baxter asked.

"I don't know. Somethin' his daughter said."

"What?"

"Never mind. It probably was an accident. Coincidences do happen, ye know."

"Maybe. Well, it isn't your problem. We'll look into it as best we can. You might as well head back home."

"I'd like to, but I got mugged, remember? I've no money."

There was silence for a moment before Baxter said, "You want me to send more money? Is that it?"

Billy didn't like Baxter's tone. "Aye, since I wouldn't be here if it wasn't for ye. I don't need much. Just enough for grub, and t' take a taxi t' the station. An' of course, buy a ticket back t' Dunfrior," he added, realizing he might as well get as much as he could. "They took that too."

There was no response from Baxter.

"Unless ye don't want t' meet me in Dunfrior. Then I'd need t' get back t' Belfast. Ye could send the money through the Post Office."

He heard Baxter suck in a deep breath. "Did you look around to see if there was anything that looked like whatever you were supposed to pick up?"

Billy hesitated. Baxter's tone indicated that if he gave the wrong answer he wouldn't be getting any money. "I haven't had a chance yet, but if ye'll send the money, I will. I could get his daughter t' help me."

"What? You're offering to stay?" Baxter sounded disbelieving.

"Well, I'm here now, an' if Mallory's death was an accident, there's a good chance the package is somewhere around." He decided to push a bit. "But if ye don't want me t' look for it, I'll set about makin' me own way home."

It worked. "OK. I'll send you some money. Which Post Office?"

Billy peered through the kiosk glass. "Connevarve."

"Wait," Baxter said. "The Post Office isn't going to give you money without any identification, and I suppose you lost that too?"

"No. All they got was the money an' the train ticket."

Baxter oozed sarcasm. "Very convenient. If I find out you lied about this…" He paused for effect, then continued, "Fifty pounds. That's it."

"Fine. Just make it fast."

"It'll be there this morning. And Billy, you be careful what you tell his daughter."

"Ye don't need t' worry about her. I'd trust her before I'd trust ye!" Billy snapped.

"Really? And you just met her yesterday? She must have made quite an impression on you, Billy boy. Is she the real reason you want to stay? Strike your fancy, did she?"

"Just send the money! Fast!" said Billy hotly. "I'll be in touch."

Slamming the phone down, he left the kiosk and went over to the Post Office. A sign in the window announced that it would open at nine. It shouldn't take more than a couple of hours to get the money from Belfast. He'd come back around noon. He began the walk back to the cottage, feeling better at the thought that he'd soon have some money again.

———

Flipping off the switch on her switchboard, Sheila Brannigan pulled the headset from her ears and let it hang around her neck. The conversation she had just eavesdropped on had been very interesting. A call to Belfast, a dead man, a missing package, money being sent from up north. She couldn't make head nor tail of it and it might all be innocent enough, but David might be interested. Since becoming a detective he'd encouraged her to keep her ears open and share any suspicious conversations with him. He was ambitious and who knew, this just might give him an early lead on a case that would bring him to the notice of his superiors.

And this was an opportune time. He'd been avoiding her lately and she suspected he was seeing another woman. When he heard the details of this conversation, though, he'd at least want to stay in touch with her, and that was all she needed. Her other attributes would hold his interest.

But he'd want every detail and realizing that, she reached for a pen and paper and copied the phone numbers and names of the parties involved from her log. Then she began to write down as much of the conversation as she could remember.

————

Bernadette awoke with a shiver, followed immediately by a sense of confusion and panic before she remembered where she was. She could tell by the light coming through the window that it was not very early. Her watch confirmed this, showing eight ten.

With sudden fear, she realized that the room was empty. Only the discarded sleeping bag and crumpled bedclothes proved Billy had been there and was not a remembrance from a dream. She sat for a moment then realized he had probably not wanted to waken her. He would be downstairs. Walking to the door, she called, "Billy?" There was no response.

She repeated the call, louder this time. Again only silence answered.

Mechanically, she folded the sleeping bag and straightened the bedclothes. She felt confusion and anger at his ingratitude rising in her, then realized that it was really disappointment. She wanted to talk to him some more, but denied it had anything to do with an attraction to him, and told herself she wanted only to find out more about her father.

She went downstairs, rubbing at her aching neck. He wasn't there. She was hungry, but more than anything her aching body craved a hot bath and a long sleep in a comfortable bed. Pulling on her coat, she looked around the cottage once more, then stepped outside, closing the door behind her.

The rain had stopped but a cold wind blew in gusts, whipping at her legs, and stinging her eyes. Her forehead throbbed and she rubbed the lump that had come up overnight from bumping into the staircase beam. Pulling her coat tightly around her neck she walked to the road. Mud sucked at her shoes, as if making a determined attempt to detain her.

She took the road to the right, knowing the Starry Plough was on the edge of town, just past the estate. She regretted telling the priest it was where she'd stay. It was the only hotel she could think of, although she knew there must be better ones in a town the size of Cork. Of course, she didn't have to stay there. She could look for a better hotel, but her luggage was at the Starry Plough now, and unless it turned out to be an unbearable flea pit, it seemed like a lot of trouble to be hauling luggage around Cork. She was too tired for that.

She reached the Starry Plough at nine fifteen. As she expected at this early hour, the front entrance was closed. The pub wouldn't be open for a while yet. She went to the side entrance which was reserved for hotel guests. It was locked too, so she headed around to the back, where the owner had his living quarters. Someone should be awake by now. She knocked and listened for a responding sound from within. The door opened almost immediately and she faced a middle-aged, balding man who held a spatula in one hand and did not seem surprised to see her.

"Ah, ye'll be Bernadette?"

"Yes. You got my luggage, then?"

"I did. Father Mallory himself dropped it off. I was expectin' ye last night, Did ye have a problem?"

"No problem. Can I come in?"

"Aye, come on. I'm just cookin' myself some breakfast. I'll see ye t' your room."

He stood aside and Bernadette found herself in a small kitchen. The smell of frying bacon reminded her how hungry she was. The man laid his spatula on a small gas stove where the bacon was frying. He turned down the flame beneath the frying pan, and motioned Bernadette through the kitchen and across a hallway which brought them out behind the bar. The aisle behind the bar was blocked with cases of beer. Squeezing past her, the man cleared a path by hoisting the beer onto the bar. He worked his way toward a staircase to the right of the bar. Her suitcases sat in a corner, behind the bar, near the foot of the staircase. The man picked up both suitcases.

"Like I say, I was a wee bit worried when ye didn't show up by the time the bar closed. I tried phonin' Father Mallory t' find out where ye were, but I never got an answer."

They began to climb the stairs. "I stayed at my father's cottage," Bernadette explained.

The landlord stopped in mid-climb. "I'm terrible sorry t' hear about your father. Terrible sorry."

Bernadette nodded an acknowledgment and they continued the climb.

The staircase led to a long, straight landing with three closed doors spaced along each side of its length. "I didn't know if ye'd be wantin' a room wi' a private toilet, at five pounds, or a room sharin' a toilet, at three pounds?"

From what the priest had said about no-one staying here, Bernadette figured that a shared toilet would in effect be private, but answered "Private." anyway.

The landlord was pleased. "Ye can have number one, then." He set the suitcases down and turned to face her. "O' course there'd be the matter o' last night's room."

"What do you mean? I wasn't here last night."

"True enough, but I thought ye would be an' so I couldn't rent the room t' someone else."

"If you expect me to pay for a room I didn't use…"

"Well now, understand, I could've maybe rented that room."

"How many people are staying here?"

The landlord looked like he wanted to avoid answering the question. "Tell ye what, I'd be willing t' take half the cost an' call it quits." He beamed at her, then seeing her tightening expression, hastily added, "I'll throw in yer breakfast too. Mind, if ye want it brought t' yer room it'd be another twenty pence."

"All right. I'll agree to pay half the cost of a room I didn't have last night. I would have taken the room with a shared bath last night, so I figure I owe you one pound fifty pence for that, and another twenty pence for breakfast in my room. That makes one pound seventy pence. Agreed?"

The landlord scowled slightly at first, then brightened. "Aye, all right. Agreed. Ye drive a hard bargain."

"I'll take breakfast as soon as you can bring it, with orange juice and decaffeinated coffee."

The landlord looked apologetic. "I'm afraid I've nothin' like that. It'd be the usual, fried eggs, bacon, sausages, potato bread, soda farls, an' tea. Mind, if ye don't want all o' that, ye could just have some."

"OK. I'll have just a soda farl and some bacon then."

She saw him calculating. "Mind, it'd cost the same. I have t' use the same dishes whether I make a whole breakfast or half o' one."

"But you wouldn't have the cost of the eggs and bacon, would you?" responded Bernadette. "But I won't argue. If it costs the same, I'll have the whole breakfast." She smiled sweetly.

The landlord frowned. "Aye, well this'll be yer room, if ye wouldn't mind openin' the door?" He nodded at the first door on the right, at the same time picking up the suitcases again.

Stepping past him, Bernadette held the door open. He set the suitcases on the floor just inside the door. "I expect ye'll still be tired after
yer trip from…?"

"America," Bernadette answered.

"Aye, of course. America. I wasn't sure. Ye might ha' been a Canadian."
Seeing her look around the room, he continued, "Sometimes the toilet
doesn't flush right. If that happens, take a glass an' fill it wi' water from the
sink. Pour three or four glasses int' the toilet. It'll work fine then." Her
look of distaste made him hurriedly add, "The man was supposed t' come
an' fix it last week. I'll remind him again."

Bernadette said nothing.

"There's soap an' a towel in the cupboard under the sink. Will ye be
needin' anythin' else?"

"Don't you want me to register or something?" she asked.

"I won't tell anybody ye're stayin' here if ye don't." He winked at her.
The universal sign of tax evasion.

"What about a key?"

He looked disappointed. "I'm afraid the lock's broke." He smiled
sheepishly, showing smoke-stained teeth. "I'll away an' make yer breakfast.
Do ye know how many nights ye'll be stayin'?"

"I'm not sure," she replied.

"I need to know in case…"

"Yes, in case someone else wants the room." She smiled at the thought.
The musty smell confirmed that no-one had stayed here for months. "I'll
let you know," she said. "Now, I'd like to wash up."

He knitted his brows, puzzled.

She smiled again. She had forgotten the language barrier. "I mean I'd
like to freshen up, not wash the dishes."

"Oh, I see," he looked sheepish again. "Ye were talkin' American. If
there's anythin' else ye'd be needing, just bang on the floor wi' yer shoe."

"I will. By the way, I don't think I caught your name."

"O'Grady. Gerry O'Grady."

"I'll be expecting breakfast shortly then, Mr. O'Grady. You'd better get back to the bacon or it'll be burned to a crisp."

"Ye're right. I forgot all about it. I'll bring yer breakfast in a wee while." He hurried from the room and Bernadette closed the door behind him.

She stood, looking around the room. On her right was an old, wooden dresser with a pitted mirror. The dresser had one large bottom drawer and two smaller drawers above that. She opened the top drawer. It was lined with faded newspaper and she noted the date as two years ago. Running one finger along the top of the dresser, she was pleased to find less dust than she'd feared. Squeezed between the dresser and the bed was a single, high-backed wooden chair. Approaching the bed, she pushed down on it with one hand. The mattress didn't yield easily, which made her hopeful. Turning back the bedcovers, she examined the pillow and sheets. They seemed clean. Lying on the bed, she found it comfortably firm. She was also happy to note that the ceiling appeared clean and she couldn't see any hanging cobwebs.

The back wall of the room, to the right of the bed had a window with heavy green curtains which were pulled back, exposing a half-drawn blind.

Getting off the bed, she looked out the window. Below was a narrow street. Across the street was a tall brick wall and behind that was a small factory. She couldn't tell what kind of factory it was, but could see trucks in the yard and beyond them, entrance gates which opened into another street. She hoped the trucks wouldn't be coming and going all night.

The bathroom was to the left of the window. She went in. There was a small sink with a mirror above it with the cupboard the landlord had mentioned, below. She confirmed that there was a folded towel and an unopened bar of soap on the top ledge of the cupboard. Turning on the faucet, she found the pressure was good and the water was hot almost immediately. To the left of the sink was the bathtub. It stood on claw legs and had been hand painted all over, but the paint job was good enough to give the tub a certain charm. She tried the tub faucet. Again, plenty of hot water. She turned it off.

The toilet bowl was slightly rust-stained around the base, but not enough to cause concern. She flushed the toilet. It worked fine, but she noticed that it refilled slowly and with an irritating gurgling sound. All in all, though, she was satisfied.

She imagined the hotel had mostly been used by sailors back when Cork was a more important port than it was today, and pictured sailors wandering up from the harbor, drinking all night in the bar and collapsing in a stupor, or maybe getting lucky with a drunken local girl or a prostitute.

The only other people she could imagine staying here were hippie tourists, or unfortunate older tourists who hadn't planned ahead and found themselves in Cork during the Blarney Festival with no other hotel room available for thirty or forty miles around.

Going to her suitcase she pulled out her overnight case. Removing a face cloth she returned to the bathroom and was about to peel off her blouse when there was a knock at her door. It was the landlord, balancing a tray with her breakfast on it. "I brought ye the whole pot o' tea," he announced.

"Thank you," Bernadette said, taking the tray.

"Is everythin' all right? Would ye maybe like another blanket? It gets nippy at night an' I can get ye one from another room."

"I think I'll be OK," she responded.

The landlord shuffled his feet nervously. "I hate t' ask, but usually I require payment in advance. No reflection on ye, of course."

"Of course," she answered. "I should have realized. Five pounds wasn't it? And I already owe you one pound seventy."

"Aye. It'd be six pounds an' seventy pence, includin' the breakfast."

"Traveler's check all right?" Bernadette dug in her bag while she spoke.

"Ye wouldn't happen t' have cash? The last time I took one o' them traveler's checks, the bank gave me a terrible time about it, said it was signed in the wrong place." The landlord sounded sorry.

"I've only four pounds in cash," Bernadette said, fishing the notes from her purse and holding them up as proof.

"It'll do until ye can get t' the bank. Ye can pay me the rest later," the landlord said eagerly.

Bernadette handed the notes to him.

"Thank ye," he said. Folding the bills into precise halves, he continued "Ye were from here originally, then?"

Bernadette watched him squeeze the tiny, folded bills into a small, belt purse. "Yes," she answered. "I was born here. I remember when old Protestant Brian used to own this place, but that was a long time ago."

With the money safely tucked away, the landlord seemed to lose interest in further conversation. "Aye, well I'll be away. Ye'll be wantin' t' eat yer breakfast while it's hot." He turned and walked from the room, leaving the door open behind him. Bernadette closed it.

The tea was strong, somewhere between burnt coffee and molasses, but she forced herself to drink it. Looking onto the street below she saw it was raining again. From around the street corner came the tired clop of horse hooves. Bernadette saw a tired old nag came into view, pulling a cart piled with large oil drums. From her childhood she recognized this as the rag and bone man, returning after a day spent swapping chipped cups and saucers for the edible garbage of the town, which he fed to his pigs. She wondered if such an entrepreneur could survive in America.

In the distance, a ship's fog horn sounded from the harbor. Its sad sound made her feel lonely and to dispel the feeling, she concentrated on her breakfast, eating hungrily. She was surprised how good it tasted. When she finished, she stretched out on the bed. It felt wonderful after the chair she had slept in the night before. Weariness and a full stomach overtook her and she fell asleep.

———

Again she awoke to the brief panic of strange surroundings. On remembering where she was, she relaxed and looked at her watch which showed two ten. She realized she should get to a bank and cash some traveler's checks. The anticipated luxury of a hot bath would have to wait.

From below she could hear the sounds of a busy pub, but as soon as she reached the bottom of the staircase and was in full view of the patrons, the hubbub died into sudden silence, like a loud radio being snapped off. She immediately realized her mistake. The bar was for men only. O'Grady was nowhere in sight and Bernadette guessed he must be on the other side of the pub, serving customers in the saloon.

Bernadette had known this bar from those Friday evenings when her mother sent her to get money from her father, before he could spend all his pay on drink. She winced at the memory. Her father's mates found it hilarious to keep reminding him that his "wee guardian angel" was here. She knew things were good when her father sat her on his knee and ordered lemonade for her, a sure sign that he was at the early, happy stage of drunkenness. Other times, he would scowl at Bernadette and yell about her mother not trusting him. Often, he hurled his open pay packet at Bernadette who learned that this usually meant he'd lost money gambling. Not only did she have to endure the crawling on the floor to retrieve the money, but when she brought it home she had to face her mother's cursing and crying about feeding a family of three on a few shillings. How different from America, where her Friday evenings were eagerly anticipated, reserved for boyfriends, girlfriends, movies, necking.

A voice cut through the silence, snapping her back to the present.

"Women belong in the saloon!"

The man who spoke stood in front of Bernadette, his stale breath heightening the memory of those ancient Friday nights. Resentment swelled within her, but she realized she was in the wrong. "I'm sorry. Excuse me."

She turned to leave, but the man spoke again. "Yer Bernadette Mallory, aren't ye?"

Everyone in the room awaited her answer.

Bernadette studied the man. "Yes. Do I know you?"

"Ye don't remember me? Aye, well, I've changed over the years. Paddy Mc Clean."

The name stirred recollections within Bernadette. Paddy "too keen" Mc Clean. He had been handsome once, but that was when he was a tall, gangling youth, before the incessant scrubbing of poverty and alcohol. Bernadette couldn't believe that the gat-toothed, bald, bulbous nosed character who stood before her now was the same person. "Paddy. Of course I remember you. How are you?"

"As long as I've a drink in me hand, I'm all right," he said, raising his glass of stout and gulping it dry. Wiping his chin on his sleeve, he belched.

Her eyes darted around the room. Even the old men in the corner ignored their dominoes to crane their necks at her.

Mc Clean belched again. "Me woman'll be interested t' hear ye're back."

Bernadette looked at him quizzically.

"Katie. Katie Mulgrew ye knew her as. She's Katie Mc Clean, now. Weren't yous best friends when yous were wee girls?"

"Katie? Yes. How is she? I'd like to see her."

"Aye, well I'll tell her ye're here." Mc Clean turned towards the bar. "But ye'll have t' meet her in the saloon. Women aren't allowed in the bar," he said loudly over his shoulder.

O'Grady appeared from the saloon side of the pub and intervened. "Now, Paddy, ye settle down. Miss Mallory's a guest here. I'm sure she won't want t' be in a bar wi' the likes o' ye." The landlord's scowled at Mc Clean, then turned his attention to Bernadette. "Can I help ye, Miss Mallory?"

"I need to get to a bank. Is there one nearby?"

"Just turn right outside the door an' there's one on the next block." He glanced at the huge wall clock behind him. "I'm afeard you'd be too late for the bank. They close at three."

Bernadette nodded and smiled. "Thank you. Guess I'll have to wait until tomorrow, then. I'll just go for a short walk instead. I'll stay in the saloon from now on." She walked to the door and exited to the street. Behind her the atmosphere in the pub returned to normal.

———

Carefully raising the latch, Billy slowly opened the cottage door. Slipping inside, he took great care to close the door gently behind him in case Bernadette was still asleep. He stood for a moment, considering what to do. Maybe he should light the fire. She would appreciate that. It was always a pleasure to get up to a cheery hearth. He stepped gingerly over to the fireplace. There weren't many ashes from last night's fire, so he wouldn't have to empty the grate. There were matches on the mantelpiece and some newspapers beside the hearth.

Picking up the matches he knelt and reached for a few sheets of the newspaper. Twisting each sheet into a tight wad, he laid them in the grate. Next, he put a couple of pieces of peat on top of the newspapers. Striking a match, he applied the flame underneath the newspaper kindling. A few wayward wisps of smoke curled their way around the mantelpiece and up the wall. Billy watched the small flames he had started, silently coaxing them to full life. They died. The fire wasn't hot enough to draw properly.

He reached for another sheet of newspaper. This one he didn't crumple, but instead spread out beside him. Striking another match he again lit the crumpled newspapers under the peat. Then he picked up the spread-out sheet and held it against the mantle so that it entirely covered the fireplace opening. He waited, feeling the slight tension as the newspaper was drawn towards the fire by the draught he was creating in the chimney. He could make out the glow of yellow flames behind the newspaper which he held tightly in place. The tension increased, sucking the center of the newspaper toward the fire. The newspaper began to turn yellow, then brown. He drew it away from the flames, pulling a cloud of smoke into the room. The newspaper kindling was well ablaze, and the peat already showed a few white patches where it was drying out from the heat. It should burn now. Satisfied, he crumpled up the newspaper and stuffed it under the peat. He returned the matches to the mantelpiece.

He thought about going into the scullery and making some tea. He might even find something to eat, maybe make breakfast for Bernadette, even if it was only tea and toast, but he finally dismissed the idea as too forward. He'd wait for her to get up. Sitting, he watched the peat catch fire and enjoyed the first weak warmth that was beginning to emanate as a result of his efforts.

Looking over to the coffin he saw that the candles had burned out and thought that was somehow sacrilegious, like the corpse was being neglected. He went over to the coffin. A brown envelope, half protruding from under the head of the coffin caught his eye. Wild hope leaped up within him for an instant. Could this be what he'd been sent for? The hope was immediately tempered by the realization of improbability. Still, there was a slim chance.

He pulled out the envelope. It had a business logo in the top left corner. "Brown's Funeral Parlour—Rest With Dignity". He turned the envelope over. It was a clasp type and wasn't glued down. He supposed it contained either a contract or a bill, but opened it anyway and pulled out three sheets of paper. Two were stapled together, underneath a single sheet which he saw right away was a signed agreement, itemizing services and costs. He noted the signatures at the bottom, 'Dan Fogarty, Priest' and 'Richard A. Brown, Director'. Billy shuffled the sheet behind the other two.

The next sheet was a death certificate. Billy scanned it, seeing the name of deceased, date, time and place of death. He read the bottom section carefully.

"Cause of death—morphine overdose.

Method of death—injection.

Comments—bruise, left arm. Verified point of injection.

Finding—accidental death"

There followed various signatures, but Billy didn't read them. His eyes were frozen on the 'Comments' line, specifically the words "left arm". Joe Mallory had been left handed and Billy was forming a picture it in his mind of a left -handed man injecting himself in the left arm. Billy bent his right wrist toward his right shoulder, as if to inject himself. It didn't work very well, and why would a person inject themselves in the shoulder anyway, rather than the forearm?

He read the line again, to make sure he wasn't mistaken. He questioned his recollection, but there was no doubt. Joe Mallory had been left-handed. Billy remembered making a joke about it, ribbing that he hadn't realized Catholics really were left-handers and not left-footers as they were known up north. He slid the papers back into the envelope and put it back where he had found it.

What had Bernadette said? The needle broke off in his arm, he remembered that much, but had she said which arm? He couldn't recall, and it was also important exactly whereabouts on the arm the injection had been made. Billy pretended to inject himself in a few different positions. He decided it might be possible, but it didn't seem likely or natural.

A morbid thought crossed his mind. There was one way to find out for certain. He looked at the corpse and shuddered inwardly. A crazy idea. He'd have to pull back the shroud and maybe even remove some clothes. He couldn't tell because the shroud was covering the neck. Leaning forward, he pulled the shroud back. A jacket and a shirt, buttoned at the collar. Replacing the shroud, he turned away.

What was he thinking? He'd have to raise the body to a sitting position, and could he even do that with rigor mortis? Then he'd have to slip off the jacket, unbutton the shirt, and slip that off. Then he'd have to put everything back on the corpse again. And all this assumed Bernadette wouldn't come walking down the stairs and find him undressing her father's body. The absurdity of it made him want to laugh. And yet...It would tell him if Mallory's death could have been accidental, or...Or what? Murder, as Baxter had suggested?

He returned to his seat by the fire. If Mallory had been killed, chances were that it was because of what he was about to hand over to Billy, and probably the killer had taken the package. On the other hand, if Mallory's death was accidental, there was a good chance that the package was still around the house somewhere. It might even have been found by

Bernadette. He could resolve that easily enough by asking her, but what if she didn't know anything about a package? Would she help him look for it? And if she did, and they found nothing, should he tell her of his suspicion that her father may have been killed? What purpose would that serve? He could fantasize about tracking down the killer, retrieving the package, and being a hero in Bernadette's eyes, but he wasn't a character in some cheap novel and a more likely outcome of such bravado was that they might both wind up dead.

He looked imploringly at the ceiling, willing Bernadette to get up. When that didn't work, he decided to wake her. He began by scraping his chair against the linoleum, then throwing peat noisily onto the fire. Going into the scullery, he slammed some cupboard doors. He strained to hear a response from upstairs, but there was none. Finally he determined to take the direct approach and climbed the stairs.

Finding the bedroom empty, his jaw dropped. Where could she have gone? He checked the other bedroom and realized he was alone in the house. He also realized this was a golden opportunity for him and he inwardly cursed the time he had wasted. He could search for the package and verify the exact position of the injection for himself. He would have to do the latter first though, since he might not have another chance for that, whereas he could search for the package later, with Bernadette's help if need be.

Returning downstairs, he looked out the window to make sure no-one was in sight. His mind ran through the motions of what he was about to do and he recoiled inwardly at the thought, but, he rationalized, how long could it take? A couple of minutes, at most, and what were the chances of Bernadette or anyone else returning to the house in that time? Steeling himself, he crossed quickly to the coffin. Hesitating, he silently asked the corpse to forgive him for what he was about to do. Then, like a timid bather who knew it was better to dive rather than tiptoe into the water, he screwed up his nerve and plunged into the task.

Pulling the shroud down to the waistline, he hesitated again. The next step required more girding of nerve, but finally he forced himself to do it. Sliding his left arm under the corpse's back, he lifted. The weight was incredible and he was overtaken with the fear that he'd never be able to do this, but he forced the body up, bracing his arm across the coffin and grasping the far side. That helped.

Relieved to see that the jacket wasn't buttoned, he tugged at it with his right hand. Please God, he thought, don't let anybody come now and find me like this. Working the jacket up over the left shoulder, he yanked it down to the elbow. His left arm, supporting the entire weight of the stiff body, was beginning to ache and his hand begged for relief from its tight grip on the far edge of the coffin. He considered resting his left arm and hand but immediately dismissed the idea. Time was critical.

His right hand pulled at the shirt, tugging it out of the trouser waist-band. His fingers worked feverishly at the buttons, his fumbling frustrating him. Each button took long minutes to undo and his left arm was complaining painfully at the weight it was supporting, but he shut it out and kept to his ham-handed task which wasn't made easier by the touch of the cold body against his fingers. Finally the shirt was unbuttoned, and Billy pulled frantically at it, forcing it up to the shoulder. It stuck there, and he cursed this impossible, insane act. He pulled on the shirt, gaining strength from his panic. The shirt began to tear at the shoulder seam. He panicked, but then decided he might as well be hung for a sheep as a lamb, and pulled harder. The shirt ripped some more then slid over the corpse's shoulder. Stopping, he leaned across the body, breathing heavily. Sweat trickled down his temples. His left arm felt like it was breaking and he could stand the pain no more. Releasing his grip on the coffin, he slid his arm out from behind the corpse. He felt a surge of relief and flexed the muscles in his arm.

Examining the exposed left shoulder of the body, he saw the same black bruise Bernadette had seen. He aimed an imaginary syringe at the same spot on his right arm. It couldn't be done easily. To be certain, he peered closely at the bruise. In the very center was a small dot, blacker than the surrounding area. He felt a thrill of horror at what he'd discovered, but this was overtaken by the realization that he had to put everything back, and quickly.

Sliding his left arm back under the corpse, he gripped the side of the coffin again. Instantly, his arm and hand began to protest. He was relieved to find that it was easier to pull the shirt and jacket back over the shoulder than it had been to push them off. They both slid easily back into place. Removing his left arm from under the corpse again, he let the body fall back. He now had both hands free to button the shirt, which was a pleasant surprise. He had expected to endure the same one-handed fumbling he had suffered removing the buttons.

Beginning at the neck, he worked his way down the buttons and had reached the third one when he heard a sound that made his blood freeze. It was a fumbling at the latch of the door. Someone was entering the cottage.

Yanking the shroud back up to the corpse's neck, he left the shirt and jacket open from the middle of the chest to the navel. Crouching over the casket he smoothed the shroud, his heart racing.

The door opened and Billy turned his head to see an old woman enter. She hadn't noticed him yet. Turning his attention back to the shroud, he decided it would have to do and tried to compose himself.

Old Mrs. Slaugherty stopped in mid-movement when she saw the young man by the coffin. She didn't recognize him, but then, she expected there would be lot of strangers showing up, and she wouldn't interfere with their private moments of respect. "Never mind me, young'un. Ye go right ahead. I'll just be takin' care o' a few things around the cottage." She was taken aback at the burning fire. "Fire's already lit," she said, disbelievingly.

Billy walked over to the fireplace, to put some distance between himself and the coffin, "Aye, I lit it."

The old woman looked at him, chewing her gums. "Aye. Well, good. I hate t' come int' a cold room an' have t' build a fire." She squinted toward the coffin. "Candles've burnt out."

Billy knew it was irrational, but he sensed that she was blaming him for allowing this to happen, for having his priorities wrong. The candles were more important than the fire. "I didn't know if there were any more," he offered.

Without removing her coat and head scarf, she crossed the room and reached under the gurney which supported the coffin. There was a small ledge there and she extracted four large, white candles. She laid them beside the coffin, on top of the brown envelope. She began to pick at the candle holders, removing the spilled wax and burnt out remnants of the old candles. "Would ye be friend or family?" she asked over her shoulder.

"Friend," Billy answered. "Although it's a while since I saw Joe."

The old woman was straining to fit the last of the new candles into its holder. Horror seized Billy when she dropped the candle into the coffin. He held his breath as she bent over to retrieve it. His heart pounded as he watched her pick up the candle and smooth out the shroud where it had wrinkled from the impact. "Ye don't sound like ye're from these parts," the old woman continued as she twisted the fresh candle into the holder. "Could ye bring me the matches from the mantelpiece?"

Picking up the matches, Billy walked over to her. "No, I'm from up north." Striking a match, he lit each candle in turn.

The old woman looked appreciative. "Would ye like a cup o' tea? I'm going t' make one for meself."

Billy was tempted, but more than tea he wanted to be out of the house. "No thanks. I have t' get t' the Post Office."

Nodding understanding, the old woman headed into the scullery.

A thought occurred to Billy. "Would ye happen t' know where Joe's daughter might be?"

There was no response from the old woman.

Walking over to the scullery, he said loudly "D' ye know where Joe's daughter is?"

The old woman went about her business of filling the kettle. "Daughter?" she answered, "I thought she might be here. She was last night, but she's maybe not left the hotel yet. She'd a long trip from America."

"Hotel? Which hotel would that be?"

Stopping, the old woman touched a finger to her chin. "See if I mind, now. Ach aye, it was the Starry Plough, right enough." She seemed pleased at remembering and went back to her task.

"Starry Plough," Billy repeated. "Is that in town?"

"'Tis down the road, past the council estate."

"Right. Well, I'll be goin' now. I'll maybe see ye again, Mrs…"

"Slaugherty. Aye, ye'll likely see me. I take care o' things here. Make tea, light the candles, make the fire…" She was bent now, reaching for something under the sink. "What's this, now?" She held up Billy's grip.

"Oh, that's mine," said Billy hastily, stepping forward and taking the bag from her.

Her look demanded an explanation for the grip being where she had found it.

"There's some pills in it I have t' take. I came in here t' get some water an' I set the grip down," Billy offered. "It's good ye found it or I might have gone off without it," he added.

The old woman nodded. She was used to looking after men.

"I'll be away, then," Billy said quickly.

Old Mrs. Slaugherty had turned her back to rummage in a cupboard and made no reply. Billy turned and walked back through the living room to the front door. An intense relief flooded over him when he stepped out into the cold morning air. He headed back to the Post Office to pick up the money from Baxter.

13

Bernadette returned from her walk looking forward to a hot soak in the bath, but as she was about to turn on the water, there was a knock at her door. She opened it, expecting to see the landlord. Instead it was a woman. "Yes?" said Bernadette.

"Ye don't recognize me..." the woman began.

Realization dawned on Bernadette. "Katie?" she whispered.

"Aye. I heard ye were home." The woman paused. "I'm sorry about yer father."

A flood of girlhood memories overtook Bernadette. Warm memories of confidences and laughter shared. Stepping forward, she hugged her childhood friend. "It's good to see you. Come in."

Katie smiled at the warm earnestness in Bernadette's voice. "I've a better idea. Why don't we go down t' the saloon an' have a quiet drink?"

"Sure," agreed Bernadette quickly. "Let me grab my coat and purse." She reached behind the door where her coat hung, then crossed over to the chair by the bed and retrieved her purse. "I'm ready."

Bernadette headed for the stairs leading to the bar. Katie touched her elbow. "Let's go out the side door. It's closer t' the saloon entrance."

They headed down the hall in the opposite direction, to another staircase. At the bottom was a heavy wooden door. Katie tugged it open and they were on a sidestreet. Katie led the way along the sidewalk to the main street and around the corner to the left. The door to the saloon was right there. They entered. Bernadette looked around. Along one wall hung a huge mirror, beneath which was a row of snugs. Katie led her to one of these and they sat across from each other. "What'll ye have?" asked Katie.

"Gin and tonic, but let me get them." Bernadette began to slide out of her seat.

Katie held up a hand. "Ye can get the next one."

Bernadette acquiesced and Katie went to the bar to order. Returning with the drinks, she slid back into her seat.

"To old friends," said Bernadette holding her glass up.

Katie clinked her glass against Bernadette's. "Old is right."

They both smiled and sipped from their glasses. Looking around the saloon, Bernadette said, "Remember when we used to come in here to buy a bottle of sherry for my mother and old Mrs Malcolmson to share on Saturday nights?"

Katie nodded. "Saturday's still women's night off, except now they don't have t' drink in secret at home. Come in here now on a Saturday night an' the place is jammed wi' women. O' course the men still go t' the bar. Some family night, husbands an' wives drinkin' separately.

Remember the time we bought the wine for yer Ma an' went behind the convent wall t' have a sip?"

Bernadette remembered. They had egged each other on and giggled nervously to hide their apprehension. She realized now that their good fortune in having a bottle with a screw cap was a measure of how cheap the wine was. They had hesitated and argued over who should commit the sin of having the first drink. Since the wine was for Bernadette's mother, the honor fell to her. She remembered it tasted like semi-sweet vinegar and wouldn't swallow it until Katie took a sip. They both looked at each other in horror and promptly spat it out. This caused another outburst of giggling and sour faces. Why would anyone drink that stuff?

Bernadette's mother had smelled it on her breath right away and gave her a slap which made her lip bleed. "No friggin' daughter o' mine'll be drinking at age eleven!" she had screamed.

Bernadette had run from the house, tears stinging her eyes, more from guilt than physical pain. She hadn't returned until after ten o'clock and expected another smack for that. Instead, her now drunk mother was maudlin. "Ach, sure I'm sorry, darlin'. Ye know I wouldn't hurt ye for the world. Ye know that don't ye?"

The memory hurt Bernadette, so she shut it off. "Yes," she sighed. "We had some times together didn't we?"

Katie nodded, eyes alight with remembered pleasures.

"I want to hear all about you," continued Bernadette. "Everything."

Katie laughed. "That'd be a lot. How old were we when ye left? Nine? Ten?"

"Eleven. I met your husband earlier and I want to hear how you two got together."

Katie lowered her eyes. "Oh aye, Paddy. He told me ye were here. We've been married for seventeen years. He's a good man, just has a problem wi' the drink."

"Do you have any children?"

Katie shot Bernadette a glance which made Bernadette feel that Katie thought she must know something to have asked that question.

"A son. Roy. He's eighteen. He'll be goin' t' college next year." She was obviously proud of that.

"You and Paddy. Who'd have thought it? I'm happy for you both."

"He's not Roy's father," Katie stated emphatically.

Bernadette was stunned. Not at the news itself, but rather at the vehemence with which it was stated. She waited for Katie to explain.

"Durin' me teens, I never got along wi' me Ma. Ye know, the usual stuff. I wanted t' dress up, be out t' all hours an' so on. I finally left school at sixteen an' got a job in the bakery down the High street. I hated it. Had t' be there by five am every day, includin' Saturdays. I helped wi' the bakin' an' served the customers, an' that was the worst. They complained about everythin'. The crust on the loaves was burnt or not done well enough, the cake was too moist or too dry, the buns were stale. Things like that. Drove me mad. I walked outside for me break one mornin' an' never went back.

Me Ma was furious. Ordered me out o' the house. I'd saved a few shillin's an' in a fit I packed me bags an' took the train t' Dublin." She looked at Bernadette and smiled sadly. "I suppose I was lucky. A young girl from the sticks just showing up in the big city, not knowin' anybody. No idea where I'd stay or what I'd do." She took a sip from her glass.

"Like I said, I got lucky. Went t' a bar on O'Connell street. A group o' young people came in. I envied them their brash confidence an' cama-raderie. I suppose they felt sorry for me. Anyway, one o' them, Kevin, started talkin' t' me an' invited me t' join them. I was too shy at first, but he insisted, an' he wasn't bad lookin'." She smiled again. "So I joined them, an' after they heard me story, one o' the girls, Patsie, offered t' let me stay in her flat until I could find me feet. Kevin said he'd an uncle who owned an office supplies business an' was lookin' for a secretary t' handle the orders an' billin'. I told him I couldn't type, but he said not t' worry, I'd learn."

Her face took on a regretful look. "I should have known that his uncle didn't hire me for me office skills. But I'm gettin' ahead o' meself.

Things worked out great at first. I got the job an' I got along well wi' Patsie. We moved into a bigger flat together. Kevin became me boyfriend." She looked Bernadette straight in the eye. "Me lover."

If she expected a reaction from Bernadette, she got none.

"Things were goin' well. Kevin was a helper for a delivery truck driver. Sometimes he'd be gone overnight, but when he was home, we had some great times. Pubs, movies, parties. Young love. Of course it couldn't last.

I didn't think anythin' o' the way Kevin's uncle paid special attention t' me, always remarkin' how pretty I was an' how I should be a model. I thought he was just bein' nice t' me because I was Kevin's girlfriend, an' I have t' admit I was flattered. Maybe I even led him t' think…"

Looking into her glass, she sighed. "One day he asked me t' stay late t' help wi' some work he needed t' do. He knew it was a night when Kevin would be gone. I agreed. Ye can maybe guess what happened."

Her voice became a whisper. "I tried t' stop him but he threatened t' tell Kevin I'd come on t' him. I loved Kevin an' didn't want anythin' t' come between us.

After that first time I was trapped. He wanted me every time Kevin was gone, an' I didn't know what else t' do." She looked at Bernadette with pleading eyes.

Bernadette instinctively reached for Katie's hand and stroked it gently.

"Kevin never knew anythin' about it," Katie continued quietly. "After about a year I got pregnant. I knew it was Kevin's child. The night I told him he was thrilled an' talked about gettin' married right away. I thought everythin' would work out, even hoped his uncle wouldn't bother me anymore now I was pregnant."

She laughed bitterly. "I was right about that, anyway. He went crazy. At first I thought he was afraid it was his kid, but it didn't help when I told him it wasn't. He fired me on the spot, gave me the wages I was due, an' turned me out onto the street. He threatened t' tell Kevin about us if he ever saw me again.

At first I was scared, but then I realized that I was at least rid o' Kevin's uncle an' could find another job. Me only worry was tellin' Kevin why I'd lost me job wi' his uncle." She took a drink and shook her head slowly. "I needn't have worried. Kevin wasn't all he'd seemed t' be either.

I found out he'd been arrested. Seems his driver had a deal goin' on the side, smugglin' guns up north. I went t' visit Kevin in jail. He thought that since this was his first offense, an' he was just a young lad an' it was his driver's fault anyway, he'd just get probation. He even had me convinced when I left. I didn't doubt he loved me, an' I knew I loved him, an' things always work out for young lovers, don't they?" She looked at Bernadette again, a rueful smile on her lips.

"They gave him ten years. I was so shocked, I almost had a miscarriage, He pleaded wi' me t' wait for him, rantin' about appealin' the sentence an' insistin' he was too young for this t' be happenin' t' him.

I realized then that he was right. He was too young. Too young t' be a father. He just had no idea. Really expected me t' have the baby an' wait for him t' get out o' prison. Then he began t' accuse me o' bein' the one who had brought us t' this, because he'd only wanted t' pick up a bit o' extra cash for me an' the baby. I was terrified, still a kid meself an' maybe that was good, because just like a child I ran back home, t' me Ma. Walked away from Kevin like I'd walked away from the bakery." She looked Bernadette in the eye again. "D' ye suppose I was able t' do that because I didn't really love him?"

Bernadette saw the guilt in Katie's eyes and her need to be reassured. "You were young, confused, frightened." Bernadette realized this wasn't enough. "I would have done the same thing," she added.

That seemed to be what Katie wanted to hear. "I dreaded goin' back home. I was sure me Ma an' Da would send me packin', but they didn't. Oh, they yapped at first, but when I finally got the nerve t' blurt out that I was pregnant, me Ma became a different woman, concerned, understandin'. I couldn't have made it through the birth without her.

Me Da, on the other hand, sulked all through the pregnancy. I don't know if he was angry at me or he thought that the baby would take his place in me Ma's life. He changed after Roy was born though, an' became a doting grandda.

Me life settled into a routine again. I went back t' work in the bakery an' me parents were delighted t' have so much time wi' Roy. I even began t' date again. O' course, nothin' ever came o' it once they found out I'd a kid.

Two years went by. Then me father died an' it hit me Ma like a hammer. Overnight she became worn out, complaining constantly o' aches an' pains an' spendin' most o' her time in bed. Roy was too much for her t' handle an' I had t' quit the bakery again t' look after him. I was beset wi' worries. What would happen to us now? What if me Ma died too?

I still hadn't taken responsibility for me own life an' now I was responsible for a toddler too. It was a rough few months an' I began t' resent me Ma, an' Roy, an' Kevin. Especially Kevin. I realize now I was goin' through what he went through, thinkin' I was too young to have this happen to me an' blamin' him for it.

Then Paddy came on the scene. He wasn't much t' look at. Maybe he thought a woman like me, wi' a kid, would have a hard time findin' a man, an' he certainly couldn't find a woman, so it must have seemed like a perfect match t' him.

At first I tolerated him just for the company. He'd bring drink over t' the house an' we'd get drunk together. Then I began t' use him. Paddy, could ye run an errand for me? Paddy, could I borrow some money? Paddy, would ye look after Roy for a while? I became dependent on him. In return he wanted sex, which didn't bother me, although it wasn't the same as it had been wi' Kevin.

We became like a family, an' after me Ma died, Paddy proposed. It took me a while, but I finally resigned myself t' the idea that I had no other choice."

She sighed heavily and drained her glass. "Lord, I've really bared me soul, haven't I? I'm embarrassed. I don't know why I told ye all that. Maybe because ye're the first woman friend I've talked t', I mean really talked t', in years."

Bernadette reached across the table and gently touched Katie's hand. "You've nothing to be embarrassed about."

They sat for a moment, eyes locked in understanding.

"Don't get me wrong," Katie continued. "Paddy's been a good husband an' a good father t' Roy. I can't complain about that."

Bernadette nodded. She sensed that Katie was on the verge of breaking into tears, and she didn't want that, so she seized the opportunity to say, "Here, let's have another drink." Taking Katie's glass she slid out of the booth, relieved to be away from the intense atmosphere Katie's revelations had engendered.

When she returned with the drinks, Katie had composed herself and was smiling. "OK, yer turn now, an' don't leave anythin' out."

Bernadette gave a summary of her life, omitting the fact that she'd had any feelings for Mike. By the time she finished, their glasses were empty again.

"I'd better be goin'," Katie said reluctantly. "Roy'll be comin' home from school an' I've dinner t' make. Can ye come an' have dinner wi' us one night? I'll get somethin' special an' ye can meet Roy."

"Sure, I'd like that," Bernadette answered sincerely.

"Maybe the day after the funeral. When is that, by the way?" Katie continued.

Bernadette was stunned by the question. "I don't know," she finally confessed.

Katie looked embarrassed for an instant. "Well, I'll find out."

She slid out of the booth. "It was good t' see ye, Bernadette."

"Yes. Good to talk to you too, Katie."

There was a pause. "I'll be seein' ye then," Katie said.

"Yes," Bernadette answered.

Katie looked as if she wanted to say something else.

"What is it?" Bernadette encouraged her.

"It's Kevin. He's come back into me life." Katie said this despairingly, but before Bernadette could react, Katie turned and strode quickly from the saloon.

Bernadette stared after her, then turned her gaze to her empty glass. She tried to rationalize that she shouldn't feel guilty because she didn't know when her father was to be buried, but unable to do so, she finally forced herself out of the booth and went back to her room.

14

Bernadette spent a glorious hour soaking in the tub. When she had finished and dressed, she began to think about eating. After dinner, she
would walk over to the Father Fogarty's church to ask when the funeral
would be. Better yet, maybe she would take the priest to dinner as a small
token of her gratitude. As she thought about this, there were two light taps
at her door.

"Yes?" Bernadette called. There was no reply.

"Who is it?" she called more loudly.

"It's Billy," came the muffled reply, loud enough for her ears but no-
one else's.

Bernadette was glad to hear his voice but resented him for having left
that morning without any explanation. She would deal with him carefully
this time, so as not to leave herself vulnerable again. She smoothed her
dress and ran her fingers through her hair, pulling it behind her ears, then
opened the door a crack. "What do you want?" she asked coolly.

Glancing over his shoulder toward the stairs, Billy coughed nervously
into his fist. "Can I come in?" he muttered.

Aware of the absurdity of conversing through the crack, Bernadette
conceded. "I suppose so."

She stepped aside, holding the door open. Billy looked furtively toward
the stairs again then stepped quickly into the room. He stopped in the
middle of the floor, as if awaiting instructions. Closing the door,
Bernadette motioned him to sit on the chair, while she herself sat on the
edge of the bed. Billy's eyes darted around the room avoiding her look.

"Why have you come?" she finally asked.

He looked up, genuinely surprised. "Ye were gone when I got back t'
the cottage," he answered, as if it were self-evident and explained everything. Indeed his tone implied that it was he who was due an explanation.

Resentment swelled within Bernadette. "You were gone when I woke
up!" she retorted, but she didn't like how it sounded, like they were
teenagers having a spat. She stood and walked to the window, folding her
arms and feigning interest in the street below. "You might have at least
said you were leaving."

Billy winced and ran his fingers through his hair. "I had t' make a
phone call."

Bernadette was disappointed. "If you only went to make a phone call,
why did you take your bag?" There was a clear triumph in her voice.
"And couldn't your phone call have waited until I woke up?" She turned
to face him, her eyes searching his face for a clue as to whether he would
explain honestly.

"I didn't take me bag," he answered quietly. " I crept down t' the
scullery so I wouldn't wake ye. I washed an' left me bag under the sink."
His cheeks reddened, and he pulled his lower lip between his teeth. "I had
arranged t' phone someone at a certain time. I thought ye'd still be there
when I got back."

Knowing immediately that his explanation was honest, Bernadette was
embarrassed at the conclusion she had leapt to, but she wasn't ready to
apologize yet. "How did you know where to find me?"

"There was an old woman at the cottage when I got back," Billy responded. As an afterthought he blurted "Ye're not angry wi' her for telling me?"

Smiling at his concern, Bernadette shook her head gently. "No. I'm not angry."

She walked back to the bed and sat down again. Sighing, she leaned forward, and laid her hands on Billy's. "You're a strange one," she rebuked mildly. Then she squeezed his hands softly. "I'm glad you came back. I was afraid I'd never see you again."

Deep in her eyes Billy saw that she was sincere and would have been hurt if he'd left for good. He felt a surge of tenderness. "I'm glad t' be back," he whispered.

They both knew they had passed the stage of being polite strangers, but neither knew how to proceed. Finally, Billy's face adopted a serious look. "Can I ask ye somethin'?" he said slowly.

Bernadette nodded and waited for him to continue.

"About yer father. Ye said he accidentally injected himself."

"Yes," Bernadette confirmed, wondering where this was headed.

"In the shoulder?" Billy asked.

She nodded again.

"D' ye know which arm?"

In her mind Bernadette saw the swinging arm in the mortuary. "His left arm. When I was at the funeral parlor I saw the bruise where the needle broke off. Why?"

Billy took a deep breath. "Does that not strike ye as strange?"

Bernadette looked puzzled. "I don't know what you mean. I suppose it was a strange way to die."

Billy realized she was not making the connection. "Yer father was left-handed," he stated.

His words hung in the air for a moment, as if Bernadette was awaiting further explanation, but her mind was imagining her left-handed father, trying to inject himself in the left shoulder. She saw that it would be unnatural and clumsy at best, and she was angry for not having thought of it herself, for having a stranger point it out.

Suddenly, the enormity of the implication hit her. "Are you saying that he didn't inject himself? That someone gave him the injection?" Her voice was rising in panic. "That's crazy. The police, the coroner, the priest, they would know."

Alarmed at her growing agitation, Billy regretted telling her and tried to retreat. "Ye're right. There must be an explanation."

But it was too late. Bernadette sank onto the bed. "No," she said softly, shaking her head. "The priest told me that the men with my father found him alone, injecting himself. They said they tried to stop him and the needle broke off in his arm. The room was ransacked in the struggle to get the needle away from him. Why would they lie about it?" She looked at him with pleading desperation.

Looking away from her, Billy realized he was committed now. "Maybe they had a hand in it. Maybe the room was ransacked because they were lookin' for somethin'. Maybe they were interrupted."

Bernadette studied him intently. "You know something about it! " she finally accused.

Shocked by her intuitive guess, he shifted uncomfortably in the chair, shaking his head quickly. "No. I just…"

"You're lying," Bernadette stated softly. "Why would you think they were looking for something?"

He made no reply.

Turning from him, Bernadette hugged herself tightly. "My God! You come in here and tell me my father's been…and you know something about it! Shit! I believed you were his friend. I trusted you." Throwing back her head, she began sobbing.

Billy lowered his head. He felt cowardly and wanted to ease her pain and restore her faith in him. "All right," he said finally. "I didn't just drop by yer father's cottage. He sent for me."

Bernadette stop sobbing and sat up. "Why?"

It was Billy's turn to walk over to the window, because he didn't want her to see his face when he lied to her. "He wrote me a letter, askin' me t' come here an' get a package from him an' deliver it t' someone in Belfast."

Knowing that her father was involved with the IRA, this explanation sounded plausible to Bernadette. "What was in the package and who were you to deliver it to?"

Billy took a deep breath but continued facing the window. "I don't know. The letter said I'd find out when I got here."

Having reached a dead end, Bernadette thought again about the fact that her father might not have died accidentally. "Why did you tell me about the injection? That my father couldn't have done it himself?" she asked softly.

At last he could turn from the window and face her again because now he didn't have to lie. "I'm worried about ye. I was afraid that if the men didn't find the package they might think ye had it…"

This time the implication of what he was saying was not lost on her. "You mean I might be…"

Coming on top of the knowledge that her father's death might not have been an accident, and her suspicion that Billy knew more about it than he was saying, this latest realization was too much for Bernadette. She jumped up off the bed and began pounding Billy on the chest. "Why are you telling me all this? It's crazy! I have enough to cope with! I can't take any more!"

Billy grasped her wrists to stop the pounding. "I'm sorry. I shouldn't have said anythin', but I thought ye deserved t' know the truth. Yer father was a good friend t' me an' I want t' know why he died. I owe him that."

Bernadette's arms relaxed in his grip and she began to sob again.

Billy gently pulled her toward him so that her face was buried in his chest. "I thought ye'd feel the same way," he added quietly.

The remark cut into her and she pushed him away. "That's not fair!" She turned and fell onto the bed. "I can't take all this in. I can't even be sure of your part in it."

It was Billy's turn to become defensive. "What d' ye mean?"

"Why didn't you tell me all this last night?" Bernadette challenged.

Billy's shoulders slumped at the question. "I didn't know last night. When I got back t' the cottage this morning I noticed an envelope by the coffin. It was the death certificate. That's how I found out the injection was in the left arm."

"You were looking for the package," Bernadette guessed.

Billy lowered his eyes. "Aye."

"And you didn't find it so you wondered if I had it."

He nodded, keeping his eyes down.

"Well, I don't. Which means that either the men who ransacked the room have it, or they didn't find it either and it's still in the cottage somewhere, or someone else has it."

Billy raised his eyes. "Who else would have it?"

Bernadette shrugged. "I don't know. The priest? No, he'd have given it to me." She sat up on the bed. "We must find it," she stated.

Billy shook his head quickly. "No. The package isn't important. I'm more concerned about ye an' about findin' out what really happened t' yer father. If he was…well, they shouldn't get away wi' it…"

Bernadette's body went limp and she closed her eyes. "You're right. I want to find out what happened too." She opened her eyes again. "But right now I'm drained."

There was no mistaking the plaintive urgency in her look. Billy hesitated then sat down beside her on the bed. Turning away from him toward the window, she curled into a fetal position. "Hold me," she whispered.

Lying down beside her, he wrapped his arm around her waist. She began to sob and rock gently in his embrace. After a long time her breathing became soft and regular. He too dozed off eventually.

15

Bernadette woke first. Her movement awakened Billy. She glanced at her watch. Five a.m. "My God, I slept for nine hours? And you've been here all night?"

Embarrassed, Billy began to get up but Bernadette pulled him back. "You're not leaving again," she said. "Considering what the neighbors must think about us already, you can afford to stay a few more minutes."

They both relaxed, lying on their backs. "Are ye all right?" Billy asked.

"Awful," Bernadette responded. " But I'm over the shock." She sat up, leaning on one elbow. "So what do we do now?"

Billy turned on his side to face her. "We don't do anythin'. Ye aren't gettin' involved."

"Screw you!" Bernadette snapped. "He was my father! Shit! You said you thought I'd feel the same way you did. So now you're gonna be Mr. Macho and do something on your own?"

Putting his hand to his forehead, Billy shook his head but said nothing.

"Anyway, you need me," Bernadette continued. "You're a stranger around these parts and people are suspicious of strangers. I'll take responsibility for my own safety. I'm a big girl."

Unable to refute anything she said, Billy gave in. "All right, but we do things me way." He tried to look stern.

Bernadette held up her hands in a gesture of acquiescence. "OK. So, where do we begin?"

"The priest I suppose. He might have the package and not have given it t' ye, an' its contents might provide a clue. We need t' also find out who those men were wi' yer father that night. An' if your father said anythin' that might help. Ye'll have t' talk t' the priest, but be careful, don't let him know ye suspect anythin' out o' the ordinary. We don't know who's involved in this, includin' him."

Bernadette nodded. "What will you do?"

"I'll start by goin' back t' yer father's house an' lookin' around, in case they didn't find what they were after. I didn't have a chance to search very thoroughly."

"OK," Bernadette said. "But Billy…"

"Aye?"

"Can you pronounce 'Bernadette'?"

Billy knitted his brows, puzzled. "Aye."

"Well, I think we know each other well enough by now to use our names, don't you?" She smiled.

He grinned in response.

Bernadette got off the bed. "Do you want something to eat? I could order breakfast."

"Thanks, but I don't think it'd be good for yer reputation, ah, Bernadette."

She liked how her name rolled off his tongue.

"Speaking o' which," he continued. "I should find a place o' me own. D' ye think I should take a room here too?"

Bernadette considered for a minute. "Why don't you stay at my father's? It's my house now, I guess, and I'll tell the priest and old Mrs.

Slaugherty, so they don't bother you. It'd save you some money." Then she remembered her father's body. "Unless you mind…"

Billy saw what she was thinking. "That'd be fine, if ye're sure?"

"I'm sure, but now I'm afraid I'll have to ask you to leave. I have to get ready."

Billy got up from the bed. "All right, Bernadette. Will ye just check that the coast is clear for me?"

She nodded and stepped to the door. Opening it slowly, she stuck her head out and checked the corridor and stairs. "All clear," she whispered. "Go down the corridor to your right. There's a door to the street at the bottom of the stairs."

He walked over to her. "Can we meet later?"

"Sure. Why don't you come back here? If I'm not around you can wait in the saloon."

Billy nodded and stepped quickly into the corridor. Bernadette watched until he disappeared down the stairs.

16

Bernadette went to the bank and cashed some traveler's checks then walked to Father O'Grady's church. Approaching the chapel, Bernadette noted the ornate iron railing around its perimeter, with its spiked, fleur-de-lis top and the small crosses and shamrocks interspersed along its length. These had always impressed her as true art, and symbolized the mysticism associated with religion. Now, the railing looked cheap to her.

She turned through the main gate, above which was a small metal arch containing Latin words she had never understood. She noticed some of the letters were missing. The coarse, gray gravel beneath her feet crunched a reminder that this was ground deserving muted reverence. All through her childhood she'd been told that this was Holy Ground, but she had never understood what that meant. It was what adults said to rebuke any child who dared bounce a ball, or engage in laughter or shouting as they waited for their parents to exchange pleasantries with the priest after Sunday services. What would those adults have thought if they had known what their children did around the back of the chapel on warm, summer evenings?

The memory gave Bernadette the urge to go back there again and so she followed the path around, between the chapel and the Sunday school. It led to a quiet, secluded little lawn that lay between the chapel's soaring spires on one side, the back of the Sunday school on another and squat, smoky row houses on the other two sides. It was still, she realized, an island in the sea of concrete and traffic, shielded from the noise of the city. She had often played here, usually with a few girlfriends who would act being queens and princesses, with the church their castle.

It came to her suddenly that the last time she had been here was when a gang of local boys interrupted their play. Her friend Jane had been smitten with the boys' leader and convinced the other girls to play "Hunt", with the boys as predators and the girls as prey. The boys claimed kisses when they caught the girls in the quiet, dark corners and hidden recesses of the chapel's architecture. Bernadette remembered several boys, pressing their hard young bodies against hers and groping at her chest. She recalled thinking at the time that she shouldn't be enjoying this, but she found it exhilarating to have several boys fighting for her even if the cold, gray stone, and soaring steeples seemed to rebuke her mightily. She wondered what might have happened had they not been chased away by the old caretaker, limping around the corner and waving his walking stick at them. She had suffered such a feeling of guilt that she had never gone back to this area. Looking around her now, at the balding grass and damp corners where dark moss grew thick, Bernadette saw only decay caused by years of pollution.

Continuing around the chapel, she entered it by a side door. Inside was silent, dark and cool with a musty smell. When her eyes adjusted she saw that the only other person in the church was the priest. Busy at the altar, he did not notice her enter.

She looked slowly around. The chapel was much smaller than she remembered, but the cherubs poking out from pillars, with the statues of the apostles lining the walls, and the stained glass with its pictures of pain and suffering all still conveyed a sense of intimidation. In the vestibule to her left was a life-size statue of the Blessed Virgin. The table in front of it was covered with candles, the newer ones glowing imploringly, the older ones burnt out from awaiting an answer to their owners' prayers. This had been the most fearful place imaginable to her, with its mystery, grandeur and promised retribution. Now it seemed irrelevant.

The priest interrupted her reverie. "Bernadette," he said, just loud enough to be heard while still showing respect for the surroundings.

She wondered how long he'd been watching her.

He walked toward her smiling, then stopped. "Ah, maybe ye'd like t' be alone?"

Bernadette realized he thought she might have come to pray. "No, it was you I came to see, Father, if you've a few minutes to spare."

"Of course. Why don't we go int' me office?" He waited for her.

Walking down the aisle towards him, she noticed the confessional boxes to his right. The memory of the small box, with its smells of incense and sweat and her terror at having to confess her darkest secrets caused her to hesitate. The priest noticed and looked to see the cause of it. As if to deny him the answer, she walked toward him more quickly. Touching her elbow lightly, he guided her behind the altar to a small door, which he held open. Bernadette entered a tiny room.

"Please, sit down." The priest indicated an armchair to the left of a bare fireplace. She sat while he went behind a small, wooden desk and wheeled a secretary chair from there to the fireplace. He sat beside her. "Would ye like some tea?"

"No, thanks," she answered.

The priest nodded and sank back into his chair. "How've ye been?"

"I'm OK," she answered. "You?"

He shrugged "As well as can be expected. Did they have the room ready for ye at the Starry Plough?"

Bernadette decided not to mention that she'd spent the night at her father's cottage. "Yes. Thanks for dropping off my luggage."

The priest nodded, and waited for her to state her business.

"I'm sure you must have told me, but in my state it didn't register. I don't know when the funeral is."

The priest slapped both hands against his knees. "Ach, forgive me, Bernadette. Stupid o' me. No, I didn't tell ye. It's Saturday morning at ten o'clock. I thought I could pick ye up at the Starry Plough at about nine thirty an' take ye t' the house."

"I'd appreciate that," Bernadette said, then paused, trying to think of a lead in to her next question. Unable to think of one, she decided to be direct. "My father didn't give you anything did he? I mean, to give to me?"

The priest seemed surprised at the question. "No. No, he didn't. Was there something…?"

"Oh, no," Bernadette hastily interrupted. "It was just a thought. A hope, really. You said you told him I was coming. I just wondered if he might have left something of significance. A family heirloom, or something. Do you know what I mean?"

He obviously didn't, but nodded that he did.

"Well, it doesn't matter. It was a silly idea," Bernadette continued. "Did he say anything before he died?" A small tightening of the priest's eyes told her that he had not wanted this question, perhaps feared it somehow.

"Ye mean about yerself?" He was being cautious.

"About anything," Bernadette answered. Then, before he could pin her down to more specifics, she added, "It's just that I came here expecting him to be alive and…well, I just wondered if he said anything at the end."

When there was no immediate response, Bernadette raised her eyes to meet the priest's. Averting her look, the priest examined the rosary beads around his neck, turning something over in his mind. "He was only half-conscious when I got there, ye understand," the priest began. "Kept repeatin' the same thin' over an' over. He might a' been delirious."

"I understand," Bernadette said, but in a tone that expected the priest to continue.

After a few more seconds, the priest seemed to reach a decision. "Connead Braith," he said finally.

Bernadette's look told him she didn't understand.

His face remained serious. "It's a name," he stated.

She continued to look perplexed. "Whose name?"

The priest sighed. "A woman's name."

It took a second for Bernadette to grasp the significance. She saw from the priest's eyes that he was waiting for her to make the assumption. "What woman?" she asked.

The priest shrugged. "No-one I ever heard o'." He leaned toward her. "I know what ye're thinkin', Bernadette, but it doesn't mean anythin'. He wasn't coherent."

Bernadette pulled away from him. "A woman," she whispered to herself. She looked at the priest. "A woman, but not me and not my mother. Who then? A lover? A new wife?" She stared hard at the priest. "Is that what you won't tell me?"

The priest stiffened and his tone took on a slight hardness. "I've told you everythin', an' I maybe shouldn't have told ye anythin'. I almost didn't, but ye asked."

Bernadette understood then that he priest had wanted to shield her but had finally offered her the truth. "I'm sorry. You're right. Thank you for telling me." She took a breath. "What about the men who were with him that night? Do you know where I could find them?"

The priest shook his head. "They'd already gone when I got t' the house, an' nobody seems to know who they were."

"Wouldn't the police or the coroner have wanted to talk to them?" Bernadette persisted.

Rising from his chair, the priest sat on the edge of the desk in front of her. "Bernadette, how can I say this? Yer father knew people who wouldn't want t' be around when the police came callin'. They don't want t' come in contact wi' any o' the authorities."

"I see," Bernadette responded. "It's just that they knew him and I really didn't. I wanted to find out what he was like, what he did."

The priest nodded his understanding. "I understand, but I think you'd be as well not t' find them fellas."

Bernadette saw nothing to be gained from pursuing the matter. "OK, Father. Well, I won't take up any more of your time. Thank you again." She stood and stepped toward the door.

"Bernadette," the priest said.

She stopped and waited, not wanting to turn and face him again.

"You've no reason for imaginin' this woman t' be anyone other than maybe a person yer father knew. I've not been able t' find anyone who knows her, an' besides…" This time his long pause forced her to face him. "Even if she turns out t' be what ye imagine, it is not for us t' be judgin'."

"Don't worry, Father, I'm not judging. If I'd thought about it, I would have expected it. After all, it was my mother who left him. I would just like to talk to someone who knew him day in and day out. Yes, was intimate with him even. Could describe his later years, bring him to life for me, so to speak." She sighed. "I just want to know what he was like, Father, and not feel so much like I'm here for the funeral of a stranger."

The priest flashed her a look of sympathy, then lowered his eyes. Opening the door, Bernadette hurried down the aisle before her emotions overcame her.

————

The Starry Plough was not very busy when Bernadette entered the saloon. Two young men stood at the far end of the bar, nursing Guinnesses and holding a whispered but animated conversation. In one of the snugs, three old men were intent on a game of dominoes. In the snug behind that, two old women were sipping gins and in the next snug, a young couple were giggling over glasses of lager.

Bernadette crossed to the bar. "Mr. O'Grady, do you know a woman called Connead Braith?"

The landlord kept his head down, concentrating on the pint glass he was polishing. "No, I don't think so," he answered slowly. He held the glass up to the light, admiring it. "Would she be from around these parts?"

"I don't know. She was a...a friend of my father's. I wanted to talk to her. You don't know anyone named Braith?"

After breathing on the glass, O'Grady wiped it on his sleeve. "I'm afraid I don't." Inspecting the glass again, he seemed satisfied and placed it on the shelf which ran the length of the bar, above his head. "Sorry I can't help ye." Turning his back to her, he rummaged in a cupboard beneath the bar.

Turning around, Bernadette rested her elbows on the bar. "Does anybody here know a woman called Connead Braith?" she asked loudly.

The young men at the end of the bar looked at her and shook their heads in unison, then resumed their murmured conversation. The old men gazed at her blankly as if she had committed a sacrilege. As her eyes reached theirs, the old women looked away, peering into their gin glasses. The young couple hung out of their snug, looking at Bernadette.

"I'm offering twenty pounds for information about this woman." She didn't know what made her say that, and felt foolish. It implied that she doubted their reticence.

The young men looked at her again. She could almost see their ears prick up but they said and indicated nothing. The old men continued to watch her in sufferance. The old women glanced at each other briefly then returned to staring into their glasses. The young couple hung out of their snug again but with serious looks this time.

Bernadette pushed herself away from the bar. "I'll be upstairs if any of you can help me find this woman."

"Would ye like some tea brought t' your room?" O'Grady asked, surprisingly loudly.

Bernadette turned to look at him. Something in his eyes urged her to accept the offer. "Sure," she replied.

The bartender nodded. "I'll bring it right up."

"Do you have a telephone directory?" Bernadette asked suddenly.

O'Grady walked toward the telephone which hung on the wall just outside his kitchen. From a cupboard underneath the phone he pulled out a telephone directory and handed it to Bernadette. "I'll bring yer tea up t' your room," he said, and again Bernadette was struck by the loudness of his voice.

Bernadette had already found the 'B' listings by the time O'Grady disappeared into his kitchen. There were no Braiths listed. Closing the book, she laid it on the bar and made her way upstairs, aware of the growing whispers behind her.

Knowing that O'Grady would be along in a few minutes, she left her door open. Sitting on the bed, she ran through her mind what other sources she could tap in trying to track down Connead Braith. The Post Office probably didn't keep information by name. The police probably didn't either and would want to know why she was looking for this woman. She could tell them of course, but it seemed like more trouble than she wanted. She couldn't think of any other sources. The problem was that she'd always depended on Larry and on her position to get any information she wanted. If only she could ask Larry to track down this Connead Braith for her, she'd have the information in an hour or two.

A thought occurred to her. Larry would just call the appropriate branch of government, state who he was, what information was needed and when it was needed, and then wait for a response. Maybe she could do the same thing. Of course the only people here who would be impressed by her position would be the U.S. Embassy. She could call them, speak to someone with authority and let the embassy do the grunt work. She imagined that their computers would provide easy access to numerous lists of people. She decided it was worth a try and was just about to head back downstairs to use the phone when O'Grady appeared in the doorway, tea tray in hand.

Bernadette motioned him into the room. "Just set it on the chair," she said, nodding in that direction.

O'Grady set the tray down and hesitated.

"Was there something else?" Bernadette asked.

Holding one finger to his lips O'Grady crossed back to the doorway. He glanced into the corridor in both directions, closed the door behind him and turned to face her. "About that, ah, woman. Connead Braith, I believe ye said?"

Bernadette looked at him quizzically. "I thought you had never heard of her?"

O'Grady held his palms up. "Ah well now, it's hard sometimes t' remember thin's exactly. Bein' a barman, ye see, ye deal wi' lots o' people every day. Some ye know well, some tell ye their names an' then ye never see them again, an' some names ye hear secondhand. Ye know, they come up in the course o' a conversation ye might overhear."

"I see," said Bernadette. "And you've remembered the name Connead Braith?"

The landlord smiled slyly. "I maybe do recall some such name, now that I've had a few minutes t' think it over."

When he said nothing else, Bernadette prodded. "Well?"

"You mentioned twenty pounds…" O'Grady said, almost regretfully.

Bernadette smiled to herself. She might have known. "Yes. If it helps me find the woman."

The landlord thought for a moment. "I can't tell ye where t' find this Connead Braith, ye understand, but I can give ye the name o' someone who might."

"All right," Bernadette answered.

O'Grady held out his hand. Rummaging in her purse, Bernadette produced two ten pound notes. "There's still the two pounds an' seventy pence ye owe me," the landlord said sheepishly.

Bernadette sighed and returned to her purse. She counted the money into his hand.

O'Grady repeated the ritual of gentle tugging and precise folding into the moneybelt she had seen when she last paid him. When he spoke again his voice had a serious tone. "Ye must agree not t' tell anyone I told ye.

I've me reputation t' consider. Ye'd be surprised at the private thin's people say when the booze loosens their tongues…"

"Yes, all right. Just tell me." Bernadette's impatience was clear and she tried to temper it. "My tea's getting cold."

The landlord looked at the tray on the chair. "Aye, so it is," he agreed. Then his voice dropped in volume. "There's a fella called Marty Coyne, lives at number 11 Lisbon Street. D'ye know where that is?"

"I'll find it," Bernadette responded.

"It's over by the gasworks. He can help ye, but mind, he might want somethin' for his troubles too."

"Marty Coyne, 11 Lisbon street," Bernadette repeated. "Anything else?"

The landlord shook his head.

"Well, thank you Mr. O'Grady. I'd better get to my tea."

He took the clear hint to leave. "Well, enjoy your tea now," he said loudly enough so that Bernadette thought everyone in the lounge downstairs must have heard him. It dawned on her that this was his intention. It also explained why he had spoken so loudly downstairs. He obviously didn't want anyone thinking he might have gone upstairs to do anything other than deliver tea.

———

Arriving at Joe Mallory's cottage, Billy decided he'd better knock, just in case that old woman Slaugherty was there. Knocking loudly, he was taken aback when the door opened revealing a large, hard looking old man who glared at him. The man looked so intimidating Billy didn't know what to say. "I was, er, lookin' for Bernadette. Bernadette Mallory?" he finally managed.

The man continued to glare. "There's no need t' be knockin' hard enough t' wake the dead," he reprimanded.

Before Billy could respond, the door opened wider and old Mrs. Slaugherty appeared from behind her husband. "It's all right, John. This here's the young fella was here yesterday."

With a grunt, the man turned and went back into the house.

"Did ye not find her yesterday?" the old woman asked Billy.

"Aye, I did. She's staying at the Starry Plough like ye said. I was on me way t' see her now, but since I had t' pass this way anyhow, I thought I'd just check an' be sure she wasn't here."

The old woman nodded understandingly. "No, son. She's not here. Mind, if ye think she's on her way ye could come in an' wait." She stepped aside, inviting Billy into the cottage.

"No, that's all right. I'll just go on down t' the Starry Plough an' see her there. Sorry t' have bothered ye," Billy said. He turned and walked back to the road then headed in the direction of the Starry Plough. He'd just have to wait until he could search the cottage when there was no-one around. Maybe Bernadette could arrange it and help him with the search.

As he walked, Billy paid no attention to the small blue car that passed him on its way to the Connevarve post office. The occupants of the car paid no attention to him either.

————

The car pulled up in front of the Connevarve Post Office and two men got out. The younger one was carrying a small briefcase. The elder, who had driven the car, stood in the road for a moment. He had the air of someone used to receiving and giving orders without questions being asked, an ex-military man maybe. He surveyed the street, switching his attention from the post office to the telephone kiosk. "That'll be the phone," he said to his companion.

The younger man walked over to the kiosk and reached his hand out to open it.

"Wait!" snapped the elder man.

His companion froze. The older man walked over to where he stood. "Check the handle. It's a slim chance, but who knows?"

The younger man nodded sheepishly and laid his briefcase on the side-walk beside the kiosk door. He knelt beside it and took out a small aerosol can.

"How long will it take ye?" the older man asked.

"Depends what I've got t' work wi', how many people have used the phone since yesterday, if there's any clean prints at all."

"Well, wait for me in the car if I'm not out when ye're done."

The older man turned and entered the Post Office, setting a small bell a-tinkling as he opened the door. It was a tiny office, with one counter running along the back wall. A thin, bespectacled woman appeared from a door behind the counter. "Good mornin'," she said in a businesslike tone.

The man relaxed as he approached the counter. The woman waited while he reached into his inside jacket pocket and removed his billfold. She watched him flip the billfold open and hold it up to the wire mesh which separated them. "Inspector Grindley," he stated.

The woman scanned the card displayed in the billfold. She was obviously impressed. "What can I do for ye, Inspector?"

The Inspector detected the excitement and eagerness in her eyes and voice. Closing his billfold, he returned it to his pocket. "I just need some information, Mrs, er...?"

"Smith. Grace Smith, an' it'd be Miss," the woman replied, smiling nervously.

The Inspector returned her smile. "Well, Miss Smith, it's about a transaction that took place here yesterday."

"Ah," said Miss Smith with a hint of intrigue, "It's about that fella who picked up the money from Belfast, isn't it?"

Grindley looked at her, feigning surprise. "How did ye know that?"

Miss Smith's smile broadened. "Well, Inspector, it's not every day we have a transaction like that, an' I didn't think ye'd be callin' about old Mr. Riley cashin' his pension like he's done for the past fifteen years."

Grindley nodded. "I can tell, Miss Smith, that ye're a sharp woman who takes her duties seriously. I'm sure ye made this man fill out all the proper forms, sign where he was supposed to, an' show his identification?"

Miss Smith appeared insulted. "Ye don't think I did somethin' irregular? Somethin' outside the regulations?"

Grindley held up his hands to placate her. "No, no. Just the opposite in fact. Like I said, I'm sure ye take yer duties very seriously."

"I certainly do," the woman sniffed haughtily. "I've been Postmistress here for twentysix years an' in all that time I've never had a problem followin' the regulations. Ye've only t' ask at the main post office in Cork. They send an inspector every three months t' examine me records an' make sure everythin's in order." She reached beneath the counter and pulled out a large black book. "I can show ye everythin' about that particular transaction yesterday an' ye'll find it's all like the regulations say it should be."

Grindley smiled to himself. Just as he'd hoped. No claims to confidentiality or desire to talk to higher-ups. Just wanting to prove what a devoted public servant she was. "That won't be necessary, Miss Smith. If ye'll just write down the man's name, address, phone number if ye have one, an' driver's license number or whatever identification he showed ye. I'll also need t' know who the sender was, an' where the money was sent from. Whatever information ye can give me. It's the man we're interested in, not ye."

"I've a photocopier back here. Why don't I just give ye copies o' all the documents?"

Again the inspector smiled to himself. "That would be even better, Miss Smith," he beamed. "I'll be sure t' let the proper authorities know how efficient an' cooperative ye've been."

Smiling broadly at that, the Postmistress set about making the copies. When she was finished she pushed the papers under the wire mesh to the inspector. Examining them, he saw that they contained all the information he wanted. Folding them, he slid them into an outer jacket pocket.

"Ye've been very helpful, Miss Smith. Can ye answer one more question for me?"

She nodded eagerly. "If I can, Inspector."

"Have there been any deaths around these parts lately?"

Miss Smith looked shocked. "Deaths? D'ye mean yon fellow might have…"

"No, no. Nothin' like that. It's a totally unrelated matter."

Miss Smith seemed disappointed. "Well, Joe Mallory died just a few days ago. He'd be the only one I know of."

The Inspector nodded. "Aye, he's the only one I know of too.

Well, I won't take up any more o' yer time, Miss Smith. Thanks for all yer help." He turned to leave.

"Inspector!" the Miss Smith called after him.

Grindley turned to face her.

"Ye never did say what ye want him for," the Postmistress whispered.

The Inspector touched a forefinger to his nose and smiled knowingly, then he turned again and left the Post Office, leaving a disappointed Miss Smith behind him. She lacked a vital piece of the gossip he knew she would spread about his visit.

His companion was already seated in the car. The inspector climbed into the driver's seat. "Well?" he asked.

"I got a couple o' fairly clean ones. Course there's no tellin' whose they are. Might not be able t' match them at all."

"Well, we'll find out," responded the Inspector. He sat for a moment. He could stop by Joe Mallory's place and sniff around there, but no, he'd better report back to his unofficial employer first, see what he wanted done next. He thought what a stroke of luck it was that Sheila Brannigan had told him about the conversation she'd overheard. It paid to keep a woman like that dangling, leading her on, hinting at a full commitment without ever finally making one. His unofficial employer paid well when he was interested in information and this should result in a nice bonus. Starting the car, he made a U-turn on the narrow road and headed back to Cork, passing Billy about a mile from the Starry Plough.

17

Lisbon street was a squalid line of rowhouses clinging like mold to the wall of the gasworks that ran behind them. The acrid smell that pervaded the neighborhood made Bernadette's nostrils smart. Number 11 was the meanest looking house of all. Its lower front window was smashed and had a piece of plywood jammed in it, but not well enough to prevent filthy yellow curtains from blowing through and slapping on the grimy windowsill. The front door was missing its bottom hinge and hung at a crooked angle, leaving a gap at the bottom on one side.

A marmalade cat, missing half an ear and with bald patches over its mangy body, squeezed through the opening. Pausing to mew plaintively at her, the cat raised its tail erect, shuddered a few times and finally urinated against the door. Sniffing the spot, the cat seemed satisfied and jumped daintily onto the windowsill. Ignoring Bernadette, the cat licked between its hind legs.

Bernadette almost lost her resolve but finally stepped up to the door and delivered three loud knocks with the brass knocker which was pitted with green and black spots. Immediately, a dog began to bark fiercely from behind the door. She heard cursing and shouting from further inside the house. As she stood wondering whether to go through with this, the black and white snout of a dog poked through the opening at the bottom of the door. The animal's fangs were bared, dripping slobber. Threatening growls came from deep in the creature's throat. From behind the door a man's voice shouted. "Get the hell back! Go on! Or I'll bury me foot up yer arse!" The voice sounded only a little more human than the dog. "Stupid bastard animal! Get away from that friggin' door!"

A heavy object thudded against the inside of the door. Bernadette stepped to the side, to be well out of the line of fire. The dog whimpered and its snout jerked back out of view. "Get in the yard! Go on, or I'll break yer back!"

There was another thud, this time followed by a pained whimpering. The door scraped open to reveal a man who immediately filled Bernadette with apprehension and misgiving. His bent nose and cauliflowered ears suggested that he might have been a boxer once, but the huge gut which spilled over his belt said that would have been a long time and many fights ago. He had a crew cut, a chin which hadn't felt a razor for a week, and a long, purple scar under his lower lip. He wore a gray undershirt, which had once been white and was torn below one armpit. His green dungarees were grimy with oilstains and had one pocket hanging loose. He was barefoot with black toenails. In his right hand he held a brass handled, black poker, which he brandished like a weapon. "If ye're from that bloody probation office an' ye got me out here on account of me Jimmy, I'll..."

"I'm not from the probation office!" Bernadette said hastily. "Are you Marty Coyne?"

"Never mind about that! Who the hell are ye?"

"If you are Marty Coyne, I'm here to give you the chance to earn some money without having to work. Maybe we could talk inside?" Right away, Bernadette regretted suggesting this. She could imagine what this house must be like, and would have preferred staying where she was.

Squinting, the man looked her up and down from head to toe.

"Money, eh? Well, I've never been too proud for that, especially if I don't have t' work for it. All right then, come in."

Squeezing through the half open door, Bernadette gingerly picked her way down the narrow, dark hallway, feeling along the wall to guide herself. Her hand touched something damp and sludgy and she jerked it back quickly. Feeling arched feline backs brush against her legs, she recoiled at the thought of how many fleas might decide to transfer hosts, jumping from the cats around her feet onto her. There was a constant mewing from the floor all around her.

At the end of the hall, Coyne opened a door on the right. "Min' yer step here. There's a basin o' water for the cats t' drink."

His warning came too late. Bernadette stepped in the water, not knowing if her shock was due to the wetness, or to the scummy feeling which testified to how long it had been standing there. She forced herself on, one shoe squelching with each step. The door led into what would be called the sitting room.

A peat fire burned in the room. In front of the fireplace the linoleum was scarred with burn marks. To the left was a scullery with an uneven tiled floor, cracked and stained. Dishes were piled high in the sink and counter tops. "Sit yersel' down by the fire. I've no tea t' give ye," said Coyne gruffly.

"That's fine, I just had some," Bernadette answered quickly. She didn't relish tea made in that scullery. Nor did she want to sit, but couldn't just stand there, so she cautiously lowered herself onto the lumpy sofa.

"Well, what d'ye want?" Coyne demanded.

"Some information, Mr Coyne. That's all."

"What information?" He spat toward the fire. The spittle hissed and bubbled on the tiled hearth, getting smaller and smaller until it vanished.

"I'm looking for a woman. Connead Braith. I think she was a friend of my father, Joe Mallory."

Coyne's eyes narrowed perceptibly at the name of the woman, then widened again at her father's name. "Yer Joe Mallory's girl?" he said disbelievingly.

Bernadette nodded.

He studied her with animal cunning. "An' ye're lookin' for this, er, woman, Connead Braith. Why?"

"I just want to talk to her," Bernadette replied.

Coyne laughed quickly, then narrowed his eyes at her. "An' who said I could help ye?" His voice sounded menacing.

"That doesn't matter. Can you tell me where to find her?"

Coyne looked away from her towards the fire. For a moment he said nothing, then he began passing the crooked, charred poker from hand to hand. "How much money?"

"Twenty pounds." Reaching into her purse, Bernadette extracted a ten pound note. "Half now and the rest if your information is good." She held the bill toward him.

Coyne looked back at her. He seemed amused. "Connead Braith ye say. Ye'r sure that's the name?"

"Yes," Bernadette answered, then added "It's an uncommon name. If you know her I shouldn't think there'd be any question about who I mean."

Laughing again, Coyne slapped at his knee. "Aye, there's no doubt, right enough." He continued to chuckle.

In exasperation, Bernadette said, "Maybe I'm wasting my time and you can't help me after all." She began to replace the note in her purse.

Leaning over, Coyne snatched the bill from her hand. "Don't be so fast!" he hissed.

Bernadette sat frozen for a moment, while Coyne examined the note. Finally, he nodded in satisfaction. "Aye, it'll buy a bit o' whisky, sure enough." He dropped the poker onto the hearth and it bounced on the tiles with a metallic clatter. "But I'd be wantin' the whole twenty pounds now."

"Half now and half later. That's the deal," Bernadette stated firmly.

"An' suppose I give ye good information an' ye find her, how do I know ye'll give me the rest o' the money?"

"You'll have to trust me," Bernadette answered.

Coyne smiled cunningly. "I'm to trust ye that doesn't trust me?" He shook his head. "No. It's all or nothin'. Ye came t' me an' that's me price. Anyway, ye look like ye can afford it."

Bernadette knew he had her, but made the pretense of mulling it over by biting at her lower lip. "All right," she said finally.

Reaching into her purse again, she withdrew another ten pounds, which she handed to him. "Where can I find her?"

Coyne took the money from her slowly this time. "Sure what's the harm?" he said to himself. "Enough people know about it." He looked at Bernadette with a broad grin on his face. "She's at the bottom o' the Atlantic Ocean."

Bernadette looked at him stupidly for a minute, causing his grin to widen. "You mean she drowned?" Bernadette managed finally.

"Not exactly." Coyne continued to grin at her, obviously enjoying this.

"Then what?" Bernadette said, irritated. "Is she dead?"

"Not exactly," Coyne repeated, his stupid grin widening even further.

Bernadette flushed with frustration. "I didn't come here to play games. I gave you the money. Tell me what you mean." Her voice had a sharp edge to it.

Coyne kept his eyes fixed on her. "Connead Braith was a boat. It sank between here an' America last month." He seemed to exult as the color drained from Bernadette's face.

"A boat?" she repeated slowly. She seemed not to understand the word. Then she recovered her composure. "What did my father have to do with this boat?"

Coyne shook his head slowly. "Ah, sure I can't be tellin' ye that. It's a secret, but ye can take it from me that yer da was interested in that boat. Very interested."

"How do you know about it?"

Coyne smiled. "Because I could've been on it. Lucky for me they wouldn't take me because they were afeard I'd get a few drinks in me an' start talkin' about it. Well, they're at the bottom o' the sea feedin' the fish now an' I'm here talkin' t' ye, so who's better off, eh?" He held up the money she had given him. "An' I made twenty pounds int' the bargain."

Her feeling of revulsion was too much for Bernadette. Springing from the sofa, she tore the bills from Coyne's hands, but she wasn't quick enough to avoid his reflexive shove which knocked her sprawling back onto the sofa. Throwing himself on top of her, Coyne snatched at the money. Bernadette held it above her head and his hand missed its mark. He lunged again and once more she jerked the bills out of his reach. This move stretched her dress strap to its limit, and on their way back down his fingers caught the strap and it ripped. The momentum of his hand extended the tear across the front of her dress and uncovered her right bra cup. Bernadette instinctively threw her left hand across the exposed area but still kept the notes in her right hand stretched away from Coyne's reach. His weight was crushing her. He was panting heavily but she felt his body relax from the stretching position he was in. Grabbing the arm covering her bra, he forced it away from her chest. "All right," he snarled. "If that's how ye want it. I'll take it out o' yer hide!"

Bernadette's head was bent back over the side of the sofa and she couldn't see what he was doing. She screamed when she felt his free hand tear at the bra and the strap cut into her shoulder. She struggled but was pinned helplessly. Finally the bra strap snapped and Bernadette felt Coyne's hand grasp her exposed breast. Terror overtook her. "All right!" she screamed. "I'll give you the money!" She thrust the bills in his direction.

Relaxing his grip on her wrist, Coyne snatched the money, stuffing it into a trouser pocket, continuing to breathe hard. "Ye shouldn't have done that. We had a deal, an' yer tit felt good. Got me excited, if ye know what I mean!" he growled.

Grabbing Bernadette's wrists, he forced her arms behind her back and underneath her body. His weight kept her arms pinned there. She felt his knees digging into the front of her elbows. Although she felt hysterical, the scream deep inside her wouldn't come out. One hand grabbed her bared breast again and squeezed hard. Finally the scream erupted from Bernadette's throat.

"Go ahead an' scream," Coyne hissed. "Nobody's goin' t' pay any heed. Yous women always start out like that an' then yous end up beggin' for it. When I get through with ye, ye'll be purring wi' pleasure, like them cats when they get fed."

Bernadette felt his hand reach between her legs, pulling her dress up. She struggled with strength she didn't know she had but he was stronger. His feet kept her legs pinned apart and his hand tore at her panties. Drained of strength and willing herself to faint so she would not have to endure the coming ordeal she lost herself in her screams as if they could block out the sensation of one hand on her breast and the other between her legs.

Just when she had almost succeeded in screaming herself into oblivion, the door burst open and Billy stumbled into the room. He and Coyne froze at the same instant. Billy recovered more quickly and reached into his pocket, pulling out his gun. Despite his shock and nervousness he remembered to flip off the safety and to hold the weapon in both hands, at arms length. "Get off her!" he yelled, motioning Coyne away from the couch.

The latter held up his hands. "Don't shoot! I'm movin'." Lifting his left leg over Bernadette, he slid his right foot to the floor. Balancing on one foot for a moment he swung his left leg clear of the couch and stood facing Billy. His trousers slid below his knees. "Can I pull up me trousers?"

The question sounded stupid to Billy but he flicked his head in approval, keeping the gun pointed at Coyne. At the same time he reached out to Bernadette with his right hand. "It's all right. Get up." He looked at her.

Coyne, hands down around his ankles, gripping the waistband of his trousers, saw his chance. Reaching for the poker lying on the hearth, he brought it up in a wide swing. Bernadette screamed at the movement but

Billy reacted too slowly and the poker smashed into his arm. The gun went off with a sharp crack before it was sent flying across the room. Coyne staggered back with a wild, scared look on his face. His head hit the mantelpiece and snapped forward. He crashed to the floor face first and didn't move.

Bernadette and Billy looked from the body to each other. "You've killed him!" Bernadette screamed.

Billy began to tremble. He knew she was right and fear seized him. "C'mon. We've got t' get out o' here."

He reached out with both hands to help her up. She stared blankly at him, her breast still exposed. Billy hesitated, then pulled the torn corner of her dress to cover her. Seeing what he was doing, she recovered somewhat and pulled her coat around her. There was a hint of embarrassment between them. "Yes," she muttered, "Must get out of here."

Billy used his right hand to guide her by the elbow. His left arm throbbed and hung limply at his side, singing with pain. He stopped and looked around the room. The gun caught his eye. "Shit!" he said. Stepping across the room, he picked up the gun and put it back in his pocket. He stood for a moment, scanning the sofa and floor. Satisfied, he crossed back to where Bernadette stood shaking. Grasping her by the elbow again, he led her quickly down the hall. Even in her daze, Bernadette noted that there were no cats. Probably scared off by the shot. Stupid thing to think of, she thought. The front door was open to the street.

"Wait!" Billy commanded. Stepping ahead of her, he slid along the hall with his back to the wall. At the door he squinted into the street, first one way then the other. "Quick!" He jerked his head at her.

They stepped into the street. The light blinded her for a moment but the cool air felt good on her face despite the odor of gasworks it carried. Gripping her elbow again, Billy marched her across to the other side of the street. He walked so quickly that Bernadette had to half run to keep up. His eyes darted around constantly and every few seconds he cast a nervous glance behind them. With one such look he saw two men turn the corner behind them, on the same side of the street as Coyne's house. With another glance back a few seconds later he saw the men hesitate at Coyne's door, then step into the house. He quickened his pace, dragging Bernadette with him.

They reached the end of the block and turned before he finally relaxed his pace, but he still kept a firm grip on her and continued to look over his shoulder. There was a pub at the end of the block. "We need a drink," he stated.

He led her into the saloon and over to a snug. Going to the bar he ordered two large brandies.

"Two pounds twenty pence," stated the bartender, setting the drinks in front of Billy. "Are ye all right? Ye look pale," he continued.

"I'm fine," answered Billy. He handed the money to the bartender and crossed back to the snug. He pushed one of the drinks over to Bernadette, taking a large slug of his own as he did so.

"You killed him ," Bernadette whispered.

"Don't talk about it here," Billy snapped. "Take a shot o' the brandy. It'll help ye calm down."

Bernadette obeyed and he watched her face grimace as she swallowed the drink. "We must call the police," she whispered hoarsely.

Reaching across the table, Billy gripped her wrist. "No!" he said through gritted teeth.

"But he's dead."

"We can't be sure o' that!" Throwing back his head, he drained his glass. "Take another drink."

Bernadette did as he said and felt calmer. "Billy, we must do something. If he's only injured we should call an ambulance, and if the police become involved it'd be better if we told them what happened. I'm a witness. He tried to rape me and you shot him by accident. We can't just sit here and do nothing."

The pub door opened the men Billy had seen enter Coyne's house came into the lounge. Billy cursed inwardly. "We may not have t' report it," he whispered.

Bernadette looked puzzled then followed his eyes to the men. They looked flustered, as they approached the bar. "I need t' use yer phone," one of them said to the barman.

The phone sat on a countertop behind the bar. The barman picked up the receiver. "What's the number?" he asked.

"Dublin 81650," came the reply.

Billy was surprised that the men were not phoning for either an ambulance or the police. He repeated the phone number over and over in his head.

"Long distance. That'll cost ye," stated the barman.

"I'll pay," answered the man.

After dialing the number, the barman handed the receiver to the man, who nodded in appreciation then turned his back to the bartender indicating the privacy of his call.

"Who are those men?" whispered Bernadette.

"I don't know, but I saw them go int' Coyne's house right after we left. Finish yer drink an' let's be goin'." He stood.

Bernadette lifted the glass to her lips and drained it. They left the pub.

"He didn't call the police or ambulance," stated Billy once they were back on the street.

Bernadette stared at him. "What does that mean?"

"I don't know, but remember this number, Dublin 81650. Now let's get back t' yer room. Fast."

The walk from the Starry Plough to Coyne's had taken Bernadette forty minutes. It took twenty to walk back. During that time she threw questions at Billy. Who could the men be? Why hadn't they called the police or ambulance? Maybe Billy was mistaken and it wasn't Coyne's house the men went into. Or maybe they didn't go all the way in to the sitting room.

Billy's only response was that they would talk about it when they got to her room. They used the back entrance to get there.

Bernadette's emotions caught up to her immediately and she collapsed onto the bed and began sobbing. Going into the bathroom, Billy examined his arm. It throbbed incessantly and was already swollen to twice its size but he could flex his fist, even though painfully. Deciding that nothing was broken, he splashed cold water on his face then returned to the room. Bernadette was where he had left her, still sobbing. He sat on the edge of the bed, beside her. "It's all right," he whispered. "Everythin's OK." Reaching out, he hesitantly stroked her shoulders with his good hand.

She stopped sobbing and turned to face him. Her eyes were red and had a haunting look. "Hold me," she whispered. "Please hold me." Sliding over on the bed, she invited him to lie down. He did, wrapping his good arm around her.

"I'm scared," she sobbed. "How did this happen? "

Billy held her more tightly, as much for his own benefit as hers. "It's all right," he repeated.

"You had a gun..."

He held her shoulders and pushed her away from him at arms length. "It was an accident. I didn't mean t' shoot him, but he was..."

Bernadette pulled herself back against his chest. "I know, I know. You saved me, and I know it was an accident. How did you know I was there?"

"Old Mrs Slaugherty an' her husband were at yer father's so I couldn't look around there. I came back t' the Starry Plough lookin' for ye. The landlord told me where ye were."

"Thank God you showed up," she sobbed.

"I heard yer screams from the street..." Realizing she wouldn't want reminding, he allowed his sentence to trail off.

Bernadette was grateful for that. She stopped sobbing and sighed heavily. "What are we going to do?"

Billy gave a deep sigh in return. "There's only one thing we can do."

Pulling away from him again Bernadette studied his face. Her own eyes showed fear and confusion. She looked so vulnerable that Billy wanted to hug her again, protect her again. She saw the tenderness in him. "Report it to the police?" she asked hopefully.

His head shook slowly. "I can't do that, Bernadette. What d' ye think they'd do? First they'd look up me record an' as soon as they had it I'd have no chance. They'd throw away the key to the cell this time."

"But I'm a witness. They'd listen to me, to the truth."

"Maybe," he said. "But I can't take that chance." He reached out and took her face in his hands. "Ye call them if ye want, but if ye do I'll be long gone."

His threat sent an involuntary chill through her. She realized she cared more about him than she admitted to herself. "And if I don't? What then?"

He shrugged. "The only lead we have now is the number the man in the bar called."

"No, there's something else," Bernadette said softly. "A boat. It may not mean anything, but Father Fogarty told me my father kept repeating a name right before he died. Connead Braith. I thought it was a woman, but Coyne said it was a boat that sank in the Atlantic about a month ago, and that my father had some connection to it."

Billy sat up. "A boat? What was the name again?"

"Connead Braith." She spelled it for him.

"There must be some record o' that. We could find out who owned it an' what it was carryin'."

Bernadette sat up beside him. "Billy, this is crazy. We're not detectives. Why don't we tell the police everything we know? Let them handle it? I don't want anyone else getting killed, especially not you."

He heaved an exasperated sigh. "I can't do that, Bernadette. I have t' follow through now, even though I feel like runnin' back home."

This last possibility frightened her again and she gripped his shoulders. "Promise you won't leave me. Promise we'll stick together, whatever happens."

They looked deeply into each other's eyes, both searching for confirmation that this was a commitment the other wanted to make. "I promise," he said finally.

"Do something else for me?"

"What?"

"Get rid of the gun."

He couldn't do that. He felt that he might need it now more than ever, but, at the same time, he was horrified that he'd actually used it to shoot someone, even by accident. He didn't want to do that again. Also, he knew it could be damning if it were found in his possession. "All right. I'll get rid of it," he lied.

Kissing him gently on the cheek, Bernadette worked her mouth around to his lips, pecking gently and quickly. His mouth responded, wanting to catch and hold her in a longer, deeper kiss. Her hand slid down his body to his thigh. His body stiffened and he tried to pull away but she held him tight. "Please," she whispered. "I need you."

His body was reacting to her stroking. "No," he answered without conviction. "Ye're in shock. Ye don't know what ye're doin'."

She kissed him again in response. "Yes I do. I need to know that it's OK. That it can feel good with a man I care about."

Her hand continued to explore, gently massaging the inside of his thigh. His body was responding fiercely. Undoing his belt and fly, her hand found his hardness and she fondled him gently. Rolling onto her back, she opened her legs. Knowing it couldn't stop now, he knelt over her, lifting up her skirt. Bernadette arched her back and her panties slid off easily. Using her hand, she guided him into her.

Along with the pleasure, they both experienced intense relief and lay for a long time afterwards, aglow in the radiant fullness they felt. Eventually getting up, they showered together, dressed and went to a small cafe where they ate dinner.

"What now?" asked Bernadette as they walked back to the Starry Plough.

"I don't know about ye, but I'm exhausted," Billy said.

"Yes," Bernadette agreed. "I'm tired too and there's the funeral tomorrow."

Billy was ashamed to realize he hadn't given a thought to Joe Mallory's funeral, and didn't even know when it was. Trying to sound as if he did know, but it had slipped his mind for a moment, he said, "Aye. What time is it again?"

"Ten," Bernadette replied. "Father Fogarty is going to pick me up at nine thirty and bring me to the house. I'll see you then."

Billy hesitated.

"What's the matter?" asked Bernadette.

"I'll be at the funeral," responded Billy. "But I don't want t' draw attention, so I'll be stayin' in the background."

Bernadette was disappointed. She had felt that being with Billy would help see her through the coming ordeal, but now realized that this might have been unfair to him. "I understand," she said.

They had arrived at the side entrance to the Starry Plough. "I'll see ye after the funeral, then," Billy said awkwardly.

"Yes," Bernadette answered.

They shared a long kiss before Billy turned and began the walk to Joe Mallory's cottage. Bernadette watched him turn the street corner before going up to her room.

18

Bernadette lay fully clothed for half an hour before deciding she wasn't ready for sleep. Realizing that it would still be afternoon in Washington DC and that she should have called Larry to let him know she had arrived safely, she made the sudden decision to call him now.

Going down to the saloon, she asked O'Grady for the telephone. He handed it to her and she dialed her office. Hearing the faint ringing thousands of miles away, she had a fleeting sense of just how far removed she was from her normal life. Long seconds passed before Larry answered. "Hello?"

Thinking it odd that he hadn't announced she had reached Representative Mallory's office, Bernadette said, "Larry, it's me..."

"Bernadette! Thank God! You got my telegram then?"

"What telegram? Where did you send it?"

"I sent it to that Father Fogarty, care of the Main Post Office in Cork. I didn't know what else to do. So you don't know what's happened here?"

Bernadette had a sinking feeling. "No. What?"

Larry took a deep breath before he answered, "You're under investigation by the FBI."

Bernadette was stunned. "What! What for?"

"They say you've been taking money from the IRA. They've frozen your bank account and taken over the office, won't even let me in. They're going through all your files. I managed to get Sam to intervene and transfer the phone to his office so I can at least answer calls. They've been to your apartment, too."

This last sentence made Bernadette feel violated. The thought that strangers were, maybe even now, sifting through her belongings and private things tore at her. The phone hung limply in her hand.

"Bernadette, are you still there?" Larry asked urgently.

She snapped out of her shock. "Yes, I'm here. What the hell's this all about, Larry?"

"I don't know. All they'll say is you've been getting money from the IRA. I do have an idea..." he added reluctantly.

"Yes?" said Bernadette, annoyed at his hesitation.

"Remember I told you about the ten thousand dollars that showed up in the bank account?"

Bernadette remembered. "Yes."

"Well, another ten thousand dollars showed up the day you left for Ireland."

Sensing a noose tightening around her neck, Bernadette felt a surge of anger toward Larry. It subsided quickly when she realized he wasn't to blame. It was her own fault. "Have you contacted my attorney?" she asked.

"Yes," Larry replied. "He's doing what he can but he told me this morning things don't look good. He wants you to call him right away."

"Yes, all right. Can you transfer me to him when we're done?"

"Sure."

It suddenly struck Bernadette that there was might be a tap on the phone. "Larry, I need you to do something. You know my friend who works for the firm? Don't say his name on the phone, but you know who I mean?"

"Yes?" Larry sounded puzzled.

"I want you to call him right away. From a pay phone. Give him this name, Connead Braith." She spelled the name. "Got it?"

"Yes. Connead Braith," Larry repeated.

She glanced at her watch. It was seven thirty. "What time is it there? Two thirty?"

"Yes," Larry answered.

"Tell him I'll call him at five o'clock tonight, Washington time, at the restaurant. He'll know where it is."

"Do you need the number of the restaurant?"

"No. I'll get it through directory assistance."

"If you'll give me the name, I can get it for you," Larry offered.

Bernadette sighed. "Larry, there may be a tap on this phone, which is fine, since we have nothing to hide, but I have to protect my friend's identity. That's why I want you to call him from a pay phone. I don't want the FBI showing up at the restaurant. Other than that, we cooperate fully with them. Understand?"

"Yes, of course." Larry sounded somber. It had not occurred to him that the telephone might be tapped.

"OK. You can transfer me to Don now."

"Right. Do you want his number in case we get cut off?"

"Good idea."

Larry recited the number then said, "I'll transfer you now."

Bernadette heard a click on the line and waited for what seemed a long time. Another click, then the voice of her attorney. "Bernadette?"

"Don. What's going on?"

"I was hoping you could tell me."

"I don't know anything. Larry handles the bank account and I'm sure he's told you all he knows."

"Yeah, but it wasn't much. All we know is someone's been depositing a lot of money into your bank account. The deposits were wired from Dublin. None of this means anything to you?"

"Only that I'm being set up."

"Set up? By whom? What for?"

"I don't know, Don, but I have a suspicion. Look, I know this doesn't help you, but I can't deal with this right now, with my father and all."

"Yes, of course. I'm sorry, Bernadette. You take care of things there and I'll take care of things here until you get back. Any idea when that will be?"

"The funeral's tomorrow morning, so maybe Monday or Tuesday. I'm not sure when I'll be able to get a flight."

"OK. Well, I'm doing what I can. I've requested a restraining order on the basis that by taking over your office they're interfering with your ability to represent your constituents. They'll probably argue national security overrides that. There will be a hearing on it tomorrow.

I've also got a call in to Speaker Sullivan. Maybe he can do something to stall them until you get back, but I've got to tell you Bernadette, from what little I know so far, and from what you said, this could be dirty."

"I think it already is," Bernadette said. "And Don, they may have a tap on my office phone."

"They do. I saw the court order. But they better not be listening in now to an attorney and his client." He shouted this last sentence into the phone, for the benefit of eavesdroppers.

"Don, I know you'll take care of things. I'm sorry I can't be there…"

"Don't worry, Bernadette. A few days won't make any difference."

"I suppose not. Well, I guess there's nothing else to say right now. Thanks, for your help."

"Yeah. Well, I'll see you in a few days then."

"OK. Goodbye." Replacing the receiver, she stood for a moment breathing deeply. It was an effort, but she realized she had to put this all out of her mind and deal with one thing at a time. Politics would have to wait.

O'Grady was standing beside her and took the phone from her hand. As he replaced the receiver he said, "Near enough twelve minutes t' America."

"Put it on my bill!" Bernadette snapped.

"All right," stammered O'Grady, shocked at her temper. He slunk away to the far end of the bar.

Returning to her room, Bernadette wracked her brains trying to make sense of what was happening. She wished Billy was with her.

———

On his way to Joe Mallory's cottage, Billy passed a telephone kiosk and decided he too would make a call. He dialed the number he had overheard the men from Coyne's house call from the pub.

A man's voice, with an American accent, answered. "Yeah?"

"Hello," said Billy, then tentatively, "Is this Dublin 81650?"

"Who are you calling?" the man asked, suspiciously.

Billy tried to imagine who the men at Coyne's might have called. After a minute, and before Billy could think of anything, the man at the other end hung up.

Billy next dialed Baxter's number. He stated that he had nothing to report yet, but he was getting close. In the meantime, he needed some help. He gave Baxter the name Connead Braith and the Dublin phone number he had just called, and asked him to run them through whatever computers he had access to. Baxter was not happy, and threatened Billy that this had better be important and had better have something to do with the assassinations of the British politician. Billy lied, assuring Baxter that it did. He asked when he could call back for an answer.

"Is it that urgent? It's Friday night, you know," Baxter said huffily.

Billy couldn't resist the chance to cause Baxter some discomfort. "Aye, it is that urgent. If I don't get the information tonight, I might miss out on somethin'."

He heard Baxter suck in a deep breath. "Phone back in a couple of hours. You'd better not be screwing me about…"

"I'll call back at ten," Billy said, hanging up.

―――――

A few minutes before ten p.m. Bernadette went back down to the saloon and asked O'Grady if she could use the phone again, in private. He seemed hesitant when he found out she would be calling America again, but a twenty pound note dispelled his qualms and he allowed Bernadette to make the call from his kitchen, away from the bar.

Five minutes passed while Bernadette got the restaurant number from directory assistance, called the restaurant and had her party paged. She hoped he hadn't left already, and was relieved to hear his voice on the other end of the line. "Bernadette?"

"Roger. How are you?"

"I'm fine. I heard about your father. I'm sorry."

"Thanks. I don't want to keep you any longer than is necessary. Did you find out anything about Connead Braith?"

"Not much. There is a file, but I can't access it. It's high level."

"There was nothing? No information at all?"

"It's a Level One file, Bernadette. Nobody can get to it without going through the director. I assumed you didn't want me to try that."

"You've no friends who could see the file?"

"Not a Level One. It means what it says. They even trace attempts to access it, but I used an expired logon, so they won't be able to trace me.

All I could tell from the screen was that the file number contained a code number, a reference to one of our embassies. I looked that up and it turned out to be the Irish embassy in Dublin."

"What does that mean?"

"At some point the file was open to somebody at the embassy, but it isn't now. I tried going in that way."

"I see. Well, thanks for trying, Roger."

"No problem, Bernadette. I'm sorry I couldn't be more help. Maybe we can get together for lunch when you get back?"

"Sure. I'll treat. Thanks again."

"Any time. See you."

She heard the click as the connection was severed.

―――――

Baxter was upset when Billy phoned at ten o'clock. "Damn you. You've put me to a lot of trouble and it better be worth it. I stuck my neck out for you. Trying to get this information was like pulling teeth. I wound up in a fight with MI5 and had to call the Home Secretary's office."

"Ye must've found somethin' important, then?"

"Get this straight. What I'm going to tell you is top secret. If you breathe a word of it, you'll be a marked man, and I won't be able to protect you. Understand?"

Billy was in no mood for this. "It's yer choice. If ye want t' know who bumped off yer politician, tell me. If ye think this secret is more important, then don't tell me. I don't care!"

The sigh from Baxter told Billy that he'd won. "All right. Some genius in MI5 decided that a good way to track the IRA arms supply network would be to supply them with some guns, then follow their import and distribution chain. So, they set up shop as an arms dealer in Mexico and made sure the IRA heard about their cheap prices, top of the line merchandise and no questions asked policy. It worked. The IRA came sniffing and struck a deal for enough arms to start a war. They loaded them onto your boat, the Connead Braith. Then a complication arose.

The Connead Braith sailed across the Caribbean and up the Florida coast. MI5 didn't want the operation blown by the American Coast Guard, so they told the Yanks what was going on and requested that the boat not be interfered with. The Americans agreed, but they would not allow MI5 to monitor the boat while it was in American waters. The Yanks would do that themselves. Once it left their jurisdiction, they would inform MI5, who could take over the surveillance again. MI5 wasn't happy, but they had no choice, so they agreed, and waited to hear from the Americans.

When they did hear, it was a shock. The Connead Braith exploded and sank in the Atlantic Ocean. The Americans said it happened so fast that the cutter they had tailing the Connead Braith couldn't get to it in time to do anything. There were no survivors.

MI5 thinks there must have been a fire on board the Connead Braith which caused the ammunition and explosives to blow up. End of story. Now you know why it's top secret."

Billy whistled lightly through his teeth. "No wonder MI5 didn't want t' tell ye."

"Right. Anyway, does any of this help you? Can you tell me now who it is we're looking for?"

"Not yet, but things are comin' together. What about that Dublin phone number?"

"It belongs to the U.S. Embassy."

Billy said nothing for a moment. That explained why an American voice had answered the phone when he'd called the number.

"Are you still there? Do you want to know exactly who at the embassy has that number?"

"Aye," answered Billy quickly.

"Captain Orville Sudice. Officially he's an assistant to the ambassador. Does any of this help? Are you going to tell me what it's all about?"

"I'm not sure yet, but it's all connected somehow. I'll be in touch." He hung up before Baxter could react.

He felt a definite satisfaction in treating Baxter so cavalierly, but it was a short-lived feeling. His mind was already wrestling with the American connection to the boat and to Coyne. Most of all he wondered about another American, Bernadette. Of course he trusted her, but was it coincidence that she was here for her father's funeral, or was there some other connection? Pondering that question, Billy walked back to spend the night in Joe Mallory's cottage.

19

Father Fogarty showed up at Bernadette's room at precisely nine thirty. She felt self conscious because she was not wearing black, and noted the priest's slight surprise at the color of her outfit, but he was polite enough to say nothing and they drove to her father's.

Entering the cottage, Bernadette found herself in a room full of strangers who fell silent and respectfully edged away from her. She couldn't help looking for Billy, even though she knew he would not be there. She noticed the glances she received and heard the murmurings about her clothes. She wanted to shout that there had been no time to buy something black and that powder blue was no insult to the dead.

Noticing her discomfort, Father Fogarty approached her. "Sure that's a pretty outfit," he said loudly. "Nice t' see some color for a change, instead o' all this black." Looking slowly around the room, he dared anyone to contradict him.

Bernadette felt like an actress, playing a role. Strangers came up and mumbled their condolences. They seemed as embarrassed as she felt, and appeared relieved when she merely nodded acceptance of their sympathies.

One man however, introduced himself in a whisper as Tom Bradon and asked if he might speak to Bernadette for a moment. He guided her gently to the scullery and out the back door into the yard. "Yer father was a good friend o' mine," the man began. "Did some work for me."

"What kind of work?" Bernadette asked.

The man smiled. "That's not important." His eyes twinkled. "What is important is that just before he, uh, passed on, yer father phoned me about some papers he had."

A chill passed through Bernadette, intensifying when the man looked deep into her eyes.

"He said he'd save copies o' them for me. I wondered if ye'd come across them maybe?"

Bernadette licked her lips. "What kind of papers are they?"

The man continued to study her intently. "Government papers. American government, in fact. Official telegrams."

Bernadette tried to sound innocently curious. "Why would my father have papers like that?"

The man continued to scrutinize her. "They were stolen an' he wanted t' be sure they got t' the, uh, proper people."

Bernadette realized the man must be in the IRA, and was telling her only as much of the truth as he had to. "Well, if I do find the papers, shouldn't I just return them to the American government? I'm American myself, and part of that government."

"Aye, I know about ye," said the man. "House of Representatives, isn't it?" He didn't wait for Bernadette to answer, but instead sighed. "It'd be nice if it was that simple, but I think ye'd do better t' give the papers t' me." There was a tone in his voice which left no room for further discussion.

Bernadette forced a smile. "Well, I haven't found any papers, but if they turn up…"

The back door opened and Father Fogarty poked his head through. He smiled when he saw Bernadette. "Ah, there ye are, Bernadette." His face fell when he noticed the man she was with. "Mr. Bradon, it's been a while," he said with some distaste.

"Aye, Father," Bradon responded. "An' a sad occasion it is." Reaching into his breast pocket, he extracted a business card which he handed to Bernadette. "Ye can reach me there." Nodding at them both, he went back into the house.

Feeling the priest's disapproving eye on her, Bernadette nervously twisted the business card between her fingers. "I suppose we'd better go back inside," she said finally, starting toward the door.

The priest grabbed her elbow. "What did that man want, Bernadette?"

She cast a disapproving look at his hand on her elbow and, embarrassed, he let go. "He was a friend of my father's, just being kind. Said I should contact him if I needed anything. That's all."

The priest nodded to indicate that he knew differently. "Stay away from him, Bernadette. He's one o' them that got yer father in trouble." He turned and went back inside the house.

Following him, Bernadette dropped James Bradon's business card into her purse.

"We should get goin' while the rain's still holdin' off," the priest announced to the room. Then, with an irritated tone he said loudly, "Would yous pallbearers stop tryin' t' hide that drink under yer chairs an' place the coffin in the hearse?"

The four men looked at each other, guiltily. "Right y'are, father." said one, standing. "C'mon boys, let's be at it."

There was a shuffling throughout the room as people edged over to the walls to make space around the coffin. One pallbearer stood at each corner of the casket and on the count of three, they hoisted it unsteadily onto their shoulders.

"Steady now," said the leader. "Open the door wider." They inched unsteadily across the room and out to the shiny, black hearse.

Bernadette watched through the window as they lowered the coffin until its front end rested on the chrome fenders. "All right, boys, when I give the word, push," the leader said.

The front of the coffin was lifted slightly and guided onto the thin, metal tracks which ran into the back of the hearse. "Push!" barked the leader. They strained and the coffin slid into the curtained hearse. "There now, that went well enough." said the leader, closing the hatchback door of the hearse with a slam which embarrassed him.

"Will ye be wanting t' go t' the cemetery?" the priest asked Bernadette.

She knew it wasn't the custom here. Women did not go to the cemetery. The priest had said it to let the others know she might, and nobody had better say anything about it.

"Yes." she replied softly.

"Right then," said the priest, in a tone which dismissed all thought of criticism. "Ye'll be in the first car with me an' Mr. Allen."

Bernadette had met the undertaker earlier.

"The rest o' yous share the other cars," the priest said loudly to the other people in the room. "Are we ready Mr. Allen?"

"Aye. Please, let's be goin'," the tall, thin man answered, frowning at his watch. He was thinking of Elsie Copeland, his next appointment. She was one of three sisters, all in their eighties and the undertaker was confident of further business in the not too distant future, if he made a good impression by being punctual for Elsie. He slipped on his white gloves and held the door for Bernadette. "After you, Miss Mallory," he said formally.

The priest took Bernadette's arm and walked her to the car.

After they were seated, the undertaker peered through the rear window, watching until the other cars which would follow in the procession were ready. He then turned to the driver and said "Proceed, John."

The car jerked into motion. The absence of a warning about driving no faster than fifteen miles per hour told the driver that his boss was in a hurry, but the driver resented working two jobs early on a Saturday morning, and so deliberately held his speed to ten miles per hour.

The priest squeezed Bernadette's arm. "Are ye all right, Bernadette? Ye look a wee bit pale," he said softly.

Bernadette forced a half smile in response. "I'm fine."

"Don't let these people bother ye wi' their ideas about what's proper," the priest said.

Bernadette looked out of her side window. They had reached the outskirts of town. People stood on the sidewalks, men removing their caps and women holding frisky kids to attention as a mark of respect to the dead.

The undertaker turned to the driver. "I think we can go a wee bit faster, John."

Understanding the implied threat in his boss's voice, the driver, cursing under his breath, pressed the accelerator. Nothing more was said until they reached the wrought iron gates of the cemetery.

"We'll be walkin' from here t' the final restin' place," announced the undertaker. "I'll go ahead an' make sure everythin's ready."

Bernadette got out of the car and looked around. The dark gray sky warned of rain.

"C'mon, Bernadette, we'll walk right behind the pallbearers." said the priest, taking her elbow.

They began the formal march along the black, tarmac path. Bernadette thought she saw Billy some distance ahead and off to the side of the path, but the man disappeared behind some trees before she could be certain it was him. She wondered where the grave site was.

"It's not too far," said the priest. "Right over by thon big oak tree."

Her eyes followed the direction of his nod. She could see the diggers, leaning on their shovels, smoking. They tossed away the cigarette butts and straightened up as the procession approached.

The coffin was set down beside the grave, on top of two lengths of rope which stretched across the open hole.

Bernadette noticed the uneven sides and bottom of the grave, caused by gouging shovels. It was not like her mother's neat hole in the ground. That grave had been dug by a machine and was sheer and smooth, with white roots dotted throughout, like shaved whiskers. A machine had also lifted her mother's coffin above the grave and lowered it slowly, with a soft mechanical whirring. It had been a hot, humid day in late August and the grass was parched brown. Bernadette remembered the shiny black limos, shimmering in the heat, and the crickets that jumped through the brittle grass just ahead of her feet as she walked. The grass never browned in Ireland, and no crickets jumped. The land here seemed tamer.

The group formed a semicircle, with heads lowered and hands clasped in front of them. The priest stepped up to the coffin and turned to face them. He adjusted the sash that was draped over his shoulders.

"Dear friends, we have come here today t' lay to rest a man who was known to us all as a good neighbor an' an honest Christian. Joe Mallory goes to a far better place than he leaves behind, but in his leaving, he makes all of our lives a little poorer. A little bit of us all is lost in his passing. Perhaps John Donne put it best when he wrote 'No man is an island'."

Leaning over the coffin, he extracted a small vial of holy water from beneath his vest. "In Patrias Nomini," he intoned solemnly.

Bernadette didn't hear his words. She was fixated on the finality of what was happening. Her father was about to be planted deep into the earth where his body would decay and disintegrate finally into...what? She wondered if her mother and father had already met again in some metaphysical world. The intonations of the priest stopped and the sudden silence acted like a sound which called her attention back to the real world.

Father Fogarty's fingers sprinkled holy water onto the coffin. "May the Lord God our Father keep ye in his arms for all eternity," he finished.

Stepping back, the priest nodded to the undertaker who jerked his head at the pallbearers. Stepping forward to their positions at the corners of the grave, each man picked up an end of rope and wrapped it around his fist. Straining greatly, they balanced the coffin on the ropes, moving sideways until it was above the grave opening. When it was lined up properly, they began to unwind the rope from around their wrists. In this manner the coffin was lowered jerkily into the grave. When it reached the bottom, each pallbearer dropped their end of rope onto the coffin. In unison they stepped back from the grave's edge, each rubbing his palms together to restore the circulation that had been restricted by the tight rope. The priest began to intone in Latin again.

Stepping forward, Bernadette knelt beside the grave. Crossing herself for the first time in years, she unclipped the corsage from her chest, sniffed it once, then tossed it onto the coffin. Deep within herself, she cried, but no tears came to her eyes. She stood and walked over to the priest. He hugged her tightly.

The undertaker nodded to the waiting gravediggers, who began to shovel the pile of black dirt onto the coffin. Bernadette listened to the dirt rattle off the coffin. Large drops of rain began to fall, warning of a downpour. The diggers worked faster, keeping their eyes on the menacing sky.

"We can go now, Bernadette," said the priest quietly. "It's over."

They walked back to the car. Bernadette was afraid they would take her back to her father's cottage. She couldn't stand the thought of having to sit there while more strangers came up and offered their sympathy. "I'd like to go back to my room," she stated.

The priest looked at her, but she avoided his eyes. Finally, he said to the driver, "Did ye hear that, John? We'll take Miss Mallory back t' the Starry Plough."

Smiling to himself, the driver glanced in the rearview mirror. Even this small change in plans would be distressing to his boss since it meant the funeral procession would now have to make two stops, one at the Starry Plough to drop off Bernadette, and one at Joe Mallory's cottage to discharge the rest of the attendees. In the back seat, the undertaker glanced nervously at his watch, wondering how late he'd be for the Copeland sisters. His worried expression heightened his driver's pleasure.

20

Bernadette lay on her bed feeling completely drained. She dozed on and off fitfully, too emotionally wrought to totally surrender to sleep.

During one of her wakeful periods there was a solid knock on the door. She imagined it would be either Billy or O'Grady but was taken aback to find two policemen confronting her.

"Miss Bernadette Mallory?" said one, trying to sound friendly. Bernadette however, heard the slight challenge in his tone. "Yes?" Her own tone was reserved.

"Would ye mind coming with us, please?" the policeman asked, managing to make the request sound like an order.

"What for? What's this about?"

"We'd like ye to accompany us t' the station. We've a car waitin'."

"What for?" Bernadette persisted.

"It'll all be explained t' ye down at the station." There was a tinge of annoyance creeping into the policeman's voice.

"Am I under arrest?"

With a sigh, the elder of the two tossed an exasperated look at his partner. "No. We were just asked t' bring ye in. It'll all be explained down at
the station. It'd be easier for us all if ye came along," he added hopefully.

Hesitating, Bernadette almost said that she had just come from burying her father, but in a way she welcomed this distraction from her morbid musings and tortured emotions, so she finally shrugged and picked up
her coat and purse. She walked between them, down the hallway and
staircase, and onto the street where their small squad car sat. Motioning
her into the back seat, the elder one sat beside her, while the other drove.

"I have a right to know what this is about." Bernadette stated.

The policeman seated beside her turned his exasperated look on her. "If
I knew, I'd tell ye, but I've no idea. We're just errand boys. It'll all be
explained at the station."

Bernadette realized it was pointless to try to elicit any information and
resigned herself to the ride.

She hadn't been in a police car since the time she was picked up for
making a false fire alarm call when she was about nine years old. Katie had
put her up to it, and they both thought it was great fun, especially when
the dispatcher kept asking her questions, letting her describe the imaginary details of the fire, keeping her on the line until the police officer
opened the door of the phone booth. She still remembered the terror she
had felt at that moment.

Katie made it worse by giving a false name and address. She'd explained
later that she did it because she thought they'd just let her out of the police
car and tell her to go on home. They didn't. They took her to the address
she gave and shocked some poor woman by announcing they had her
daughter in the car. When the woman said she didn't have a daughter, the
police were not amused. Neither was Bernadette's mother when the police
handed her over with a stern warning. Her mother had really laid into her
for the disgrace of having all the neighbors see her daughter being delivered home in a police car.

The squad car finally pulled into the police station and Bernadette was led to a sterile interview room containing just a table and two chairs. The elder policeman followed her into the room and indicated that she should sit on one of the chairs, while he stood by the side of the door, obviously waiting for someone else to arrive. He avoided looking at her and Bernadette knew it would be a waste of time to try to involve him in conversation. So she sat and wondered what they wanted to see her about. Coyne probably, but how had they connected her to him? She'd have to be careful what she said.

After a few moments a plain-clothed man clutching a manila folder entered the room. He jerked his head at the uniformed police officer, who slid out of the room, closing the door behind him.

"Miss Mallory," stated the newcomer, crossing the room and taking the chair across the table from Bernadette. "I'm Inspector David Grindley." He laid the manila folder on the table in front of him. "Would ye like some tea?"

"No," replied Bernadette. "What's this about?"

The inspector studied her for a minute then leaned across the table. "D'ye know a man called Coyne? Marty Coyne?"

Looking away, Bernadette feigned thinking about the name. "I don't think so."

The Inspector raised his eyebrows. "Ye don't think so? Are ye not sure?"

Feeling herself getting flustered, Bernadette tried to steady her voice. "I don't recognize the name."

Leaning back, the inspector balanced his chair on its two back legs. "I see. Would ye mind tellin' me where ye were between three an' five o'clock yesterday?"

Again Bernadette looked away. "Yesterday?"

"Aye," answered the inspector serenely. "Just one day ago."

"Well, let's see. I believe I went to the bank. I remember it was just before closing time and I had to hurry to get there."

"Which bank would that've been?"

"Bank of Ireland, on Magrug street."

"Aye, I know it. What did ye do there?"

"I cashed some traveler's checks."

The inspector nodded. "Then where did ye go?"

"Nowhere. I walked back to my hotel."

"But that didn't take ye two hours, did it? What did ye do until five o'clock?"

"Actually, it did take about two hours. I stopped into a few stores."

"I see. Did ye buy anything?"

"No. I browsed. Look, Inspector, what is this about? I'm not sure I have to answer these questions."

"It would help us if ye did. Ye see, Marty Coyne was murdered yesterday at about four p.m."

Bernadette did not have to fake shock when she heard the word 'murdered'. "That's terrible, but what does it have to do with me?" she managed to say after taking a moment to compose herself.

The Inspector held up his palms. "I don't know that it has anythin' t' do with ye Miss Mallory, but here's the thing. In one o' Mr. Coyne's pockets we found a couple o' ten pound notes. A lot o' money for a man like Coyne to be carryin'."

A knot gripped Bernadette's stomach.

"One o' the notes had most o' a bank teller's datestamp on it," Grindley continued. "It was from the Bank of Ireland, Magrug Street branch." He let the words hang, studying her face intently.

Although her throat was dry, Bernadette dared not swallow under his scrutiny.

"We checked wi' the bank. Lucky for us they stay late on Fridays t' balance their books for the week. Sure enough, we found the wrapper with the missing piece o' the datestamp still in the teller's drawer. They save them, ye know, t' help balance their cash.Anyway, the teller remembered openin' a fresh bundle o' tens t' serve an American lady who cashed some traveler's checks. The traveler's checks had yer name on them, an' of course, ye gave yer address as the Starry Plough. That's how we found ye."

The Inspector was smug, obviously trying to impress on her the futility of trying to hide anything from such a sleuth as himself. "So, yer story fits perfectly with what we know from our investigation so far."

A surge of relief swept through Bernadette and she dared hope that maybe the interview was over.

"Of course," continued the inspector, his brows knitting, "There is one thing I don't understand." He stopped, as if puzzling something over in his mind.

"Yes?" asked Bernadette finally.

"If ye got the money from the bank, an' ye didn't spend any, an' ye don't know Coyne, how did he end up with two o' the notes the bank gave t' ye?" This time the Inspector fixed Bernadette with a look that was both challenging and threatening.

She felt the knot in her stomach again, tighter this time. A truthful recollection seemed to offer her salvation and she blurted it out without thinking. "I didn't buy anything in the stores, but when I got back the Starry Plough I paid a bill I had run up there. Twentytwo pounds and some odd pence."

The inspector looked disappointed. "I see. Well, that might explain it. Coyne was known t' drink in the Starry Plough from time to time. He maybe was in there after ye paid yer bill an' the notes got passed t' him that way."

Again Bernadette felt a surge of relief, even though she detected a hint of regret in the Inspector's voice.

"We'll have t' check with the Starry Plough of course, but I'm sure that's only a formality," continued the Inspector.

Bernadette's stomach knot tightened considerably as she realized the possibility of the police finding out that she'd been given Coyne's name and address by O'Grady.

"Well, I think that pretty much clears things up as far as ye're concerned, Miss Mallory. We didn't really consider ye a suspect, ye understand, but we did have t' clear things up about the ten pound notes."

Bernadette nodded weakly and the Inspector got to his feet, closing the manila folder and tucking it under his arm. "Ye're free t' go. I'm sorry for any inconvenience we've caused ye. I'll have a car take ye back to yer hotel."

"Thanks, but I think I'll walk," Bernadette responded softly, rising from her chair.

The Inspector held the door open for her. As she was about to walk through, he clicked his fingers as if just remembering something. "I don't suppose ye've come across anybody from England, or maybe up north, hanging around the Starry Plough?"

Bernadette froze, and immediately aware of her reaction tried to hide it by forcing herself to continue walking. "No, I don't. Why? Do you have a suspect?"

The Inspector waved his hand dismissively. "No, it was just a chance. The bullet that killed Coyne came from an unusual gun. A Waltham 45. Unusual but not totally unknown t' us. It's standard issue t' British Intelligence. Coyne was involved with the IRA an' I wondered if the Brits maybe sent one o' their agents t', ah, remove him, as they say. Well, never ye mind, we'll figure it out. Thanks for yer help."

Managing another weak smile, Bernadette walked from the police station into the welcome, cool street. Two thoughts dominated her mind. First, that the police seemed dangerously close to knowing something about Billy's involvement in Coyne's death, and second that Billy was an agent of British Intelligence. She didn't know which revelation shocked her more but she was determined to warn Billy about the first and confront him about the second.

Arriving at her father's cottage she entered without knocking. Billy was not downstairs, but she could hear noises from upstairs. Climbing the stairs she came upon Billy in her father's bedroom, searching the dresser drawers.

"Billy," she said firmly.

He spun around, startled, but relaxed when he saw Bernadette. "Hello," he answered.

"Did you find what you're looking for?"

"No. I searched downstairs already. I don't think it's here."

"I didn't see you at the funeral," she said softly.

He swallowed hard, realizing she should have been his immediate concern. Crossing the room he hugged her tightly. "I was there," he whispered. "I stayed in the background. How are ye doin'?"

Bernadette was glad to hear him finally ask that. "I'm fine. Really." She forced a smile to convince him.

Walking into the room, she sat on the bed. "Come and sit down," she said, patting a spot beside her.

He sat beside her. "Is there somethin' else?" he asked.

"Why do you ask that?"

Billy shrugged. "I don't know. Ye seem like there's somethin' else on yer mind."

She studied him for a minute and Billy knew there was something.

"Where did you get the gun?" she asked finally. Watching him carefully, she detected the guilty look that played about his eyes before he recovered.

"Why d' ye want t' know that?" he answered carefully.

"Where?" she persisted.

He looked away from her. "I bought it in Belfast, from a man in a pub."

Reaching up, she placed her hands on his cheeks, guiding his face toward her. "Why?"

He managed to still avoid her eyes. "I thought I might need it when I came here, for self-defense. I was wakin' into an IRA den, after all. I didn't intend t' use it, just wanted t' be able t' scare people off if I had t'."

"I don't believe you," she stated.

Giving her an angry look, he stood up. "What does that mean? Where d' ye think I got it?" His eyes met hers now, flashing defiance.

"From your employer."

Billy looked puzzled. "Me employer?" He was thinking of Harland and Wolff.

"Yes, your employer, British Intelligence." Bernadette kept her eyes locked into his.

Blinking rapidly, he looked away. "Who told ye that?"

"The police."

His head whirled back to face her. He looked scared.

She pulled him back down to sit beside her on the bed. "I just came from the police station. They questioned me about Coyne, said the bullet came from a gun issued to British Intelligence agents. They're looking for someone from England, or up north."

Billy slumped forward. "Jesus," he muttered. Then, sitting up with a look of genuine alarm he said, "How did they link ye t' Coyne?"

"It's a long story and not important. I think I've convinced them there's no connection between us, but I have to get to the landlord at the Starry Plough before they do."

Billy buried his face in his palms. "Jesus," he repeated. "What are we gettin' int'?"

Bernadette gently pulled his hands away from his face. "Why didn't you tell me you worked for British Intelligence? The police think they might have sent someone here to kill Coyne. Is that why you're here? Was it a coincidence that I happened to be at Coyne's house?"

His face took on a horrified look. "No! It was an accident. Ye were there. Ye saw...."

"OK. OK." She patted his hands to calm him down. "But why didn't you tell me you worked for them? And what else haven't you told me?"

Billy gave a heavy sigh. He was humiliated. "All right. I didn't tell ye the whole truth. Yer father didn't contact me, he contacted British Intelligence in Belfast, but he did ask that I be the one t' come here. Believe me, I didn't want to."

"Then why did you? Why didn't you just refuse?" Bernadette challenged, unsure if he was being truthful.

He shook his head in resignation. "Remember I told ye the Irish wanted t' make an example o' me, t' show how tough they could be wi' terrorists?" Bernadette nodded.

"Well, they gave me twenty years. Can ye believe that? Twenty years at age eighteen! I'd a' been an old man when I got out.

Anyway, soon after me sentencin', two men came to visit me. One was from British Intelligence and one was from Irish Intelligence. They were trying to work out a prisoner swap. The Irish were holdin' two agents the British wanted freed, and the British had some Irish fella. They'd a good idea who robbed the bank wi' me an' suspected them o' killing other people north and south, so both sides wanted them put away. Givin' them t' the Irish would even up the swap.

They offered me a deal. I wouldn't have figured in at all, except they needed me t' testify against me accomplices. In return, they'd reduce me sentence." He paused and averted Bernadette's eyes. "I took the deal."

She sighed. "Then they threatened to tell someone what you'd done."

"Aye. They could tell either the IRA or the UVF. The IRA'd be after me because o' the fella killed in Dundalk, an' the UVF'd kill me for turnin' in their men."

"I see," said Bernadette, disappointment clear in her voice.

"I had no choice!" Billy said imploringly, his wide eyes meeting Bernadette's again. "I've an ex-wife an' an eleven-year-old daughter in London. They threatened t' harm them."

Bernadette was shocked. She stared blankly at him then stood and walked around the bed to the window which overlooked the back yard. Billy's eyes followed her. She pulled back one side of the window curtain. "Well, so far I've found out you have a wife, a daughter, and you're working for British Intelligence. Is there anything else I should know?" Her voice wavered between sarcasm and disdain. "How often do you see them?"

"She's my ex-wife. We got married because she was pregnant, not because we had any great love for each other. I wanted t' do the right thing, but it turned out t' be the wrong thing an' we grew t' hate each other. She took the girl an' went t' London two years ago. I haven't seen either o' them since."

His voice cracked at this last remark, causing Bernadette to turn around and face him again. He sniffled and she felt an overwhelming urge to comfort him. She walked to him with her arms outstretched. "I'm sorry," she said. "I didn't know." She squeezed him to her bosom.

At first he just sat there, unresponsive, but as she hugged him and caressed his forehead, he began to melt and returned her embrace. Finally, he sighed and whispered "There is nothing else, Bernadette. I didn't tell ye because I didn't think it mattered. I wasn't trying t' deceive ye."

"It's OK," she whispered. She gently broke their embrace and smoothed his hair. "But you must be careful. The police will be on the lookout for anybody from up north.

We may have to hide your accent by pretending you can't speak," she added with a smile which he returned half-heartedly.

She suddenly felt an overwhelming desire to protect him, to keep him with her in this room, away from the police, the IRA, the UVF, everyone. She pulled him to her, hungrily kissing and caressing. He responded, and they made feverish love on top of the bedcovers. Afterwards, worn out, they crawled under the sheets and slept.

21

They woke to a church bell summoning local worshippers. and enjoyed the sound for a while before Bernadette finally said she was hungry. Billy was too, so they walked into Connevarve, where they found a small cafe open. They each ate a large, greasy breakfast of eggs, bacon, and soda bread washed down with lots of tea. Sated, Bernadette asked, "How would you like to go for a walk? I'll take you to a place I used to go when I was a girl."

"Lead the way," answered Billy.

She led him out of the village and across the fields, stopping to show him a stream where she would go with her father to catch frogs for use as fishing bait. From Billy's expression she saw that she had triggered some unpleasant thought in him. "What is it?" she asked.

"Nothin'," he answered quickly.

"Tell me," she urged.

He sighed. "I was just thinkin' about...Ah, nothin'."

Suddenly Bernadette knew. He was wondering what his own daughter was doing right now, who might take her for walks, and whether she thought of her father at all. Feeling guilty that she had caused his depression, and not knowing what to say, Bernadette squeezed his hand comfortingly. Returning the squeeze, he smiled weakly. They continued in silence until they reached their destination.

As far as Bernadette could tell, nothing had changed about the hill. The sheer granite cliff known as Cromwell's Nose sneered above the town. Scattered about the scree below the cliff were short, straight trees, sticking out like week-old stubble on a chin. She marveled at how they stood proudly among the rocks, defiantly surviving.

In the distance sat the town, squat and dirty, with plumes of black and gray smoke rising from its innards, a malignant tumor on the face of the green, rolling landscape. Beyond the town, the gray sea looked painted and unsympathetic.

They sat on the grass, Bernadette welcoming its cool dampness. Plucking a blade, Bernadette was about to put it between her lips when Billy reached over and pulled it from her hand. He ran his thumb and forefinger along its length. "Didn't anybody ever tell ye not t' suck grass? It might have worm's eggs on it," he said holding the now de-egged grass out to her. "An' they might hatch in yer stomach."

"Oh? And I'm supposed to feel better now that you've wiped it off with your sweaty fingers?"

Billy smiled. "Some people get turned on by sweat."

Looking at him coyly, Bernadette ran her tongue slowly along the length of the grass blade.

"Ye'll get a cut doin' that," he admonished mildly.

"Yeah? Well, there's always some risk with aphrodisiacs, isn't there?" Bernadette replied with a twinkle in her eyes.

Billy shook his head in mock resignation.

Her tongue found the grass surprisingly sweet. Lying back she pulled Billy down beside her, holding his hand. They lay for a moment looking at the puffy white clouds which sailed above them. "What do you see?" Bernadette asked.

"Where?"

"In the shapes of the clouds."

Saying nothing for a moment, he studied the cloud formations. "I see a wizard ridin' a camel," he announced finally.

"Where?"

He pointed with his free hand. "There. See, he's got a pointed cap, a curved nose, pointy chin an' a flowin' robe. He's sittin' side-saddle on the camel, between its two humps."

"What an imagination," Bernadette said. "I can't see anything like that."

"Well, what can ye see?"

Placing the blade of grass between her teeth, she concentrated on the clouds. "Ships. A great armada sailing across an ocean of blue."

"Maybe they're alien spaceships," Billy said.

Bernadette turned and poked him gently. "I didn't make fun of you…"

Their eyes locked. Reaching out, he slid the grass from between her teeth, letting it drop to the ground. Putting her hand on the back of his neck she guided his lips onto her own. The kiss was sweeter than the grass had been. Closing her eyes, she savored the silence, and the sensuous moistness of his lips.

Suddenly a dog barked. Bernadette sat up abruptly. Down the path, a young couple walked toward them, arm in arm. Ahead of them stood the dog, twitching his nose at the air and holding his tail erect. He barked again, in the direction of Bernadette and Billy. "Blackie!" called the young man. "Come back here!"

Billy tried to pull Bernadette gently down beside him again, but she felt the loss of their privacy and said. "Let's go." Standing, she brushed at her dress.

Billy continued to lie for a moment, then realizing too that their moment had passed, he sighed and stood beside her.

"We can find another spot," she assured him, with a look of promise. Looking around, she saw the old stone wall that ran to the ruins. She led Billy in that direction, away from the couple.

The ruins had changed. She remembered them as almost spiritual. The gray, stone walls which had soared to the heavens above her as a child, now seemed small, three stories high, perhaps. No comparison to the modern monuments to bureaucracy in Washington. They entered the small, square tower.

From the history she had learned in school, she had always thought of the walls as being soaked in monks' blood from Cromwell's visit. Damp moss clung in the dark corners and a rusted, iron ring still hung on the back of the rotted door. The sense of history though, had fled, replaced by crushed Coke cans and broken beer bottles. The ashes of many fires covered the ground and the walls were smoked black in places. Urine stains fouled all four corners.

A sadness came over Bernadette. The monastery had always been special to her. A place to be alone when she needed to escape the squalor of her daily life. Her greatest pleasure had been to imagine these ruins as her private mansion, with the cloisters her country garden. Now the vines were gone, replaced by patches of nettles, which seemed to exult in their invasion. She wondered how the ancient monks would feel if they could see now what had been their home.

Billy looked disgusted. "I hope this isn't the spot ye had in mind."

The sound of voices and nearby barking of the dog told them that the young couple were also headed to the ruins. Girlish giggles and insincere protestations made Bernadette imagine they had come here for cold sex, and she resented this final act of sacrilege, even though the place had been a thrashing ground for couples for longer than she knew. She also felt hypocritical. What was she looking for, after all, but a place to enjoy the man she was with? But she told herself it was different, she and Billy had feelings for each other. "No. I can't stand this place, and I want us to be alone."

She led Billy through a gap in one of the walls and they cut through ferns and nettles to hook up with the path again, avoiding having to pass the couple and their dog. Bernadette continued quickly along the trail.

As they rounded a sharp turn in the path, a figure stepped from behind a tree, into their path.

It was Katie.

"Katie! What are you doing here?" Bernadette asked.

"I was lookin' for ye. O'Grady down at the Starry Plough didn't know where ye were. When I didn't find ye at yer father's cottage, I thought I might as well check here, since it's on me way home anyhow." She looked from Bernadette to Billy.

"This is Billy Kingston, a friend of my father's," Bernadette said, then added "A friend of mine too. Billy, this is Katie Mc Clean. We were best friends when I was a girl."

Billy nodded at Katie, but neither of them greeted the other.

"I'm glad you came," said Bernadette, to break the silence. " We had some good times playing in the old ruins, remember?"

"Aye, we did." Katie said softly. There was a hint of remorse in her tone. Then she returned to the present. "Can I talk t' ye alone? It's about Kevin. An' your father."

Bernadette looked at Billy who shrugged slightly and began walking down the path ahead of them.

Bernadette turned back to face Katie. "What about my father?"

Walking over to a large rock at the side of the path, Katie sat on it, beckoning Bernadette to sit beside her. Bernadette did. Katie brushed her toe in the dirt keeping her eyes fixed there, away from Bernadette. "I don't know where t' start. I suppose with Kevin. I told ye he'd turned up again. Just showed up on me doorstep one night, about ten o'clock. Thank God neither Paddy nor Roy were home. I didn't recognize him at first. He was different, harder somehow. I was terrified, afraid o' what he wanted, an' feeling guilty. I was scared Paddy or Roy'd come home , so I got him t' agree t' go for a walk with me, t' get him away from the house.

When I told him I was married, he said he'd expected that an' I shouldn't worry, he didn't intend t' upset me life, just wanted t' see his child. He didn't even know if it was a boy or a girl.

He wanted t' know what Roy was like, his characteristics an' such. I told him, an' explained that Roy'd be goin' to college next year. I tried t' explain that the boy didn't need any disruptions at this point o' his life. Kevin said he understood, but he wanted t' meet him. Said I could tell Roy he was just an old friend. I tried arguin' against it, but me heart wasn't in it. I mean, how could I deny him the right t' meet his own son?

So, I arranged it. I think Roy knew right away that Kevin was more than a friend. In fact he jokingly asked me if he was an ould flame o' mine." She glanced at Bernadette and smiled forelonely. "Anyway, they met a few times an' got along well. I don't know if it was because they were father an' son, or if it was the stories Kevin told. Roy's at an impression-able age an' he thought Kevin had led an exciting life.

Then, one night Kevin showed up unexpectedly. I knew right away something was wrong. He gave me an envelope an' said that if anythin' happened to him, I was t' give the envelope t' yer father. In the meantime I was t' hide it in a safe place. He said he'd still be meeting Roy the next night. Then he left.

I knew he was in trouble again, but I didn't want t' know what it was, so I didn't even open the envelope, just hid it in me dresser drawer.

The next night, Roy came back early. Kevin hadn't shown up. I knew then that whatever it was he'd been afraid of must have happened. In a way, I hoped it had. He was beginnin' t' influence Roy t' the point that he talked about not goin' t' college. Said that Kevin might be able t' get him a job.

Was that terrible o' me, t' hope somethin' had happened to Kevin an' he'd be gone from me life again?" She looked at Bernadette.

"It's understandable," Bernadette reassured her. "Did you give the envelope to my father?"

"Aye. I brought it over t' his house last Sunday evening. He opened it right away. I could tell by his face that it was somethin' shockin'. He asked me where I got it but I said I couldn't tell him that an' he didn't press me further. I watched him put the envelope in that little cupboard by the fireplace. He thanked me for deliverin' it, an' I left.

The next day, two men showed up at me house. They wouldn't say who they were, but I could tell they weren't friends o' Kevin. They wanted t' know if I'd seen him. I said no. They said I was lying, that they knew he'd come t' me. They searched the house for him, then they began about the envelope. Had he given me anythin'? Where was it? I denied everythin', but they kept on, threatenin' t' tear the house apart lookin' for it.

Then Roy came home, an' they smiled at me. Evil smiles. They whispered that if I didn't tell them where either Kevin or the package was, they'd hurt Roy..."

She grabbed Bernadette by the arm. "What could I do? I didn't know where Kevin was an' I was terrified they'd hurt Roy!" She began to sob hysterically. "But please God, Bernadette, I didn't know they'd hurt yer father! I thought he'd give them the envelope!"

Bernadette gripped Katie's shoulders. "It's all right Katie. I don't blame you. Tell me what happened."

Sniffing her sobs into subsidence, Katie scraped at her eyes. Her voice was unsteady when she continued. "They got int' a car an' drive off.

I set out for yer father's house right away, t' try an' warn him. I ran all the way, thinking I might get there ahead o' them if I cut across the fields, but I was too late. When I got there, I could hear their voices upstairs. It sounded like they were tearin' the room apart. I got scared and left before they found me there."

She lowered her head into her palms. "I'm sorry, Bernadette. Maybe I could have done something...told somebody..."

Putting her arm around Katie's shoulder, Bernadette stroked her old friend's hair with her other hand. "You couldn't have done anything and might have wound up getting hurt yourself. You don't have any idea who the men were?"

Katie shook her head. "None. I'm terrified they'll come back."

"And you never saw what was in the envelope?"

"No." Katie's reply seemed a bit too fast and emphatic.

"That's too bad," said Bernadette. "If we knew..."

Katie looked at her. "Kevin knows."

Bernadette looked perplexed. "But you don't know where Kevin is."

"He delivered a message to Roy at school yesterday, an address. I was t' meet him there immediately. I went yesterday evening, after I left ye. He was angry that I'd taken so long t' get there. I told him I'd been with ye an' had come as soon as I got the message. He wanted t' know if I still had the envelope. I told him I'd followed his instructions, that when he hadn't kept his appointment with Roy I'd assumed somethin' had happened t' him an' took the envelope t' yer father. Then I told him about the men. He was angry at first, but finally admitted that I'd only done what he'd asked.

He kept pacin' up and down, thinkin' hard, an' then he stopped, like he'd had an idea, but he wouldn't tell me what it was. Suddenly he wanted to know all about ye. He's in some terrible trouble, Bernadette, an' he won't say what it is, but for some reason he seems t' think ye can help him."

She stood up and turned to face Bernadette. "He wants t' meet ye."

Bernadette took a second to register the sentence, then stood up too. "When and where?"

"As soon as ye can. I'm t' take ye t' him."

"OK, but I want to bring Billy."

Katie looked at her pleadingly. "He said only ye."

"I'm bringing Billy. I won't go otherwise."

Katie's shoulders sagged. "Then I've no choice."

They walked quickly down the path. Billy was waiting for them, leaning against a tree. He threw a questioning look at Bernadette.

"Katie wants us to meet someone who may know something about my father. We have to go now."

Billy hesitated.

"It's OK," said Bernadette. "I trust Katie."

Katie gave Billy a weakly reassuring look. Wondering what they were getting into, he told himself to be careful and to say as little as possible.

23

Becoming extremely nervous when they reached the outskirts of Cork, Katie led them through a couple of narrow alleys, constantly looking over her shoulder. She explained that Kevin had told her to do this, in case they were being followed. Next they boarded a bus, Katie making sure they were the last ones on. Getting off the bus on a quiet street, they immediately caught another bus going back the way they'd just come. Finally, after entering a pub through the front door and leaving by the side entrance, they stopped in front of an unmarked door, beside a laundromat. Scanning the street before hurrying them inside, Katie quickly closed the door behind them.

They were in a dim hallway, illuminated only by an unfriendly, naked bulb. The hallway led to a staircase. Katie led them up, to another hallway which had a door on either side. Crossing the hallway, Katie stopped before the first door. Putting a finger to her lips, she knocked lightly four times. She craned her ear against the door, then obviously in response to something only she could hear, whispered urgently, "It's me, Katie."

The door opened a crack and an eye peered out. It looked at Katie, then examined Bernadette for a long second. The crack widened, but when the eye noticed Billy, the door quickly closed to an inch again. "Who's he?" a man's voice hissed.

"A friend o' Bernadette's," Katie answered. " She wouldn't come without him. Let us in, Kevin. Ye don't want us standin' out here d' ye?"

The eye in the crack glinted resentfully at Katie, but finally the door opened and Katie stood aside, beckoning Bernadette and Billy inside.

Kevin stood behind the door. Once the trio was inside his tiny flat he scanned the hallway then shut the door quickly, chain-locking it with his left hand. When he turned to face them, he had a gun in his right hand, pointed at Billy.

"I said she was t' come alone," he said, rebuking Katie while keeping his eyes on Billy.

Stepping in front of Billy, Bernadette stated, "We'll leave if you like, but if you want to talk to me, Billy stays."

Kevin kept the gun pointing, although its target was now Bernadette.

"Kevin," implored Katie, "Put that thing away before somebody gets hurt. If it goes off, the cops'll be here in no time."

Kevin kept his eyes on Bernadette for a few seconds with the gun still pointing at her, then he suddenly shoved it into his waistband. "All right. Let's all sit down." He motioned to a sofa, seating himself in a chair facing the door.

Katie, Bernadette and Billy sat on the sofa. No-one spoke for a moment, while Kevin studied Bernadette and Billy intently. Finally Bernadette said "You wanted to talk to me?."

Kevin nodded. "Maybe. I need t' get some things straight first."

"What?"

"Katie says ye're a big shot in the American government."

"Depends what you call a big shot. I'm a member of the House of Representatives. Do you know what that means?"

Kevin ignored the question. "Are ye one o' Ganera's people?"

Bernadette smiled. "No. In fact, I'm not very popular with the president right now."

"Is that so?" Kevin's voice showed genuine interest. "Why not?"

Katie sighed. "I didn't come here to talk about my problems."

Kevin held up a hand. "I have t' be sure ye're someone I can talk to."

Bernadette hesitated, then said. "I'm holding up the release of some money which might help Ganera win re-election."

Nodding slowly, Kevin seemed to make a decision. Abruptly he said, "Katie tells me ye're interested in a woman, name o' Connead Braith. Have ye found her yet?"

He studied her face intently, which made Bernadette suspect that he already knew the answer. "I've found out that Connead Braith is not a woman," she responded evenly.

Kevin cocked an eyebrow. "She's not?"

"No," Bernadette kept her eyes fixed on his. "I was hoping you could help me...."

Kevin nodded slowly again. "Maybe, but first we must agree on what that help might be worth."

Bernadette shrugged. "What do you want?

Trying to make his voice firm, Kevin succeeded only in betraying a slight desperation. "T' get out o' this country. Go t' America maybe. Could ye arrange that?"

Slowly, Bernadette answered. "I'm not sure how I..."

Interrupting her, Kevin's voice took on a hopeful edge. "Get me diplomatic immunity, an' a flight out o' here."

Bernadette studied him, thinking. "Maybe. I have to hear what you've got to say first."

Kevin smiled thinly. "All right. Just remember that what I tell ye might put ye in some danger."

He waited, but Bernadette did not betray any effect the words may have had on her.

"Maybe Katie's already told ye somethin' about me?" Kevin continued.

Bernadette glanced at Katie who lowered her eyes. Turning back to Kevin, Bernadette answered. "Only how you met and that you were in prison."

Kevin nodded slowly. "Aye, well there's things about me she doesn't know." He looked at Katie as if to apologize for what he was about to say. "I was the mate o' a truck driver for a supermarket chain. I didn't do any driving, just helped load an' unload the truck. I enjoyed going all over the country, especially up north. It's like a foreign country up there.

It was all pretty routine for a couple o' months. Then one night me driver asked if I could use a few extra pounds, an' if I could keep me mouth shut. I said I could. We were t' go t' Newry that night an' he told me we'd be makin' a side trip, t' see a man about some butter. He had a scam goin' wi' the warehouse foreman t' load some extra butter on the truck, but they couldn't carry it off without me, because we all had t' sign off that the load was what been ordered.

I asked if crossing the border would be a problem. He said the Irish side was taken care of an' we both knew the northern side didn't bother as much as they should have. They figured the Irish had already checked things out and me driver had made a point o' gettin' t' know the British customs men.

It was scary that first time, but we went through with no problem. We stopped at a farm outside Newry an' unloaded six cases o' butter. I watched the farmer countin' money into me driver's hand, an' we were on our way. I got twenty pounds, which was a lot o' money back then, an' it had been easy."

"This is all very interesting," said Bernadette, "But I don't see where it's leading."

"Ye'll see soon enough," Kevin responded. He continued, "Now that he knew he could trust me, we made side trips every time we went up north. Sometimes it was butter, sometimes bacon. Wi' all the extra twenties I was gettin', I had a good thin' goin'." He shook his head. "Funny, just when things are goin' great an' ye're sure it'll last forever..." Looking at each of them in turn, he shrugged.

"One night, there was a different crew workin' the Irish side o' the border. Me driver wasn't prepared for that, an' I was smitten by his fear, but there was no turnin' back. I knew we were goners when they took us out o' the truck an' put us in a small room wi' two soldiers. It took about ten minutes before the customs men came back an' nodded at the soldiers. They'd found guns, packed in wi' the butter."

I was so angry I took a swing at me driver, but the soldiers separated us an' marched us off at gunpoint. I tried to tell them I knew nothin' about guns, but they weren't interested. Just told me t' be glad I got picked up on the Irish side.

They wanted t' know who all was involved, but I had the sense t' keep me mouth shut about the warehouseman. I told them I didn't know anythin', that it was all the driver's doing. I think they finally believed me, especially since they'd seen me try to punch him.

I couldn't believe it when I got ten years. When you're that young, an' yer parents have always been there t' bail ye out o' trouble, ye think somebody'll save ye again. It's hard t' realize that ye're suddenly on yer own.

The hardest part was what I'd done t' Katie." He fell silent for a moment. "But I've already gone over that wi' her."

Katie smiled weakly in acknowledgment.

"The other hard part, the part Katie doesn't know about, was what happened t' me in prison. It's a tough place, especially when you're young n' good lookin'. There's a lot o' men who haven't seen a woman in years…" His voice trailed off and he licked at his lips. "I had t' take a protector. I wouldn't have survived otherwise."

Getting up from his chair, he walked over to Katie, holding out his hands to her. "I'm sorry."

Shock registered in Katie's eyes and she made no effort to reach out to his outstretched palms. He hesitated, seemingly on the verge of imploring, then let his hands fall back to his sides. "It was either that or be raped every night," he stated. There was a plea for understanding in his voice.

Bernadette touched Katie's hand lightly. "You didn't have to tell us that," she admonished Kevin.

"I did. It's important, the only reason I'm still alive."

This focused everyone's attention on Kevin again. Returning to his chair, he ran his fingers through his hair. "He wasn't so bad. We developed a relationship. I actually grew t' like him. He got out a few weeks before me, but cared enough t' arrange another protector for me, an' told me t' come an' see him when I got out."

He looked at Katie. "I thought about looking for ye, Katie. Honest, I did, but I felt so....I thought ye'd be better off without me, an' I couldn't face me child."

Katie made no visible response, but she squeezed Bernadette's hand hard.

"I went t' live wi' him in Dublin when I got out. I knew he was in the IRA, but I didn't know he sold information about them. Who d' ye think he sold it to?"

"The British, I suppose," answered Bernadette.

Kevin shook his head. "No. He sold it to yer guys."

Bernadette looked uncomprehending for a moment. "You mean the American government?"

"Aye, the embassy. They paid him a wage, every week, just like a regular job."

"Why did they want information about the IRA?"

"I don't know, an' I'm sure he didn't either, but ye don't look a gift horse in the mouth.

He asked how I'd feel about doin' it. I told him I had no information t' sell since he was the only IRA man I knew. He said he'd introduce me. He couldn't keep tabs on all the groups by himself anyway, an' told me it was easy, so I agreed. Thinkin' back on it, of course, smugglin' butter had been easy too." He laughed to himself.

"Anyway, one day he took me t' meet a guy from the embassy. It was in a pub, an' I remember all the time thinking they shared some secret, but I couldn't put me finger on it. They went off on their own for a while an' when they came back, me friend was visibly upset. I figured they didn't want me. God, was I wrong about that.

No offense, but Americans are pretty blunt, an' this one just came out an' stated what the problem was. He an' me friend had been lovers for a while. I could get on the payroll, an' I could keep me relationship wi' me friend, but I had t' have a relationship wi' the American as well. Me friend told me I could refuse, an' we could carry on as we were, but I knew if I did refuse, he might get kicked off the payroll. It wasn't such a hard decision anyway. I was already in one relationship an' had grown used t' it. How hard could it be t' get used t' another one? So, I agreed."

More to break the embarrassing atmosphere that had developed, than anything else, Bernadette asked, "Who was the man from the embassy?"

"Sudice. Orville Sudice. He's a captain in the marines but I think he really runs the embassy."

Billy made a conscious effort to conceal any sign of recognition of Sudice's name.

"What do you mean?" Bernadette asked.

Kevin shrugged. "He made all the decisions. Never needed t' ask approval or check wi' anyone, an' always talked about the ambassador, Humphrey, as if he were an idiot."

"What kind of information did you give them?" Bernadette continued.

"Not much. Names, addresses, where people went, who they hung out wi', what they talked about. Not very excitin' stuff, which isn't surprisin' since all the action's up north, but they took it an' the checks kept comin'. I came t' think it was all a sham, maybe just a way for Captain Sudice t' pay for his pleasures discreetly.

Then, one day he came t' see me at me flat. He'd never done that before, we always met in a hotel room he rented, so I knew somethin' was wrong. He said me friend had been killed in a car accident. I was shocked, of course, but me reaction was nothin' compared t' Sudice's. He cried. I never imagined him capable o' that. He always acted tough an' used t' lecture me about how important it was t' be mentally strong an' self-reliant, but he cried for hours, begging me not t' leave him. I told him I wouldn't an' he finally cried himself t' sleep in me bed.

The next mornin' he was his old self, like nothin' had happened. He didn't come t' the funeral an' I don't recall him ever mentionin' me friend again, an' if I mentioned him, Sudice'd fly into a rage an' remind me about toughness Still, I think Sudice came t' be dependent on me. For what exactly, I don't know, but he always treated me well an' our relationship became...."

He paused and Bernadette ventured "Maybe it wasn't dependency. Maybe he had to take care of you because you knew the truth about him. Not the sexual thing, but you'd seen him cry and maybe that meant more to him."

Kevin seemed surprised at the thought. "Maybe, I never thought o' that...

Anyway, things went on much the same for about a year. Durin' that time I'd become part o' the IRA an' was pretty well known among them in Dublin. I carried messages between units an' once in a while delivered things I didn't care t' know about. Then I found out about the Connead Braith." Bernadette's ears perked and she thought everyone in the room must have noticed.

"The IRA found an arms dealer in Mexico who could supply them wi' a lot of cheap weapons. The purchase was arranged but they needed a boat t' pick up the goods. They came up wi' the Connead Braith. The plan was t' sail her t' Mexico, load the weapons, an' sail back along the American coast before strikin' out across the Atlantic to Cork.

That's where yer father came in. As leader o' the Cork unit, he was responsible for seeing that the boat landed safely, was unloaded an' her cargo shipped up north. The people in Dublin worried that he was too old an' sick, but he'd served his time for them an' they couldn't just cut him out. So they told him he'd be in charge o' that part o' the operation. At the same time they picked another man who would really run things if yer father proved not t' be up t' it. All that was needed now was a dependable crew.

I reported all this t' Sudice, an' for the first time he seemed genuinely interested in the information. Told me t' find out the name o' the dealer, what weapons were being bought an' the exact route the boat would travel on the return trip. It was askin' a lot, but I was so insinuated in the IRA by then that I managed t' get the information."

He stopped, and shook his head, laughing to himself again. "I thought he'd be pleased enough that he might give me a bonus. What d' ye think he did instead?"

No-one answered.

"He told me I had t' be a member o' the crew! I asked him why, an' he told me his plan. He'd arrange for a U.S. coastguard cutter t' intercept the Connead Braith on the return trip, shortly after she turned out t' sea, for Cork. He couldn't take a chance that the boat might escape. That's where I'd come in. I'd make sure the boat stayed on course, an' if I had to, I'd keep the crew covered wi' a gun while the intercept was made. He stressed that things probably wouldn't come t' that, that the Connead Braith would almost certainly surrender without a fight. What choice would they have, in the middle o' the ocean, knowing the U.S. navy would be called in t' deal wi' them if they didn't follow the coast guard's orders?

I told him he was crazy. There was no way I'd do it. Even if I didn't have t' keep the crew covered, it was either spend a lot o' years in an American prison wi' the rest o' them or, if Sudice somehow helped me out, risk having the IRA realize I was the traitor.

He told me that if things went according t' plan, nobody would go t' an American prison. His interest was the weapons. The boat an' men could go free once the guns were transferred t' the coastguard cutter. What could the IRA do? Report t' the police that they'd been hijacked? They'd just have t' put it down t' experience.

I asked him what he was planning t' do wi' the weapons but he wouldn't tell me, just said he'd put them t' better use than the IRA. As for me havin' t' cover the crew, he assured me it almost certainly wouldn't come t' that, but even if it did, he guaranteed that I'd be given a new identity an' a place t' live in America where the IRA could never track me down.

We fought about it for days. He told me his entire career depended on this. It meant glory or oblivion for him, an' there was no real risk t' me, but if he went down, I went down wi' him. His threats an' pleas had no effect. I was adamant that nothing could make me do it.

Then he played his ace. If I didn't cooperate, the Irish authorities could be convinced t' lock me away for a very long time. After all, he'd a lot o' evidence concerning me activities for the past year an', if the U.S. embassy leaned heavily enough, I might wind up rottin' away in prison.

That's when I realized how much I hated him an' hated the life I was livin'. I desperately wanted t' get out o' the whole mess an' just disappear.

I ended up telling him that if I did this, I wanted a lot of money. Five thousand pounds. I thought wi' that much money I could be free o' him an' the IRA . I thought I could disappear an' set meself up nicely someplace where nobody'd find me. So the deal was struck. Little did I know that instead o' tickets t' freedom, each one o' those five thousand pound notes would be a death warrant with me name on it." He paused again.

No-one in the room stirred. He had their rapt attention.

"We set sail about a month ago. I'd never been on a boat on the ocean an' was sure I'd be seasick, but mercifully it was a smooth crossing. We docked one night at a village called Tres Rios in the Yucatan. Trucks came out o' the jungle an' peasants from the village loaded the crates on board. Guns, grenades, mortars, enough t' equip a small army, which, of course, is exactly what was intended.

We were sailing out t' sea again before dawn."

He told them about the Connead Braith's encounter with the U.S. Coast Guard cutter. Bernadette, Billy and Katie sat in horrified silence as he recounted the sinking of the boat.

"I'd no idea they would sink it," he continued, softly, as much to himself as to anyone in the room. "I asked t' speak t' the captain, but was told that no-one on the cutter was allowed t' talk t' me. I was confined t' a cabin an' ignored except when they brought me food." He looked at each of them in turn, obviously ashamed and appealing for understanding.

"Go on," said Bernadette tersely.

He sighed deeply. "We sailed back past Mexico, to a small port in Belize where we were met by a small army o' guerrillas. The weapons were unloaded an' packed into trucks that drove off into the jungle.

We headed back t' Florida where I was put on a flight from Miami t' Dublin. God, I was terrified. An' furious. I was met at Dublin airport an' taken to Sudice's office at the embassy.

He was all smiles an' asked if I'd had a nice trip. I screamed at him about the sinkin' o' the Connead Braith, an' about me being brought back t' Dublin of all places, where I'd be easily recognized. I demanded the five thousand pounds, so I could take off immediately. He laughed some more, then swiveled around in his chair an' opened a small safe behind him. He took out a wad o' notes an' tossed them on the desk in front o' me.

"Here's a hundred," he said "You'll get the rest later. I've some other jobs I want you to do first."

I screamed at him that I had t' get out o' Dublin before I was seen. He told me not t' worry, he'd get me a new identity, even plastic surgery if I wanted, but all in good time.

That's when I lost control. I picked a heavy ashtray off his desk an' smacked him across the head wi' it. He collapsed like a sack o' spuds. Before I knew what I was doing, I was around t' the safe an' took every-thin' out o' it, which was another wad o' bills, this gun, an' some papers. Then I beat it.

When I had a chance t' look at the papers I thought I had him, figured he'd pay me even more than the five thousand t' get them back. I hid out that night an' phoned him the next day. He wasn't dealin', but told me if I returned the papers he wouldn't have me killed. I didn't believe him.

I guessed they'd be watching for me at the airports an' harbors, so I couldn't leave the country, but I couldn't risk remaining in Dublin in case

I ran into somebody who knew I was part o' the Connead Braith crew. I could only think o' one place t' go, an' that was here, t' Katie. I was on me way before I realized that I'd told Sudice about her and where she lived, an' I'd be putting her in danger when he figured out I might come here. Still, I was so sure that I wouldn't survive for long that I suddenly had an overwhelming urge t' at least see me child before they caught up t' me. I'm sorry, Katie. It was selfish o' me."

Katie's eyes narrowed slightly but she said nothing.

"So you gave the papers to Katie and she gave them to my father," said Bernadette.

"Aye, that was another mistake. Can't blame Katie, though, she only did what I told her."

"Why didn't you show up for your meeting with Roy that night?" Katie asked suddenly.

"Two fellas were waitin' outside me digs. I was lucky t' spot them before they saw me. I had t' find a new place t' stay. I did try t' keep the date, but there were two other fellas hangin' around your house. Since ye've no phone, I had no way t' contact you or Roy."

Bernadette spoke. "OK. Now for the sixtyfour thousand dollar question. What was in the papers?"

Kevin smiled. "They were dynamite, all right. Approval from yer president for the whole Connead Braith operation. The idea was t' divert the guns t' Kurdish rebels in Iraq, so they could overthrow Saddam Hussein."

Bernadette gasped.

"I think Sudice even made some money on the deal," Kevin continued. "I saw a lot o' money change hands in Belize. Mind, there was nothin' about that in the president's cable. He just approved the plan, promised all the help he could an' praised Sudice for his ingenious thinking of ways t' work around the communist congress."

Bernadette's face flashed anger but before she could say anything, Kevin continued. "There was something else in the papers, approval of another scheme. If ye think the Connead Braith was bad, what d' ye think the other scheme was?"

No-one answered.

"T' kill a British politician!" Kevin stated dramatically.

"Why would the president of the United States approve the assassination of a British politician?" Bernadette challenged.

"It's all in the papers," Kevin answered. "Sudice got a secret message from Gerry Evans of the IRA, wonderin' what it would take to set up a meetin' between Evans an' the president. Sudice clears it wi' the president that a meetin' can be arranged in return for a large contribution t' the president's reelection campaign."

"Why would Gerry Evans have to pay t' meet the president?" Billy blurted out. "Seems t' me like they're ould friends."

Bernadette held up a finger. "This administration has made an art of selling access, and in this case, everybody wins. The president scores points with Irish American voters, who want to see Britain out of Ireland. Evans, meanwhile, gets respectability. In fact, the IRA was removed from the list of prohibited terrorist groups shortly after Evans met with the president, meaning the IRA can raise money again in the U.S.—far more than the campaign contribution would have cost them."

Bernadette nodded slowly to herself, content that everything so far made sense. "You were going to tell us about the British politician," she continued, turning to Kevin.

"British Intelligence found out about the contribution, and could prove that it came from the IRA. The evidence was turned over t' the Northern Ireland minister. He held on t' it, tryin' to figure out how to use it for his own political gain.

In the meantime Sudice found out that the minister knew, an' received quick permission t' remove, that's their word, remove the minister before the information could be passed on."

Bernadette nodded again. "If people found out that the president of the United States had taken a campaign contribution from the IRA…

So, Sudice hired the assassins and the IRA got the blame."

"Aye," Kevin said. "Who'd imagine the American government was behind it? Even if they did, inquiries would go nowhere. Sudice has a lot o' influence wi' the Irish government, an' I know he owns the police in Dublin, an' probably here too. Why d' ye think there was no inquiry into yer father's death?"

For an instant, Bernadette was shocked by the rhetorical question, then she sighed. "So Sudice probably has the papers back."

"They could still be somewhere in yer father's house." said Kevin, hopefully.

"We looked. They aren't there, and the place was ransacked. They must have found them," Bernadette answered.

"I could still be a witness, testify," said Kevin eagerly, but with diminished hope.

Bernadette studied him for a moment, torn between sympathy and revulsion. "That wouldn't be enough. If we had the papers…"

"Ye won't try t' get me out o' the country, will ye?" Kevin stated, his voice devoid of hope.

"I'm not sure I could, even if we had the papers." She felt a wave of nausea course through her body, but fought it back. "Let's go," she said to Billy and Katie, rising from her seat.

"But I could testify. Surely an eyewitness…" Kevin said loudly, in final desperation.

"I'm sorry," Bernadette answered. "Without the papers we have nothing, and to say anything publicly would put all our lives in danger."

"So ye're not goin' t' do anythin'?" It was less of a question on Kevin's part than a reluctant acceptance.

"I'm sorry. I need time to think…" Bernadette faltered then began walking toward the door.

Billy and Katie rose from the couch and followed Bernadette across the room and out of the flat. Once they were back on the street, walking away from Kevin's flat, Katie no longer seemed concerned about stealth.

"I need a drink," Bernadette stated.

They entered the first saloon they came to. Billy ordered drinks and brought them to the snug where Bernadette and Katie were seated.

"Can ye not help Kevin?" Katie asked Bernadette.

Billy responded. "Can we even believe him? No-one's seen the papers but him."

"But if he's tellin' the truth, about what the papers said, is there no way t' help him?" Katie persisted.

Bernadette looked pityingly at her old friend. "Katie," she said slowly, "I don't know how to put this, but Kevin isn't exactly a nice person. He left you in the lurch, spied on his fellow countrymen for a foreign government, indirectly caused the deaths of his supposed comrades....I'm not sure I even want to help him."

Katie looked hurt. "Everythin' ye say is true, an' I don't like him much either anymore." She looked from Bernadette to Billy and back to Bernadette. "But we were in love once an' he is the father o' me son...."

Bernadette shook her head understandingly. "Maybe you're right. He's more pitiful than anything, but I don't see how I can help him. If only we had the papers...."

"If ye did, could ye get him out o' the country an' over t' America like he said?"

"I don't know. Maybe, but what's it matter? Sudice must have the papers."

Katie's head drooped slightly and she lowered her eyes. "No, he doesn't. I have them."

Both Bernadette and Billy gaped at her, then at each other.

"I didn't tell ye the whole truth about when I went t' yer father's house that night," Katie continued. "I heard the men upstairs shouting at yer father that if he didn't know what they were talkin' about, they'd have t' go back t' the bitch who sent them there an' beat the truth out o' her. That made yer father admit that he had received the papers but he'd already given them t' someone else.

I knew he was only saying that t' protect me, an' I didn't think he'd had time t' do anything wi' the papers, so I sneaked over t' the drawer I'd seen him put them in. They were still there, so I took them an' sneaked out again."

"Why didn't you tell this to Kevin?" asked Billy.

"I was going t', then I got this idea in me head that maybe I could make a deal wi' them an' Kevin could go back t' wherever he'd come from, an' I wouldn't have t' worry about Roy gettin' mixed up in this. I just wanted it all t' end an' have things go back t' the way they were before Kevin showed up. After what Kevin just said though, I know things are beyond that."

She raised her eyes to look at Bernadette again. "If I give them t' ye, can ye get him out o' the country?"

"Katie, I can't promise anything. I'll do my best to help Kevin, but I must see those papers. Where are they?"

"At me house. I figured the men who came looking for them wouldn't come back after yer father told them I'd given the papers t' him."

"I think we'd better get them," said Billy softly. "Now."

They went straight to Katie's house. She retrieved the envelope from a corner of a cupboard in the kitchen, where she kept her pots and pans. Resisting a strong urge to tear open the envelope and read its contents there and then, Bernadette said to Katie, "If I can figure out a way to get Kevin out of your life, I will."

They heard a key in the front door. "It'll be Roy," said Katie anxiously.

A moment later her son came into the kitchen. He looked at the strangers, surprised, then relaxed. "Hello, mum." He waited for introductions.

Katie appeared flustered. "Hello, son. This is Bernadette Mallory. Joe Mallory's daughter, from America. She's back for the funeral, an' this is her friend Billy, ah…"

"Kingston," offered Billy, nodding a greeting at Roy.

Roy returned the nod. "I'm sorry about yer father," he said to Bernadette.

Bernadette noticed his eyes fall on the envelope she held. "Thank you," she said. She put the envelope into her purse as if it were an inconsequential afterthought.

"They were just leavin'," Katie said hastily, her look urging Bernadette and Billy to go now.

Seeing the earnest wish in Katie's eyes, Bernadette nodded. "Yes. We've already taken up too much of your mother's time. Nice to have met you."

Leaving Katie's, Bernadette and Billy hurried back to Bernadette's room. Right away Bernadette noticed the envelope on her bed. It was the telegram Larry had sent to Father Fogarty. Although she knew it was foolish, she didn't like the idea that someone had been in her room when she wasn't there. Quickly reading the telegram, she set it aside. Sitting on the bed, she removed the manila envelope from her purse. Billy sat beside her and they scanned the papers together.

"Exactly what Kevin said, but are they genuine?" asked Billy.

"As far as I can tell," Bernadette replied.

"Why would Sudice risk keeping them? Why didn't he destroy them?"

Bernadette shrugged. "Insurance t' cover himself in case somethin' went wrong? It would give him something on the president"

"And now ye've somethin' on both o' them," Billy stated quietly. He sounded less than happy.

Bernadette nodded. "Damn right, and I intend to use it."

"How?"

"I'm going to pay a visit to Captain Sudice and tell him I have the papers. I'll promise not to release them to the press if he'll let Kevin go. Then I'll go to the president and demand that he stop the frame-up he's pulling on me."

"That's it?" Billy said doubtfully. "Ye don't think they'll want the papers returned t' them first?"

"They're not in a position to argue," said Bernadette with certainty. "They'll have to trust me to keep the papers out of circulation."

"An' will ye?" Billy's voice sounded hopeful but dubious.

"No. I'm going to hold a press conference on the steps of the capitol in Washington D.C. and release the papers to every news organization on earth. I'm going to destroy Ganera and Sudice and all the other faceless people who think they're above the law."

Billy seemed deflated. "I see, an' ye'll be a powerful woman, I imagine."

"Damn right, I will. This will give the election to Daleman and I'll be able to have any job I want."

"An' what job would ye want?"

"I don't know. I haven't thought about that yet." She looked at him quizzically. "Billy, what's bothering you? You seem like you don't want me to do this. Have you forgotten these people killed my father and are doing their damnedest to destroy me?"

"No. I can understand ye wantin' revenge."

"What then?" Before he could answer, her face took on a look of sudden understanding. "I know what it is. You want the Connead Braith papers to turn over to British Intelligence. But they'll find out when I release them, Billy. It'll only take a couple of days longer. Just tell them you couldn't find…"

"It isn't that," Billy snapped. Then he recovered. "I'm sorry, it isn't that. I decided I'd be better off not givin' them anythin'. That way they'll write me off as useless. If I gave them the papers I'm afeard they'd think I might be useful the next time they need somebody."

"What then? Something's bothering you. Can you see a problem with what I'm going to do?"

"I wonder if ye or Kevin will ever be safe," Billy said softly. "They might take revenge too. They're still powerful men aren't they?"

Bernadette touched his shoulder. "Don't worry. Once I go public, they won't dare try anything. As for Kevin, I'm afraid he'll have to fend for himself. I'll do what I can to help him disappear."

Sighing resignedly, Billy tried to adopt a convincing tone. "I suppose ye know best. I'm just worried. When will we go t' see Sudice?"

"We?" Bernadette stressed the word.

"We're in this together. Remember?" Billy said sternly. "I won't let ye go alone."

Bernadette smiled and draped her arms around his neck. "We'll go tomorrow. Right now I'm ready for bed." She pulled him onto the bed on top of her.

Her lovemaking was frenzied, like nothing Billy had ever known. She seemed intent on satisfying some intense craving that went beyond either of their physical needs or capabilities. It frightened him and he was relieved when she was at last sated and they both fell into an exhausted sleep.

25

Billy awoke to find Bernadette already dressed and applying makeup in front of her dresser.

"Good morning, sleepyhead," she said with a large smile. "I already had a bath and did my toilette, so the bathroom's all yours."

"What time is it?" Billy asked groggily.

"Eight o'clock," Bernadette answered, turning her attention back to her makeup.

Sliding his legs from under the bedcovers, Billy sat on the edge of the bed. "Where are ye goin' t' put the papers when we go t' see Sudice?" he asked.

"What do you mean?" Bernadette asked without looking away from the mirror.

"Well, ye're not going to carry them in yer purse I hope?" Billy said, stretching his arms and legs.

Bernadette stopped applying her lipstick. "You're right. I hadn't thought about that."

"We need t' give them t' someone for safekeeping," Billy said.

"Yes," Bernadette agreed. "I think I know someone we can trust, Father Fogarty."

Billy nodded, satisfied. "Good," he said. Getting off the bed, he went into the bathroom.

When he reappeared about fifteen minutes later, Bernadette was sitting on the bed. "All set to go?" she asked. "I thought we'd have breakfast here, then I'll call Fogarty and Sudice."

"Aye, I'm ready, an' hungry."

Leaving the room, they went downstairs to the empty saloon. The landlord stood behind the bar, as if expecting them. He scowled when he saw Billy.

"Good morning, Mr. O'Grady," beamed Bernadette.

"Mornin'," the landlord responded, continuing to scowl at Billy.

Bernadette felt she had to offer an innocent explanation. "This is my friend, Billy. He came in through the side entrance. We're going to Dublin today."

Billy nodded toward the landlord who ignored him.

"Did ye find the telegram I left on yer bed?" O'Grady asked.

"Oh, you put it there? Yes, I did. Thank you."

"Father Fogarty brought it. He waited awhile for ye but finally asked me t' give it t' ye. I waited for ye, too, but when it got late…Well, I thought ye'd want t' see it as soon as ye got back, it being a telegram an' all."

"Yes, thanks again," Bernadette said. "I wonder if we could have breakfast?"

O'Grady glanced at Billy then looked back to Bernadette. "Both o' yous?"

"Yes. Whatever you can come up with. Scrambled eggs and toast would be fine."

The landlord glared again at Billy, but continued to address Bernadette. "Will ye be wanting it in yer room?"

"We could eat it down here, in one of the snugs, if that's OK?" Bernadette answered. "It'd save you a trip up the stairs."

O'Grady hesitated for a second then nodded. "I suppose it'd be all right. Scrambled eggs an' toast it is." He turned toward the kitchen.

"Can I use the phone while we're waiting?" Bernadette asked.

Reaching under the counter, O'Grady produced the phone, and placed it in front of Bernadette. "Is it a local call?" he asked.

"One is. To Father Fogarty. The other one's to Dublin. I'll pay you, of course."

The landlord nodded and trudged off to the kitchen.

"Friendly, isn't he?" muttered Billy.

"He's all right," replied Bernadette. "Why don't you go and sit down and I'll make the calls."

Billy walked to one of the snugs while Bernadette picked up the telephone receiver. She dialed directory assistance and got the numbers for Father Fogarty and the American embassy in Dublin.

She called the priest first. "Father? Hello, it's Bernadette Mallory. Yes, I got the telegram. Thanks for bringing it. No, it wasn't anything bad, just business. In fact I called my office yesterday and they told me about it, but thanks anyway.

Father, I wondered if you would do me a favor?

I'd like to leave some documents with you for a while. It's just some stuff I'd rather not carry around with me and since there's no lock on my door, I don't want to leave them in my room when I'm gone. You would? Great. Will you be at home for a while? I can come over. It'll take me about an hour...Oh, that's very kind of you. I'd appreciate it a lot. Thanks. I'll see you soon then? Goodbye."

She set the receiver down. "He's going to drive over here," she said to Billy.

"Good. Saves us a walk," answered Billy.

Bernadette smiled. "I'll call the embassy now, to make sure Sudice can see us today."

"Maybe ye should call about trains first, so we've an idea when we'll get there." Billy suggested.

"Good idea," said Bernadette, picking up the receiver and dialing the operator again. After obtaining the number for the railway station, she immediately dialed it. As she received the train times, she called them out to Billy. "Ten o'clock, then one o'clock. Yes, and how long does it take? Three and a half hours? Fine. Thank you." She hung up again. "I'm not sure we can make the ten o'clock," she said to Billy.

Billy glanced at the huge clock above the bar. It showed five past nine. "Depends what time the priest gets here," he observed.

Bernadette nodded agreement. "I'll call the embassy anyway. At least we know we can be there sometime this afternoon."

She dialed the number. "Hello. This is Bernadette Mallory. I'd like to speak to Captain Sudice, please." She smiled at Billy while she was put on hold.

O'Grady appeared from the kitchen, carrying a tray with their steaming breakfast. He went over to Billy and set the tray down. "Will there be anythin' else?" he asked coldly.

"No. This is fine," Billy responded, looking him straight in the eye.

The landlord ambled back into his kitchen, glancing at Bernadette on the way.

Putting her hand over the receiver, Bernadette said to Billy, "You go ahead while it's hot. I'll only be a minute."

Billy began eating.

"Hello?" said Bernadette into the telephone, "Ah, Captain Sudice. Yes, that's right. I wondered if I could come and see you today? Yes, I understand you must be busy, but I think you'll want to see me." She lowered her voice. "It's about a friend of yours, Kevin." She winked at Billy.

"Hello? Captain Sudice, are you still there? I was thinking this afternoon, I'm not exactly sure what time, depends what train I can get. Good. I'll see you this afternoon, then. Goodbye." Replacing the receiver, she walked over to the snug and slid in opposite Billy.

"What did he say?" Billy asked.

"He tried to put me off at first, but when I mentioned Kevin, he somehow found time to see us," Bernadette answered, smiling. "The bastard's going to be squirming and sweating all day, wondering what it's about."

"Aye," Billy agreed, softly, then added ominously, "I just hope he waits for ye t' show up an' doesn't do somethin' before then." He instantly regretted saying it. "I mean…"

Bernadette concentrated on her scrambled eggs. "He won't." She looked up, smiling. "Besides, you'll protect me, won't you?"

"Aye," Billy said quickly. "We're in it together. I'm…"

"Don't say you're sorry," Bernadette interrupted, waving her fork at him, half threateningly. "It'll be fine. Finish your breakfast and let me get on with mine. I'm starving."

Billy smiled in return and nodded.

O'Grady returned , carrying a teapot and they both accepted a refill.

"How much for the phone calls and breakfast?" Bernadette asked.

"Well, let's see now. One local call, that'd be fifty pence. An' a call t' Dublin. Hard t' say how much that'd be. How long did ye talk?"

"About three minutes."

"Well, call that three pounds, then. An' then there's the breakfasts."

Bernadette grew impatient with the computations. "Will ten pounds cover it?"

"Ten pounds? Aye, I suppose so." The landlord was delighted.

Reaching into her purse, Bernadette handed him a ten pound note. "One last thing, do you have any scotch tape?"

"Scotch tape?" O'Grady seemed puzzled.

"Sorry, cellotape," Bernadette interpreted.

"Oh, cellotape. Now I understand. I never heard o' scotch tape before. All the tape I have is Irish." He smiled and waited for a reaction to his joke but there was none.

"I just need enough to seal an envelope."

"Aye, right. Are yous done with these?" the landlord said sullenly, indicating the breakfast plates.

Bernadette nodded. Picking up the dishes, O'Grady headed back to his kitchen, reappearing a moment later with a roll of scotch tape which he laid on the table.

"How much will that be?" Billy couldn't resist asking.

Without looking at him the landlord answered, "Depends how much ye use." Turning, he retreated back to his kitchen.

Smiling at Billy, Bernadette shook her head disapprovingly. From her purse she removed the envelope containing the documents. She was about to apply a strip of tape when Billy reached over and stopped her.

"Maybe we'd better make copies," he suggested. "T' prove t' Sudice that we've really got the papers."

"You're full of good ideas," said Bernadette. "But I wonder if we have time before the priest arrives?"

At that moment there was a loud knocking on the front door of the saloon.

"I guess not," said Bernadette, in answer to her own question. "That's probably him now."

O'Grady came out of his kitchen. "Who on earth can that be, at this time o' day?"

He addressed the question to himself, but Bernadette answered. "I think it's Father Fogarty. He's said he'd meet us here."

Crossing to the stained glass doors, the landlord opened one of them. Father Fogarty stepped into the saloon. "Good mornin', Gerry," he greeted the landlord.

"Good mornin', Father," O'Grady mumbled in return.

Looking around the priest saw Bernadette and Billy. "Ah, there ye are." He strode across the room to their snug, O'Grady closing the door behind him.

"Good mornin', Bernadette," the priest said, then looked at Billy, obviously awaiting an introduction.

"Good morning, Father. This is Billy Kingston. He was a friend of my father's."

Standing, Billy held out his hand. "Pleased t' meet ye, Father."

Grasping Billy's hand, the priest held it tightly. "Don't tell me, now. You're a Belfast man, right?"

Billy nodded. The priest shook his hand. "I've never been there meself, but I'd an aunt used t' live there. She moved across the water when the troubles started." Deciding that wasn't an appropriate subject to pursue, he quickly added, "Well, where's this package ye want me t' look after?"

Bernadette glanced at the landlord who stood behind the priest, paying keen attention to everything. The priest took Bernadette's hint. "Gerry O'Grady," he said sternly to the landlord. "Have ye nothin' better t' do than stand around eavesdropping on private conversations?" He glared at the landlord.

Blushing, the latter stammered, "I'm only waitin' t' see if they're done wi' their tea so I can take the cups."

"Can ye not see they're empty, man? Take them an' yourself away."

Slinking past the priest, the landlord picked up the cups. He hesitated. "Are ye done wi' the tape?"

"No," answered Bernadette. "I'll give it back to you when I'm finished."

The landlord slouched off to his kitchen, the priest watching his back till he disappeared. "I tell ye, I never saw such people for nosiness," he muttered. Then he turned to Bernadette. "Is this the package?" He pointed at the envelope.

"Yes," answered Bernadette. "But I need to make some copies first. Do you know of a place nearby?"

"Aye, there's a shop on Conmeath street. Come on an' I'll drive us over there."

"Is it far? Only we'd like to try and catch the ten o'clock train to Dublin." She glanced at the bar clock.

The priest followed her look. It was nine fifteen. "We can just make it if I give yous a lift t' the station, but we'd better get goin'." He started toward the saloon doors. Bernadette and Billy followed him.

The priest waited in the car while Bernadette and Billy went into the store and made the copies, which Bernadette put into her purse. She then took the envelope with the originals and taped the open flap. Next, she took a pen from her purse and signed her name across the tape she had just applied and then across every seam on the envelope.

"What are ye doin' that for?" Billy asked.

"Just so we can tell if anybody opens the envelope," Bernadette answered.

Rummaging in her purse, she finally pulled out the business card James Bradon had given her at her father's funeral. She taped the business card to the back of the envelope.

"Who's that?" Billy asked.

"Someone I met at my father's funeral," Bernadette replied. "He'd be interested in what happened to the men on the Connead Braith and I think he'll at least take care of Sudice if something goes wrong. Let's go."

Hurrying back to the priest's car, they climbed into the back seat. Bernadette laid the envelope on the passenger seat beside the priest, who sped away from the store. "D' yous have yer tickets?" the priest asked, keeping his eyes on the road.

"No," answered Bernadette.

The priest tutted. "It'll be a close call, then. Better hope there's not a long line." He sped up.

———

Dropping them at the side entrance to the station, the priest said, "The ticket counter's t' the left. You'll have t' hurry."

They got out of the car and Bernadette went to the priest's window, which he lowered. "Thank you, Father," Bernadette said. "If one of us doesn't pick up the envelope from you by midnight, I'd like you to mail it to the address on the back. Don't give it to anyone else, only Billy or myself."

The priest's face took on a look of puzzlement and fear. "Bernadette, if ye're in some kind of…"

"I'm not in any trouble. Just being cautious. Will you do it?"

"Well, of course, but…"

"I have to run," Bernadette interrupted. "Thanks for everything. See you later." Turning, she took Billy's elbow and they ran into the station.

The priest sat looking after them for a moment, then picked up the envelope and read the address on the back. "Dear God, I hope ye know what you're doin', Bernadette," he whispered to himself.

There was no line at the ticket office and they made the train with minutes to spare. Finding an empty compartment, they sat across from each other. The train began to lurch its way out of the station.

They said nothing for a while, then Bernadette leaned toward Billy. "I think it's time we talked about us," she said, staring earnestly into his eyes.

"Aye, I've been thinkin' the same thing." he answered.

Bernadette waited.

"I don't see where we can go wi' this, Bernadette," Billy stated.

"What do you mean?"

"We want different things. Ye want revenge, an' I understand that, but ye also want power, an' I don't understand that."

"You don't understand why I'd want the chance to be able to make decisions and have the power to get things done? To get rid of people like Ganera and Sudice and begin doing some good for people, like politicians are supposed to?"

Billy sighed. "D' ye think Ganera an' Sudice entered politics t' hatch plots an' kill people?"

Bernadette leaned back in her seat. "I don't know. They certainly have shown they have that capability…"

"But did they start out that way? An' if they did, what makes ye think Daleman is any different?"

"I just think he is. My God, Billy, if we give up believing that things can be improved, what hope have we?"

"But what if they don't improve?" he persisted. "What would ye do if ye found out that the same kinds of things went on under Daleman?"

"I suppose I'd have to fight him too, then."

"An' could ye do that as a member of his government?"

"I could try, and if I had to, I'd leave his government."

"Then ye'd be back where ye are today."

Bernadette made no answer.

"On the other hand," continued Billy, "What if Ganera an' Sudice entered politics wi' the same high ideals as ye, but wi' different ways o' getting there? Isn't that really what politics is about? Everyone is for peace, freedom an' prosperity but they argue over how t' accomplish those goals?"

"Yes, I suppose so."

"Well, then, couldn't it be that the system dictates how people like Ganera an' Sudice come to be? Maybe they're required t' be that way in order t' survive. T' retain power so they can accomplish what they see as the greater good."

"I don't understand where you're going with this. I thought we were talking about us?"

"What I'm trying t' say, Bernadette, is that I don't think we can be together. I don't want t' live a political life. Ye do. Ye've geared yer whole life toward accomplishing somethin', an' that's fine, but it's not for me. I want t' live me life away from the scheming an' intrigue. I've seen too much o' it."

"You think I could become like them?"

"I don't want t' find out."

Bernadette was stung by his answer. "What am I supposed to do? Just walk away? " She leaned toward him again. "Look what they've done, Billy! To me, my father, those men on the Connead Braith, the British politician. Christ! They're murderers, and we can prove it!" She slumped back into her seat. "We can't just ignore it. At least, I can't.

Anyway, I thought you wanted to find out who killed my father?" She shot him an accusing glance. "Bring them to justice?"

"I do," Billy answered steadily. "But ye know, Bernadette, yer father told me once that there could never be peace in Ireland because people were too caught up in revenge. At some point, someone has t' decide that the cycle must be broken, so people will stop killin' each other. They have t' do that before they can start talkin' and learn t' live wi' each other. I think that's why he took me under his wing in prison. It was his way o' showin' that such a change is possible, but it has t' begin wi' individual people."

"You think if I forgive Ganera and Sudice and do nothing with the papers they'll treat me and everyone else kindly?" Bernadette said sarcastically.

"I don't think tryin' t' destroy them will make them stop trying t' harm ye," Billy answered evenly.

Bernadette stared at him. "You're really something, you know. If I didn't know better I'd say you were a coward."

Her slap had no effect on him. "Something else I've learned is not t' do somethin' just t' prove ye're not what somebody else says ye are," he said softly.

"I'm not giving this up, Billy. I can't," Bernadette said with finality.

Shrugging, Billy turned to look at the fields streaming by outside the window. "I'll do me best t' help ye, then, an' hope everything works out like ye expect."

Bernadette was stunned at the realization of what he was saying. He was serious about ending their relationship. "What will you do?" she asked finally.

Billy shrugged again and kept his face turned to the window. "Go back t' Belfast, t' workin' in the shipyard. Try t' see me daughter as often as I can. Live out me life." He made an attempt to break the tension between them. "Maybe I'll see ye on TV."

Swallowing the lump that was forming in her throat, Bernadette whispered, "And that's final? There's no possibility you'd come to America with me?"

He turned to look at her. She could see he was suffering as much as she was. "No. I'd like t' share me life wi' ye, Bernadette, but not that kind o' life." He kept his eyes fixed on her. "Anyway, I could never be that far from Susan."

Her sudden expression made him realize she didn't know who Susan was. In the same instant he knew she thought it was his ex-wife. "Me daughter," he added quickly. "If I moved to America I'd maybe never see her again."

Bernadette's look softened. She thought of her own father and how she'd moved away to America and had never seen him again. How could she blame Billy? She loved him more for wanting to be near his daughter, but she was unable to give up her need for revenge. Her sigh was the final suppression of the sadness welling up inside her. "Then I guess we're back to what we were a few days ago. The daughter and the friend of Joe Mallory."

Billy made no reply.

26

Bernadette had been to Dublin twice before. Her parents had taken her to see the Easter Rising parade when she was five or six years old. She remembered her mother had pinned white lilies on each of their chests and Bernadette thought they were dressing fancy until she saw that everyone was wearing a white lily that day. It made her feel secure that all these people shared something, even if she didn't know what. She remembered men marching and bands drumming. Everybody was happy.

They visited the zoo in Phoenix Park where her mother and father oohed and ahhed as they pointed out each exotic creature to Bernadette. Her recollection was that the animals looked sad. Resigned to their unnatural life behind bars, they showed no interest in anything. After the zoo, Bernadette and her parents picnicked in the park, eating egg sandwiches washed down with warm lemonade, a real treat.

Her second trip to Dublin was when she went to see her father, in prison. She realized now that he had seemed like one of the animals in the zoo. The cold gray walls of Mountjoy and the smell of fermenting malt that seemed to pervade the city that day had formed her lasting impression

of Dublin. She detected the smell now, as she and Billy approached the
large white concrete and glass office building that was the American
embassy. The building seemed brash and ugly among the Georgian houses
which dominated the neighborhood.

They checked in at the reception desk and a secretary notified Sudice
by phone that they had arrived. He came to the lobby to meet them and
was younger than Bernadette had expected, in his mid-thirties maybe,
with a crew cut and handsomely chiseled features. His crisp army uniform
was immaculate, with sharp creases, perfectly straight and symmetrical.
She was impressed by the medals and ribbons on his chest, and even by
his shoes which positively gleamed as he approached them with a meas-
ured stride.

"Representative Mallory," Sudice said loudly, holding out his hand to
her. Bernadette ignored it. Sudice pretended not to notice, and withdrew
his hand discreetly. "And this is?" Sudice continued.

"A friend, Billy Kingston," Bernadette replied.

The captain did not offer his hand to Billy. "Let's go back to my office."
He indicated a corridor to their left where they had to pass through a
metal detector. "Just a precaution," beamed Sudice. "We don't want any
guns, cameras, or recording devices.

I'm glad to see you don't have any," he added as they passed through
the screener without setting off any alarms.

He led them down the corridor to a door which opened onto a stair-
well. They descended, Bernadette surprised that they were going into the
basement. The walls were unpainted mortar and there was a loud hum of
machinery in the corridor they had now arrived in.

Sudice indicated an unmarked office across the hallway and held the
door open for them. The office was small and plain. In its center sat a
metal desk, with a computer off to one side. On the floor to the left of
the desk was a safe. Next to that, in a corner, was a file cabinet. There
were four chairs in the office, one behind the desk and three arranged in

a row in front of it. Sudice motioned them to sit, seating himself behind the desk.

"Coffee? You probably haven't had any good stuff since you left the U.S."

"Not for me." answered Bernadette, looking at Billy who shook his head.

They sat in identical straight-back vinyl chairs with wooden arms. The captain leaned back in his own chair and put his feet on the desk. Bernadette perceived in this a gesture designed to demean their meeting and to repay her for the failure to shake his hand. She wondered if she was being paranoid.

"Well, how can I help you, Representative Mallory? I believe you said it concerned Kevin?" He beamed across the desk at them.

Bernadette found this disconcerting. She had expected Sudice to be more apprehensive. "Let's get to the point, captain. What do you know about a boat named the Connead Braith?"

"What do you know about it?" Sudice responded coolly.

"We know everything. About the people on board who you ordered killed in cold blood, the guns for Iraq, the fact that you made money on the deal." She leaned toward him. "And we know about the British politician."

Sudice grinned. "Kevin has been talkative. I suppose he said that I planned the assassination of the politician, and you believe him?"

"Yes," stated Bernadette.

Lifting his feet from the desk and swinging his legs down to the floor, Sudice leaned across the desk. "Then why aren't you talking to the police?"

Holding his look, Bernadette replied, "I want to make a deal."

The captain raised his eyebrows. "A deal?" He reached down beside him. His briefcase was on the floor, leaning against the desk. From it he produced a newspaper. "This deal wouldn't have anything to do with this would it?"

He threw the newspaper on the desk so that it faced Bernadette. It was the Washington Post. She hadn't made the headlines, but was on page one—" FBI investigating congresswoman. Suspected links to IRA." She didn't read any more, but pushed the paper back toward Sudice.

"You can keep it if you want," he said. "We get about a dozen flown over every day."

"Yes, that's part of the deal. I want that bullshit stopped immediately," said Bernadette vehemently.

"Part of the deal?" said Sudice, stressing the first word. "You mean there's more?" He seemed to be enjoying himself and it was beginning to worry Bernadette.

"Yes. There's Kevin."

"What about Kevin?"

"He gets paid the rest of the money you owe him and flown to the U.S."

Laughing, Sudice shook his head. "Now, tell me, why would I give money to a dead man and fly his body to the U.S.?"

At first she thought he meant that Kevin might as well be dead. Then a sickening fear overtook her.

Sudice watched the color draining slowly from her face. "Ah, you don't know about Kevin. I only found out a couple of hours ago myself. You were probably on the train when it happened."

"What happened?" Bernadette demanded, her voice on edge.

"Blew his own brains out, I guess," said Sudice calmly.

Reaching across the desk, Bernadette slapped him across the face.

For an instant he wore a ludicrous expression of incredulity. Billy leapt to his feet, ready to intervene.

"You bastard," Bernadette spat.

Rubbing his cheek, Sudice glanced at Billy. "I had nothing to do with it and you can check that out. There was a witness, a woman who was there when it happened."

Exchanging looks, Bernadette and Billy both thought of Katie. "If that's true, take the slap for my father instead," hissed Bernadette.

Sudice dropped his hand from the cheek he had been rubbing. It was already bright red. "What happened to your father wasn't intended. My men knew him and didn't want to hurt him. They gave him the injection to knock him out so they could search for my stolen documents. They didn't know he'd already had an injection earlier."

Bernadette didn't believe him and Sudice didn't care. "There'll be no deal," he added with finality.

"If you think we have no evidence with Kevin gone, think again," Bernadette said coldly. Reaching into her purse, she pulled out the photocopies, throwing them on the desk.

Picking up the copies, Sudice examined them with a look of derision. "Photocopies? Hardly evidence. Anyone can doctor copies of any number of documents and produce one good-looking photocopy." He pushed them back to Bernadette. "I don't think they'll hold up in a court, or even in a congressional investigation."

Bernadette opened her mouth to say something, but before she had a chance, Sudice continued "Oh, you're going to tell me you have the originals. So what? What's likely to happen if you release them? We'll claim they're forgeries and have them examined by the FBI—our FBI—and they'll agree. You'll call in your experts who'll say they're genuine, and the whole thing will never be resolved to anyone's satisfaction. Meanwhile, we'll be ramming home the point that, as someone who hangs out with terrorists and receives money from them, you'd naturally concoct some outrageous forgery to save your skin. By the time anybody cares, the election will be over. President Ganera will have four more years, and you'll be in a federal prison."

Bernadette stared at him in disbelief. "Ganera would take that risk with the election coming up?" she challenged.

Sudice's shrug told Bernadette that the president knew nothing about this. "The president doesn't know, does he?" she said softly.

Shrugging again, Sudice responded, "I've talked to his most trusted advisors. The president will do whatever they suggest." He narrowed his eyes at her. "You see, it's a problem of trust. Would you be willing to give me the originals before the investigation of you was completely and irrevocably quashed?" He didn't wait for an answer. "No, I didn't think so. Should I trust you to give me the originals after the investigation is called off? I'm afraid not. What would prevent you from releasing the documents anyway?

So there's the problem. It's a deal that can't be made." He leaned back in his chair. "But I have another deal. One I don't think you'll be able to turn down.

I've been in this line of work for a long time, and what it comes down to is this, people who want money need information to sell, and people who want information need money to buy it. I'm fortunate, I have both money and information." He beamed as if explaining the secret of life.

"What are you talking about?" asked Bernadette peevishly.

Sudice leaned back in his chair. "I've been in the army since I left college. Never wanted to do anything else. Weapons fascinate me, but I was posted to Intelligence. I wasn't happy at first, until I learned the power of information. Most people know that without information, such as knowing when, where and how to effectively use them, weapons are useless.

On the other hand, if you have the right information, you can render worthless whatever weapons are ranged against you.

The beauty is, I love gathering information. Digging carefully, finding a nugget here and there, uncovering the relationships between them, storing them away until the day they're needed..."

Bernadette sensed the growing excitement in him. "Captain..."

He abruptly switched subjects. "Have you ever played 'Guts' Ms. Mallory?"

Bernadette sighed. "No."

Narrowing his eyes at Billy, Sudice asked, "What about you, Mr. Kingston?"

"Never heard o' it," answered Billy.

"It's a card game," continued Sudice. "We used to play it a lot at the academy. Each player gets three cards, face down. The idea is, you turn up a card at a time until you've beaten your opponent's hand. You can bet on every card, so the stakes can get pretty high. One thing to remember, there's only one joker in the deck and it beats everything."

"I don't have time for…" Bernadette began.

Holding up a finger, Sudice continued, "People think it's purely the luck of the draw, and it would be, if not for the gambling. There's no bluffing, of course—everyone can see each other's cards as they're turned up, but you can force people out of the game by betting enough. You see, everyone has the same information, what cards have been dealt, and therefore, which are still available, but most people don't know how to use that information. They can't figure the odds of what a particular card may be, based on the cards already showing."

Leaning forward again, he placed his elbows on the desk. "We're about to finish a game right now," he said with a deadly softness, smiling thinly. "You turned the first card—stalling the appropriation. Not a bad start. Want to bet on it?"

Bernadette merely returned an expression indicating that she was indulging a child.

"No? Then we turn our first card, the Chinese threat. Beats yours. We also won't bet yet.

Your next card, a request for more time. You know we need an answer now, so that beats us. Bet?"

Bernadette's expression turned to a look of disdain.

Keeping his eyes fixed on her, Sudice continued, "Our next card, planting money in your bank account. We're ahead again and we each have one card left." He looked from Bernadette to Billy. "Does anyone have the joker, I wonder?"

Bernadette decided Sudice was crazy.

"Your turn. Last card, the documents. An ace, at least, might even be the joker. Depends what our last card is." He stopped and leaned back in his chair again. A stupid grin crossed his face.

"Well?" asked Bernadette, finally. "Are we going to see your last card or do you concede?"

"I never concede. Remember we can bet on each card. I'm willing to bet everything on my last card. My entire career. Are you willing to bet everything, Ms. Mallory? Risk your career, your status, your reputation? Or do you concede without seeing my last card? How certain are you that I can't win?"

Exasperated, Bernadette replied, "Let's see your last card."

Grinning again, Sudice reached for his telephone. Holding down the speaker button, he said "Send in the joker." Leaning back, he folded his arms across his chest.

After a moment the door opened and Inspector Grindley walked into the room. Closing the door behind him, he leaned against it.

"I think you know the Inspector," Sudice said to Bernadette. "A moment ago I said that some people want money and some want information. The inspector wants money. I want information. We have an arrangement which satisfies both our needs.

Why don't you explain, Inspector?" he continued to the policeman.

"Miss Mallory," the inspector nodded at Bernadette. Then he turned to Billy. "An' ye'd be William Kingston, from Belfast."

"Aye," answered Billy reluctantly, fighting back the nerves that were clawing at him.

"Aye. Sent here by British Intelligence." He held up a hand to forestall Billy. "Don't deny it. We know all about Mr. Baxter an' why ye came t' Cork. We also know all about Marty Coyne." He stopped and there was silence for a moment.

It was broken by Bernadette. "What about Marty Coyne?"

Raising his eyebrows, the Inspector turned toward Bernadette. "Ye o' all people should know, Miss Mallory that Mr. Kingston here murdered Coyne in cold blood."

Jumping to her feet, Bernadette protested. "That isn't true! It was self defense. I was there. Coyne was assaulting me. Billy stopped him. There was a struggle and the gun went off accidentally."

Studying her intently, Grindley said slowly. "But Miss Mallory, when we talked about Coyne, ye stated ye knew nothin' about his death."

Bernadette blushed. "I didn't tell the truth."

"Why should I believe ye're tellin' the truth now?" The Inspector asked, grinning slyly.

Billy stood up. "She's tellin' the truth. Coyne coulda killed her. The gun went off by accident."

"Sit down, Mr. Kingston," said the inspector with a menacing tone.

Billy felt anger welling up inside him, but a glance from Bernadette made him obey the inspector. Bernadette sat down again too.

"Why didn't ye report this, ah, accident?" Grindley continued.

His question was addressed to Bernadette, but it was Billy who answered. "She wanted to. I forced her t' say nothing."

"An' how did ye force her?" asked Grindley.

Before Billy could think of an answer, Sudice cut into the conversation. "OK, that's enough." He looked at Bernadette. "The point is, the police have enough evidence to convict Mr. Kingston here of murder. I'd say it looks very bad for him. A British agent. Fingerprints on the murder weapon. Witnesses who saw him enter Coyne's house at the time of the killing…"

"Ye couldn't have found the gun!" Billy snapped.

"Oh?" interjected the Inspector. "Why not? D' ye still have it?"

Regretting his protest, Billy mumbled. "No. I got rid o' it. Threw it in the river." He avoided looking at anyone.

"The point is," continued Sudice. "We have a gun. We also have your fingerprints. Taken from a glass you drank from at the Starry Plough and transferred to the gun which we say is the murder weapon."

There was a momentary stunned silence from Bernadette and Billy, before the latter ventured, "These witnesses, I suppose they'd be the men I saw enter Coyne's house? The men who telephoned ye immediately? What were they doin' at Coyne's?"

"Coyne had been known t' shelter IRA men on the run..." Grindley began.

"Shut up!" Sudice snapped, glaring at the policeman, who looked stupid and flared embarrassment.

"So, they were looking for Kevin," Billy stated.

"Never mind about Kevin," Sudice barked. "If you hadn't interfered we'd have found him and the documents, and we wouldn't be having this conversation." He breathed heavily, then recovered his composure. "As to the witnesses, they'll be anybody we damn well choose. Understand?"

Billy stood again. "Yous bastards..."

"Mr. Kingston," Sudice said calmly, "There are two more police officers outside the door. Now, shut up and sit down or you'll be arrested and taken to jail right now."

Billy read the look in Sudice's eyes and sat down.

"Good," continued Sudice. "Believe it or not, I'm trying to save you." He turned back to Bernadette. "So, this is my deal, either you give me those originals or your friend here goes back to Mountjoy. What do you think he'd get, Inspector?"

Sucking in a breath, Grindley said. "Well now, let's see, second time, British agent, open an' shut case." He shrugged. "Life, if he survives that long."

Sudice smirked at Bernadette. "There you have it. Are you willing to have your friend here rot in prison? Maybe be sliced up by some IRA boys?"

Bernadette felt fury and fear raging inside her. She fought to control both emotions. "Why?" she asked softly. "Why are you doing this?"

Looking at her with derision, Sudice seemed to relish the chance to explain . "Two reasons. First, I'm a patriot. People like you are destroying the United States. You're a communist. Always have been, ever since college. You'd love to see Nicaragua fall to the commies. It's not enough that we have that asshole Castro thumbing his nose at us. You won't be content until you've reduced the United States of America to the status of a third world country, but I'm not going to let you. The president under-stands. He'll thank me for this.

That's the second thing. I'm too good to be here. I belong in D.C. where the real action is. I could make a big difference there, serve the president personally."

For an instant his eyes glowed at the thought, before he returned from his reverie. "Now you know the deal, what's your answer?"

Bernadette looked at Billy. His eyes said not to do it. Bernadette's mind raced for a way out, some greater threat she could make to Sudice. A more powerful joker she could throw in his face. She could not come up with one. "All right, you win, but I won't give you the documents until Billy's safely back in Belfast." She realized it was a foolish condition as soon as she said it. Why would Sudice agree to give up his joker?

"No, Bernadette!" Billy stood, fists clenched.

The Inspector moved toward him.

Sudice held up a finger toward them both. "I agree," he announced calmly. "But you both should understand something. If Mr. Kingston makes it back to Belfast, and I don't have the documents in my hands by this time tomorrow, it will be you, Ms. Mallory facing the murder charge. It will be your prints we found on the gun and you our witness saw."

"Don't do this, Bernadette," Billy pleaded through gritted teeth.

She looked into his eyes. "Let's go," was all she said.

He decided he had a better chance of convincing her if they were alone. "All right," he answered.

They stood to leave.

"The Inspector will be going with you," Sudice stated. "He'd better have the documents by this time tomorrow." There was no mistaking the menace in his tone.

Grindley stood away from the door. "Don't try anythin' foolish," he said to both of them, "It wouldn't be the first time someone got badly hurt trying t' resist arrest."

The three of them walked from the office. Outside, the inspector stopped and exchanged some whispered words with two obviously plain-clothed policemen, then he followed Bernadette and Billy in the direction of the railway station.

They walked quickly through the busy streets. Grindley kept pace with them. Because of this, Bernadette and Billy said nothing. Instead, they each wracked their brain for a way out of the trap they were in.

Billy hoped Grindley would need to purchase a ticket, allowing Billy and Bernadette a few minutes alone, but the Inspector already had his ticket and insisted on sitting on the bench next to them while they waited for the train.

"Ye could get a train from here t' Belfast," Grindley remarked to Billy. "Why go back t' Cork an' then have t' come back through Dublin again?"

"I left me belongin's in Cork," Billy answered. "An' if it's OK by ye, I'd like t' spend as much time as possible wi' Bernadette. Sudice said we had until tomorrow t' give ye the papers."

Grindley shrugged. Apart from this brief exchange, he was content to observe Billy and Bernadette, annoying them by his presence and the chilling effect it had on their ability to talk openly. Boarding the train, Bernadette sought out an empty compartment and sat in a corner by the window. Billy sat across from her, forcing Grindley to choose whom to sit beside. He chose Bernadette.

"How did you come to be involved in this?" Bernadette suddenly asked, turning to face the policeman squarely. "What has Sudice got on you?"

Grindley raised his eyebrows. "Got on me? Nothin'. I'm in it for the money like he said."

Bernadette glanced at Billy, then back to the Inspector. "What if I offered you more money?"

The policeman held her look. "I'd consider it for about ten seconds an' then turn ye down."

"Why?" asked Bernadette, perplexed. "If money's your only interest…"

Grindley cocked his head at her. "Money's me main interest, but it's not me only interest. I'd also like t' stay healthy enough t' enjoy the money, an' if I helped ye, Captain Sudice would not be happy. He's a powerful man t' have as an enemy, as ye've found out. I don't think I'd survive for long. He has a lot o' people workin' for him. People I'd rather not…"

"Yes!" snapped Bernadette. "He has you for one!"

"Hey!" The inspector held up his hands defensively. "Don't take it personally…"

Standing, Bernadette spun to face him. "Don't take it personally!" she said, stressing the last word. "Oh, that's good. Don't take it personally that you're a police officer, and you're doing your damnedest to…"

"That's enough!" snapped Grindley. "Save it. Let's just get this over wi', then we'll be out o' each other's lives."

"There's no point, Bernadette," said Billy calmly. "Inspector, could I have a word wi' ye?" He stood and nodded toward the compartment door.

The inspector looked from Billy to Bernadette, whose eyes blazed at him. He shrugged at Billy and went out into the corridor.

"It's OK," Billy said softly in answer to Bernadette's questioning look. He followed the inspector out of the compartment.

Walking to the end of the corridor, Grindley leaned against a window. Billy lurched along the corridor and stopped beside him.

"Are ye goin' t' offer me a bribe too?" The inspector's tone was short.

Billy shook his head. "No. I want t' ask ye a favor." He watched Grindley's face to gauge the reaction.

"What favor?" Grindley asked, the question heavy with suspicion.

"Ye know that Bernadette and I have feelings for each other. Since I may not see her again after today, I wondered if ye could give us some time alone. Ye know, t' talk, privately." Billy hated Grindley for having to ask this.

Narrowing his eyes slyly, Grindley whispered. "Ye're not thinkin' o' givin' her one last poke, right there in the compartment, are ye?"

Billy bit back his anger. "Ye know how women are. If ye give us some time alone, it'll make it easier for ye t' deal wi' her after I leave."

Grindley studied Billy. "I really don't have anything against either one o' ye personally," he stated. After a moment's hesitation he added, "OK. I'll be in the compartment next t' yous." He held up a finger in Billy's face. "I'll be sitting on the corridor side, so I can see if either one o' yous leaves the compartment. Don't try anything daft."

Billy nodded. "Thanks."

They both stumbled their way back down the corridor. Grindley entered the compartment before Billy's, leaving the door open. When Billy reached his compartment, he looked back and could see Grindley leaning into the corridor, watching him. Billy entered the compartment and slid the door closed behind him.

"Where is he?" asked Bernadette immediately.

Billy sat opposite her again. "In the next compartment. He said he'd just as soon not have t' listen t' us appealin' t' his nobler spirit all the way back t' Cork. He can see the corridor from where he is, so we can forget about tryin' t' get off the train without him, unless ye want t' try an' squeeze out that way." He nodded toward the window away from the corridor, where the green countryside was flashing by.

"So, we're alone," Bernadette stated.

"Aye."

Now that they had the opportunity to speak privately, neither was sure what to say and they sat in silence for a moment. "So, what are we goin' t' do?" Billy asked finally.

Bernadette laughed hollowly. "Give him the documents after you're in Belfast. What else can we do?"

Reaching over, Billy took Bernadette's hands in his own. "What if we could give Grindley the slip, get the documents an' head for Belfast?"

"Then what?" Bernadette asked, unenthusiastically.

"Give the documents t' the British. They'd surely expose the whole thing, an' take care o' Sudice."

"Would they? I'm not sure they could do anything to Sudice. He has diplomatic immunity. They might strike a deal to have him removed, but I doubt they'd risk accusing Ganera or the U.S. Government of anything. That's not how things are handled at that level. What could they do anyway? Sudice's right. The U.S. would claim the documents were forgeries and the British couldn't call the president a liar."

Billy sighed. "I was thinkin' about us. No matter what happens, we'd be out o' it."

Leaning forward, Bernadette squeezed his hands. "If I thought that's all there'd be to it, I'd do it in a minute, but we're talking about somebody who has people killed. In Ireland, at sea, in England. How safe would we be? Could we live every day, each worrying about the other when we're apart? Our hearts pounding every time there was a knock at the door?"

Releasing his hands, she leaned back in her seat again. "No, Billy. I can't subject you to that. They'll leave you alone once they have the papers. It's me they're after."

Knowing the answer to the question he was about to ask, but not sure Bernadette had thought about it, Billy swallowed, then said, "What if ye give them the papers an' they go ahead an' charge ye wi' Coyne's murder anyway?"

Bernadette's steady look told him she had considered the question. "That's a risk I have to take."

Sagging back in his seat, Billy shook his head. "No. There must be some way…"

"Billy." Bernadette's voice was firm but tender. "There is no way out, short of Sudice and Grindley dropping dead."

Leaning forward again, she cupped his chin in her hands. "I want you to promise me that you'll go back to Belfast and phone me when you get there. There's nothing you can do and I don't want you dead. Promise?"

Seeing the moistness growing in her eyes, Billy's throat began to knot in response. Sliding out of his seat, he crossed the carriage and sat beside her. They held each other tightly. He could feel her weeping softly in his arms. His love for her, and something she had just said forged a grim decision in his mind. "Suppose somehow we could get out o' this?" he whispered.

She sighed audibly, not wanting to listen.

"Let me finish," he continued. "Suppose they keep their word. I get back t' Belfast, ye give them the documents an' they lose all interest in us. Then would ye consider stayin'? We wouldn't have t' live in Belfast. We could go t' England. Would…"

Sitting up, Bernadette looked into his eyes. She considered the question to be moot, and therefore had no trouble answering sincerely. "Yes, if things worked out that way, I'd stay with you."

His eyes reflected the happiness he felt.

Bernadette liked seeing that look, and so, added, "And I'd love to be Susan's stepmother."

Now it was Billy who felt like crying.

28

When the train pulled into Cork, Grindley followed them down the corridor and onto the platform. They headed for the taxi ramp.

"We can share a taxi. Yous two can get out at the Starry Plough an' I'll stay on t' yer father's house," Billy said.

He saw the look on of surprise and disappointment on Bernadette's face. "I…"

"No," Billy interrupted. "I'm not one for long good-byes." He tried to sound unemotional.

Dropping her eyes, Bernadette turned her head away. "Yes, you're right," she said quietly.

Grindley shook his head. "I don't think so. I want t' see what's so important that ye had t' come all the way back t' Cork for it."

Trying to hide his disappointment, Billy shrugged. "Fine. If ye've never seen a man's personal belongin's before…" His mind began to race, trying to figure out a way to avoid having Grindley discover the gun.

"I was thinking of going to my father's house anyway," said Bernadette.

"Good," announced Grindley. "Then it's settled. We'll all go there together."

Grindley sat in the front of the taxi. Bernadette and Billy were alone in the back. The driver struck up a conversation with Grindley about the national soccer team and whether it had a chance of qualifying for the World Cup. Grindley didn't want to talk, but the driver was a garrulous, persistent type, forcing reluctant responses. Seeing his chance, Billy pulled Bernadette to him, turning her face against his own. Grindley caught a glimpse in the rearview mirror. To him it looked as if they were kissing and he was mildly disgusted. The driver diverted his attention with another question.

"Listen," Billy whispered urgently. "I have somethin' in me grip. I can't let Grindley find it. He has t' be distracted somehow."

Bernadette's eyes widened and her head jerked back reflexively. Holding her cheeks, Billy pulled her back to him.

"The gun?" Bernadette whispered. "Why? What does it matter now?"

"No, not that. Somethin' else. I can't tell ye what, but it could cause me a lot o' trouble if it got into the wrong hands." He thought he was a good liar and forced what he felt to be a desperate and sincere look into his eyes.

Bernadette was not fooled. "It is the gun. Don't deny it, I know it is. You're going to…"

"I'm not goin' t' do anythin'." Billy had a hard time holding his voice to a whisper. "I need it for when I get back t' Belfast."

With his tight grip and the edge in his voice, Bernadette wavered. "You must swear…"

"I'm not going t' do anythin'," Billy hissed.

Her love for him overcame her doubt. "All right, but he won't be separated from you now. I have an idea. It may not work, and even if it does it's risky."

"I've no choice," Billy answered.

"Where is the grip?"

"Under the bed."

Bernadette pulled herself back from him. "Wait, stop the car," she said in a loud voice.

Looking at her in the rearview mirror, the driver eased his foot off the accelerator. Grindley turned to look at her. "What for?"

"I need to make a phone call," Bernadette said.

Grindley squinted his eyes at her. "Who to?" he demanded.

"To the person who's got the papers. I don't want to run into them and have them say something so you'd know where the papers were before Billy can leave." There was a tone of finality in her voice.

Grindley hesitated, but it sounded plausible. "All right. There's a phone booth on the next block."

The driver coasted to a halt, keeping the engine running. The phone booth was on the opposite side of the street. Bernadette got out of the cab and crossed the street. They watched her fumble in her purse, lift the receiver, dial, and insert her coin. What they couldn't see or hear was Bernadette's relief that the phone was answered by Father Mallory. "Father, thank God. It's Bernadette."

"Bernadette..."

"Listen Father, I haven't much time, and I need your help, and above all, your trust."

"Well, aye, of course, but..."

"I need you to go to my father's house immediately. Under the bed, you'll find a grip. In it is a gun..."

"A gun! Good heavens, Bernadette! What are ye askin'..."

"Please, Father. This is a matter of life and death. You must trust me. I'm not asking you to do anything illegal or dangerous. I just need you to get the gun and hold onto it until Billy comes to get it from you. I prom-ise I'll explain it all to you, but I can't right now. I need you to trust me."

"But a gun, Bernadette. I don't know..." He fell silent for a moment. Looking toward the taxi, Bernadette could see the three occupants watching her. The priest spoke again. "I don't know what ye've gotten into, Bernadette. That fella ye addressed the package to…If ye'll swear by yer father…"

"I do. Thank you, Father. You don't know how much this means to me. Please hurry. It's critical that you get there and away again as quickly as possible.

And one other thing, Father. If you should happen to run into me or Billy and we're with someone else, don't say a word about the gun or the package.

I can't thank you enough, Father, and I will explain it all, I promise, but please hurry."

"I'll leave right away. But Bernadette, ye be careful."

"I will. I must go now." She replaced the receiver.

Her mind was already calculating. The priest was maybe five miles closer to her father's house than they were, and he wouldn't be slowed by down-town traffic. He should easily make it there ahead of them. Still, it wouldn't hurt to buy him a few extra minutes. So she took her time crossing the street, waiting until there wasn't a car within two blocks of her.

Reaching the taxi, she knocked on Grindley's window. He lowered it. "Nature calls," said Bernadette. " I'm just going to run into that pub." She nodded at the pub at the far end of the block.

Grindley sighed. "Just hurry, will ye? The meter's runnin', ye know."

Bernadette hurried until she was inside the pub then she slowed down. She spent a full five minutes in the ladies room before deciding she'd bet-ter not overdo it. She hurried back to the taxi. "Sorry," she said as she climbed back in beside Billy. "Had to wait for a stall."

"Spare us the details," answered Grindley gruffly. "Let's go," he said to the driver. "We've wasted enough time."

Bernadette hoped so. Leaning over to kiss Billy, she silently mouthed the words 'Father Mallory'. Billy squeezed her hand lightly in gratitude and to show that he understood.

Reaching Joe Mallory's house, Grindley instructed the driver to wait. He allowed Billy to enter the house first, then followed him closely, stepping ahead of Bernadette.

"Let's see this treasure, then," he said to Billy.

Fighting desperately to stay calm, Billy avoided looking at Grindley but stepped aside to let the policeman pass. "There's a grip upstairs, under the bed." He feared that his voice betrayed his anxiety.

Grindley turned to face Billy. "You sound a wee bit nervous."

Billy forced himself to hold Grindley's look. The Inspector was wearing a smirk. Stepping over to stand beside Billy, Bernadette and her arm through his, squeezing as she did so.

"D' ye want t' look in the bag or not?" Billy forced himself to say.

Grindley nodded slowly, searching Billy's face. Billy wanted desperately to wet his stone-dry mouth, but he resisted.

"Do you want me to get the grip?" Bernadette asked, stepping forward. In her mind was some wild idea that she could sneak a glance inside, and if the gun was still there, she could hide it somehow without being seen.

Grindley held up a hand which stopped her in her tracks. "Let's all go upstairs and get it. I've been lookin' forward t' this."

They climbed the stairs, Bernadette leading the way, followed by Billy then Grindley. When they reached the bedroom Grindley pushed past them and strode to the bed. Reaching under the bed he pulled out the grip, which he hoisted it like a trophy, all the while grinning broadly. Setting the grip on the bed, and keeping his eyes fixed on Billy, he slowly undid the zipper the full length of the bag, one notch at a time, or so it seemed to Billy.

With his eyes still on Billy, Grindley reached into the bag. He produced a shirt, which he dropped to the floor. Next came a pair of trousers, then underpants, followed by socks and another pair of underpants. He glanced into the bag and the smirk which had been fixed on his face faded. Billy and Bernadette exchanged a tight hand-squeeze. Rummaging about in the bag, Grindley's hands explored the side lining, looking for a hidden pocket. Examining the outside of the grip, he tried to pry apart the seams.

"Satisfied?" Billy asked.

Dropping the bag to the floor, Grindley wagged a finger at Billy. "There's somethin'," he said flatly. "I don't know what. I thought maybe it was the gun ye used on Coyne, but there's somethin'. Nobody travels from Dublin t' Cork an' back again just for this."

"I do," Billy replied. "Now, are ye goin' t' let me go, or was that all bullshit?"

"Pack it up an' let's be goin'," answered Grindley tersely. "We'll see ye t' the station."

Billy's heart sank at these words, but he could think of no response. Kneeling, he began stuffing his belongings back into the grip.

"I'm staying here," said Bernadette.

Grindley shot her a look.

"I thought I'd look through the house. I haven't had a chance to sort out what I want to take back with me," she offered as explanation. "And I hate long good-byes too. I just want Billy gone and this whole thing over with." A lump seized at her throat when she said this, and along with the release of tension from Grindley's search of the grip, forced tears to well up in her eyes.

Billy held her tightly.

"All right, then I'll stay here wi' ye." Grindley was exasperated. "Ye," he said to Billy, "Finish pickin' up that stuff, say yer good-byes an' get on yer way."

Stuffing his belongings back into the grip, Billy zipped it shut. He clasped Bernadette by the shoulders.

"Please," she whispered hoarsely, "Just go, please."

"I love ye, Bernadette," he said softly.

"I love you too, Billy, but go now, please. I can't stand this any longer."

Cupping her chin in his hands, he looked deeply into her eyes. "I'm glad I met ye Bernadette Mallory. Don't worry, everythin' will work out. I promise."

Bernadette recoiled slightly at his words, but before she could formulate a response he strode quickly from the room. Standing numb, she fought back tears and the impulse to run after him.

She heard him descend the stairs and open the front door. The slamming of the taxi door felt like a body slam to her. With the revving of the engine she imagined her heart being ground up. A slight dizziness swept through her head. As the sound of the taxi backing up, turning and driving away reached her ears, she wanted to scream, convinced that, like a sinkhole, she would inwardly collapse from the emptiness his departure left.

———

"Back t' the station?" said the driver with a puzzled tone. "Did ye not just come from there?"

Billy wasn't in the mood for talking, especially when it was none of the driver's business. Now that the die was cast, he wanted to get it over with. "St. Matthew's chapel first, an' step on it. An' no talkin', I'm tryin' t' think."

With a look of resentment, the driver said huffily, "Right y'are, sir." He managed to make the last word sound like an insult.

They drove in silence to the chapel and stopped in front of the main entrance. Billy got out and surveyed the soaring limestone tower. Being a Protestant, he'd never been in a chapel. A woman with a shawl pulled over her head emerged and peered at him with a quizzical look. Realizing it must seem odd, him standing there, and not wanting to draw attention to himself, Billy suddenly entered the chapel.

The sweet smell of incense assailed his nostrils. He'd forgotten Catholics used incense. He did expect to see idols since it was well-known that Catholics worshipped idols. Sure enough, he was confronted with a statue of the Blessed Virgin, cradling the baby Jesus to her breast. The bright blues, golds and whites surprised him. He was used to holy pictures and statues being more conservative.

Walking to the right, past the glowing candles he came to an aisle which opened into the main body of the chapel. Again he faced a huge statue, this time of the crucifixion, and again he felt the bright hues cheapened the art and should have been more somber to reflect the act portrayed.

He saw the priest walking away from him, toward what he assumed must be the confessional boxes, to one side of the altar. A quick look around told Billy the chapel was otherwise empty. If this had been a church, Billy would have walked after the priest, not wanting to break the silence, but this was a chapel and held no special reverence for Billy. "Hello!" he called. He would not call the priest "Father".

Spinning around, the priest peered in Billy's direction.

"It's Billy Kingston. Bernadette Mallory's friend."

The priest jerked his head, in recognition, then hurried toward Billy. "Where's Bernadette?" he asked when he reached Billy.

"At her father's house." Billy didn't want to spend any more time here than he had to. "I've come for the, uh…"

"Aye, I know what ye've come for," said the priest with resentment. "It's a fine thing Bernadette asked me t' do…" Realizing he was becoming agitated, the priest brought himself under control. "But this is no place t' be talkin' about it an' I suppose ye're only doin' what Bernadette asked ye t' do."

Billy was grateful to quickly agree with that. "Aye."

"C'mon then," said the priest walking toward the side entrance, "It's over in the rectory." He held the door open for Billy. As they crossed the gravel path to the priest's home, the priest became agitated again. "Can ye not tell me what's going on? Is Bernadette in trouble?"

Billy adopted a serious tone. "I really can't tell ye much."

The priest registered his exasperation with a sigh.

"But we're not in any danger or anythin' like that," Billy continued, trying to reassure the priest.

Stopping, the priest fixed Billy with a withering look. "Where there's guns, there's always danger," he said solemnly.

Returning the priest's look, Billy shrugged. "I'm sorry, I'm not hidin' anythin' from ye, but I've nothin' t' tell ye. I'm only doin' what Bernadette asked."

The priest continued to look at Billy, who finally looked away. "You're not a Catholic, are ye?" the priest said finally. It was more of a statement than a question.

"No, I'm not." answered Billy, with a measure of innate defiance.

The priest nodded slowly. "That explains why ye can stand there, showin' me no respect, an lyin' so brazenly,"

Billy started to object, but the priest continued, "It doesn't matter. Whatever's going on is between ye an' Bernadette. I trust her, an' I know she trusts ye. I just wish yous could both trust me." He continued the walk toward his home.

Standing for a moment, Billy thought he should apologize to the priest, but what would be the point? He couldn't tell him anything, so he put it out of his mind and followed the priest up to the door of the rectory, then inside.

The priest crossed over to his desk while Billy stood by the open door and waited. The priest turned to face him. In one hand he held a tea towel with something wrapped in it. Obviously the gun. In his other hand the priest held the envelope Bernadette had given him at Cork station. "You'll be wantin' this too, I suppose." said the priest holding the envelope toward Billy.

"No!" said Billy quickly.

The priest looked surprised.

"Ye must keep the envelope. Give it only t' Bernadette. That's what she said," he added.

Sighing in resignation, the priest returned the envelope to the desk drawer. Walking over to Billy, he handed him the tea towel.

Unwrapping the gun, Billy examined it. He was about to stuff it into his pocket when he thought better of it. "Can I keep the towel?" he asked.

The priest said nothing, but nodded his head once.

Billy felt uncomfortable, keenly aware of the priest's cold look which seemed to demand an explanation more than words could. "I'm sorry. There's just nothin' t' tell ye. Ye've been a big help t' meself an' Bernadette, but believe me, there's nothin' for ye t' worry about."

The priest remained silent.

"I have t' go. I may not see ye again. I'm going back t' Belfast."

The priest's eyes betrayed a hint of surprise.

"I want t' thank ye," Billy blurted out. He held out his hand.

The priest looked at the outstretched hand, then clasped it in both his own. "Ye have the look o' a desperate man. I pray that the Lord will be with ye."

Taken aback at the priest's words, and at the man's perceptiveness, Billy quickly turned and hurried out the door, back toward the waiting taxi, clutching the gun tightly to his chest. He was careful to climb into the back seat of the taxi, where his grip was. He stuffed the tea towel inside.

"What've ye got there?" asked the driver, starting the motor.

"None o' yer business!" snapped Billy. "Just drive t' the station."

"Right y'are, sir." snarled the driver.

29

"I'm going back to my room," Bernadette announced.

Grindley looked surprised, and suspicious. "I thought ye were going t' go through yer father's things?"

"I'm too upset. I just want to go to bed."

Grindley studied her intently. "Somethin' went on here. Why'd ye really come back t' this house? It couldn't have been for his clothes."

Bernadette smiled ruefully. "I'm going back to the Starry Plough." She walked toward the cottage door. Grindley stood for a minute, slowly shaking his head, then he followed her out of the cottage and along the road. They made no conversation during the walk, which suited them both fine.

They entered the Starry Plough through the side door and climbed the stairs. At the door to her room Bernadette turned and said to Grindley, "You can find me here in the morning."

Grindley nodded. "I think I'll stay here meself. Can't let ye out o' me sight now."

Bernadette shrugged. "You'd better go talk to the landlord about a room, then." She turned from him and went into her room, closing the door behind her.

Grindley stood in the corridor, considering. Then he walked along the corridor and down the stairs leading to the bar. There weren't many customers and O'Grady saw him right away. He fixed Grindley with a look of displeasure and waited for the newcomer to explain why he'd entered the bar from the staircase. Recognizing the look, Grindley decided to be direct. Reaching into his jacket pocket, he produced his wallet, flipping it open so that his police I.D. could be seen by O'Grady. The latter's look turned to one of apprehension.

"How can I help ye, Inspector?" The landlord's tone was solicitous and worried.

Grindley was gratified. "I'll be staying here tonight. In Miss Mallory's room." Again he recognized the look of disapproval on O'Grady's face. "It's not what ye're thinkin'. It's official business. For her protection."

O'Grady glanced nervously around the saloon, but no-one was paying them any attention. Leaning across the bar, he whispered, "Is she in some sort o' danger?"

Grindley said nothing immediately.

"I've a right t' know," prodded O'Grady.

"Don't concern yerself about it. I'll be here an' I'll take care o' it. There's nothin' for ye t' worry about."

O'Grady did not seem reassured.

"I'll be takin' a mattress from one o' the other rooms an' movin' it into Miss Mallory's room," Grindley continued, "I don't want us disturbed."

"Now, wait a minute," said O'Grady, flustered. "This doesn't seem right. I mean, comin' in here talking about protection an' moving me mattresses around. I've a right t' know what's goin' on. I've me customers safety t' think about."

It was Grindley's turn to lean across the bar. "Do ye want t' see the police here every day, checkin' things out? Especially at the stroke o' closin', when we better not find one person in the bar one minute after closin' time? Is that what ye want?"

Looking scared, the landlord quickly shook his head.

"Then go about yer business an' leave us alone. I'll be gone in the mornin'. All right?"

O'Grady's head nodded rapidly.

"Is there anyone else staying here?" asked Grindley.

O'Grady shook his head.

"Good," said Grindley. "See that nobody comes up the stairs, including yerself."

O'Grady swallowed hard. "I will." he said, his voice shaking.

Grindley turned and walked back to the stairs. Only a couple of the patrons paid desultory attention to him. Climbing the stairs, he walked to the room opposite Bernadette's. It contained one twin bed, which suited his purpose. He slid the mattress off the bed and onto its side. It slid easily across the floor as he dragged it out of the room and into the corridor. Propping it against the wall of Bernadette's room, he knocked lightly on her door. After a minute she opened the door with an exasperated look on her face. "What?" Then she noticed the mattress and shot him a quizzical look.

"I need ye t' hold the door open for me," he stated, gripping the mattress and pulling it out into the corridor at an angle so that it would slide through the door into Bernadette's room.

"What are you doing?" demanded Bernadette, unwilling to believe what the inspector was clearly planning.

Continuing to pull the mattress, Grindley forced her to stand aside and allow him and his load into the room. He ignored her until the end of the mattress cleared the door. "Ye can close the door now," he said, balancing the mattress on end in the middle of the room.

Bernadette made no attempt to close the door. "You can't do this," she stated. "It's ridiculous."

Grindley sighed. "I don't like it any more than ye do. But I can't afford
t' have ye sneakin' out on me in the middle o' the night, so I'm going t'
put this mattress up against the door an' I'm goin' t' sleep on it. That way,
ye won't be able t' get out without steppin' on me."

"Oh, for heaven's sake!" snapped Bernadette. "You are not sleeping in
this room, and if you try, I'll scream."

Grindley looked genuinely shocked.

"If you want to piss about like this, fine." Bernadette went on. "You can
just as easily put the fucking mattress on the other side of the door, and
sleep in the damn corridor. All I know is, you aren't sleeping in here."

She was breathing heavily and Grindley could see that she was so emotionally wound-up that the wrong reaction on his part would result in her
making good on her threat to start screaming. He held his hands up
defensively. "All right, calm yerself. I'll get out o' yer room."

Stomping across the room, Bernadette opened the door again, glaring
at him. Grindley hauled the mattress back into the corridor and
Bernadette slammed the door shut behind him. He stood for a moment,
feeling like an idiot. He'd half a mind to tell her that if she imagined he
had any ideas about him forcing himself on her, she must be crazy, but he
finally dismissed her with a shake of the head and maneuvered the mattress around, sliding it along the floor until it was tight against the door,
then he let it drop. Now all he had to do was lie down and sleep till
morning. It wouldn't be the most comfortable night he'd ever spent, but
it wouldn't be the worst either.

Across town, Billy arrived at the railway station. Going straight to the men's toilets, he transferred the gun from his grip to his pocket. He then spent a few minutes examining himself in the mirror. Finally, he was satisfied that there was no suspicious bulge from any profile.

He next checked the daily timetable for trains to Dublin, then found a bar on the station concourse. The more he thought about what he had to do, the more he felt like drinking, but he knew that to carry out his plan required just the right amount of bottled courage and so he paced his drinking accordingly. By the time the bar closed, he felt ready. Walking to the taxi ramp outside the station, he approached the first taxi.

"Where to?" asked the driver.

"The Starry Plough," Billy replied.

By the time they arrived at their destination the streets had emptied of late-night revelers. Billy paid the driver and watched as the taxi pulled away. He was alone on the sidestreet. Walking to the corner, he checked the main street in both directions. Except for the odd, passing car, the street was deserted. Walking back down the sidestreet he stopped at the side entrance to the Starry Plough. After a look over his shoulder, he tested the door. It opened quietly.

Stepping inside, he closed the door quietly behind him. It was dark on the stairway and there was no light from the corridor above. He tried to recall how many rooms there were, and wondered which one Grindley would be in. He had no doubt Grindley would be here, he'd never let Bernadette out of his sight now. Billy decided he would have to check each room in turn. Standing still for a moment, he strained to detect any sound from the corridor at the top of the stairs. There were none. Expecting the stairs would creak, especially in the center, where most of the traffic was, Billy cautiously placed his weight on the outside of the first step. There was no creak. Satisfied, he began to stealthily climb the stairs, at the same time reaching into his pocket for the gun.

When his head reached the level of the corridor Billy saw a glow which he realized would be coming from lights left on in the saloon, or perhaps from O'Grady's kitchen. In the faint light he could see well enough to identify the doors to each of the rooms. He could also make out the silhouetted shape of something lying on the floor by the door to Bernadette's room. He froze and his mind raced to come up with something that fit the shape he could see, but it was his ears which provided the answer. Grindley was snoring.

The realization that it was a man lying up against the door caused Billy to take a step down, removing himself from view by the figure. It had to be Grindley. The realization provoked competing hopes and fears in Billy. First, he'd found Grindley, which was good. Second, Grindley had better not wake up before Billy got to him. Finally, Bernadette had better be asleep and not awaken either.

Screwing up his nerve, he again began a furtive ascent of the stairs. Once in the corridor, Billy realized he needed to move quickly now. He sneaked along the corridor wall and bent over the sleeping figure which he could see now was indeed Grindley. He placed his hand firmly over

Grindley's mouth, at the same time holding the gun directly in front of the sleeping man's face.

Grindley sputtered awake. In the space of a few seconds his face registered confusion at where he was, panic that he couldn't breathe, and fear at the sight of the gun. Jerking his head, Billy touched the gun against his own pursed lips to indicate that Grindley should get up very quietly. He kept his hand pressed over Grindley's mouth to emphasize the point. Grindley understood and rose to his feet awkwardly but quietly. Putting his lips against Grindley's ear, Billy whispered, "Keep yer hands by yer side, an' don't be makin' any sudden moves."

He motioned Grindley to walk along the corridor, away from the saloon. Grindley complied and Billy shadowed him, keeping his hand over Grindley's mouth, and pressing the gun into the policeman's back. When he judged they were far enough away from Bernadette's room, Billy whispered, "I'm goin' t' take me hand away from yer mouth. Keep walkin' an' don't be makin' a sound." He removed his hand.

"Where are…" Grindley began.

"I said, don't make a sound!" Billy hissed through his teeth. At the same time he jammed the gun deeper into Grindley's back.

At the bottom of the stairs, he ordered Grindley to stop. "I'll take yer gun, now," he said. "Where is it?"

"Under me left shoulder," Grindley said, licking his lips nervously.

Keeping his eyes and his own gun on Grindley's face, Billy reached under the policeman's jacket and pulled that gun from its holster. He stuffed it into his jacket pocket. "Good," he whispered. "Now, we're goin' for a walk. Don't try anythin'."

"Where are we goin'?" Grindley sounded scared.

"Ye'll see. Open the door quietly."

Grindley hesitated. He'd been trained for situations like this, but now that it was happening he was panic stricken. "Ye won't shoot me?" he muttered desperately. "I'm a cop."

"Ye're a bastard," answered Billy calmly. "I've already shot one man. Another one won't make any difference. Cop or not, ye'll die like he did. Now move."

"That was an accident," said Grindley. "Ye couldn't shoot a man in cold blood." He sounded hopeful.

"It looked like an accident t' Bernadette, but I killed that bastard because I wanted to," Billy lied. "An' he did a lot less harm than ye. Now, I'm going t' count t' three an' if ye're not movin'…"

"OK! I'm goin'," stammered Grindley, quickly.

They went into the street. Billy placed the gun in his pocket, keeping his finger on the trigger. "Head for Joe Mallory's place an' remember, I've a gun aimed at yer back."

They walked through the deserted streets and soon were on the outskirts of the city. "Cut across the fields here," Billy ordered.

"Ye're goin' t' kill me," Grindley said suddenly. "Jesus, please don't. I'll do anythin'. I'll help ye an' Bernadette t' get away." Stopping, he turned to face Billy. There were tears in his eyes.

"I'm not going t' kill ye if ye don't do anythin' stupid." Billy stated. "Now cut across the fields, it's a shortcut t' Mallory's."

Grindley began to walk across the field. "What are ye goin' t' do?" He sounded like he had to hear the plan to confirm that his death wasn't part of it.

"We're going t' Joe Mallory's place. I'm going t' tie ye up an' leave ye there."

Grindley stopped and turned toward Billy again. He had an eager look on his face. "That's good! Then yous'll both be away tonight. Sudice was plannin' t' kill ye, ye know. He's got it all arranged. They were goin' t' get ye in Belfast, as soon as ye called Bernadette."

Billy stopped. "What about Bernadette? What has Sudice planned for her?"

"She'll go down for Coyne's murder," Grindley said. "I can stop that," he continued eagerly. He began to walk toward Billy. "I'm in charge o' the case. If I…"

Billy wasn't listening. The futility of his plan hit him like a hammer. Bernadette had been right. Sudice would never leave them alone. Hatred of Grindley and Sudice flared within him. "I knew that's what ye had planned," he said quietly. "Bastards like yous don't deserve t' live."

Grindley stopped. "I can help yous…" His voice was hysterical.

"Shut up!" screamed Billy.

Convinced that Billy intended to shoot him there and then, Grindley suddenly turned and began running across the field, stumbling through the long grass, waving his arms wildly and screaming for help at the top of his lungs.

Billy stood transfixed for a moment, then realized that if he didn't act quickly Grindley might get away. Pulling the gun from his pocket, he aimed at the fleeing figure. "Stop!" he yelled.

Grindley heard the command but it seemed only to add to his panic. He continued his wild run through the grass.

Billy cursed to himself. He had to do something quickly. Releasing the safety on the gun and holding the weapon in both hands at arms length, he squeezed the trigger.

The bullet missed Grindley, but fear made him fall forward, arms outstretched. Billy ran quickly to where he lay. Grindley was sobbing and covering his head with his hands. "Don't kill me, please God, don't…"

Consumed by thoughts of what this man had planned for Bernadette and himself, Billy didn't hesitate. He fired again. The bullet struck Grindley in the chest. He shuddered once, then collapsed face first into the grass.

Falling to his knees, Billy began to retch. His body shivered uncontrollably. This lasted for about ten minutes before the shock began to wear off. It was such a release of tension that he wanted to stay lying there, close his eyes and allow the long grass to swaddle him, caress him to sleep. His brain, though, took over. Realizing he must get away from the scene, he forced himself to his feet, took a long look at Grindley's body, then began walking quickly back across the field the way they had come.

He was tempted to go back to the Starry Plough, back to Bernadette. He relished the thought of being in her warm bed, feeling her soft arms around his body and her warm breath on his neck. If he could just spend one more such night.

Of course, he knew he couldn't, so he walked back into town, and as he walked he thought about what he had just done. Killed a man in cold blood. No, not that. It was self-defense. Kill or be killed.

He was surprised that he could accept what he had done so calmly. Was it part of a natural progression? At the bank in Dundalk he had been involved in the death of a man, although he hadn't pulled the trigger. Still, he had been shocked and scared. A lot of that was because of his age and the fact that he'd been caught, but he'd also been horrified that he could have been involved in a man's death and had spent many nights praying for forgiveness. With Coyne, he had fired the gun, albeit by accident. Coyne's death had still shocked and scared him, but not to the degree that he couldn't act in his own interests, and he had not prayed for forgiveness. With Grindley there was no denying that he had deliberately killed a man. He hadn't planned it, but he had executed a policeman. No, not really a policeman, a criminal, someone who hurt innocent people. Who might even have killed innocent people. No, Billy hadn't killed an innocent man in cold blood. He'd acted in self-defense. It was justified, and maybe that explained why he was able to be so calm about it. His conscience was clear.

Rationalize as he might, though, Billy couldn't totally block out the small voice in his head which kept whispering, "Say what you like, but you murdered a man. How will you justify it the next time?" The only answer Billy had to this was to keep repeating to himself "Self-defense."

By the time he reached the railway station it was past one a.m. and the station was almost deserted. A uniformed worker swept one of the platforms, while a couple of maintenance workers hauled large bags of garbage from the toilets. Otherwise, the only people were a couple of old winos, each stretched out on a bench for the night.

Walking to the platform where the trains to Dublin departed from, Billy saw that the next train wouldn't leave until six a.m. He wondered if he could sit on a bench and doze for four or five hours, but was afraid the police might come along and bother him. He couldn't risk that.

So he went into the Railway Hotel, just off the main concourse. There was a young, managerial type behind the registration desk. He regarded Billy with some distaste, whether because of Billy's appearance, or because he hadn't expected to be disturbed at this hour, Billy couldn't tell. "I'd like a room," Billy stated.

The young man studied him for a moment. "Single?" he asked.

"Aye."

The young man nodded. "I'll need ye t' fill out a registration card." Reaching under the counter, he produced a white card which he slid toward Billy along with a pen.

Billy began to complete the card.

"Just arrived?" asked the young man, clearly disinterested.

"Aye, by car. Just passing through," Billy answered while continuing to complete the form.

"Luggage?"

"Just me grip here, I'll leave the rest in the car." Billy pushed the completed form back to the young man.

The latter reviewed the form and seemed satisfied. He initialed the top right corner, then turned and selected a key from a cabinet behind him. He handed the key to Billy. "Room 201, second floor. Checkout by ten."

"I'd like t' be on the road by six. Can I get a wake-up call at five?"

"There's an alarm clock radio in yer room," the young man said. He began to sort through an index card file, showing no interest in his customer. Picking up the key, Billy headed for the staircase to his right.

The room was small, but clean. Billy set the alarm clock. He was so tired he didn't even brush his teeth, just dropped his grip beside the bed, removed his clothes and slid under the bed covers. It felt wonderfully soft and warm and within minutes he was sound asleep.

———

He was awakened by the banter between co-hosts on the local morning radio show. It was five o'clock. Although still tired, he felt relieved that morning had arrived. He got up, showered and brushed his teeth extra carefully, to make up for the brushing he'd missed last night. He put on his clothes from yesterday, but stopped when he got to his shoes. They were caked with what he knew to be blood. Tearing off his clothes again, he examined everything and was relieved to find only a few specks on the lower legs of his trousers. "Christ!" he thought. "What an idiot! I could have been covered in blood when I got here, and I didn't even think about it."

He rinsed the bottoms of the trousers in hot water to remove the stains and did the same to his shoes. Anyone noticing, he thought, would assume he'd just spilled water on himself.

After checking out of the hotel, he headed for the main platform. By now it was five-thirty. He was hungry and decided he had just enough time to eat some breakfast, so he went to the platform cafe where he ordered tea, toast and scrambled eggs. He ate quickly and went to board his train. On the way he bought the morning paper and scanned it quickly. There was nothing about Grindley. He decided he would call Bernadette when he got to Dublin. He had to know if Grindley's body had been found yet, and if it had, whether any connection had been made to her or to him.

31

Bernadette woke with a start. She had been having a bad dream in which she, Grindley and Sudice were playing cards. At least, the figures in her dream had the faces of Grindley and Sudice, but their bodies were skeletons. She didn't want to play but they kept dealing and she was compelled to look at her cards. Each one was the jack of hearts and each bore Billy's face. She threw the cards down in terror and demanded to see Billy. They took her to Brown's funeral parlor, to the room where she had seen her father's body, but when Sudice triumphantly pulled back the sheet which covered the body, it was Billy who was revealed. She awoke clutching her ears to drown out the maniacal laughter from Grindley and Sudice.

Looking at her watch, she saw it was ten minutes before eight and imagined Billy would be home by now, unless something had happened. Shivering, she pulled the sheets up to her chin. It was only a dream, she told herself, but another part of her wanted to fling open the door to her room and demand that Grindley prove to her that Billy was OK. Then she realized that to do that would be awfully close to her dream. She tried to put it out of her mind. They wouldn't risk doing anything to Billy, not without the documents. Sudice wasn't that stupid, and besides, they had her.

Realizing that things were beyond her control now, she decided the best way to occupy her mind was to busy herself, so she got up, had a bath and dressed. She felt ready for breakfast and opened her door.

She was taken aback to see the empty mattress on the floor of the corridor, but immediately assumed Grindley must have already risen and was probably downstairs. Stepping over the mattress, she made her way down to the saloon.

O'Grady was in his kitchen and saw her approach the bar. He came to greet her. "Good mornin'," he said slowly, stressing every syllable.

Bernadette picked up on the inference in his tone that something wasn't normal and needed explaining. "Good morning," she replied, cautiously.

"Ye'll be wantin' breakfast, I expect?"

She nodded. "I'll eat it down here."

O'Grady nodded in return. "What about the police officer?"

Bernadette shrugged. "I thought he was down here already."

O'Grady eyed her suspiciously. "I've not seen him."

Bernadette shrugged again. "Well, I don't know where he is."

"He's not in yer room?" asked the landlord stupidly.

"He never was in my room," answered Bernadette tersely.

"But he said…" O'Grady began.

"I don't care what he said," Bernadette interrupted. "As far as I know, he spent the night sleeping on the floor outside my room. His mattress is still there."

"The floor?" O'Grady was sounding stupid again. "I don't understand."

"He put a mattress on the floor outside my room," Bernadette explained patiently. "I suppose he took it from one of the other rooms. It's still there if you don't believe me."

"It's not that I don't believe ye," O'Grady said quickly. "It's just…"

"Go and see for yourself," Bernadette instructed.

O'Grady slowly climbed the stairs, stopping halfway to turn and look at Bernadette as if expecting her to confess that she was kidding. Bernadette folded her arms and waited. The landlord continued his climb. Hearing him move down the corridor, opening and closing doors, Bernadette realized that she should have checked the other rooms herself. Of course, that's where Grindley must be. He probably realized how foolish it was to spend an uncomfortable night on the floor when he could as easily be tucked in a soft, warm bed in a room of his own.

After a few minutes O'Grady returned. "He's gone, right enough. He's not in any o' the rooms."

Although surprised, Bernadette acted as if she'd been vindicated. "So, can I have breakfast now?"

O'Grady nodded sheepishly. "Would ye like t' sit in the kitchen while I make it? It's warmer in there an' ye can have a cup o' tea while I'm making the breakfast."

This sounded good to Bernadette so she followed him into the kitchen. Motioning her to sit at the small table against the wall by the stove, O'Grady retrieved a cup from a cupboard and poured tea from the teapot on the stove. Bernadette wrapped her hands around the cup and took a sip.

O'Grady busied himself gathering bread, eggs and bacon into a pile on the countertop on the other side of the stove. He lit the gas burner and placed a frying pan on it. Into this he spooned some lard. Bernadette winced slightly at the thought of the fat she'd soon be consuming. As he tinkered, the landlord spoke. "He said he was protectin' ye."

Bernadette didn't want to talk about Grindley. "Did he?" she responded.

"Aye, he did, but he wouldn't say who or what he was protectin' ye from." The expectation of an explanation was clear but Bernadette ignored it.

"Are ye in some kind of danger?" O'Grady continued, finally.

Not knowing what to respond to that, Bernadette remained quiet.

O'Grady stopped what he was doing. "I've a right t' know," he said, hopefully. "I mean, I am the landlord here, an' if ye are in danger, an' wi' him gone an' all…"

"I'm not in any danger," Bernadette cut in. Then she relented somewhat. O'Grady was right, he had to be told something. She didn't want to risk him going to the police. This thought reminded her that she had not had a chance to talk to the landlord about Coyne having been in the Starry Plough and getting her ten pound notes that way. "There is one thing I wanted to warn you about," Bernadette said slowly.

O'Grady looked worried, sure that he was now going to get the truth about the strange goings-on in his pub, and that he wasn't going to like what he heard. "Aye?"

"It's about that man you sent me to see, Marty Coyne. You know he was killed?"

O'Grady stiffened slightly. "Aye, so I heard. I had hoped ye weren't involved in that."

Bernadette chose her words carefully. "I didn't kill him, but he had some money on him which I'd given to him. The police traced it to me. I didn't think you'd want to get involved in explaining why you told me about Coyne." She awaited confirmation.

"No, I don't want anything t' do wi' that," agreed O'Grady.

"Well," Bernadette continued, "I told them that I had used the notes to pay you."

The color drained from O'Grady's face. "Why did ye do that?" he said hoarsely.

"Don't worry," said Bernadette. "They knew Coyne drank here sometimes and figured he got the notes from you as change."

The landlord's face relaxed. "I see," he said.

"All you have to do is verify that I paid you over twenty pounds, which is the truth."

O'Grady nodded slowly. "Aye, I'll tell them that, an' if they ask about Coyne having been in here, I've only t' say he might have been. After all, they can't expect me t' remember everybody from every day, can they?"

"No," agreed Bernadette, relieved that this small conspiracy had been arrived at so easily.

O'Grady, however, was not ready to leave it at that. "But why are the police still hangin' around ye?" he asked.

Bernadette thought quickly. "I'm one of the last people to see Coyne alive. The police think I can help them find out who killed him, that he might have said something, or I might have noticed something. They keep asking me questions, trying to jog my memory." She realized she was not doing a very good job.

"But what are they protectin' ye from?" O'Grady persisted.

Bernadette sighed. "They say they don't want to risk anybody trying to intimidate me into not helping them."

O'Grady did not look satisfied.

"And to tell you the truth, I think they want to be certain I don't leave the country just yet," Bernadette added.

O'Grady was wavering. "They don't think ye were involved in Coyne's death, do they?" It was clear from his tone that the landlord did not believe Bernadette had been involved.

"I don't think so," she answered. "But I suppose until they have a firm suspect they must keep everybody in mind as a possibility."

Finally the landlord seemed satisfied. "Well, I wonder where this Inspector went?" As he asked this, O'Grady put a fried egg, two pieces of bacon and a slice of toast on a plate which he set on the table in front of her. He then refilled her cup with tea.

"Maybe he went out to breakfast or to get something from his office. I don't know, but I'm sure he'll be back soon," Bernadette said.

O'Grady shook his head. "Strange he'd sleep on the floor like that."

"I guess he takes his job seriously, and I wasn't about to let him sleep in my room."

"No, of course not," said the landlord quickly, sounding as if the idea were outrageous.

"Could I get a knife and fork?" asked Bernadette.

Opening a drawer, O'Grady handed her the items.

"I think I will eat in my room after all," Bernadette said. "By the way, I'm expecting a long distance telephone call."

O'Grady nodded acknowledgment. "I'll come an' get ye when it comes."

"I'll see you later then," Bernadette said, balancing her breakfast and leaving the kitchen as quickly as she could without spilling her tea.

32

The train to Dublin was an express and Billy arrived in the city at eight-thirty. He had expected to hang around all day waiting for Sudice to quit work, but now there was a chance he'd be able to get to Sudice before he began work. Hurrying to a phone booth, he looked up the U.S. embassy in the tattered directory and dialed the number.

A female voice answered. "United States embassy. How may I help you?"

"Captain Sudice, please."

"I'm sorry, Captain Sudice hasn't come in yet. Is there someone else who can help you?"

"No. D' ye know what time he will be in?"

"He usually arrives at about ten o'clock, sir. Perhaps you want to try again then?"

Billy smiled to himself. "Aye, right." He hung up. It was less than a twenty minute walk to the embassy, so he had plenty of time.

He dialed the number of the Starry Plough. O'Grady answered "I'd like t' speak t' Bernadette Mallory," Billy said.

"Hang on," O'Grady replied, then as an afterthought, added "Who's calling?"

"It's her friend, Billy Kingston. Ye remember me, I had breakfast wi' her an' we got some cellotape from ye."

"Aye, right," said O'Grady with obvious displeasure. "She's in her room. I'll go an' get her."

While he waited, Billy thought about Sudice and whether he drove to work, took a taxi, or walked. Bernadette's voice interrupted his musings.

"Billy?" Her voice was full of relief.

"Bernadette..."

"Where are you, Billy? Are you home? In Belfast?"

Billy hesitated. "Aye. I made it back all right."

"Thank God," said Bernadette. "I was worried. Grindley's gone off somewhere. I haven't seen him since last night. I thought maybe..." She left the sentence unfinished.

"Gone? Did he say anything?"

"No. Just disappeared. He slept in the corridor outside my room last night so I wouldn't be out of his sight. When I woke this morning, he was gone."

"What are ye goin' t' do?"

Bernadette sighed. "I'm sure he'll come back."

"What if he doesn't?" Billy asked.

"Why wouldn't he?" countered Bernadette.

"I don't know. But if he doesn't..."

"I'm sure he will," Bernadette broke in. "God knows what he's up to. If I hadn't heard from you I'd be worried that he'd done something to you..."

"He hasn't," Billy quickly assured her. "So, what would ye do? I mean, ye'd have the documents an' I'm safe."

Bernadette knew what Billy was getting at. She had agreed to live with him if the documents were turned over to Sudice and no harm came to her. He was asking if she would feel the same way if she had the documents and was free to leave Cork. Confronted with the question and certain that Billy was safe, she realized that she missed him already. Hearing his voice again, she knew now that if she returned to America, no matter what the outcome of releasing the documents and no matter what her reward, she would not be happy. She wanted Billy more than she wanted power.

"Funny how you can live your life, proud of being independent, confident of what you want and how you'll get it," she said slowly. "Then suddenly, you meet someone and it all gets turned upside down. You want something completely different, and maybe you don't know how to get it, and you don't want to be independent anymore. You want to be involved in someone else's life.

I guess I'm trying to say I love you, Billy Kingston, and yes, I'll come to Belfast when this is over, no matter what."

Billy's heart leapt. "Ye've made me very happy, Bernadette. I love ye too."

There was silence between them for a moment.

"Well, I'll call ye later then, t' see what happened an' arrange t' meet ye," Billy said finally.

"Yes, call me later."

Reluctantly, Billy hung up the phone. His feeling of happiness clouded over when he remembered the one problem that could interfere with his being with Bernadette. Leaving the station, he began walking in the direction of the American embassy.

———

Arriving at the embassy, Billy surveyed the building from across the street. The rising sun reflecting off the glass doors prevented him from being able to see inside the building from his present position, but he knew that right behind the main glass doors, two marine guards were posted, one on each side of the hallway.

He walked around the building, staying on the far side of the street. Sudice would almost certainly have a car and Billy wondered if the building had an underground car park. There had been no sign of a car park when he had visited the building with Bernadette, although they hadn't seen the back of the building.

Turning onto the street that ran behind the embassy, Billy saw that there was a car park adjoining the rear of the building. He observed that the parking area was accessible only through a manned barrier. There were about six flagstone steps leading from the parking lot to the building's back door. A smooth concrete banister defined the steps on either side. Billy noted that the parking stalls closest to the rear entrance were marked RESERVED in large letters and bore the title of the person to whom the parking spot was assigned. He didn't know Sudice's title, but this didn't bother him. There were only about ten reserved spots, all in a row and Sudice would surely have one of them.

Continuing walking on the far side of the street, he tried to make out who might be in the booth which sat between the entrance and exit lanes of the parking lot. A car approached the entrance and Billy slowed his pace. The car turned into the embassy and stopped at the barrier. An old man leaned his head out from the booth and exchanged some words with the driver of the car. The red and white striped barrier rose and the car entered the lot. Billy was relieved that the booth was not manned by a U.S. marine. Crossing the street, he approached the booth.

There was a single seat in the booth and the old man was hunched over, reading a newspaper. Billy knocked lightly on the window. The old man looked up, then stood and slid the window open.

"What time does the embassy open?" asked Billy.

"Nine o'clock," responded the old man, glancing at his watch. "About five minutes. Ye'll have t' go around t' the front. The back door's for staff only."

"I'm waitin' for someone who works here," answered Billy.

"Aye, well ye could wait inside. They'll be open by the time ye walk around to the front an' there's free coffee in the lobby."

"I wanted t' surprise them," Billy responded. He noted the look on the old man's face that wasn't exactly suspicious, but that asked for a further explanation.

Billy thought fast. "It's a woman. We haven't seen each other in a while an' she's not expecting me."

He lowered his voice and beckoned the attendant to come closer. "I've been at sea for six months. I was hopin' I could maybe wait for her beside the steps, in the corner over there. You know, so she'd go up the steps without seein' me an' I could sneak up behind her an' put me hands over her eyes." He winked at the old man.

The old man grinned back. "Ye're a sly dog," he said. "Women love that stuff."

He withdrew his head back from Billy's. "But I can't let ye do it. If anybody saw ye, they'd want t' know why I was lettin' let ye hang about there. I might lose me job." He seemed genuinely sorry.

"I'll make sure nobody sees me, " Billy said earnestly. "An' if they do, an' want t' know how I got there I'll say I went in the front door an' out the back. Sure there's no harm in it."

The old man wavered. "I have t' see what's in the bag." he said eventually.

Since Billy hadn't seen the old man search the car that had just entered the lot, he figured the old guy was trying to show that he took his job seriously. "Just dirty clothes," he responded, holding the bag up. "I'll leave it wi' ye, if ye like."

The old man considered. "Aye, all right then. Ye can pick it up on yer way out."

Billy passed the grip through the window. "Thanks," he said. "I appreciate it."

The old man waved him away with a smiling shaking of his head and closed the window.

Billy walked across the parking lot and leaned against the wall in the corner where the steps met the building. He was again surprised at how calm he felt and put it down to the fact that this was his and Bernadette's only chance. She would certainly be free, and he stood a good chance himself, especially if there was only the old man in the parking booth to worry about. Self-defense, he reminded himself.

The minutes passed slowly. Billy tensed whenever he heard someone approach the steps. By craning his neck he could see them clearly from behind. He'd have no trouble seeing Sudice.

By five past ten, he was worried. No-one had entered the building for a while and most of the reserved parking spots were occupied. He began to think that maybe Sudice wasn't coming to work today, or maybe he had already entered the building through the front door. Resigning himself to the idea that he would have to come back in the afternoon, when Sudice left work, Billy saw the door of the parking booth swing open and the parking attendant beckon to him. He would be wondering what had happened to Billy's woman. Billy started to walk toward the booth but he had only taken a few steps when a car pulled up to the striped barrier. The old attendant went back into his booth to attend to the car and Billy saw the barrier rise. He couldn't make out the driver of the car, but turned quickly and retreated to his hiding place. He'd give himself this final chance.

The car parked in one of the last two available reserved spots and Sudice climbed out. Billy's adrenaline began to flow. Sudice opened the back door and leaned into the car. He retrieved a brown briefcase, slammed the door shut and began to walk toward the steps.

Not yet, thought Billy, let him get clear of the cars so he has nothing to hide behind.

Sudice was a few paces from the steps when Billy stepped from his hiding place and confronted him.

Startled by the figure which appeared in front of him, Sudice's surprise deepened when he recognized who it was. "What are you doing here?" he demanded.

Billy walked toward him and stopped about ten feet away. Sudice stood erect, demanding an answer. Reaching into his pocket, Billy produced the gun and raised it in both hands. His expression turning to horror and fear,

Sudice turned to flee into the building, managing to leap up the first two steps before Billy fired.

The bullet hit between Sudice's shoulder blades, bending him over backwards. The briefcase fell from his grasp and slid to the bottom of the steps. Sudice tottered , clutching at air. Billy fired again, hitting his victim in the neck. Sudice's head jerked forward, and a stream of blood pumped from his throat. His body finally collapsed, rolling down the steps, and landing face up, at Billy's feet. Holding the gun inches from his victim's temple, Billy fired again. Sudice's head opened and blood spurted over Billy's shoes.

He was about to squeeze the trigger again when the embassy door opened and two marines, pistols drawn, burst onto the steps. Billy's trance was broken. For the merest split second he considered shooting at the marines but realized he wouldn't have time to get both of them. Dropping his gun, he raised his arms in surrender, satisfied that he had done what needed to be done.

The marines crouched, keeping their guns aimed at Billy. They took in the scene. "Don't move!" yelled one.

The other looked from Sudice's bloody body to Billy, who stood with a smile on his face. "You fucking bastard!" the marine said quietly and squeezed the trigger of his pistol.

The bullet hit Billy in the forehead, just above his left eye. He was still alive when his body crumpled on top of Sudice's. He died regretting that he had probably cost the old parking attendant his job.

33

Bernadette felt better after Billy's call. At least she didn't have to worry about him any more. Grindley still hadn't shown up and she waited, passing an hour reading the morning paper.

After another half hour, Bernadette telephoned the local police station and asked for Inspector Grindley. He wasn't there and was believed to be in Dublin. Did she want to leave a message? Bernadette hung up.

Since she would need them whether or not Grindley came back, she decided to retrieve the documents from Father Fogarty but there was no reply when she phoned the priest. She considered going over to the church but decided not to, in case Grindley showed up. So, she stayed in her room, and dozed on her bed.

Deciding that lunchtime would be a good time to try the priest again, she went down into the saloon just after noon. By now she was used to the customers and paid them no attention, going straight up to O'Grady and indicating that she wanted to make a call. He nodded his head, giving permission.

There was still no answer and Bernadette hung up. One of the saloon customers asked O'Grady to turn on the television. Bernadette watched the landlord jump up on the bar to fiddle with the television knobs. She decided she would call her office in Washington, to see what, if anything was happening there.

She dialed the operator to place the call, and while the number was ringing she looked idly at the television screen. Her body froze at the picture on the screen. It was Sudice. Bernadette held the telephone away from her ear to hear what was being said by the television announcer. The news bulletin concerning the assassination of a U.S. embassy official in Dublin that morning and the death of his assassin caused her to drop the telephone receiver. The feeling of horror rising within Bernadette made her certain she was about to faint. She was oblivious to the small, tinny voice of the phone operator coming through the dangling receiver, "Hello? Can I help you?" Then, slightly louder, "Hello? Can I help you?"

Bernadette suddenly shrieked, "Nooooo!" and swayed on her feet.

Everyone in the saloon turned their heads to look at her. O'Grady, rushed toward her from behind the bar and was able to catch her in time to lower her limp body to the floor.

34

With the help of some of his patrons, O'Grady carried Bernadette to her room. He called a doctor and Father Fogarty, but before either of them arrived, Bernadette came to. O'Grady fussed over her, asking if she wanted smelling salts, tea, or water, or if she was going to be sick. Ignoring him, Bernadette lay on the bed, staring vacantly into space.

The doctor and priest arrived almost simultaneously. Bernadette ignored them also, continuing to lie and stare at the ceiling. After a cursory examination, the doctor confided to the priest that she was in shock and there wasn't much they could do but wait for her to come out of it. He'd give her a sedative to make her sleep, since that was the safest and fastest route to recovery. Still Bernadette ignored everything going on around her.

Rummaging in his black bag the doctor extracted a syringe and a small vial of clear liquid. The priest, sitting on he chair by the bed, watched as the doctor poked the needle through the vial cap and drew some of the liquid into the syringe, then shot a tiny stream of the liquid out of the needle tip until the amount of liquid in the syringe was precisely right.

The doctor approached Bernadette. Sitting on the edge of her bed he put his arm under her left elbow, to raise her upper arm so he could deliver the injection.

She suddenly screamed and sat bolt upright. "Get away from me! You're trying to kill me, like you killed my father. You're a murderer! Get away from me!"

The doctor dropped the syringe in his initial shock at this outburst. He tried to calm Bernadette. "There now, don't be alarmed. Ye've had quite a shock, that's all. Ye'll be fine."

"Get him away from me!" Bernadette screamed, appealing to the priest.

Father Fogarty stood. He remembered the dangling arm in Brown's Funeral Parlor. "I think maybe ye should let her be, doctor," he said.

The doctor read something in the priest's eyes. "Aye. It'd be better not t' force the sedative on her." He bent and picked up the syringe from the floor. "But she needs t' sleep,"

"I'll see she does," responded Father Fogarty. "But I think it might be as well for ye to go. I'll look after her, an' I'm sure ye've other patients t' see."

The doctor nodded. "Aye. She'll be fine, right enough. Just see she gets some sleep."

The priest nodded assuringly and the doctor left.

Bernadette, who had sat upright this whole time, with her body tensed tightly, collapsed back onto the bed and resumed her empty staring.

"Go to sleep, Bernadette," Father Fogarty said quietly.

Bernadette gave no indication at first that she had heard him, but after a few minutes her eyes closed.

When he was satisfied that she was sound asleep, the priest tiptoed out of Bernadette's room and went downstairs to the saloon. O'Grady stepped toward him right away. "How is she, Father? Is she goin' t' be all right?"

The priest nodded. "Aye. The doctor says she just needs t' sleep an' she's doin' that now.

I have t' go somewhere for a while, so I want ye t' keep an ear open in case she wakes up. An' ye could maybe look in on her about every hour or so. I'll be back in three or four hours."

The landlord nodded. "Don't worry, Father. I'll look after her."

The priest gave a satisfied nod and left the saloon.

———

It was twenty past five when Father Fogarty returned to the Starry Plough. He'd been gone a little less than four hours. O'Grady approached him immediately.

"Is she still sleepin'?" the priest asked.

"No, Father. She came down here about an hour ago and made a phone call. Airplane reservations."

The priest's eyebrows lifted slightly. "Did she seem all right? Did she say anything t' ye?"

"No, Father. Just if she could use the phone."

"Is she back in her room now?"

The landlord nodded and the priest climbed the stairs to Bernadette's room. The door was open and he could see Bernadette lying on the bed, staring at the ceiling again. "It's Father Fogarty. Can I come in, Bernadette?"

He was surprised when she answered, "Yes. Come in if you want."

Walking over to the chair by the bed, the priest sat down. "How are ye, Bernadette? Are ye feelin' better?"

"Yes," she stated, keeping her eyes fixed on the ceiling.

"Ye'd a bad shock…"

"I don't want to talk about it."

"I suppose not," responded the priest. "It's too early…"

"I don't ever want to talk about it. Not now and not later," Bernadette interrupted, without moving her eyes from their spot on the ceiling.

The priest felt that Bernadette was not in her previous state of shock, but was now deliberately choosing to isolate herself from the world. He resented this, and wasn't sure how to proceed, but after a few minutes he asked "D' ye know when ye'll be goin' home? Back t' America, I mean?"

"Tomorrow," Bernadette answered.

The priest seemed agitated at the response but diverted his look away from her. "I was thinkin' I'd offer t' bury Billy here if they can't find any relatives...it's either that or he'll get a county burial somewhere in Dublin. I thought maybe ye'd..."

"I'm going back to America tomorrow," Bernadette said forcefully. "I won't be attending any more funerals."

The priest suppressed his urge to confront her and demand an explanation of everything that had happened. This wasn't the time. "What time will ye want t' be at the station?" he asked.

"About ten, but you don't have to..."

Now he did turn to glance at her again and she finally diverted her eyes from the ceiling and return his look. "I want to," the priest said simply.

35

Bernadette was packed and sitting on the edge of the bed when Father Fogarty arrived. They exchanged pleasantries but there was a strained feeling between them, which made her feel guilty. The priest loaded her luggage into his car and they set off for the station. She had no idea when there was a train to Dublin but her flight from there to London wasn't until six pm so she had plenty of time. She just wanted to be gone from Cork

"What will ye do about the cottage?" the priest asked. "Will ye be sellin' it?"

"I suppose so, I've no use for it."

"I was wonderin' if I could ask ye a favor concernin' it?"

"Yes?"

"Well, the church is always lookin' for places t' house missionaries. They spend a few years in Africa or somewhere an' come back t' Ireland for a few months t' attend conferences an' update their trainin' an' such like. It's always difficult t' find accommodations for them. Hotels are too expensive, an' me parishioners don't have rooms available. They usually end up staying wi' me an' that can be difficult, three an' sometimes four grown men living together for months in a house built for one." He shot her a glance.

Bernadette nodded, encouraging him to continue.

"I've a couple o' them comin' next month, an' I know it's a lot t' ask, but I wondered if ye'd consider lettin' the church use the cottage? Just while ye're trying t' sell it, ye understand." He looked at her sheepishly.

Bernadette smiled in return. "I've a better idea. Why don't I give the cottage to the church? Then it would always be available."

The priest's look changed to one of startlement, but with a hint of joy. "Ach, I couldn't..."

"Please," Bernadette interrupted. "I want to, and my father would have wanted it. I'll have the paperwork taken care of when I get home. In the meantime, consider it your own. Use it however you want."

The priest beamed. "I don't know how to thank ye. We'll have other uses for it. I've always wanted t' have some kind of place, like a camp, where we could take some o' our troubled youths, t' teach them teamwork an' livin' together. It would work fine for that too."

Bernadette smiled at the priest's happy face. She wanted to hug him but was restrained by the guilt she still felt. In a somber voice she said. "We didn't do anything wrong, Father."

The priest looked perplexed, thinking she was referring to them.

"Billy, I mean. That whole business. We were victims, or at least the intended victims." She suddenly didn't know how to explain. "I'm sorry you became involved," she stated finally.

The priest's tone was equally serious when he replied. "Billy killed a man. That's wrong."

"You don't understand," Bernadette said softly.

He shot her a look. "Then tell me, Bernadette. I've a right t' know. I did give him the gun, after all. I'd never have done that if I'd known. An' ye're the one who asked me t' get it for him." He glanced at her again. "I should tell the police what I know." It wasn't a threat, more the appeal of someone wanting to be assured that he shouldn't tell the police anything. Someone caught in a moral dilemma.

"If you hadn't given Billy the gun there might be more people dead, and believe me, the man he killed was no saint," Bernadette said with vehemence.

"If we were justified in killin' everybody who isn't a saint, there'd be nobody left. We can't be judgin'..." the priest began.

Bernadette held up her hands. "You're right. That was a dumb thing to say." She took a deep breath. "But dammit, I didn't know what he was going to do either! Do you think I'd have asked you to get the gun if I'd had any idea? If he hadn't been so stupid he'd still be alive..." Her voice was rising with each sentence.

"Ye're angry with him," the priest stated, his words cutting into her. "Because ye loved him an' ye feel betrayed. Is that why ye don't want t' be at his funeral?"

She recoiled at hearing her feelings described so accurately and wanted to scream denial, but in the priest's presence she couldn't. She had to confess. "Yes," she whispered, then buried her face in her hands. "I don't understand. I thought he loved me." She began to shudder with sobs.

The priest put one arm around her shoulder. "I think he did. Wrong as it was, I've a feeling that's why he did what he did."

Bernadette sobbed for a while then subsided into sniffles. "That's what makes it so hard," she said thickly. "I feel like he betrayed our love."

"Love's a strange thing," stated the priest. "It gives exquisite sensitivity t' emotion. That's what makes it so pleasurable, an' sometimes so painful." He squeezed her hand. "I'll see he has a proper burial."

They pulled into the station. The priest wanted to park and wait with Bernadette for her train, but she convinced him not to.

"Ye're a good woman, Bernadette. Yer father would have been proud o' ye. I'll write an' let ye know how things work out wi' the cottage ...if ye wouldn't mind."

"I'd like that," she answered.

"Will ye ever come back t' Ireland?"

"I don't think so. This wasn't an enjoyable trip."

The priest nodded. "Aye. Well, I'll bid ye goodbye an' God bless."

Bernadette felt suddenly overwhelmed and threw her arms around him in a crushing hug. "Thank you for everything, Father."

He returned her embrace for a long moment, then stepped back.

She watched him climb into the car. As he pulled away he looked over his shoulder and waved to her. She lifted her hand in silent response.

36

Back in her apartment, Bernadette dialed the number of the Speaker of the House. She was nervous but excited.

"Speaker Sullivan's office," came the pleasant voice on the other end of the line.

"This is Representative Bernadette Mallory. Could I speak to the Speaker, please?"

"One moment please, Representative Mallory."

Bernadette waited.

"Bernadette?"

It was a voice she didn't recognize. "Yes, hello…

"Speaker Sullivan is unable to take your call."

"Who is this?" she asked.

"Tom Larson, Chief of Staff."

"It's very important that I speak…"

"I'll be honest with you, Representative Mallory. The Speaker won't be taking your call, not now and not in the future."

"What…"

"So please don't call again."

"But you don't understand. I have…"

"He can't talk to you. Don't you get it? You're poison, with all this stuff in the press. Didn't you read what Daleman had to say about you yesterday? We're lucky to have wriggled out of any connection to you."

"I've been out of the country. What…"

"I'm sorry. I can't talk to you any more."

"But if you'll just let me…"

"Goodbye, Representative Mallory. Please don't call again." He hung up.

Bernadette kept the telephone to her ear, disbelieving. Then anger swelled up in her and she slammed the phone down.

————

Bernadette was back in the Oval office. Butz, the chief of staff, George Schultz, the Secretary of State, and the president were in the room with her. She detected smugness in their looks and it made her rage inside. Unlike the first time they had met, the president came from behind his desk and crossed the room toward her. His hand was outstretched and he adopted a look of sympathy. Its patent falseness made Bernadette seethe all the more. "I'm sorry about your father…" the president began.

Reaching out, Bernadette delivered a ringing slap to his face, relishing the look of shock and fear the strike produced.

Both Butz and Schultz jumped to their feet.

"That's for my father and for Billy," Bernadette said calmly.

Butz picked up the phone. "Get security in…"

The president, recovered from the slap, held up his hand. "It's all right." He rubbed his cheek where she had hit him.

Butz spat "Never mind!" into the mouthpiece and replaced the phone. He glared at Bernadette. "Goddam you!" he snarled. "Who the hell do you think you are?"

"I said it's all right," snapped the president, glaring at Butz. The latter looked aggrieved at the rebuke and threw himself back down on his chair.

The president returned his eyes to Bernadette. "Maybe you'd like to tell me what that was for."

Bernadette narrowed her eyes at him. "You know damn well what it was for. My father's dead because of you."

The president nodded slowly. "And who's Billy?"

"He's the man who killed Orville Sudice. I assume you know who Sudice was?" Bernadette sneered. She saw the look on his face that acknowledged recognition.

"Yes, Captain Sudice was a patriot who died serving his country. At the hands of some terrorist you hung out with, I might add."

Bernadette fought back the impulse to attack him again.

The president turned and walked back to his desk. He sat on the edge of it, facing her. "You're in enough trouble already," he stated. "According to what I read in the papers."

"I have the documents showing you authorized Sudice's activities." Bernadette announced.

She savored the worried looks this caused all three of them to exchange. "They're not with me and they're not at my apartment or office either, in case you get any ideas. They're with a friend, someone who doesn't know what they are but will turn them over to the media if need be."

Schultz spoke. "Any documents you may have purporting to be from the president authorizing covert activities must be forgeries."

Bernadette turned to face him. "I've already been through that shit with Sudice. I came here to make a deal, but if you want to have the documents made public right before the election, fine."

Schultz glanced at the president, then turned his attention back to Bernadette. "What deal?"

"I want the investigation of me ended. In return I'll give you the documents and I'll pass your damned appropriation."

Schultz raised an eyebrow.

"I want out," Bernadette continued. "I'm sick of politics and people like you. But I want my reputation intact."

She saw the faint smile play about the Secretary's lips, a smile which said they'd won after all.

"I think we can make a deal along those lines," said Schultz. "When do we get the documents?"

Bernadette shook her head. "No. First you stop the investigation. I want to see it in the papers tomorrow morning."

A frown crossed Schultz's face. "We'd need the documents first. Then we'll call off the investigation, then you pass the appropriation."

"You're not listening," Bernadette said loudly. "The deal is that you end the investigation first."

Schultz sighed and looked to the president. The latter betrayed no sign of interest. Schultz turned his attention back to Bernadette. "Tomorrow morning's papers would be impossible..."

"Then forget it!" snapped Bernadette. Turning, she stomped toward the door.

"Wait!" It was the president.

Bernadette stood where she was, refusing to face him.

"She's got us by the balls, George, and she knows it."

Bernadette smiled to herself and turned around.

The president's expression was grim. "Take care of it," he snapped at Butz.

"But how do I explain..."

"Jesus Christ! Just tell them it was an FBI screw-up. Somebody there will have to take the blame and I don't care who it is. Just get it done!"

"Yes, sir." Butz said softly and began moving toward the door.

"I don't want any possibility that the investigation could be re-opened," warned Bernadette.

Butz glared venom at her.

"Take care of it," said the president to his chief of staff.

Butz hurried from the room.

"Satisfied?" asked the president.

Bernadette nodded. "Maybe. We'll see what the papers say in the morning."

"I want you to give the documents to George, here."

"Fine," answered Bernadette. "I'll bring them to his office. Maybe we can do lunch."

The president scowled. "And the appropriation? When can you take care of that?"

Bernadette shrugged. "I'll schedule a committee meeting for the day after tomorrow."

The president nodded. "Good enough." He walked over and stood in front of her. "I'm putting an awful lot of trust in you. I hope you have the brains to keep your end of the bargain, otherwise you will cause us both a lot of trouble, but especially yourself. I am still president and I can still hurt people who cross me."

"Yes," said Bernadette, looking him straight in the eye. "I've seen what you can do to people."

The president mistakenly took this as an admission of fear and seemed satisfied. "Tomorrow then, by noon. Work it out with George." He returned to his desk and sat down, pretending to busy himself with some papers. The meeting was over and Schultz held open the door for Bernadette to leave.

Home again, jet lag finally overtook Bernadette. She was ready to collapse into bed when the phone rang. She considered ignoring it, but finally picked up the receiver. "Hello?"

"Bernadette! It's Don. Have you heard?"

She became immediately alert at her attorney's excited tone. "Heard what?"

"I did it, Bernadette. I got them to drop it! You're off the hook! It'll be in the papers in the morning. They're blaming some monumental screw-up at the FBI. But, damn, I know it was my threat to…"

Bernadette didn't want to hear her attorney exult over something he had nothing to do with and she couldn't fake excitement right now. "Don, that's wonderful. I can't believe it! But I have someone here right now. Can I call you back?"

"Er, sure. Of course. This is going to do wonders for both our careers…"

"Yes. I'll call you back. OK?"

"Sure, yeah…"

She hung up the phone, crawled into bed and was asleep within five minutes.

———

The phone woke her and she slapped around for it sleepily. "Hello?"

"Representative Mallory?"

"Yes."

"Tom Franks, Washington Post. We just got word that the FBI investigation of you is being dropped. I wanted to give you the chance to comment so we can include it in our lead story."

Bernadette pulled her small alarm clock up to her face. The green luminescence of the hands told her it was ten p.m. She was angry that she'd had only two hours sleep. "No comment for now."

"Did you know they were going to…"

"No comment!" She hung up and fell back onto the bed.

The phone rang again. She sighed inwardly and picked up the receiver again. "Hello?"

"Representative Mallory, Doug Rowntree, DC Inquirer…"

"No comment." She depressed the hang-up button on the phone then laid the receiver on her bedside table. She waited until the loud beeps warning that the phone was off the hook stopped, then again surrendered herself to her overwhelming need for sleep.

When Bernadette awoke again, it was to a restrained but persistent knocking on her door. Her clock showed seven fifty. She ignored the knocking for a few minutes, hoping that whoever it was would go away. They didn't, and she finally slid out of bed, pulling on her slippers and nightrobe. "Who is it?" she asked through the closed door.

"It's George, the doorman, Miss Mallory. I'm sorry to disturb you but I must talk to you."

Bernadette opened the door a crack. "Yes, what is it?"

"Begging your pardon, Miss Mallory, but we have a situation downstairs."

Bernadette waited for more.

"It's the press, Miss Mallory. The lobby and sidewalk are full of them. It's as much as I can do to stop them from coming up here. I tried to call you, but your phone's busy. It must be off the hook." He said the last sentence with a slight tone of rebuke.

"Yes, it is. I unhooked it because they've been calling me all night."

"I see." The doorman did not sound sympathetic. "Well, the thing is, they've been gathering since the wee hours. There must have been ten of them waiting outside when I got here at six. Now there's about twenty. Their TV cameras and microphones and cords are interfering with people . coming and going. I've already had several complaints. I don't know what to do. They're threatening to come up here like I said. Of course I won't allow that, but I'd rather not call the police…"

It was an appeal from someone out of their depth, and Bernadette responded. "I'll take care of it, but I need a few moments to get ready. Maybe you could put them in the party room and tell them I'll be down shortly."

The doorman beamed. "Yes, the party room. Of course I couldn't let them in there before, but now that you've agreed…"

"Yes. I'll take full responsibility. Go back down and I'll get ready."

Turning, the doorman headed quickly toward the elevator. Bernadette picked up the newspapers from the hallway floor by her door. She'd made all the headlines.

———

She entered the party room to a barrage of flashbulbs and shouted questions, none of which she could make out in the din. The crowd of reporters surged toward her. Holding up her hands, Bernadette shouted "Please! Everyone be quiet! Please! I'll answer all questions but first I have a statement to make."

The reporters closest to her quieted those around them and after some final jockeying for camera positions the room was relatively quiet.

"I'm grateful to have been fully exonerated by the FBI in their recent investigation of me. The charges brought against me were not only ludicrous but were maliciously manufactured in a scheme to influence the workings of the House appropriations committee of which I am chairperson."

There was an audible gasp from the reporters. "Are you blaming the administration?"

Bernadette didn't know where the shouted question had come from. She held some documents in her hand, high above her head. "I am blaming the president of the United States and this is the proof. These documents show that our president has been involved in illegal and murderous activities!"

Bedlam broke out as the crowd surged forward, shouting questions and pointing microphones and cameras in Bernadette's face.

——

Across the city, George Schultz rushed into the president's suite. The president and his wife were enjoying breakfast together. The look on the Secretary of State's face alarmed the president. "George! What is it? What the hell's happened?"

Schultz made no reply but crossed to the TV in the corner and switched it on. They all watched as Bernadette talked about a plot to divert arms to the Kurds and the assassination of the British politician. The president swallowed hard. "The bitch crossed us! What's the backup plan, George?"

Schultz stared at him. "There's no backup plan, Mr. President. We're finished. The election's lost. We'll be lucky to stay out of prison."

The president clutched Schultz by the shoulders. "What do you mean? We've got to fight! Crucify that bitch! If you can't do it, I'll find someone who can!"

Schultz shook his head pityingly. "It's over. Nobody can touch her now that she's gone public."

"But we can stall, till after the election! Claim the documents are forgeries, like you told her."

Schultz shook his head again. "We can't stonewall this. The press is in a frenzy. They'll dig to the bottom of it. There's no way we can win the election, and even if by some miracle we did, you'd be impeached within months."

The president's eyes showed that he knew what Schultz said was true, but he couldn't accept it yet. "Then what?" he half-whispered, fearing the answer.

Schultz sighed. "I don't want to sound selfish, but we've got to start thinking about covering other things. And we have to figure out pardons."

The president looked at him uncomprehendingly. "Pardons?"

Schultz looked embarrassed. "You have the power to grant pardons to anyone involved…"

The president recoiled slightly. "I pardon everybody, is that it? And I take all the crap for that? And what about me? Who pardons me, George? Have you thought about that?"

Avoiding the president's eyes, Schultz responded, "The only way you can be pardoned is to resign and let Darnage take over, then he can pardon you…"

"And what if I don't issue any pardons and don't resign?" the president snapped.

"Then we all go to prison together," Schultz replied.

The president's wife screamed and dropped the cup of coffee she'd been cradling.

———

One evening a few days later, Bernadette went for a quiet walk through her neighborhood. Approaching a street corner she saw a young woman, passing out leaflets and haranguing passers by. As she drew closer, Bernadette could make out that the young woman was demanding the immediate impeachment of president Ganera, and urging people to vote for the Socialist Workers' Party of America. She stepped in front of Bernadette. "Hey, lady! Take a pamphlet!" She pulled a sheet of paper from the stack she clutched under one arm and thrust it in Bernadette's face.

Bernadette shook her head, declining the offer.

"No time to read a pamphlet? OK. How about a contribution then?"

Bernadette smiled and shook her head again, continuing on her way along the street. Behind her she heard the young woman shout, "That's great, lady! Don't read a pamphlet! Don't get involved! It's because of apathetic people like you that we have a pig for a president!"

Bernadette almost turned to respond, but her mother whispered into her ear. She continued walking.

Printed in the United States
3308